THE BRIDES OF THE
BIG VALLEY

*3 Romances from a Unique
Pennsylvania Amish Community*

THE BRIDES OF THE
ℬIG VALLEY

WANDA &
BRUNSTETTER
JEAN BRUNSTETTER
& RICHELLE BRUNSTETTER

SHILOH RUN PRESS
An Imprint of Barbour Publishing, Inc.

Deanna's Determination ©2019 by Wanda E. Brunstetter
Rose Mary's Resolve ©2019 by Jean Brunstetter
Leila's Longing ©2019 by Richelle Brunstetter

Print ISBN 978-1-68322-886-8

eBook Editions:
Adobe Digital Edition (.epub) 978-1-68322-852-3
Kindle and MobiPocket Edition (.prc) 978-1-68322-853-0

All scripture quotations are taken from the King James Version of the Bible.

This book is a work of fiction. Names, characters, places, and incidents are either products of the author's imagination or used fictitiously. Any similarity to actual people, organizations, and/or events is purely coincidental.

Cover Design: Buffy Cooper
Photograph by Richard Brunstetter III; RBIII Studios

Published by Shiloh Run Press, an imprint of Barbour Publishing, Inc., 1810 Barbour Drive, Uhrichsville, Ohio 44683, www.shilohrunpress.com

Our mission is to inspire the world with the life-changing message of the Bible.

Member of the
Evangelical Christian
Publishers Association

Printed in Canada.

INTRODUCTION

In Mifflin County, Pennsylvania, lies an area known as the Big Valley—also called the Kishacoquillas Valley. In 1791 several Amish families from Lancaster County purchased land in the Big Valley. By the 1840s the Big Valley congregation grew so large it had to be divided into three districts. There are now three distinct groups of horse-and-buggy Amish living in the Big Valley.

Those in the Byler Amish Church, descended from Bishop Samuel B. King, are distinguished by the yellow tops on their buggies, earning its members the nickname "yellow-toppers." While it wasn't always that way, of the three Amish groups, the yellow-toppers are currently the most progressive.

Yost B. Yoder, an Amish bishop originally from Nebraska, helped another group get started. The people who belong to this more conservative group are referred to as the Nebraska Amish and are known as "white-toppers" because the fabric used for their buggies is white. The men from this community do not wear any suspenders. Many of the Nebraska Amish live in very simple homes with no indoor plumbing. Their barns are not painted, and the doors on their homes are often painted blue.

The Peachey or Renno Amish, also known as "black-toppers," are another group of Amish who live in the Big Valley. The Peachey Amish started from a conflict between the upper district's bishop, Abraham Peachey, and the middle district's bishop, Solomon Beiler. The black-toppers are stricter, especially in regard to the ban, than are their yellow-top Amish neighbors.

In addition to these three main Amish groups, there are also several Mennonite churches in the valley, as well as some Beachy Amish who allow cars, electricity in their homes, tractors for field work, and two suspenders, unlike the yellow- and black-topper men, who wear only one suspender.

While to many the Amish may all seem alike, the cultural diversity in the Big Valley proves otherwise. Despite the differences of the three distinct groups, they have all retained their Amish identity, which is based on a deep religious system that expects its members to live a peaceful life with nonconformity and simplicity.

DEANNA'S DETERMINATION

by Wanda E. Brunstetter

CHAPTER 1

Deanna Speicher hurried to set up her table at the flea market, all the while trying to keep her five-year-old son in tow. The place bustled with activity as other vendors did the same, unpacking boxes and putting prices on the articles they hoped to sell. Serious shoppers usually came before the initial crowds arrived, looking for the best bargains, freshest baked goods, and newly harvested produce—all part of the flea market appeal.

"*Mammi*. Mammi." Abner tugged on Deanna's dress with one hand while pointing in the opposite direction. "*En sack voll eppel!*"

"*Jah*, there are many sacks of apples. We will get some later." Deanna spoke in Pennsylvania Dutch so Abner would understand. He knew only a few words of English but would learn more when he started school next August. One of the teachers would teach him, along with three other special-needs children. The other teacher in their Amish schoolhouse would give lessons to the remainder of the students.

Deanna removed several colorful quilted table runners and pot holders from the box she'd set on one of her tables; at the same time, she tried to keep an eye on her rambunctious son. Abner had

9

been born with Down syndrome. He was full of affection to those whom he recognized, but sometimes the child acted overly friendly with strangers. The latter gave her reason for concern. Here at the flea market, where Deanna came nearly every Wednesday to sell her quilted items, many strangers came and went, as well as people she and Abner knew. One person in particular always caught her son's attention whenever he visited the market or came by their house.

Deanna smiled. Elmer Yoder had been a good friend even before the tragic death of her husband a little over a year ago. Simon died after falling from their roof, attempting to replace missing shingles.

She had spent three months trying to manage on her own while dealing with the shock of losing him. Elmer had stepped in and given of his time during those painful days, coming over often to help with chores and entertain Abner while Deanna got other tasks and some quilting done.

One month later, Deanna's world fell apart again when her mother died from a brain aneurism. Her father was devastated by the loss of his wife of forty years. A few weeks after her mother's funeral, Deanna sold her house, and she and Abner moved in with her dad. It turned out to be a good arrangement. Dad helped them financially, and Deanna cooked his meals and took care of the house, since his pallet-making job kept him busy most of the day.

Deanna's stomach gurgled as the tempting aroma of fresh herbs, apple cider, and smoky cured meats reached her nostrils.

A good many people milled around, talking with friends, while others introduced themselves to sellers, but she saw no sign of Elmer.

Deanna sighed. *If he's here, I hope he drops by—at least to say hello. If he isn't too busy shoeing horses today, I'd like to invite him over for supper tonight.*

She turned her head abruptly when Abner shouted, "*Hundli!*" Deanna looked in the direction he pointed. An elderly English woman moving past her tables had not a puppy but a full-grown dog walking in front of her on a leash. The woman wore a pair of dark glasses, which to some might seem strange on this overcast day in October. It didn't take Deanna long to realize the woman was blind; her dog was a service animal. Deanna wondered how it felt to live in a world of darkness. It would certainly be a challenge. She closed her eyes and opened them quickly, unable to imagine going through life with no vision.

As a man joined the woman and took hold of her arm, Abner hollered: "*Die hundli is gross.*"

"Yes, it is big," Deanna responded in Pennsylvania Dutch. "Only it's a dog, not a puppy."

Abner's pale eyebrows furrowed, but he didn't argue with her. She guessed to him all dogs were puppies.

What a shame your daadi *isn't here to see how you're growing.* An image of Deanna's tall, blond-haired husband invaded her thoughts as she placed the rest of her quilted items neatly on the tables. Abner took after his dad with sandy blond hair and pale blue eyes. Simon had been a hard worker and always provided well for them through his carpentry work. Now the responsibility of raising their son fell mostly on her.

If she made enough money today, Deanna hoped to use some of it toward a gift to give Abner for his birthday next week. Of course, her option was to make something for him, the way her father had been doing out in the barn the past several weeks after Abner went to bed. Dad loved his grandson, and Abner couldn't get enough of him either. Deanna's father didn't have many free hours at home, but he always made time to spend a few minutes each day with her son.

Deanna's musings evaporated once more when a middle-aged English woman stopped at her table. "How much are your pot holders? I'm doing a little early Christmas shopping, and these will make nice gifts for some of my family and friends." She gestured to a stack of the more colorful ones.

"I am asking five dollars apiece."

The woman's eyebrows raised a notch. "Seriously?"

Deanna gave a nod. "Is it too much?" She'd never had anyone question the price of her quilted items before.

"No, not at all. I've seen pot holders like this go for ten dollars down in Lancaster County. Yours are quite reasonable." The customer picked up twenty pot holders and handed them to Deanna. "I'll take these as well as ten of your table runners."

"Those are fifteen dollars each," Deanna explained.

"Not a problem."

Deanna accepted the woman's money and put the items in a plastic sack. She'd no more than handed over the purchase, when Abner whipped around the front of the table. "Daadi! Daadi!"

A lump formed in Deanna's throat, watching Elmer approach, pick up Abner, and lift the boy onto his shoulders. In his enthusiasm, Abner knocked Elmer's straw hat off his head, revealing the lanky man's full crop of auburn hair. When it landed on the floor, she picked it up. In the time her son had known Elmer, he'd never called him "Daddy" before. Could it be because Elmer came around so much and spent a good deal of time with Abner that the child now thought of him as his father?

Elmer grinned when Deanna picked up his hat and placed it on one of her tables. She looked so perky this morning, like everything was right with her world—a far cry from the sadness he'd seen in her brown eyes after Simon died. Elmer shared in Deanna's grief, for he and Simon Speicher had been close since boyhood.

Elmer stood silently, holding Abner's legs securely as he watched Deanna wait on a young English couple who had stepped up to her table. He'd never admitted it to anyone, but Elmer fell hard for Deanna way back when they were teenagers. But she and Simon began courting before Elmer had a chance to voice his feelings for her. Even if he had, she may have rejected him.

When Deanna married Simon, Elmer found it difficult to watch his best friend in the position he'd dreamed of holding. Because he cared about them both, Elmer wrestled with his unwanted feelings for his friend's wife. His heart ached whenever he'd seen them at church or any social event. Most times when he saw Deanna and Simon together, Elmer felt conflicted. It pleased him to see his best friend so happy, but at the same time he envied their contentment with each other. So as not to jeopardize his friendship with Simon, Elmer kept his emotions in check. As far as he knew, no one suspected how he felt about Deanna.

As time went on, Elmer accepted the strong bond of friendship with both Deanna and Simon. Inside, his conscience won out, for it was wrong to long for someone not meant for him. With God's help, Elmer had managed to let go of his feelings for the woman who could never be his. Instead, he focused on his job and leisure activities, always praying that someday he would find the same kind of happiness his best friend had with a very special wife.

When Deanna became pregnant with her and Simon's child, Elmer faced another hurdle. Since he had never met a woman he cared about as much as Deanna, Elmer resigned himself to the likelihood that he might remain a bachelor, never knowing the joy of married life or experiencing the rewards of fatherhood.

Unaware of Elmer's original desire to make Deanna his wife, Simon had invited him over for supper many times for special occasions or simply to get together. Then after Abner came into the world, Elmer became like an uncle to the precious little boy. He loved Deanna's son as if he were his own. The little guy illuminated happiness right from the start, willing to give pure, innocent affection to everyone. When Abner learned how to walk, he never hesitated to go to Elmer, holding his arms out to be picked up.

Now his best friend was gone, and without planning it, Elmer's feelings resurfaced for Deanna. Until recently, he'd fought his emotions, guilt eating away at him for how he felt. But as time went on and Elmer offered his support and help to Deanna, he sensed her healing process had begun. Only then did he slowly reveal how he felt about her.

A few months ago, he'd begun courting her. Although Deanna had never spoken words of love to Elmer, the evidence showed by the way she reacted to him whenever he came around—like now, as their gazes met and a warm smile spread across her pretty face. Elmer had to hold himself back not to shout to the world that he was in love with this special woman.

"*Gaul reide!*" Abner gave Elmer's hair a tug.

Deanna shook her finger at the boy. "Not now, Son. Elmer didn't come to the flea market to give horse rides, and you need to let go of his hair."

"Aw, it's okay." Chuckling, Elmer bounced his shoulders up and down. "How's this, little man? Does that feel like a bucking horse?"

Abner giggled. "Gaul reide! Gaul reide!"

"Okay," Elmer relented. "I'll give you a short ride, but then we're gonna come back here and help your *mamm*." He looked at Deanna to gain her approval and felt relief when she nodded.

"We'll be back soon." Holding tightly to Deanna's precious boy, Elmer trotted off at a fairly good clip. As he made his way around the exterior of the market, passing cars and plenty of white-top, yellow-top, and black-top buggies in the parking lot, Elmer's smile grew wider. Several people looked his way and waved. Elmer gave a nod in their direction, and Abner kept laughing. Elmer wished the game of horsey ride could last forever, but unfortunately, he had a real horse to shoe on the other side of town. Later this evening though, he planned to stop by Rufus Kanagy's place to see Deanna. If things went well, by the end of the day, he'd be counting the weeks till his and Deanna's wedding.

CHAPTER 2

Reedsville, Pennsylvania

Elmer stood at the pump outside his house, washing the grime from his face, hands, and arms. An evening breeze swept across the yard, rustling the colorful leaves remaining on the trees and stirring those on the ground. The cool air made him shiver.

At moments like this, Elmer wished he had indoor plumbing. If he wasn't in a hurry to get over to Deanna's, he'd fill the wash-tub with warm water heated on the stove and soak awhile.

Before Elmer had left the flea market that morning, Deanna had invited him to join them for supper this evening. So if he wanted to be there on time, taking a hot bath was out of the question.

As Elmer finished washing and drying off, he rehearsed in his mind the exact words he hoped to say to Deanna. Saying them to himself was simple, but looking into Deanna's eyes could easily make him forget the perfect speech he wanted to memorize. It was important to word his proposal just right. If Elmer didn't say it properly, she might turn him down. *"Deanna, will you marry me?" or "Deanna, will you be my wife?" Should I just blurt it out or say something else to lead up to it?*

One thing was for sure. Elmer had no intentions of admitting how his love for her reached all the way back to their teen years.

Woof! Woof!

Elmer looked across the yard and saw his dog, Freckles, heading his way. The German shorthaired pointer, with a white body and liver spots, always seemed eager to see his master—especially during bird-hunting season. In Mifflin County, small game–hunting season started in ten days. Elmer wasn't a serious hunter; he simply enjoyed the time in the fields, hunting with his dog and watching Freckles go into a point when a rabbit or pheasant crouched nearby. When he gave the command, Freckles flushed out the animal. It was gratifying when he and Freckles worked together to bring a pheasant home for supper or to share with his parents.

Freckles brushed against Elmer's leg and let out a few more barks.

"Not now, faithful *hund*. I don't have time for play, but soon you and I will have some time to hunt the fields together." Elmer leaned down and gave the dog's head a few pats. "I'm going to see my girl and need to get changed in a hurry."

Freckles cocked his head to one side and stared up at Elmer with pathetic brown eyes. Too bad the dog didn't talk. Elmer felt certain he'd ask to come along. Under different circumstances, Freckles might be going. Abner always got a kick out of tossing a stick and watching Freckles bring it back. But tonight, Elmer didn't need the hassle of being responsible for the dog's every move.

With one more quick pat, Elmer left Freckles and went into the house. Hopefully, he had a clean white shirt and pair of brown trousers to wear. He chuckled, remembering the time an English boy he'd met asked why he and the other Nebraska Amish who lived in the Big Valley didn't wear suspenders, while Amish from the other districts wore one suspender across their right shoulder. Elmer had replied: "Don't rightly know. That's how it's always been."

When Elmer arrived at Rufus's home, it surprised him to see Deanna outside taking laundry off the line. It was almost six o'clock. He figured she'd be inside fixing supper by now. With it being flea market day, Elmer wondered if Deanna had gotten home later than normal.

Should have considered how busy she'd be and declined her supper invitation, Elmer berated himself. *I could have come by after the meal. Well, I'm here now, so I may as well offer to help her.*

Before he went over to join Deanna, Elmer sat quietly in his buggy a few minutes, watching her. Was it any wonder he felt the way he did? Even as she took clothes off the line and folded them neatly where she stood, one could see how she did this task with care. Deanna had been a good wife to Elmer's friend. Simon had mentioned numerous times how blessed he felt to have a woman like Deanna. Without a doubt, she was a loving mother to Abner too. Elmer would never be able to fill Simon's shoes, but if Deanna accepted his proposal, he'd work night and day to make her happy and be a good role model for Abner.

After Elmer climbed down from the buggy and secured his horse to the hitching rail, he gave his shirt a tug. It felt awfully tight around his throat. Walking toward Deanna, Elmer's sweaty hands trembled, but his eyes never drifted from her lovely face.

Deanna smiled when Elmer approached. "Am I here too early?" he asked.

She shook her head. "You're right on time. Chicken's in the oven, and mixed vegetables are on the stove. My *daed*'s keeping an eye on Abner while I get the clothes off the line."

"Here, let me help you." Elmer removed two towels and put them in the wicker basket by Deanna's feet.

She flapped her hand in his direction. "Oh, no need. Why don't you go in the house and visit with Dad and Abner? I'll be in shortly, and then we'll eat."

"If it's okay, I'd rather help you." Elmer pulled another towel down and shuffled his feet a few times.

Is he nervous about something? Deanna wondered. *If so, what could it be?*

When everything was off the line and the basket filled with clothes, Deanna bent to pick it up, but Elmer beat her to it. He stood staring at her with the oddest expression. Elmer wasn't acting like himself this evening.

"Is something wrong?" She looked up at him, tilting her head to one side.

Blinking rapidly, beads of sweat erupted on his forehead. "I uh. . . Th–there's a q–question I want to ask you."

"What is it, Elmer?" Deanna had never heard him stutter before.

He took a step forward then two back. "The thing is. . ." Elmer paused, dropping his gaze to the ground. "I wondered if you. . ."

His words were cut off when Abner came out the door, waving his hands and shouting, "*Sis zeit fer's nachtesse!*"

"Jah, we know it's time for supper," Deanna called to him. "Go back inside now, Son. We'll be there in a few minutes."

Abner's chin jutted out, and he pouted. Deanna hoped the boy obeyed and didn't embarrass her in front of Elmer.

A few seconds went by, and then Abner turned and went back in the house.

Deanna faced Elmer. "Now what was the question you were about to ask?"

Gripping the laundry basket, he gave a brief shake of his head. "Doesn't matter. It can wait till later. Your son sounds like he's *hungerich*, so we'd better go eat."

Deanna followed Elmer to the house. *Maybe once Elmer has a warm meal in his stomach he will be ready to talk.*

"This chicken is sure good." Elmer glanced at Deanna from across the kitchen table and smiled. "How'd you find time to bake it with the busy day you've had?"

"I had it all ready to go, so when I got home from the flea market, all I had to do was put it in the oven," she replied.

"I woulda put it in for her," Rufus spoke up, "but I worked late in the pallet shop." He glanced at Deanna and nodded. "My *dochder* takes good care of me, so I try to help her out as much as I can."

Before Elmer could respond, Abner shouted, "*Meh hinkle!*"

Deanna put a finger to her lips. "There's no need to holler. If you want more chicken, please ask for it nicely."

Abner's forehead creased as he looked at his mother as though he didn't understand. Since Deanna had spoken to him in Pennsylvania Dutch, Elmer felt sure her meaning had been clear. Even though Abner was a special-needs child, he understood most things said to him.

Elmer reached over and patted the boy's shoulder. "Can you say please to your mamm?"

Abner sat staring at his plate for several seconds. Then he leaned toward his mother and said, "*Sie so gut.*"

Deanna gave a nod and forked a drumstick off the platter and onto her son's plate.

"Now say '*danki*,'" Elmer prompted.

"Danki." Abner picked up the drumstick and took a bite. After chewing the piece of chicken, he smacked his lips.

Elmer held back telling the boy it was impolite to smack his lips. After all, there was a time and place for lip smacking. Elmer had done it himself on more than one occasion, not only as a child but since he'd become an adult.

"Did you do well at the flea market today?" Rufus looked at his daughter.

"I sold all the pot holders I brought with me today and also a good many table runners. I'll have to get busy and make more before next Wednesday." Deanna ate some green beans and took a drink of water. "None of my full-size quilts sold though."

Her father's brows furrowed as he pulled his fingers through the ends of his thinning brown hair. "Too bad. Quilts are what bring in the most money."

She gave a slow nod. "Maybe closer to Christmas I'll sell more of those."

Elmer was tempted to say that if Deanna married him, she wouldn't have to worry about money. But with Rufus sitting across from him, now was not the time to bring up the topic. Elmer hoped for the chance to ask her before the evening was over.

Soon after the supper dishes were washed, dried, and put away, Rufus took Abner's hand. "It's time for bed."

Abner yawned and made no fuss.

"I'll take him upstairs. Looks like the day's activities wore him out."

"Danki, Daed." Deanna pressed two fingers to her smiling lips.

"Let's sit in the sunroom," Deanna suggested after Rufus and Abner went upstairs.

"Jah, sure." Elmer rubbed his bare chin, hoping she hadn't noticed his nerves taking over, making his fingers tremble.

As they entered the sunroom—an extension of the living room featuring more windows—Elmer noticed the cardboard box that normally sat under the window had been tipped over. Most of Abner's toys were spilled out on the floor.

"Sorry about the clutter. When we got home from the market this afternoon, while I started supper, Abner came out here to play. I didn't realize he'd made such a mess till now." Deanna went down on her knees to pick up the toys, and Elmer joined her.

"Why don't you rest and let me do this?" he offered.

"Danki." Pushing a wisp of brown hair back under her white head covering, Deanna rose and took a seat on the cot. It was the same cot Elmer had seen Abner napping on when he stopped by on other occasions to visit since she'd moved in with her father. The small bed was obviously more comfortable than sitting on the floor or in one of the straight-backed chairs inside this long, narrow room.

Elmer compared the furniture in some of the black-top and yellow-top homes he'd been in over the course of his life. Not only did they have more furniture, but the chairs were cushioned, and some even had full-length couches and comfortable easy chairs. Elmer had grown up as a Nebraska Amish in the white-top community, so he'd never expected to have anything more than a sparsely furnished home like this one.

Fancy furniture doesn't matter, Elmer told himself as he set the box up straight and put the toys inside. *As long as Deanna and Abner are in my life, I can be happy living the way we do.*

After Elmer stood to take a seat on one of the wooden chairs, he noticed Deanna sat with her head tipped back against the wall and eyes closed. Her heavy breathing indicated she'd fallen asleep.

So much for asking her to be my wife. Guess it was not meant to happen tonight.

Elmer draped a quilt over Deanna's lap and stood gazing at her several seconds before slipping quietly out of the room. *Maybe soon I'll get another chance to ask my question.*

CHAPTER 3

Deanna shook her head in disbelief. The past week flew by in a blink, and here it was Abner's birthday. She grabbed a pen and paper to jot down a list of things she planned to accomplish before supper. *I cannot believe my son is six years old already.* Deanna stared into space, recalling an image of Abner being placed in her arms for the first time. It had been a special moment for her and Simon. One she would never forget.

In an effort to keep from giving in to sadness because her husband was gone, Deanna turned her thoughts back to the day ahead of her. *I'm glad I chose not to attend the flea market today. It will give me more time to make sure my son's birthday turns out well.*

Since the chilly temperatures were characteristic for the month of October, and rain had been predicted for later this morning, the flow of customers would no doubt be sparse at the market anyhow. Once the weather became bitter cold and snow covered the ground, Deanna would cut back on the days she went to Belleville for the flea market. When she did attend, she'd get one or two tables inside a building, not outdoors in the open air like she did during the rest of the year. Since the outside tables and booths were the first thing most people saw when they arrived at the market, most of the time Deanna opted for tables out in the open. Summer could be hot, and storms at times forced her to pack up early, but feeling the breeze and fresh air coming through the Big Valley was more gratifying than being stuck indoors.

Humming softly, Deanna finished mopping the kitchen floor and opened the oven door to check on the chocolate cake she would serve after supper this evening. Abner loved chocolate cake. For that matter, so did she. At supper, she planned to serve ham, boiled potatoes, cooked carrots, and whole-wheat rolls. Her sister-in-law, Sue Ellen, had volunteered to bring a Jell-O salad, which the children would enjoy. She looked forward to spending time with everyone and hoped Abner would be on his best behavior.

There'd be a full house, so last evening Deanna had put an extra leaf in the kitchen table and asked her father to bring in a second table he kept in the barn. They would set up the tables in the living room since it was larger than the kitchen and held few pieces of furniture. In addition to her brothers, Emmanuel, Saul, Noah, and Leroy, as well as their wives and children, she'd also invited Elmer to join them. Deanna looked forward to seeing him again and was certain Abner would enjoy Elmer's company too.

After testing the cake with a toothpick and seeing it was baked all the way through, Deanna removed the pan and placed it on a cooling rack. Then she took a seat to check her list. One of the remaining tasks was making pickled eggs to serve with supper. But with all the planning for Abner's birthday, she'd have to forgo having them tonight. The eggs should have been done at least two days ago to give them time to pickle and turn a nice deep purple.

Peeling the eggshells, Deanna sighed. *It's too bad we can't have these tonight, but at least I'll have them to serve if Elmer comes for another meal soon.*

She rose from her chair to get the beet juice out of the cooler, when Abner dashed into the room, slipped on a wet spot, and landed on his knees. His small mouth quivered as he looked up at her through slanted eyes.

Deanna expected him to begin wailing, but her son got right back on his feet without shedding a single tear.

My boy is special in more ways than one. She knelt down and gathered him into her arms. Soon after they discovered her son had Down syndrome, Deanna had been told that it was the most common genetic disorder in America. In fact, more than twenty thousand cases were reported every year in the United States alone. The condition happened when children were born with an extra copy of their twenty-first chromosome. This extra chromosome caused problems as the brain and physical features developed. The risk factors for a woman giving birth to a child with Down syndrome included being over thirty-five, having a family history of Down's, and being a person who carried the genetic translocation. Since Deanna had been twenty-five when Abner was born, the first risk factor could be ruled out. To Deanna's knowledge, no one in her family had a history of the syndrome. That meant either she or Simon must have carried the genetic translocation.

Pushing her thoughts aside, Deanna took Abner's hand, led him across the room, and asked him to sit in a chair at the table.

Then she got out a cookie and handed it to him.

"*Kichlin*," he said with a grin.

"Jah, it's a peanut butter cookie." She took one too and sat in the chair beside her special little boy.

Deanna was well aware that children with Down syndrome could have mild to moderate disabilities, and many of those disabilities could be lifelong and possibly shorten the life expectancy of the individual. But recent medical advances and support, like those used at the clinic in Belleville, provided families with many ways to deal with challenges. For her, every day spent with Abner was special and not to be taken lightly. Deanna's biggest goal in life was to be a good mother.

Abner's somewhat flat face and nose; small ears, mouth, hands, and feet; slanted eyes; depressed nasal bridge; and skin folds at the inner corners of his eyes were typical of someone with Down's. He had also been slow learning to walk, talk, and run. Yet Abner seemed quite intelligent for a boy his age with or without a disability. Despite this, he did exhibit impulsive behavior and sometimes a short attention span. Early on, the doctors informed Deanna that Abner might be more prone to respiratory, skin, and urinary tract infections. He could also develop a heart condition sometime later in life. She was also told that, although there'd be challenges along the way for Abner, there was no reason her son couldn't live a full life. It was good to know all the facts and important to have normalcy in her son's life.

When Abner asked for another cookie, Deanna obliged. After all, today was his birthday. All birthday boys deserved a second cookie.

As soon as Elmer entered Rufus Kanagy's house that evening, he was greeted by Abner, hugging his leg and shouting for a horsey ride. It was a little hard to comply with so many people milling around, but Elmer managed to sit the boy on his knee and bounce him up and down a few times. For now, it would have to suffice.

As much as Elmer enjoyed being here with Deanna's brothers and their families, he doubted there'd be any chance of him speaking to Deanna alone. It was too bad he couldn't pop the big question last week or find time between then and now to speak to her alone. But work got in the way, leaving little opportunity for anything but going home, cooking a simple meal, and collapsing into bed. Elmer was so tired, he wouldn't have been good company anyway. If anything, it gave him more time to practice what he wanted to say.

Within five minutes of Elmer's arrival, Deanna announced that supper was on the table, and everyone gathered around for silent prayer. In addition to thanking God for the food, Elmer prayed the Lord's blessing on everyone.

When all had finished praying, Rufus, who sat at the head of the larger table, passed the food around. The succulent aroma of ham reached Elmer's nose, and he drew a deep breath. The cooking he did for himself in no way compared to this good meal. If Deanna agreed to become his wife, he'd not only be getting a fine wife but a good cook besides.

After everyone finished eating, Deanna and her brothers' wives cleared the table and did the dishes while the men visited and the children played.

Soon it was time for chocolate cake and coffee, as well as milk for the children. This was followed by the opening of Abner's birthday presents.

Elmer leaned his elbows on the table, watching as Abner opened his gifts—mostly homemade toys and a few items of clothing. He couldn't help glancing at Deanna. The love she felt for her son radiated in her smile. His heartbeat increased as he continued to watch her. It seemed Elmer had loved Deanna for a lifetime. *She was my first love, but Simon was hers. Can I make her as happy as he did?*

When the boy opened the paper sack Elmer had given him, he squealed and jumped out of his chair. Carrying the miniature horse and buggy Elmer had made, Abner went down on the floor with the wooden toy. Elmer, along with everyone else at the table, laughed when Abner made some high-pitched whinny sounds as he crawled behind the horse and buggy, moving it around the room.

Seeking Deanna's approval, Elmer looked over at her again.

"I'd have to say, my son likes your gift very much." Offering him a genuine smile, she nodded.

Elmer grinned. "I kinda hoped he would."

All the other gifts Abner received—a few books, box of crayons, red ball, pair of pajamas, and a new straw hat—went by the wayside. Elmer wasn't sure if it was because the boy liked horses so much or if it had more to do with the connection he'd made with Abner from the time he was a baby. Of course, others, such as Abner's grandpa, had made a connection with the boy, but a special bond between Elmer and Deanna's son had developed even when Simon was still alive. Elmer hoped the day would come soon when he'd become Abner's stepdad.

Abner's cousins, Jacob and Joseph, joined him on the floor, both wanting a turn at pushing the horse and buggy around. Elmer kept his attention on the boys, waiting to see how Abner would handle it. Since this was a new toy, and a birthday gift, no less, Elmer expected Abner to put up a fuss and refuse to let anyone else play with it. To his surprise, however, Abner handed the toy over to Joseph without hesitation.

Not a selfish bone in that boy's body, Elmer mused. *His mother and grandfather have taught him well. And someday, Lord willing, I'll have the opportunity to teach him too.*

"Danki for inviting us to join you tonight." Deanna's brother Saul rose from the table. "Work comes early tomorrow, so I'd best gather up my family and head for home."

"Same here." Noah glanced at his wife, Sue Ellen, and without a word of protest, she gathered up their children, and everyone was soon ready to leave.

Determined to speak to Deanna privately after the others had gone home, Elmer made no effort to leave, staying put in his chair.

Glancing across the room to where Abner lay curled up on the floor next to his miniature horse and buggy, Elmer noticed Rufus staring at him with a quizzical expression. Several awkward moments passed, and then Rufus bent down and scooped Deanna's son into his arms. "Guess I'll take the boy upstairs and put him to bed. Too much celebrating got the birthday boy plumb tuckered out."

Deanna nodded. "Danki, Daed."

It's now or never. As soon as Rufus disappeared from sight, Elmer got up and moved his chair closer to Deanna. "There's

31

something I want to ask you." His fairly relaxed state of mind went into panic mode when the words he'd practiced to say to her turned to mush. With heart pounding in his chest so hard he felt it might explode, he lowered himself into the chair.

"What is it, Elmer?"

He cleared his throat, gave his left ear a tug, and blurted, "I love you, Deanna, and I'd be honored if you would agree to become my *fraa*." This wasn't exactly the way he'd practiced saying it, but he was happy to get the words out.

At first Deanna sat staring at her hands, clasped in her lap; but then she lifted her head and answered in a near whisper, "Jah, Elmer. . .I accept your proposal."

He drew a deep breath and relaxed in his chair until another question came to mind. "How long do you think we should wait?"

Her cheeks colored a bit as she looked directly at him. "Would next April be okay?"

"April?" he almost shouted. "But that's six months away."

Deanna leaned back with forehead wrinkled, and a giggle escaped her lips. "Six months isn't that long to plan a wedding. Even though this will be a second marriage for me, I'd like time to make a new dress and do several other things in preparation for our wedding." She touched his arm lightly. "Is that okay with you?"

"Jah then, April will be fine." What else could he say? He didn't want to appear pushy, and if he wanted Deanna Speicher to become Mrs. Elmer Yoder, then as hard as it would be, he was willing to wait awhile longer.

CHAPTER 4

Heading down Route 655 toward Belleville with her horse and buggy, Deanna glanced over at Abner. With eyes tightly closed, he slouched in his seat. They were only a few miles out of Reedsville, yet her boy had fallen asleep.

"Poor little guy," she whispered. "Guess I got you up too early this morning."

Deanna wanted an early start since they had so many places to go. The first stop would be the clinic for Abner's wellness check. When they finished at the clinic, Deanna needed to stop at Mountain Side Shoe Shop to get a new pair of church shoes for Abner. He'd outgrown his old ones, which were quite worn in any event. Last month she'd bought him some new everyday shoes, which her father had generously paid for. Dad helped quite frequently with Deanna's expenses now that she had no husband to support her financially. It was one more reason she did her father's laundry, cleaned his house, and cooked all the meals without a word of complaint.

Once Elmer and I are married, I wonder how Dad will feel about Abner and me moving out of his house and into Elmer's place. It had been a week since Elmer had asked Deanna to marry him, and she'd informed her father the next morning. While he'd smiled and expressed happiness for her, Deanna sensed a bit of disappointment in his tone. She felt sure her father had nothing personal against Elmer. Quite likely, he simply dreaded living alone. Once Deanna moved out, Dad would undoubtedly feel the loss of Mom more than ever. She couldn't blame him. Deanna still missed Simon, even though she'd come to grips with his death.

Deanna's top teeth rested lightly on her bottom lip. *Maybe Dad would consider moving to Elmer's place or living with one of my brothers.* She shook her head. *I doubt he has any desire to leave the home he and Mom lived in from the time they got married.*

Deanna jiggled the reins to get her horse, Bess, moving a bit faster. It wouldn't be good to be late for Abner's appointment.

For the next few miles, Deanna tried to concentrate on the fall foliage along both sides of the road. A layer of fog rose off the fields and hung low over the mountains bordering both sides of the valley. It was hard to focus on the changing leaves with the thought of marrying Elmer on her mind.

After losing the wonderful man she'd been married to for eight years, Deanna felt uncomfortable at first, learning that Elmer cared for her as more than a friend. She'd always thought Elmer was a nice person—genuine, kind, and considerate of others. It had been hard for Deanna to allow her heart to feel anything more for him than friendship. She could not deny that her son felt comfortable with Elmer or that Elmer thought the world of Abner and accepted his disability without question.

As time went on, Deanna had come to think of Elmer as more than a friend, and little by little, she'd let her guard down.

Deanna's heart finally won out, and she accepted it as God's will that Elmer was meant to be in her and Abner's life. Their relationship grew stronger, and when Elmer asked Deanna to marry him, she'd had no trouble saying yes. She also felt thankful that he was willing to wait until April. In addition to getting the arrangements made for their wedding, it would give her more time to prepare Abner for the changes to be made once Elmer became his stepfather. And there would be changes—hopefully in a positive way that would benefit Abner as well as herself.

On his way to get lunch in Belleville, Elmer enjoyed the view. His horse took the lead since they'd traveled this route many years. Along the eight-mile stretch from Reedsville to Belleville, numerous farms and acres of land dotted the landscape around every bend of the road. Silos, fences, grazing animals, and the beautiful backdrop of the mountains on both sides of the valley spelled out why so many folks loved living here.

Elmer never tired of the valley's beauty—especially during autumn. Like many of the other residents, he'd grown up here and felt blessed to call it his home.

Kishacoquillas Valley was the true name for the area, nicknamed "Big Valley." The thirty-mile stretch was nestled between two mountain ridges—Stone Mountain to the north and Jack's Mountain to the south. Both mountains were ablaze with color dotting the landscape like a colorful quilt and giving the air an earthy smell. The morning fog had lifted and created white billowy clouds drifting slowly across the sky.

Taking it all in, Elmer's smile remained. His life finally seemed to be falling into place. Soon, he'd marry the woman he loved and become father to a stepson he truly adored.

Belleville

After Abner's wellness check, which had gone quite well, Deanna and Abner stopped at the shoe store, followed by a visit to Big Valley Dry Goods for fabric and sewing notions. Afterward, she'd stocked up on supplies for the kitchen at Center Bulk Foods. By the time Deanna pulled her horse and buggy out of the bulk food's parking lot, Abner had become irritable, and Deanna's stomach growled from hunger. It was time to stop and eat lunch.

She directed Bess into Taste of the Valley's parking lot and secured the mare at the hitching rail. Lifting Abner down, Deanna led him into the small but cozy restaurant. She got Abner seated at a table then stepped up to the counter to place their order.

"I'd like a bowl of vegetable soup for my son and the Applehouse Road Salad for myself," she told the Mennonite woman who waited on her.

The woman wrote Deanna's request on a slip of paper. "Would you like something to drink?"

"Yes, please—two glasses of water and one hot peppermint tea." Deanna reached in her purse for the money to pay but paused to add a special dessert to the order. "Oh, and please include a slice of cheesecake." Since today was Thursday, they offered delicious cheesecake, same as they did on Tuesdays. The restaurant also had pie and yogurt parfait available, but dividing a piece of cheesecake with Abner sounded better to Deanna than anything else right now.

When Deanna returned to the table, she found Abner staring out the window. *"Guck emol datt!"*

"Just look at what?" Deanna asked.

He pointed. *"Es Daadi."*

Does my son see someone who looks like his daddy? She looked out the window at the area where the horses and buggies were hitched. Standing beside her buggy was an Amish man with his back toward the restaurant while securing his horse. When he turned around, her eyes widened. It was Elmer. Once more, it seemed her son considered Elmer as his daddy. She smiled. *And soon he shall be.*

The rich smell of coffee reached Elmer's nostrils as he approached the door to Taste of the Valley restaurant. *If I'm not mistaken, that looked like Deanna's horse and buggy I parked beside.* Before he reached the counter, Elmer spotted Deanna and Abner at a table. Of course, there was no way he could have missed them, with Abner clapping his hands and shouting, *"Hock dich naah!"*

With cheeks turning pink, Deanna put her fingers to her slightly parted lips. "Shh. . .Abner, please be quiet."

Holding his chin high, Elmer grinned, hearing her boy wanted him to sit by his side. But he understood Abner's mother's embarrassment over her son shouting and pointing in a room full of customers, all looking in their direction.

"I'll be there in a few minutes, Abner." Elmer gave the boy direct eye contact. "Just need to order my food."

Apparently not satisfied with what Elmer said, Abner got out of his chair, zipped across the room, and grabbed hold of Elmer's hand. Elmer couldn't help the sense of satisfaction he felt observing how excited Abner got over seeing him. With his other hand, Elmer patted the boy's head. Then he glanced over at Deanna to make sure she approved. When Deanna lifted her shoulders and gave him a wide smile, Elmer took Abner's hand, stepped up to the counter, and placed his order for a Saddlers Run sandwich, consisting of turkey, bacon, avocado, mozzarella cheese, and tomatoes on sourdough bread. He also asked for a cup of black coffee. The tantalizing smell made it hard to resist. After paying for the items, he brought Abner back to where his mother waited. They'd obviously not been here long, for no food or drinks sat on the table.

"Sorry about that." Deanna spoke quietly. "My son got so excited when he saw you, I couldn't react quickly enough to make him stay put."

"Not a problem." Elmer chuckled and took a seat opposite her while Abner climbed into the chair next to him. "It's nice to know Abner loves me." He reached over and gave the boy's shoulder a squeeze.

"He certainly does," Deanna agreed. "He talks about you a lot and every day has been playing with the little wooden horse and buggy you gave him."

"Nice to hear." *But do you love me, Deanna?* Elmer had a hard time sitting still while keeping his thoughts to himself. Even though she had agreed to marry him, Deanna hadn't actually expressed love for Elmer. Sometimes the way she looked at Elmer made him believe he saw love in her eyes. But other times he found himself doubting. For all Elmer knew, she might still be in love with Simon and would never feel anything more than a strong friendship for him. Had Deanna agreed to marry him because she needed a father for Abner? It didn't matter, because in six months he and Deanna would be married, and Elmer had enough love in his heart for both of them. Between now and then and even after the wedding, Elmer would do everything in his power to make Deanna fall deeply in love with him. It was the only way he'd ever be truly happy. One thing was for sure—Elmer did not want to walk in the shadow of the man who had left Deanna a young widow because he'd fallen from their roof.

CHAPTER 5

Reedsville

Elmer opened the back door to take out the trash. When a blast of chilly air hit him in the face, he shivered and looked toward the sky. "I'm not very *schmaert*." He formed an O with his lips and blew, watching the vapor from his breath disappear into thin air. "Shoulda put my jacket on. Didn't realize it was so cold."

It was the first Saturday of November, and the weather had turned wintry almost overnight. But at least no snow had been predicted. Elmer didn't dislike snow unless it turned into a blizzard; he just preferred warmer weather over the cold. He wondered sometimes what it would be like to live in a balmy climate like Florida. He'd visited Sarasota twice in his life—once with his parents and another time by himself. He still remembered how good the warm, white sand felt beneath his bare feet.

"Probably won't get back there anytime soon," he muttered on his hurried trek to the dumpster. "But maybe sometime after we're married, I can take Deanna and Abner." Elmer's voice changed to thoughts. *Bet my new stepson would have fun on the beach. Deanna might enjoy it too.*

Elmer had a vision of him and Deanna holding Abner's hand

as they stood in the warm, aqua-colored water, letting the waves lap against their legs. There were so many fun things he wanted to do with his new family in the years to come. Of course, it all depended on his financial situation. But even if they couldn't take any lengthy trips, Elmer thought of many other fun things to do, like fishing, swimming in a neighboring pond, and keeping Abner entertained with a variety of indoor and outdoor games.

After Elmer disposed of the garbage, he sprinted back to the house to warm up in the heated kitchen. Elmer poured himself a cup of coffee, pulled out a chair at the table, and lowered himself into it. His cold hands grasped the hot mug, but soon the warmth returned to his fingers. A few swigs of coffee, and his insides warmed too.

Elmer glanced at the note he'd written last evening and placed on the table. It was a reminder that he had been invited to eat supper at his folks' place this evening. His sisters, Rebekah, Eva, Winnie, and Alberta, would be there with their families, so Elmer planned to share his news about marrying Deanna with them during the meal. He figured everyone would be happy for him since, not one, but all of them had mentioned numerous times that, at age thirty-two, Elmer should have been married and starting a family by now.

He tapped his fingers on the table. "You'd think they'd be happy I'm living on my own, have a job I enjoy, and am making enough money to support myself. Even so, I am more than ready to get married and settle down."

Freckles barked, and Elmer got up to glance outside. *Looks like he chased another squirrel up a tree.* Elmer had wanted to take the dog out for a few hours to hunt today, but maybe next Saturday he'd have more time.

Elmer glanced at the battery-operated clock hanging above the kitchen window. "If I get going soon, I should have enough time to stop at the McGuires' farm to check on their son's pony."

Elmer guided his horse to the corral gate at the McGuires' residence. Mr. and Mrs. McGuire were a nice English couple who inquired about his services after purchasing their son a Shetland pony for his seventh birthday last year. Since they lived on the way to his parents' house, it was a convenient time to pay them a call and take care of the Shetland's hooves. Of course, he'd have to wash up afterward, as well as change into a clean shirt and pair of trousers, which he'd brought along.

Frank McGuire walked out of the house to greet Elmer, and his son, Robert, followed close behind.

"Good to see you again, Elmer." Frank extended his hand.

"You too." Elmer reached out to shake hands with Frank. "And how are you, Robert?"

"I'm good, but Nickie is limping." The boy frowned.

"Oh?" Elmer looked at Frank for an explanation.

"We only noticed it this morning and hoped you'd have time to check out her hoof. Sure am glad your neighbor got ahold of you with my message."

Millie, Robert's mother, came out of the house and joined them, and they all walked into the barn together.

Nickie was a pretty brown-and-white pony, a little taller than most Shetlands. She nickered softly from her stall when they approached.

"Hey there, little lady." Elmer opened the stall gate, walked up to Nickie, and waited. Robert's pony had gotten used to Elmer bringing her a cube of sugar each time he paid a visit to file her hooves. The first two times he came to see Nickie, he put the sugar cube in the palm of his hand for her to take easily. But then he started hiding it under his straw hat. After doing that a few times, Nickie knew right where to look. This evening, she used her nose to knock Elmer's hat to the ground. Elmer bent his neck, and Nickie's soft lips plucked the cube off his head.

"She found it!" Robert hollered, while Millie and Frank laughed. "My pony is so smart."

"She sure is." Elmer grasped Nickie's head and nuzzled her nose. "Okay now, let's see what the problem is and get your pony fixed up."

"She seemed to be favoring her back left foot," Millie informed Elmer.

"Yes, and I checked all her hooves and got some dirt out of them," Frank added. "But she still seemed to favor that one foot."

Elmer did an examination of each hoof, and when he picked up Nickie's left rear hoof, he found the problem. "Here's the culprit."

Robert moved closer, and his parents did the same.

"A stone is wedged in her hoof." Elmer got the hoof pick, and after a few seconds, the stone was out. "It's hard to believe a small rock can cause bruising, but that's what happened to the sole of your pony's foot."

After Elmer applied ointment to the bruise, he ruffled Robert's dark, wavy hair. "She will be good as new in a couple of days. Just keep Nickie in her stall until Wednesday of next week. Then you'll be able to ride her again."

Robert went over to hug the pony while Nickie leaned into his grasp.

"Thank you so much." Millie smiled, shaking Elmer's hand. "Our boy was so worried about his pony."

Elmer looked over at the child with his pony. "He sure loves Nickie. Reminds me of when I was a boy and how much I loved horses."

After Millie returned to the house and Frank went about doing tasks around the barn, Elmer worked on Nickie's hooves while Robert sat with him to watch.

"I'm friends with some Amish kids who live down the road." Robert seemed eager to tell Elmer about it.

"Yes, I happen to know a few of the families who live near you. I take care of their horses like I do with Nickie." Elmer finished one hoof and started working on another.

"Do you ever ride your horse?" Robert asked, looking toward the entrance of the barn.

"No, I only use him to pull my buggy."

"Oh." The McGuires' son was quiet for a minute before asking another question. "Why do you ride in a buggy?"

"The Amish have a set of rules. One of them is that once we join the church, we do not drive or own a motorized vehicle. So the horse and buggy is our mode of transportation." Elmer glanced briefly at Robert and then continued. "We do ride in cars though, as long as someone other than an Amish church member is driving it."

The boy nodded as if he understood. A few minutes passed, and then he said, "Wish we had a horse and buggy. Our car makes funny noises, and Daddy is always trying to fix it."

Elmer suppressed a chuckle. "It's just like horses and ponies. Sometimes they need to be fixed or patched up."

Robert's father came up to them. "How's it going?"

"I'm all done with Nickie's hooves." Elmer gathered his tools and put them in the case. "Other than giving the bruise a few days to heal, your son's pony is in good shape."

Frank and his son walked with Elmer to his buggy. Then Frank shook Elmer's hand and paid him. "Thanks again."

"You're welcome."

Robert came up to Elmer, reached out his hand, and shook Elmer's. "Thank you for taking care of my pony."

"I was happy to help."

Elmer smiled as he climbed into his buggy. It was jobs like this one that made him glad he was a farrier. To have a child like Robert thank him made the work he did worth all the effort.

"If you have a few minutes, can I talk to you, Deanna?" Dad asked, stepping into the sunroom, where she sat in front of her old treadle sewing machine. It used to belong to her grandmother, and when she died, the machine was given to Deanna's mother, so it had sentimental value as well as serving a purpose for Deanna's sewing needs.

"Jah, sure, Daed." She stopped sewing and turned to face him.

He pulled up one of the straight-backed chairs and sat. "I've been thinking about something ever since you told me about marrying Elmer next spring."

"What is it?"

"I assume Elmer will expect you and Abner to move in with

him since he has his own house."

"I suppose. We haven't talked about it though."

Dad leaned forward, resting his elbows on his knees. "It's important for you to know I'm okay with it. I'll miss you and Abner, but once you two are married, your place will be with him."

Deanna cleared her throat, wondering how best to broach the subject. "I have been thinking. . . What if you moved into Elmer's house or maybe with one of my *brieder*?"

With a determined set of his jaw, he shook his head. "Maybe when I'm too old to get around by myself, I'll consider living with you or one of the brothers, but for now, I'm staying put."

"Okay, but you'll be welcomed for meals at our house any-time, and if you change your mind. . ."

"I appreciate that." He stood. "Now I'd better get outside and finish my chores. Just wanted to come in and talk to you about this before I forgot." Dad looked over at Abner, playing happily on the other side of the room. "Looks like my grandson is keeping himself well entertained."

She smiled. "*Jah*, and it's allowing me to get some mending done."

"I'll leave you to it then. I should be back inside in plenty of time for supper."

"Okay, sounds good."

When Dad left the room, Deanna pressed a palm to her chest. While she felt relieved to hear him say he was all right with her and Abner moving to Elmer's home after the wedding, she felt a pang of guilt leaving her father in this big house all alone. Maybe once she and Abner moved out, he'd realize how quiet and empty the house felt and reconsider moving in with one of his children.

∽

"Come in, Elmer, and have a seat by the woodstove." Mom gave him a hug and gestured across the room, where two of his brothers-in-law sat.

"Danki, I will." Elmer hung his jacket and hat on a wall peg and greeted his sisters Rebekah and Winnie.

"Where's the rest of the family?" He looked back at Mom.

"Your sister Eva is in one of the bedrooms, feeding her baby girl, and Gerald is out in the barn with your daed, looking at a horse we may want to sell."

"I see. What about Alberta and her family? Are they around somewhere?"

Mom shook her head. "I expect they'll arrive soon, and then we'll eat."

"Okay." Elmer ambled over and joined the men.

"It's a cold night, jah?" Rebekah's husband, Gabe, stood and shook Elmer's hand. Aaron, married to Elmer's sister Winnie, did the same. After the greetings, Elmer and the other two sat down. Elmer had to admit, the warmth of the woodstove felt nice.

"What's new with you these days?" Aaron asked, directing his question to Elmer.

"Pretty much the same. Keeping busy shoeing horses. Before arriving, I took care of a little boy's Shetland pony." Elmer wasn't about to tell his brother-in-law about his future marriage to Deanna. It was something he wanted to share with the whole family once everyone got here and was seated around Mom and Dad's oversized kitchen table.

For the next fifteen minutes, Elmer chatted with Aaron and

Gabe and got caught up with their lives. Then Dad came into the house along with Gerald. About the same time, Eva entered the kitchen with little Sara, named after Elmer's mother. Eva handed the baby to Gerald, and then she set about helping Mom, Rebekah, and Winnie. Soon, Rebekah's girls, Marylou and Caroline, along with Winnie's son, Jason, came in from the living room.

"When are we gonna eat?" Marylou rubbed her tummy. "I'm hungerich."

"We're all getting hungry," the girl's dad said. "But we're not gonna eat till your aunt Alberta, uncle Seth, and cousin Tom arrive."

Marylou opened her mouth as if to say more, but she closed it and marched across the room to stand beside her uncle Gerald. "*Die boppli is lieblich.*" She stroked the infant's nearly bald head.

"Yes, the baby is adorable," Mom agreed. "But then all our grandchildren are special."

"You're right, Sara." Dad nodded.

Elmer had spent a good many years feeling envious of his sisters because they all had mates and children to raise. But now that it was certain he and Deanna would be getting married, he didn't feel jealous anymore. In addition to helping raise Deanna's little boy, Elmer looked forward to the prospect of him and Deanna adding to their family. She was still young enough to bear children, so he saw no reason why they couldn't raise as many as the good Lord gave them.

In addition to the commotion of everyone in the kitchen all talking at once, the room quickly filled with a tantalizing aroma when Mom took a plump turkey out of the oven.

Elmer licked his lips in anticipation. While today wasn't Thanksgiving, it had the mouthwatering smells of a feast, with all the food set out to eat. Now if the rest of their company would get here, they could all dig in.

Another ten minutes went by, and finally the *clippity-clop* of a horse's hooves announced that Alberta and her family had arrived. They entered the house a short time later, and handshakes and hugs started all over again.

"And now," Dad said after everyone was seated at the table, "let us pray."

After the prayers were said and the food had been passed around, Elmer tapped his water glass with the handle of his spoon. "I won't be telling anyone else this news till it's officially published in church, but Deanna Speicher has agreed to become my fraa. We're planning to be married in April."

Congratulations came from all sides of the table, and his sisters even clapped.

"Well, it's about time." Dad reached over and thumped Elmer's back. "I was beginning to wonder if you were ever gonna get up the nerve to ask her."

Elmer's toes curled inside his boots as a warm flush swept across his cheeks. "Well, you know what they say. . ." He looked at Mom and then at Dad. "Good things come to those who wait."

"That's right, Son." Mom's pale blue eyes sparkled with tears as a smile spread across her round face. "We all hope you, Deanna, and young Abner will be very happy."

Everyone nodded their agreement.

Elmer released a gratified sigh then sank his fork into the succulent meat on his plate. *Just think, after Deanna and I are married, she'll be included in all my family gatherings, and I'll join many of her family's get-togethers too.*

CHAPTER 6

Deanna shivered and hunched her shoulders against the cold as she prepared her horse and buggy for sale day at the flea market. *Too bad the tables I requested aren't available for me yet inside one of the buildings. I'm sure that's where most of the buyers will be shopping today and not outside in this bitter weather.*

Wrapping her woolen shawl tightly around her shoulders, she looked up at the thick gray clouds. Hopefully, enough customers would show up to make it worth her while. If there weren't many people toward the end of the day, Deanna would pack up a little early and run a few errands before going home. She hoped to stop at Countryside Dry Goods on Back Mountain Road to see if they had any appropriate fabric on sale so she could begin sewing her wedding dress.

Maybe after Elmer and I are married, I won't need to sell my quilted items at the sale, Deanna pondered. *I'll simply supplement our income by selling a few things from home.* Deanna enjoyed quilting and had no plans to give it up completely, but it would be nice not to be committed to attending the sale every Wednesday.

It would also be helpful for Deanna if she didn't have to take

Abner along. Keeping an eye on him there had always been somewhat of a challenge. Today, however, she wouldn't have to worry about Abner because this morning Dad informed her that his back felt too sore to work, so he'd decided to stay home and give it a rest. Deanna hesitated to leave Abner with her father when his back was acting up, but Dad insisted they'd be fine.

She'd made sure to fix them both a sandwich for lunch and set out some quiet toys to keep Abner occupied. With any luck, he'd take a nap after the noon meal and Dad could get some rest too.

With a quick glance at the house and a whispered prayer, Deanna released Bess from the rail, climbed into her buggy, and picked up the reins. Then with a snap of her wrist, she guided the horse down the lane toward the road. She anticipated that tomorrow would be a fun day for both her and Abner. Elmer had invited them to meet him for lunch at Michele's Restaurant & Pizzeria in Reedsville. He'd mentioned when he stopped by to see her Sunday evening that he had a horse to shoe on Thursday, not far from his home, and would easily be done and cleaned up before noon.

Shifting her thoughts, Deanna observed a cluster of clouds as her horse trotted along. Cloud formations had piqued her interest at a young age when she used to lie on her back in the grass, staring up at the sky. Every cloud appeared different—some looked like fluffy white cotton balls, while others were dark, suggesting a storm might be forthcoming. Some clouds even formed into shapes of animals, flowers, or funny-looking people. Of all Deanna's senses, she appreciated her sight the most. The ability to see the wonders of God's creation bolstered her faith while bringing peace and happiness to her soul. She had done a lot of cloud watching after Simon died. Looking up at the sky and watching the clouds roll by made her somehow feel closer to her husband. Sometimes Deanna wondered if Simon and others who had died and gone to heaven could look down at earth and see what went on.

How would Simon feel about my decision to marry Elmer? Deanna wondered. *Would he be pleased that I'm moving on with my life?* She couldn't help but think her late husband would give his blessing. During the eight years they'd had together, his concern for her and Abner's welfare had been evident.

"Yes," she murmured, "I believe Simon would want me to marry again, and he'd be happy I chose his good friend."

The rustle of hay and a familiar whinny greeted Elmer after he entered his barn. Walking across the creaking boards, strewn in many places with dried straw, Elmer's nose twitched. To some folks, barn odors were unappealing, but not to him. He enjoyed all the sights, sounds, and smells in this old but sturdy building. Elmer had fond memories of spending time in his folks' barn when he was a boy. While some trips to the barn meant work, a good many times he went out just to sit, think, or carve on a piece of wood. Today though, Elmer had come here for another reason.

"Okay, boy, it's time for us to get down to business." Elmer opened the stall gate and stepped inside. He snickered when the dry hairy tickle of horse lips touched his cheeks. From the time he was young, all Elmer wanted to do was be around horses. He understood them, and they seemed to understand him.

"Jah, I know. . . You love me, don't ya, boy?"

When the horse whinnied in response, Elmer gave the animal's dusty warm flanks several pats. Then he pulled a curry comb slowly over the curves of the horse's back. A little grooming went a long way in relaxing his mahogany-colored gelding.

A gray field mouse skittered across the floor, and Elmer's horse kicked up his back feet.

"Steady, Buster. You oughta know the routine by now, and you shouldn't let a little old *maus* bother you."

Elmer made sure the gelding was secured to a post and then gave the animal's neck a gentle pat. He'd chosen his horse's name because soon after he'd acquired Buster, the rambunctious animal had kicked his back feet and busted the corral gate. Elmer spent a good many weeks working with the horse after that. Even though Buster could still be a bit testy at times, for the most part, he'd settled down and become a dependable, easy-to-manage horse. At least for Elmer, the horse cooperated whenever he gave a command. That counted most of all since Elmer was the only one who ever drove the animal. Elmer never trusted Buster enough to let someone else handle him. More importantly, Elmer didn't want anyone to get hurt.

Eight weeks had gone by since Buster's last shoeing, and he definitely needed new ones. Since Elmer had no other horses to shoe this morning, it was a good time to take care of his own.

It didn't take long to remove Buster's old shoes, clear out the caked-on mud, trim the horse's hooves, and inspect each one to make sure they were healthy. After that, Elmer measured for and forged new shoes while the metal was hot. It was important for the shoes to fit properly because ill-fitting ones could cause damage to the horse.

Elmer had learned the farrier trade from his uncle James, and he'd worked at it pretty much full-time since he was eighteen years old. Back then, his mother worried when he'd first shown an interest in horseshoeing. She'd reminded Elmer of the big commitment and expressed concern because some horses were stubborn, which could lead to danger. Elmer was well aware of the risks and had a few close calls over the years, but he always exercised caution, even with a more docile horse.

In addition to shoeing for the Amish in the area, Elmer worked on riding horses, draft horses, and some that were simply pets. He had a good clientele, and the people who called on Elmer trusted him to take care of their animals. While Elmer had no phone of his own, his closest English neighbor kindly let Elmer use his phone number for advertising purposes and willingly took messages and relayed them to Elmer.

During Elmer's apprenticeship, Uncle James had mentioned several times that a farrier must have strength, endurance, and a special way with horses. "Four hours of shoeing is equal to eight hours of construction work, so you'd better be sure you're up for the job," his uncle had said.

To this day, Elmer still visualized the short-statured man pointing a finger at him and saying: "This job brings danger; even friendly horses can be spooked by any number of things. So when you're shoeing a horse, you better know exactly what you're doing."

Elmer didn't let his uncle's words of caution or his mother's concern dissuade him. If anything, it made him more aware. Even though the job was strenuous, he had strong back muscles, which was a good thing because he had to be bent over in an awkward position for long stretches at a time while working on a horse's hooves. A few years ago, Elmer had added stretching exercises to his morning routine. It helped to limber him up before his daily tasks began.

Once he'd made up his mind to pursue horseshoeing, nothing held him back. He continued to be motivated and hardworking, with a love and respect for horses. Because of his perseverance, Elmer had done well enough financially, although he certainly wasn't wealthy. He budgeted his money and lived within his means. Thanks to his frugal spending, Elmer had bought his own home. While it was certainly nothing fancy, the house was sufficient for his needs. And with four bedrooms—two upstairs and two down—Elmer could easily accommodate a wife and children.

One of the challenges Elmer faced early on was the expense of farrier tools, which added up to almost two thousand dollars. The tools included things like an anvil and stand, nippers, forge stand, shoe and nail pullers, driving and rounding hammers, hoof knife, wire brush, curved blades, rasp, and of course horseshoes. Some of the tools, like hammers and hoof nippers, would last for years; but other supplies, such as horse rasps and brushes, would need to be replaced more often. Buying supplies was an ongoing thing for a farrier, so Elmer always made his purchases count by shopping around and getting the best tools for the job—ones better made that would last a long time.

After he finished with Buster and led the horse outside to roam around in the pasture, Elmer put his tools away and washed up at the pump. While lathering his hands and arms with plenty of soap, Elmer's thoughts went to Deanna. *I wonder how she is doing today at the market. I hope she bundled up.* Elmer looked forward to seeing her and Abner tomorrow at noon to share a meal after he finished shoeing a horse in the area. Every chance Elmer got to be with the woman he loved filled his heart with joy, and tomorrow would be no exception.

Deanna arrived home by late afternoon. Since fewer customers shopped outside than in the sale buildings at the market, she'd been able to leave early. Except for a couple of stragglers walking by the outside vendors, most people stayed inside where it was warm and had plenty of food vendors.

She was glad to pack up early because even now she felt rattled. Today Deanna had seen someone at the market who completely unnerved her. She'd been sitting at one of her tables, watching people come and go. Despite the chilly weather, the morning had gone by quickly. A few people Deanna knew stopped by for a quick chat. Others whom she had never met gave a sidelong glance at her items and kept walking.

When a customer she had been talking with went into one of the buildings, Deanna rearranged the cushion on her chair and sat down. Her back went rigid when a man walked past her table. Sitting up straight, she had trouble breathing. He looked similar to her deceased husband, Simon.

Deanna tried not to stare, but she could hardly look away. Except for the man being English, he had the same color of hair as Simon's. Even his physique and height reminded her of Simon.

Deanna had heard it said that everyone had a double. She

didn't know if she believed it before, but after this, she wasn't so sure.

Did I see that man today for a reason? Deanna asked herself as she took care of her horse and buggy. *Was it a sign from God that it's too soon for me to get married again or that Simon might not approve?*

Shaking her unfounded reflections aside, Deanna brought the unsold items back into the house, where all was quiet. She peeked into the sunroom and found Dad and Abner snoozing—one on each end of the cot. Deanna yawned. Seeing them in restful slumber made her feel even more tired. After being in the cold all morning, she went to her room, hoping to get a quick nap in the warm house before it was time to prepare supper.

Kicking off her shoes, Deanna picked up the extra blanket she kept folded at the end of the bed. She snuggled down and covered herself. *It feels good to be home again.*

It could have been a better day at the market if it hadn't been for the nippy weather. Even so, Deanna hadn't done too badly with sales. Since it was getting closer to the holidays, she'd sold a quilt along with a few of her usual items.

As the warmth of the blanket enveloped Deanna, she could not keep her eyes open any longer. Before long, she fell into a deep sleep.

Deanna smelled the fragrance of flowers covering the field she walked in. Elmer held her one hand, and Abner held on to the other. As they approached a large shade tree, Simon stepped out from the shadows behind it.

"Simon! Oh Simon!" Deanna ran to him with open arms. "You've been gone so long."

When Elmer and Abner approached, Deanna stood back to let Abner get a hug from his daddy.

She watched as Simon walked toward Elmer. Without hesitation, her husband reached out to shake Elmer's hand. Then they gave each other a warm embrace, as good friends usually do.

No words were spoken, yet everything seemed understood. Simon took his son by the shoulders and gave him another fatherly hug. Then he urged Abner toward Elmer, who held out his hand to him.

Simon turned back and looked at Deanna. The smile on his face was beautiful. Deanna was mesmerized by his handsomeness as he gently cupped her face with his hands and kissed her. When their caress ended, Simon turned Deanna so she was looking directly at Elmer. Questioning, Deanna looked back at her husband, and now he pointed to his best friend.

Elmer held out his other hand to Deanna, but before she reached out to take it, she needed to look at Simon once again. This time when she did, he was gone. It was as if he had never been there at all.

Deanna coughed and sputtered, opening her eyes when she heard someone laughing. She sat up in bed, trembling as she clung to the blanket that covered her while she'd slept. The dream she'd awakened from had been so real. If only it were true. But it had left Deanna with a sense of peace about her engagement to Elmer.

The laughter continued. It sounded like fun going on in the room where her father and son had been napping.

Oh Simon. The dream I just had. I believe I understand what you were telling me.

Deanna fell back onto the pillow and smiled, looking up at the ceiling. First, she'd seen a man today who resembled her husband, and now she'd awakened from this dream, which she wasn't ready to let go of just yet. *Simon was telling me to go to Elmer, and he gave his blessing. Oh, I cannot wait to tell Elmer.*

CHAPTER 7

"Are you ready, Buster? It's time for us to go," Elmer called to his horse as he loaded the needed supplies into the back of his work wagon. Then he walked into the barn to make sure Freckles's bowls were filled with fresh water and food. Elmer was getting an earlier start than originally planned, because he now had two horses instead of one to shoe this morning. Barring anything unforeseen, he figured he ought to have them both done in plenty of time to meet Deanna and Abner at Michele's Restaurant by noon.

"I'm hungry for pizza." Elmer spoke out loud while looking at his horse. "It's been awhile, and I've got a hankering for pepperoni with extra cheese."

Buster snorted and stomped his right front hoof.

Elmer chuckled. "You wishing for a slice of pizza too, boy?"

Buster nickered, swishing his tail.

Elmer wondered how much of his words the horse understood. *Enough to obey my commands, that's for sure. I'm lucky to have Buster; he's a mighty nice horse.*

Freckles sat close by, wagging his tail. Most owners of

shorthaired pointers got the dog's tail docked when it was a puppy, but Elmer chose not to do this to his dog. Elmer had also trained his dog to keep within the boundaries of the property, and Freckles usually hung around the barn when Elmer went out on jobs.

He scratched behind Freckles's ears. "Now keep watch on the place while I'm gone, you hear?"

Freckles barked three times.

Chuckling, Elmer gave Buster a few pats then climbed into his rig and took up the reins. As he went out toward the road, he glanced back and saw his dog plop down by the barn door.

Heading down the road toward the farm where he'd be shoeing the two horses, a merry tune popped into Elmer's head, and he began to whistle. He felt great today as he breathed in the clean fresh air with such a clear blue sky overhead. On mornings like this, everything seemed right with the world—his world anyway.

Holding tightly to her energetic son's hand, Deanna led the way across the parking lot and into the restaurant. They'd arrived twenty minutes early, but she didn't mind waiting. Perhaps Elmer would show up early too.

Once inside, they waited a few minutes before a hostess showed them to a table near the window. Within the first minutes after sitting down, it became obvious that Abner had grown restless, for he picked up the salt and pepper shakers and moved them to the left and then the right, across the table in front of him. One of the shakers fell over, and some pepper escaped the lid. Deanna used her hand to push the granules into a small pile then sneezed as she brushed them into a napkin.

Deanna took the shakers from Abner and put them back in place. After a few seconds, he grabbed only the salt shaker. Instead of moving it around, he gave it a good shake, turned it upside down, and shook it again. Abner snickered as tiny flecks of white poured out onto the red-and-white-checkered tablecloth.

Exasperated, Deanna took the shaker from Abner. "You need to sit still while we wait for Elmer." Speaking in Pennsylvania Dutch, she pointed to the window. "Keep watching and tell me when you see Elmer's horse and buggy come in. Okay?"

"Jah, Mammi." Abner leaned close to the window, pressing his nose against the glass.

Deanna smiled. *No doubt my son is as eager to see Elmer as I am today.* She glanced at the clock on the far wall. Only ten minutes to go until twelve o'clock. *He should be here soon.* Containing her eagerness was hard today, especially because she wanted to tell Elmer about the dream she'd had yesterday.

Another ten minutes went by while Abner continued to stare out the window and Deanna studied the menu. If she made her decision on what to eat now, she'd be ready to order once Elmer arrived.

Abner moved away from the window and gave his belly a thump. "Hungerich."

"Jah, I'm hungry too, but it's good manners to wait to eat till Elmer gets here. It's the polite thing to do."

Abner's chin jutted out, and he smacked his hand on the table, sending the salt he'd spilled in several directions. "Hungerich!"

When the elderly English man sitting across from them looked their way with eyebrows lowered, Deanna's cheeks burned from the embarrassment she felt over her son's outburst. Abner could get this way sometimes, especially if he had to wait for something he wanted. She'd been working on it with him and seeing some improvement until now.

Deanna sighed. *Why today, of all days, does Abner have to act up?* She put a finger to her lips. "Speak quietly, Son."

"Hungerich! Hungerich! Hungerich!" Abner's breathing grew heavier and his voice louder. If Deanna didn't do something to calm her son down, he could embarrass her even further.

When she caught the waitress's attention, she motioned for her to come over to their table. "We are still waiting for our friend, but my son is hungry, so I'd like to place his order now."

"Sure, no problem." The dark-haired woman pointed to the menu. "What would he like?"

"A toasted cheese sandwich from the children's menu would be good, along with a glass of milk."

"I'll put the order in right away. Do you want to order something too?"

Deanna shook her head. "I'll probably have a cold turkey sub, but I will wait till my friend gets here to place my order for that."

"Okay, whenever you're ready." The waitress left and came back soon with Abner's milk, which seemed to satisfy him for the moment. Another ten minutes went by before his sandwich came out, and by then it was almost twelve thirty.

Deanna turned her attention to the window. *I wonder what could be taking Elmer so long. Is he running behind? Or did Elmer forget about our plans to meet for lunch here today?*

It had taken Elmer longer than he hoped to shoe Bishop Henry's buggy horse, and now he still had Henry's wife's mare to do.

It meant he'd be late meeting Deanna and Abner at the restaurant. Well, he couldn't quit now; he'd already taken off the horse's old shoes. *Guess I'll get there when I get there. Surely Deanna will understand.*

The mare Bishop Henry called "Flo" had cooperated so far. In fact, the horse kept nodding her head, acting as if she was on the verge of falling asleep.

Elmer lifted his gaze to the barn rafters. *Sure hope Flo doesn't decide to lay down while I'm trying to work on her hooves. I need to get done here so I can be on my way.*

As he worked on the horse, his thoughts went to Deanna and Abner. It had been a week since they'd last seen each other. His heart ached for both of them. Even if it had only been a day without seeing them, Elmer would still feel the same.

Next year at this time we'll be happily married. Who knows, maybe we'll be expecting a brother or sister for Abner by then.

Elmer thought of his best friend. It wasn't fair what happened to him. One day he was here, and the next, gone.

Simon, you needn't worry. I'll be the best husband to Deanna and a good father to Abner. I will never be able to replace you, and you'll always remain in their hearts, but I'll try to be the next best thing and see that neither of them wants for anything. I'll love them like there is no tomorrow, and rest assured, I shall never take anything for granted.

Trimming Flo's hooves went well enough, and fortunately she remained awake. Elmer whistled a song he'd sung many times while carving or cutting a piece of wood. Yes, he was one happy man.

Next came cleaning and applying the horse's new shoes. No problems occurred as Elmer finished with the two front hooves.

As he moved to the rear so he could work on the back ones, the bishop's cocker spaniel showed up on the scene, yapping and running back and forth in front of Flo like she sought attention or wanted to play.

But the horse didn't like any of it, and before either Henry or Elmer could call off the dog, Flo gave a piercing whinny and kicked out both of her hind legs. It happened too fast for Elmer to react. His head snapped back. His world disappeared.

By one o'clock, Deanna felt certain Elmer wasn't coming. He'd either forgotten or something had happened to detain him. It was at times such as this when she wished they both had cell phones so she could call and check on him.

Deanna looked over at Abner. He'd finished his sandwich and was playing with the salt and pepper shakers again. She was about to call the waitress over so she could order herself something to eat when she heard sirens wailing in the distance. A few minutes later, two first responder vehicles roared past.

Maybe an accident tied up traffic and that's the reason Elmer is late. Deanna pinched the skin at her throat. *I hope it didn't involve someone's horse and buggy and that no one was seriously injured.*

A tragic accident came to mind. Last fall, a truck driving between Belleville and Allensville hit a black-topper's buggy, and all the occupants were killed. Their horse sustained irreparable injuries and had to be put down. The driver of the truck sustained only minor wounds, and word had it that he'd been drinking.

Deanna moved her fingers from her throat to her temples. *Such senseless tragedies can occur because of people who drink and drive or simply aren't paying attention.*

When the waitress came over to Deanna's table and asked if she was ready to order something for herself now, Deanna declined. Just thinking about whatever happened down the road caused her appetite to diminish.

"I'll take the check now, please." She looked up at the young woman and forced a smile.

"Okay." The waitress left and came back a short time later with Deanna's bill. Deanna handed her the correct amount, including a little extra for the tip. Then she gathered up her purse, took Abner's hand, and headed for the front of the restaurant. Deanna was almost to the door when a middle-aged English couple came in. When they stepped up to the hostess, Deanna heard the man say, "There's been a mishap down the road at Henry Zook's place. An Amish farrier got kicked by a horse, and I heard he was hurt pretty bad."

Deanna's eyes widened, and her entire body broke out in a cold sweat. She needed to go to Bishop Henry's place and find out for herself what had happened, but she didn't know what to do with Abner. If Elmer had been seriously hurt, she wanted to protect Abner from seeing him like that. It would frighten her boy to no end. Dad had left for the pallet shop early this morning and wouldn't be back until later today, so taking Abner home was not an option.

While Deanna stood in the parking lot, trying to figure out what to do, her friend Ruth Herschberger along with Ruth's teen-aged daughter, Mollie, pulled in. As soon as they got out of their buggy, Deanna approached.

"I just learned there's been an accident at Bishop Henry's

place, and I believe it was Elmer Yoder who got hurt." She paused and swiped a trembling hand across her forehead. "I would like to go there and see for myself, but I don't want to take Abner."

"Not a problem." Ruth gestured to her daughter. "Mollie and I will look after your son."

Deanna exhaled with relief, touching her friend's arm. "Danki." Then she bent down and told Abner she needed to go somewhere and that he'd be spending some time with Ruth and Mollie.

Abner didn't question her announcement. Wearing a smile, he trotted off toward the restaurant with the Herschberger ladies. Deanna didn't take time to explain that he'd already eaten. After all, it wouldn't hurt the boy if he ate something more.

Hurrying to her horse and buggy, Deanna sent up a quick prayer. *Heavenly Father, please let Elmer be okay.*

CHAPTER 8

When Deanna pulled her horse and buggy onto the Zooks' driveway, her gaze came to rest on the rescue vehicles parked by the barn, their lights flashing. Fear welling in her chest, Deanna's hands shook as she secured Bess to the hitching rail. The whole way over, her mind would not let go of how she had lost Simon. Deanna couldn't stand the thought of losing Elmer too.

Nadine, the bishop's wife, came out of the house and greeted Deanna with a hug. Her tearstained face expressed the worst, something Deanna prayed she never wanted to see. "I'm glad you're here. Elmer is in a bad way."

Her voice lowering to a near whisper, Deanna asked, "What happened?"

Taking a deep breath, Nadine explained: "My horse got spooked when our dog came into the barn while Elmer was getting ready to put new shoes on the mare. The animal kicked her back feet out and hit Elmer in the forehead." The skin around Nadine's eyes bunched as she slowly shook her head. "Henry said the blow hit Elmer's skull with such force, he feared it may have killed him. And oh Deanna, there was so much *blut*."

Deanna stifled a gasp. "Did he pass out? How much blood did he lose? Is he gonna be all right?"

The bishop's wife grasped Deanna's arms and gave them a squeeze. "You need to calm down. I have no answers for you, but I'm sure the paramedics will respond to your questions once they finish working on him." She motioned to the house. "There's nothing we can do but pray for Elmer, so why don't we sit on the porch while we wait?"

Deanna shook her head determinedly. "I can't sit and wait. I need to see for myself how Elmer is doing." She dashed across the yard and into the barn.

Deanna cringed as she approached the spot where Elmer lay on a stretcher. Nadine had been right—Elmer's face was covered with blood. His eyes were shut, but at least he was breathing. Deanna felt relief seeing his chest move slowly up and down. Over and over she repeated to herself: *He'll be okay. . . . Elmer will be okay.* But it was hard to believe the words in her head.

"How bad is it?" she asked Bishop Henry, who stood nearby looking solemnly down as the paramedics worked on Elmer.

"We don't know yet. They're getting him ready to transport to the hospital in Lewistown."

"I. . .I need to go with him." Tears pricked the backs of Deanna's eyes as Nadine walked up and put a consoling arm around her waist. "Henry, would you please let Elmer's family know what happened? I'm sure they will want to be at the hospital too."

"Jah, of course. I'll go there right now." The bishop bobbed his gray head. "Just leave your horse and buggy here for now, and then you or your daed can pick it up later."

She gave a nod. "Oh, and one more thing. Would you mind going by Ben and Ruth Herschbergers' place? Ruth and her daughter are taking care of Abner for me. They need to know where I've gone. And if they can't keep Abner for the rest of the day, please tell them my daed should be back at his house by four o'clock. They can take Abner there before it's time to fix supper, and let Dad know what happened to Elmer."

Henry gave Deanna's shoulder a reassuring pat. "Don't worry. I'll see that everyone you mentioned gets the message. And remember, Deanna, we'll all be praying."

A lump formed in her throat as she looked back at Elmer being loaded into the ambulance. No doubt about it—he needed a good many prayers right now.

Lewistown, Pennsylvania

Deanna sat in the hospital waiting room with Elmer's parents, anticipating some news on their son's condition. *What is taking so long? Why haven't we heard anything yet?*

It was hard not to worry, and Deanna struggled to keep her thoughts and words positive. She wanted to offer comfort and a feeling of hope to John and Sara, but at the moment, Deanna needed someone to uplift and bolster her own faith. When tragedies such as this occurred, it was difficult to keep one's eyes on God and not give in to despair.

"I hope our daughters all got the message about Elmer." Tears welled in Sara's eyes as she clasped her husband's arm. "They need to be praying for their *bruder*." She sniffed and dabbed at the tears on her cheeks.

"Henry said he would let them all know." John patted her hand. "Wouldn't be one bit surprised if all four of our girls showed up here most any time."

"They'll have to hire a driver and find someone to stay with their *kinner*."

John nodded. "I am sure it can all be arranged. Just try not to worry. The only thing we can do for our son right now is pray."

Needing something to do other than sit and fret, Deanna rose from her seat. "Would either of you like something to drink? There's a vending machine down the hall. I'd be happy to walk down and get a hot or cold drink for both of you."

"No, thanks, I'm fine." John looked over at his wife. "How 'bout you, Sara?"

Touching her stomach, she shook her head. "My *bauch* feels like it's tied in a knot. Don't think I could eat or drink anything without it coming right back up." She turned her head in the direction of the hallway, where someone's name had been paged over the intercom. "I want to see my son and know he's all right."

"I understand, for I want that too, but we have to be patient."

Since neither of Elmer's parents wanted anything to drink, Deanna returned to her seat and picked up a magazine. Perhaps even looking at the pictures would keep her mind occupied with something other than the situation at hand.

Deanna flipped through the pages but didn't see a thing. The words and pictures all meshed into one. Fifteen minutes went by, and then, with flushed faces and wide eyes, Elmer's sisters entered the room. "Have you seen Elmer yet? Do you know how he's doing?" Alberta was the first to speak.

"All we know is he got kicked in the head by the horse he was trying to shoe." Hands pressed against her chest, Sara moaned. "The doctors are examining him now, but no one has told us anything about your brother's condition." When they all embraced in a hug, Sara began to cry.

"I'm sure we'll hear something soon." Deanna hoped her voice sounded more optimistic than she felt. The longer they waited to hear from the doctor, the greater concern she felt. If Elmer was seriously hurt, surely a doctor or nurse would have come to inform them by now. Families had a right to know how their loved one was doing.

Deanna glanced across the room, where a young couple sat huddled together. No doubt they were waiting to hear how someone they cared for was doing as well.

Life can be so cruel. How could such a beautiful blue-skied day turn so horrible? Deanna leaned her head back and closed her eyes. *Everything can be going along fine one minute, and in an instant, a person's world can be turned upside down.* That's how it had been the day Simon died. They'd had breakfast together that morning, and by noon, Deanna's beloved husband was gone. *If I could have known what was coming that morning, I would have said so many things to Simon before he went up on the roof. I would have hugged and kissed him and said, "I love you, Husband." But no, I barely responded when he kissed my cheek before heading out the door. I had some silly old chore on my mind instead.*

So many regrets, but they wouldn't change what happened. Deanna's only hope was for the chance to express her love each and every day to those she cared about.

A cool hand touched Elmer's arm and he flinched. "Wh–where am I?"

"You're at the hospital in Lewistown."

Elmer groaned as a searing pain shot through his head. "Who are you?"

"I'm Nurse Cheryl. Dr. Dennison is here with you too. The wound on your head has been stitched and bandaged. There is also a strip of gauze covering your eyes."

"Wh–what's going on?" Elmer opened his eyes, but the darkened room and the gauze made it impossible to make out a face. He tried to sit up, only it hurt too much, so his head remained on the pillow. *Do they have my eyes covered for some reason?* He reached his hand up where his arm hurt, but the same cool hand stopped him.

"Please, lay still, Mr. Yoder. An IV is in your arm."

He did as he was told and felt a blanket being pulled over him. Elmer heard voices from what sounded like an intercom. He could also hear squeaky shoes and other voices from what he assumed was a hallway with shiny clean floors.

"You've been seriously hurt. Do you remember what happened to you today?"

The man speaking to him sounded close, yet Elmer was bothered because he still could not see anyone's face. His brain felt so fuzzy, like it was filled with a wad of cotton. Try as he may, Elmer couldn't remember anything past getting ready to leave the house this morning.

He pulled the gauze off and blinked, trying to bring the

doctor and nurse into focus. "It's so dark in here. Please, would you turn on a light?"

"The lamp above your bed is on." The female voice spoke again.

"It. . .it can't be. I don't see any light at all. All I see is darkness." Elmer clenched his fists so hard that his nails dug into his palms. "What's wrong with me? I can't see a thing. Please tell me what's going on." He reached up to feel his face, but a hand restrained his movement.

"You were kicked in the head by a horse, Mr. Yoder."

"I was kicked in the head?"

"Yes, and unfortunately the blow affected your optic nerve."

"What does that mean?" Elmer's mind raced, searching for answers about something that made no sense. He vaguely remembered going over to Bishop Henry's place this morning but had no recollection of shoeing the man's horse.

"There's no easy way to tell you this, Mr. Yoder, but the injury you sustained affected your eyesight."

Every muscle in Elmer's body tightened as a sudden coldness hit the core of his being. "Are. . .are you saying that I'm blind?"

"Yes." A gentle hand touched his arm again.

"But it's just temporary, right? Once my head heals, I'll be able to see again. Okay?"

His stomach quivered as he waited for the doctor's response.

"I'm sorry, Elmer, but short of a miracle, your loss of sight will be permanent."

Maybe this is a nightmare and I haven't woken yet. But Elmer's ears roared as a guttural scream spewed from his mouth. "No! No! This cannot be true. If I am blind then my life as I know it is over."

CHAPTER 9

Deanna sat in a chair beside Elmer's bed, staring at his unmoving form. Two days had gone by since his accident, and he still wouldn't talk to her when she came to visit.

When he'd been brought to the hospital and she and Elmer's family sat waiting for news of his condition, Deanna would never forget the look of agony on his parents' faces when the doctor explained that their son was permanently blind. Her heart went out to Elmer's sisters too, listening to them sob as they gathered around their mom and dad with hugs.

Deanna hurt for Elmer as well. It was all she could do to keep her emotions in check. As she sat in his hospital room now, she wanted to reach out, clasp his hand, and offer words of encouragement and comfort. But it was impossible to offer much when he wouldn't acknowledge her. Although Elmer couldn't see Deanna, he was aware of her presence. He'd proven that by turning his head away when she'd first come into his room and spoken to him.

Getting up from her chair and moving closer to the bed, Deanna tried again. "Why are you shutting me out, Elmer? Don't you know how much I care?"

No response.

"Please talk to me." Deanna placed her hand on his arm and recoiled when he pushed it away.

"What's wrong, Elmer? Why won't you speak to me?"

"Ain't nothing to talk about," he mumbled, turning his head in her direction. "You oughta go and leave me alone."

"I don't want to go, Elmer. My place is here with you."

Elmer shook his head. "Your place is with your *familye*."

"You are part of my family. At least you will be once we're married."

"We'll not be getting married, Deanna."

"Why not?" She felt panic but did her best to remain calm. This was not the Elmer she knew at all.

"Come on. You know the answer to that. I can no longer support a fraa and a *kind*. Without my sight, I won't be able to shoe horses anymore."

"I'm sure there are other things you can do, Elmer."

"Don't *baddere* with me. You deserve better."

"Why would you say I shouldn't bother with you? I love you, Elmer, and I want to be your wife." Every answer Elmer gave to Deanna, she countered with what she hoped was a positive response. Unfortunately, he came back with a reply Deanna didn't want to hear.

"Love won't fix the problem of me being a blind man. If we got married, I'd be a burden. You'd be taking care of me instead of the other way around."

"No, Elmer, I don't see it that way. Your blindness might be a challenge at first, but we can find a way to work things out."

"I am through talking about this. We won't be getting married, so please, just go." He turned his head away from her once again and kept it that way.

Tears welled in Deanna's eyes, and as they trickled onto her cheeks, she reached up to wipe them away. "All right, Elmer, I'll go for now, but I will be back tomorrow to see how you're doing."

Elmer did not respond.

Unsure of what to do, Deanna walked over and stood by his window. The parking lot below buzzed with activity as people came and went. Some carried in flowers and balloons, while a few folks walked solemnly back to their cars. The main street in front of the hospital became a blur as tears clouded her vision. Deanna glanced back at Elmer then slipped quietly from the room.

As she made her way down the hall and past the nurses' station, Deanna remembered thinking just a few days ago how much she appreciated her sight. She could not imagine how terrible it would be for Elmer to spend the rest of his days unable to see any of the wonders God created.

But he still has his other senses, Deanna thought. *Experiencing all God made for us to enjoy doesn't come only from what a person can see. In fact, isn't it true when a person loses their sight, their other senses become stronger and more in tune with what surrounds them? We can know it through what we hear, touch, smell, and taste.*

Deanna reflected on Psalm 34:8. "O taste and see that the Lord is good: blessed is the man that trusteth in him."

"That's what Elmer needs to do," Deanna whispered. "He needs to trust God to help him deal with this infirmity and set his feet on a new path."

Elmer heard footsteps and then the squeak of a door opening and closing. He was certain Deanna had left the room. *I'm glad she's gone. It was too difficult trying to reason with her.* Elmer didn't understand why Deanna couldn't see the reality of the situation and why she would want to come back tomorrow to see how he was doing.

How does she think I'll be doing? Nothing will be any different than it is now. Elmer clamped his lips together. He would spend the rest of his life shrouded in darkness and could no longer use his farrier's trade to earn a living. He had worked hard to learn his skills and enjoyed the work he did. Now it had all been for nothing. Even if he could find a different type of work, he would still have to rely on other folks to help him get around. *No, it's better to call off the engagement now and not give Deanna any hope of us having a future together.* Elmer's blindness must be a sign that God did not mean for them to be together.

Elmer rolled onto his other side, trying to find a comfortable position. *Is this my punishment for wanting the woman my best friend married?* Even though Elmer had set his feelings for Deanna aside while she and Simon were married, he had allowed those emotions to resurface soon after Simon died. Was that wrong in the eyes of God?

In an effort to get the troubling thoughts out of his head, Elmer lay listening to the voices in the hall outside his room. Nurses perhaps? Or maybe the people talking were relatives of other patients on this floor. Either way, it didn't matter. Elmer was alone, and he preferred it that way. Whenever company came to call on him, he felt obligated to talk when he was still trying to comprehend how quickly his life had changed.

Elmer thought about all the tasks he did on a day-to-day basis—even the things he took time to enjoy. He had planned to take his dog, Freckles, on an outing of small-game hunting. *Guess my hunting days are over too. Why not—everything else is.*

Yesterday when his parents came by, Mom chattered nonstop. It seemed as if she thought talking about things going on outside the hospital would take Elmer's mind off his current situation. Well, it didn't. In fact, hearing all the news about people they knew in their community only fueled his depression. *Maybe I'll tell the nurse I don't want any more visitors.*

Elmer dreaded going home from the hospital even more. Mom and Dad made it clear that he'd have to move in with them since he could no longer take care of himself, let alone his house, animals, and property.

So instead of being a burden to Deanna, I'll be an inconvenience to my folks. Elmer's throat swelled, making it difficult to swallow. *And what's gonna happen when Mom and Dad are gone someday? Will one of my sisters be stuck with me?*

It was hard not to wallow in self-pity, but Elmer couldn't conjure up one positive thought. His future seemed bleaker than a year without sunshine. "No hope. No hope," he muttered. "I wish that horse's kick had killed me. I'd be better off dead. It should have been me who died instead of my best friend, Simon. Seems God took the wrong person from this earth."

"Now what kinda talk is that?"

Elmer jerked his head, rolling over onto his back. "Who's there?"

"It's me—Henry Zook. Didn't you hear me come into the room?"

"No, I did not. Besides, even if I had, I wouldn't have known it was you. I can't see, remember?" Elmer's caustic tone cut through the air, but he couldn't tame his tongue and didn't care how it sounded. Since the accident, whenever Elmer chose to speak, he pretty much said what was on his mind.

"I thought you'd recognize my voice. We've known each other a long time, and—"

"So why are you here?"

"Came to see you, of course."

Elmer heard the scraping of a chair to his right and figured the bishop had taken a seat—the same one Deanna had sat in earlier.

"Wish the reason was mutual." Elmer could not stop the unpleasant words. "But as you can see, I can't."

Brushing his comment aside, Henry continued. "How are you feeling today, Elmer?"

How do you think I feel? "Never better." Elmer clenched his teeth. *I wonder how you'd deal with things if you were in my place.*

"Sounds to me like you're feeling sorry for yourself."

What if I am? It's not like there's no good reason.

"No comment about what I said?"

"What do you want me to say?"

"How about you're thankful to be alive?" The bishop's voice grew louder. "That kick from my fraa's *gaul* could have been so much worse. It might have killed you."

Elmer's memory of the accident had returned, and he was tempted to voice his previous thoughts on that topic but decided to keep them to himself. *I'd like to tell him to get rid of his hund or that he should have had the dog tied, at least till I was done with my work. If not for the spunky spaniel frightening Nadine's horse, the accident never would have happened. But no point getting Henry riled up. He might end up preaching a sermon to me.*

A sermon was the last thing Elmer needed right now. All he wanted was to be left alone. Everyone—Deanna, Mom, Dad, his sisters, and some well-meaning friends—seemed to think it was their duty to cheer him up. No amount of well-meaning words could take away the pain Elmer felt at the core of his being. If he was destined to live in a world of blackness, Elmer didn't want any lectures, sermons, or pity. Maybe in time he'd come to grips with his blindness, but he would never marry Deanna, and that was the worst part of all.

CHAPTER 10

Reedsville

The days dragged on as Elmer sat in his world of darkness. He was never one to feel sorry for himself, but things had drastically changed. He'd been out of the hospital three weeks and now lived with his folks so they could take care of him. If he remained with them permanently, his house and even his horse and buggy needed to be sold. What good were they to him now anyway? The blindness took away his normal way of living, so from here on out, caring for a horse and driving a buggy were out of the question.

Elmer had no desire to do anything but lie on his bed or sit in a chair, like he'd been doing since moving in with his parents. Focusing on all that he'd lost consumed his thoughts. There was no point in trying to do anything. Whenever Elmer walked on his own, he bumped into things. He couldn't even see if his hair was combed or the straw hat he owned sat straight on his head.

Elmer refused to go anywhere in public because he didn't want people's pity. It meant staying home from church and other community functions of course, which didn't sit well with his parents. The last people he wanted to see him like this were Deanna and Abner.

Deanna had brought the boy over to visit Elmer a few days after he was discharged from the hospital. His refusal to talk to them had been upsetting to Abner. Elmer heard the child crying from behind his closed bedroom door. Elmer's mother made excuses for him, saying he was too tired for company right now. But Elmer was smart enough to know Deanna had figured out he didn't want anything to do with her now. A clean break was the best thing anyway, given the circumstances. She would eventually move on with her life and find someone more suitable to marry. Someday Deanna would realize it was for the best all the way around.

"Why don't you get up from that chair and come out to the barn with me?" Dad's booming voice drove Elmer's thoughts aside.

"What for?" he muttered. "There ain't nothing in the barn for me."

"Jah, there is. The horses need to be groomed, and the cats, as well as your dog, are waiting to be fed."

"No thanks. I can't do any of those things."

"Sure you can."

"I'm blind, remember?"

"You can still feel with your hands, can't ya?" Dad bumped Elmer's arm.

Elmer clamped his mouth shut so hard his teeth clicked together. *Wish he'd just leave me alone.* He loved his parents, and they meant well, but his blindness made everything and everyone so frustrating. *Maybe I should have stayed in my own home. At least there I could wallow in self-pity with no one urging me to do things I can't do.* But that was not possible right now. How could Elmer

86

cook or keep his house clean? He couldn't even see if the furniture needed dusting.

"Come on, Son. If nothing else, you can sit on a bale of straw and keep me company while I do my chores."

Elmer grunted and pulled himself out of the chair. If he didn't go, Dad would keep pestering him. Most likely, Mom would get in on the cajoling too. Sometimes she became overprotective, and other times she sided with Dad and tried to get Elmer to do things he wasn't comfortable with.

"Here you go, Elmer. Grab hold of this walking stick with one hand and take my arm with the other."

Elmer grimaced when the unyielding wooden stick was thrust into his hand. It felt like the same one he'd made and given to Dad for his birthday last year. Little had Elmer known when he fashioned the stick that he'd end up being the one using it.

"Just a few more steps—we're almost there."

As Elmer held on to his dad, the air felt heavy, as if the weather was about to change. *But then, how would I know? The sun could be shining, for that matter.*

He heard crows nearby doing their familiar *caw. . .caw. . . caw.* Elmer even recognized the sound of the blue jays squawking up a fuss about something. Was it him, or were sounds louder than normal?

Elmer cocked his head and listened to the barn door slide open. As they moved forward, creaking floor boards greeted them. How many times had Elmer come into this building? He and his sisters used to play here after completing their chores. Before the accident, it had been a familiar, happy place. But no longer. For Elmer, Dad's barn was a scary place where he could easily bump into something, trip and fall, or lose his way and not be able to get out.

"You can have a seat on the bale of straw to your right while I get the brush and curry comb out." Dad's tone reminded Elmer of being told what to do when he was a boy. At the moment, he almost felt like a child—vulnerable and frightened of every little thing.

"Feel around with your walking stick and you'll find the bale I'm talking about." Dad let go of Elmer's arm.

Elmer froze, rooted to the spot. His equilibrium seemed off, and the sensation of falling was so great, he didn't dare move a muscle. If not for the walking stick held tightly in his hand, he would have fallen over.

"Go ahead, Son. Take three steps to the right. The bale is there, you'll see."

"No, I won't see." Elmer spoke sharply and then regretted his tone. "Sorry, Dad. I just meant..."

"It's okay. I understood what you were trying to say."

Elmer felt a little nudge against his left shoulder. "You can do it. I'm telling you the truth—the bale of straw is where I said it was."

Gripping his stick so tightly his fingers ached, Elmer pivoted to the right and took one step, then another, and one more. *Thunk!* His stick hit something. He assumed it was the bale Dad had told him to sit on.

"Okay, you're there. Turn around and sit down," Dad coached.

Elmer's legs trembled as he bent his knees and lowered

himself. He felt relief when his backside touched the prickly bale of straw.

"See. . . You did fine. Now take a breather while I get the grooming supplies. I'm sure your gaul will be glad to see you, Elmer."

"I–I'm not gonna groom my horse." Elmer spoke loudly, not sure if his dad had walked away.

"Jah, you are, Son."

Elmer heard the squeak of a gate followed by what sounded like the huff of a horse's breath. Feeling around on the bale he sat upon, he pulled out a piece of straw. Instinctively, he lifted his hand toward his face and took a whiff. *At least something hasn't changed since I lost my sight. The old sniffer can still detect the smell of dried straw.*

Elmer continued to sniff, and other odors reached his nostrils—grain, sawdust, horse manure, and even the peculiar odor of wood—all the things he used to take for granted.

He jumped when a wet tongue slurped his hand. Elmer knew without question that his dog had come to greet him. "Hey, Freckles. How are ya, boy?" Elmer moved his hand until he felt the dog's head. It was smooth and silky. That hadn't changed.

"I'm gonna miss hunting with you, my faithful friend." Elmer grimaced. "Just one more thing I've been robbed of."

"Okay, Buster's ready for you, Son."

Elmer jumped again when his dad called out to him.

"I'm not able to groom my horse, Dad," he responded. "I can't manage the things I used to do anymore. My life as I once knew it is over."

"You need to stop this foolish talk, Elmer." Dad's voice grew closer until he stood next to Elmer with both hands on his shoulders. "You're not dead, and your life is not over. So quit fighting your blindness and learn how to cope."

Elmer recoiled at his father's sharp words. *Doesn't my daed have any compassion?* He wished he could jump up and make a dash for the house, but that was out of the question. No matter how much Elmer wanted to be out of the barn, he was trapped here until Dad said it was time to leave.

"Listen, Son. . ." Dad's tone softened. "Feelings of depression and anger are common, and I understand that everything seems difficult for you right now. But new skills can be learned. You just gotta be patient and take one thing at a time."

Elmer's toes curled inside his boots. It took every ounce of self-control to keep from falling forward and bawling like a baby.

"Would you take me back in the house, please? I can't do this right now, Dad. I'm not ready."

His father remained quiet. All Elmer could hear was the older man's heavy breathing. After many seconds went by, Elmer felt Dad's hand clasp his upper arm. "Come on, Son. I'll walk you back. We'll make another trip out to the barn in a couple of days. I'm sure you'd enjoy spending a little time with Freckles as well as Buster. Your horse has always been like a pet for you."

Elmer couldn't deny it. He had Buster eating out of his hand the first day he got him. But nothing was the same anymore. Since Elmer couldn't use the horse to pull his buggy now, the closeness they once had would soon become nothing more than a distant memory.

Gripping his walking stick as Dad led him out of the barn and through the yard, Elmer felt something wet on his cheeks.

He lifted his face and stuck out his tongue. "Is it *verschnee?*"

"Well, what do you know? You're right, Elmer. It is snowing." Dad bounced the crook of his arm up and down where Elmer held tightly. "See, you don't need your eyesight to tell you what the weather is doing. You can smell it, feel it, and hear it."

The words "So, what's the big deal" were on the tip of Elmer's tongue, but he kept his mouth shut and plodded along. When they reached the porch steps and were safely inside the house, Elmer released a deep breath. Unless something drastically changed for him over time, within the confines of his parents' house might be the only place he would ever feel safe again.

Deanna sat at the kitchen table, attempting to focus on her grocery list. Abner had been a handful this morning, whining and complaining about every little thing. Whenever she tried to get anything done, he demanded her attention.

He misses Elmer; that's the problem, she told herself. Abner mentioned Elmer almost every day and repeatedly asked when his daadi was coming to the house.

Unless Elmer changed his mind about marrying Deanna, there was no chance of him becoming Abner's daddy. It saddened her to think Elmer didn't want to see them. Apparently, he did not realize shutting himself off from everyone was not a good thing. No one should ever be alone when forging their way through deep waters. Deanna could attest to that. She would have never made it through the ordeal of losing Simon if not for her reliance on friends and family.

Deanna tapped her pencil against the writing tablet. *How can*

I get through to Elmer and make him realize he can learn a new trade and lead a productive life? Not long ago, he proclaimed his love for me. Surely his feelings didn't change just because he lost his sight.

A sense of determination welled in Deanna's soul as she reflected on the dream she'd had before Elmer's accident. She hadn't shared it with him because he'd ended their engagement and she saw no point in telling him until he was ready. In addition to continuing to lift Elmer up in prayer, she would go over to see him every day if that's what it took. And the next time she went to the Yoders' house, if Elmer said he didn't want to talk to her, she would not take no for an answer.

"*Kumme*, Mammi! Kumme!" Abner shouted from the living room, where he'd gone to play ten minutes ago.

Deanna set her grocery list aside and got up from the table to see why her son wanted her to come. When she entered the room, she found Abner with his nose pressed against the window.

"*Es hot am fenschder reigschneet!*"

Deanna chuckled. "So it snowed in at the window, did it?" Here lately, things had been far too serious. It felt good to have something to laugh about.

CHAPTER 11

"Do you have a few minutes to chat with me about something, John?" Sara joined her husband inside the stall where Elmer's horse was kept.

"As you can see, I'm busy grooming our son's gaul. But if you don't mind talking to me while I work, I'm fine with it."

"I can do that." Sara moved out of his way and positioned herself against the stall gate. "Something has to be done about Elmer. A whole month has gone by since his accident, and all he does is sit around and sink deeper into depression." Her voice cracked. "What can we do to give him a feeling of self-worth?"

John stopped combing Buster's mane and turned to look at her. "I've tried to get him to help me with chores in the barn, but he refuses. When I went with Elmer to his appointment in Lewistown two weeks ago, the doctor stressed the importance of Elmer going to the Nu Visions Center to get help and learn some coping skills."

Sara's forehead wrinkled. "How come you haven't mentioned this to me till now?"

"Thought I had." John pulled his fingers through the hair on top of his head. "Since Elmer wasn't willing, guess I forgot to say anything."

Sara fastened both hands against her hips. "I've offered many suggestions to Elmer, and so have his sisters, but he still seems determined to wallow in self-pity." She moved her head slowly from side to side. "Deanna has come by here countless times, and Elmer will barely even talk to her. That poor woman is beside herself. Surely there's someone who can get through to him."

"Guess we'd better pray a little harder then, 'cause at the rate things are going, it doesn't look like our son will ever get the help he needs." John grabbed the curry comb and began working on Buster's mane again.

"On my way home from Belleville today, I may pay a call on Henry Zook and see if he or one of the other ministers in our district would come over and talk to Elmer again."

John shrugged. "Suit yourself, but there's been plenty of talking already. If our son was gonna listen to anyone, it would have been Deanna, don't you think?"

She nodded. "I'm hoping for the chance to speak to her today too."

Belleville

Deanna had sold her last batch of quilted table runners, when she spotted Elmer's mother heading her way.

"I was hoping you'd be here at the flea market today." Sara leaned against one of Deanna's tables, which, due to the cold December weather, were inside one of the buildings.

Deanna nodded. "Since Christmas will be here soon, lots of

people are here today, looking for last-minute gifts. Thought I'd better take advantage of it since things will slow down after the holidays."

"I see your point." Sara glanced around. "I don't see Abner anywhere. Isn't he with you today?"

"He is, but my friend Ruth and her daughter, Mollie, came by awhile ago. They took Abner with them to get a hot dog and something to drink."

"How nice." Sara lifted her purse handle from the crook of one arm and switched it to the other arm. "Would you be free to leave your tables for a bit and join me for lunch?"

"I'm sorry, Sara, but after Abner left with Mollie and Ruth, I ate one of the sandwiches I'd brought with me today." Deanna gestured to the remaining quilted items on the table in front of her. "Also, I don't want to leave here for any length of time because I can't afford to miss any potential customers."

"I understand. Well, since you have no one at your tables right now, would you mind if I had a few words with you?"

"Not at all." Deanna gestured to the folding chair Abner had occupied earlier. "Please, come around and take a seat."

"Danki." Once Sara got seated, she turned to Deanna and said, "I'll get right to the point. My son is still unwilling to accept professional help in dealing with his blindness, and I was hoping you might get through to him."

Deanna blinked rapidly. "Why would Elmer listen to me? As you know, I've tried and tried. The last time I went to see him, he asked me not to come again."

Sara shook her head. "He doesn't mean it, Deanna. My son is depressed and angry about losing his vision. He does not realize

95

he can live a happy life without his sense of sight."

"I understand, but if Elmer won't seek the proper help, then there's nothing you, me, or anyone else can do about it." Deanna's frustration mounted. She'd been determined to keep seeing Elmer and make him realize they could still have a life together, but each time she went over there and he shut her out, she became more discouraged. The old saying "You can lead a horse to water, but you can't make him drink" was a reminder that no one could make Elmer do anything he didn't want to do—even if it was for his own good.

Deanna placed her hand gently on Sara's arm. "I'll continue to pray for Elmer, but I hope you understand that there's nothing else I can do."

Sara's chin trembled, and her eyes appeared watery. "Then I hope one of our ministers can make him see the light." She covered her mouth and spoke between her fingers. "I didn't mean it the way it sounded." Sara put her hand down. "What I meant to say was that I hope one of the ministers will be able to talk Elmer into going to the Nu Visions Center."

"I hope so too." Deanna tried to sound optimistic, but truthfully, she didn't hold out much hope.

Reedsville

Using his homemade walking stick, Elmer paced the living-room floor. The scantly furnished room was easier to navigate than his bedroom or even the kitchen. He felt like a caged animal, wanting freedom but afraid to step outside on his own. *What I wouldn't give to go out in the yard and see what the weather is like.* He stopped pacing and gripped the stick with such force he feared it might break. *Course, I couldn't see anything, but maybe I could feel, smell, or taste what it's like out there.*

Elmer was thirsty, so before making any decisions about going outside, he slowly made his way to the kitchen. The table and chairs were the only obstacles if he wanted to get to the cupboard where Mom kept the glasses. Holding his arm in front of him and using the other to steady himself with the stick, he inched forward, shuffling his feet.

First he bumped into a kitchen chair and then the leg of the table, but still he remained upright. Hesitating a few seconds, Elmer inhaled a deep breath to calm himself. His mother wasn't here right now, and Dad was outside, so unless he wanted to stay thirsty, he'd have to get his own drink of water. Besides, it made him feel better that no one was watching.

Bumbling forward like a child learning to walk, he reached out in front of him until he found the countertop. He went to his left and felt the dry sink. On the right side, above the sink, water glasses were kept in the cupboard.

Elmer felt relief when his fingers touched a glass. *As long as I can find the water pitcher, I won't go thirsty.* After a bit more feeling around, he located the pitcher. He held it and the glass over the sink and poured some water. Feeling the water sloshing around, he stopped pouring when he thought the glass was full enough. Elmer set the pitcher on the counter, lifted the glass to his parched lips, and gulped down the water. When his thirst was quenched, he put the glass in the sink.

A bit more confident, Elmer stumbled his way back to the living room. *Thump. Thump. Thump.* Using the walking stick to guide him, Elmer plodded across the room. *Maybe I will venture outside for some fresh air. I'll just step off the porch and stand in the yard for a bit. How hard can it be to go outside?*

Elmer felt his way along the wall until he located the front door. He didn't bother searching for his jacket. He wouldn't be outside long enough to get cold. Just a few deep breaths of fresh air—that ought to be good enough. Then he'd come right back inside to the warmth of the house.

Elmer's free hand found the knob. When he opened the door and stepped out onto the porch, a blast of cold air hit his face. He sucked in his breath and let it out in a rush. *It's a bit colder than I thought it would be.* At least, according to his father, last week's snow had melted a few days ago, so the chances of him slipping on the porch steps or in the yard were slim.

Grasping the handrail with one hand and holding firmly to his stick with the other, Elmer made his way down the steps. He stood still a few seconds, turning his head to the right and then the left. The ground felt frozen and crunchy. *I wonder if I could make it to the barn. Dad went there awhile ago. Won't he be surprised when I walk in? Maybe then he'll quit bugging me to try things on my own.*

Elmer walked cautiously in the direction he thought the barn was located, listening intently for any noises he might recognize. If he was getting close to the barn, he should hear at least one of the horses whinny. But Elmer heard nothing except the rush of wind blowing against his body and sending shivers up his spine.

Where am I? he wondered, turning in circles. His head felt top-heavy, like it weighed too much, and a spinning sensation overtook Elmer, causing him to fall on the ground. "Somebody help me," he hollered. "Help! Help! Help!"

It seemed like an eternity until Elmer felt a pair of strong hands clasp his trembling shoulders. "Kumme, Son. Let me help you up."

As Elmer rose to his feet, the emotional dam broke and tears pushed past his eyes, rolling down his cheeks. He felt like a child.

"I—I lost my way, Dad. I couldn't find the barn or get back to the house." Elmer's voice cracked. "I am never going anywhere by myself again. I was a fool to even try."

"Never say never, Son. And what you tried was not foolish. Shows you have spunk." Dad spoke with reassurance. "You'll just have to learn some new ways to help you get around and do some of the things you used to take for granted. Maybe I should attach a rope that stretches from the house to the barn."

"Don't think I'll ever learn how to adjust to this darkness— with or without a rope."

"Jah, you will, but not without the proper help." Dad guided Elmer across the yard, up the steps, and into the house. "Are you ready now to visit the Nu Visions Center in Lewistown?"

Shivering against the cold seeping through his clothes, all Elmer could manage was a nod. He wasn't convinced that anything they taught at the clinic would help him lead a better life, but if he went, no one could say he hadn't at least tried.

Of course, Elmer thought with regret, *my going there won't change anything between me and Deanna. It's over between us, plain and simple.*

Chapter 12

Lewistown

Elmer left the Nu Vision Center with a white cane and a feeling of dread. Sweat poured from his forehead as another reality settled in once again. Each step he took, which was supposed to help, seemed to finalize his blindness.

Who am I trying to fool? Elmer wanted nothing more than to break the cane in two. *This is how it's gonna be, so I better get used to the skinny walking stick being like another extension of me.*

The cane's purpose was comparable to the bulkier wooden walking stick he'd been using. The only differences were its slenderness and color. Of course, Elmer couldn't see the color of his guidance cane, but he'd been told it was white. And in the past, he'd seen blind people using white canes.

White, black, or even purple—it didn't matter what color it was. What did matter was his ability to learn how to trust. Trusting people to be honest had a lot to do with eyesight. The ability to see an expression on someone's face told volumes, particularly if they were telling a lie. Now Elmer would have to listen more carefully to the tone of a person's voice in hopes of figuring out if their honesty was genuine or not.

The cane and all the things he'd been taught at the center on learning how to cope hadn't done a thing to change Elmer's perspective. At least he'd taken a step forward, but for whom? Was it for his benefit or everyone else's?

During Elmer's time at the center, he learned about a phone he could buy that was voice-activated to answer, dial, and hang up using only his voice. He felt certain if he ever did move back home, the church ministers would grant him approval to get the phone.

In addition to learning how to get around with his new cane, Elmer had also been taught some ways to identify money. Coins, such as nickels, dimes, and quarters were fairly easy to identify because their different sizes were easier to detect. Also, quarters and dimes had ridges around them, while nickels and pennies were smooth. To keep track of his paper money, it was suggested that Elmer could either keep different bills in separate places inside his wallet or fold certain bills in various ways. It all seemed like a nuisance to him. Elmer doubted he'd ever get used to living without his sight. That unexpected kick in the head had wiped out all his hopes and dreams for the future. While touch helped to differentiate many items, Elmer would never be able to do all the necessary things in order to shoe a horse. His regular clients would have to go outside the area for a farrier now—or at least until someone who lived closer learned the trade.

The bitter taste of bile rose in Elmer's throat as his dad directed him into the backseat of their driver's van. What point was there to sit up front? He couldn't see the road up ahead of them anyway.

"Lift your foot about six inches higher, Son."

"It's okay, Dad. I've got this." Elmer answered a little too harshly even though his father was only trying to help.

Once Elmer got settled in his seat, Dad reached across him to buckle his seatbelt.

"Dad, would you please stop it? I can buckle myself in."

His father didn't say anything but delayed shutting the door until Elmer's seatbelt clicked together. Then he slid the side door shut and climbed into the front seat with their driver. Elmer's sense of hearing told him that was the case.

He gripped the armrest. *Can't blame my daed for not sitting back here with me. I'm not the best company right now.*

The rest of the trip home was silent, and Elmer reflected on how one of the counselors at the center stressed the importance of accepting his disability and trying to keep a positive attitude.

Positive attitude? How can there be anything positive about being blind?

Reedsville

"You know what you need, Elmer?" Bishop Henry asked as the men sat at Mom's kitchen table eating lemon-flavored fry pies and drinking coffee.

Yeah, a new pair of eyes. Elmer shrugged his shoulders. *How much longer do I have to put up with people telling me what I need to do?* He and Dad had only been back from Lewistown an hour when Henry Zook showed up. Instead of carrying on a casual conversation, the bishop was once again about to tell him what to do.

"You should make some birdhouses and try selling them at the weekly flea market in Belleville. If you had some already made up or could make a few before next Wednesday, they could be sold as Christmas gifts. I'm sure some people would buy them."

"That's a good idea." Dad spoke before Elmer had a chance to respond. "Until you get the hang of working without your eyes, I'd be happy to help. Since this is Thursday, if we start on the project right after lunch, it'll give us the rest of today, tomorrow, and Saturday, as well as Monday and Tuesday of next week to see how many we can get done. Jah, it's doable." Dad clapped his hand so close to Elmer's ear, it caused him to nearly jump out of his chair.

"I'll help too." Mom's tone sounded enthusiastic. "You two can build the houses and I'll do the painting. Your daed and I will go with you to the market. How's that sound?"

It sounded to Elmer like he was being forced into doing something he'd rather not do. "Isn't next Wednesday less than a week until Christmas?" Elmer asked. He'd heard his mother mention the other morning how many days it would be till Christmas.

"Sure it is, but that's when some last-minute shoppers are scurrying to find something to buy," Dad answered.

"I–I'm not sure I can build anything in the dark, but I guess it won't hurt to give it a try."

He felt a gentle pat on his shoulder and knew it was Mom's hand. Elmer wished he didn't have to try doing anything. It would be a whole lot easier to curl up and die. But a little voice in his head kept saying to him: *You are not a quitter. Just try.*

Yawning, Deanna stretched out on the cot in the sunroom. It felt good to lie down for a bit and allow the sun streaming through the windows to take the chill from her bones. Even though there was no heat in this part of the house, as long as the sun was out, it stayed pleasantly warm. She felt more tired than usual this evening and wondered if she had picked up a bug somewhere. Of course, Abner kept her on her toes most of the day while she tried to get some quilting done. No wonder she felt fatigued. Since Wednesday was the last market day before Christmas, Deanna had no time to lose to complete as many things as possible to sell.

The week or two before Christmas normally had Abner all excited, but this time it was different. The boy had been a handful ever since they stopped going over to see Elmer. Even when Deanna had been taking him to the Yoders' with her, he'd come home in a bad mood. Abner had gone over there excited to visit with Elmer but always left disappointed because Elmer either said very few words to them or didn't come out of his room to acknowledge their presence at all. Deanna did her best to explain to Abner that Elmer had lost his ability to see and was dealing with the result of the accident, but the boy didn't seem to comprehend. Abner missed the times Elmer used to give him horsey rides. He'd even cried and said Elmer wasn't fun to be around anymore. It nearly broke Deanna's heart each night, tucking her son into bed and seeing him grasp the wooden horse and buggy that Elmer had carved for him.

She yawned again. *Poor Abner—he's just a boy and doesn't understand any of this.* For that matter, Deanna didn't fully comprehend the struggles Elmer now faced. She was fortunate not to have lost any of her senses. Losing one's sense of sight would be a challenge, but Elmer wasn't the only person in the world, or even the United States, who was blind.

Deanna had read an article on blindness in a magazine at

the hospital during one of her visits to Elmer. It stated that over ten million people in the USA had a visual disability. The article also related information about how many of those sightless people had jobs, and some even lived on their own. Yes, they had to make adjustments for their disability, but many had hobbies and enjoyed taking trips and doing various fun things with their friends and family.

She rolled onto her left side, trying to find a more comfortable position. *If Elmer would only get past the idea that his life is over and accept things as they are, he might find the desire and courage to make things better for himself. He needs to learn a new trade and get help coping with his blindness. If he could earn a living, he might have hope and reconsider marrying me.*

Deanna's fingers clenched. How many times had she gone over this in her mind? And for what? It didn't change anything.

"You're awful quiet over there." Dad's voice broke the silence in the room. "If you're tired, you oughta go on up to bed. Abner's all settled in now."

"Danki for tucking him in." Deanna sat up. "I am tired, Dad, but I'm mostly concerned."

"About Elmer?"

"Jah. I only wish he would get the proper help he needs in order to deal with his disability."

"Seems to me that he doesn't wanna deal with it." Dad took a seat on the chair near the cot. "He used to be such a positive person, not to mention a hard worker. Elmer's got no gumption anymore. He's given up."

Deanna poked her tongue into her cheek, inhaling a long breath. "I don't believe he's lost his gumption. He's just caught in a trap of depression and can't find his way out."

"Jah, well you oughta forget about marrying him. Might be better for both you and Abner if you let the buggy maker court you. He was interested in you before Elmer spoke his intentions."

Deanna reached up to rub the tightening muscles in her jaw. "I have no romantic interest in Yost Hostetler."

Dad lifted his hands and raised them toward the ceiling. "So what are you gonna do—sit around forever, waiting for Elmer to come to his senses?"

She gave a quick nod. "If that's what it takes, then jah. I have patience and determination, as you well know."

Dad's lip curled slightly as he wrinkled his nose. "Suit your-self, but I think you're making a mistake. Unless Elmer gets some sense in that thick head of his, it's doubtful you two will ever get married."

Deanna hated to admit it, but her father was right. No matter how much she prayed for Elmer, perhaps God had a different plan for her, and it wasn't to be Elmer's wife. If that were the case, she'd have to accept it, no matter how much it hurt.

Elmer woke up the following morning, tired and even more out of sorts than usual. In addition to getting to bed late last night, his frustration mounted the previous day because of his inability to see. Cutting wood, hammering nails, and sanding the birdhouses with Dad was nerve-racking. It nearly drove him crazy when Dad told him what to do, and then Mom praising him for every little thing even though he failed more than he succeeded. When he got a nail hammered in, his mother actually clapped.

Elmer fought with himself all the time now. If he wasn't scolding himself for how he treated his parents, he berated himself for being negative, but somehow it couldn't be helped. Each task he tried made Elmer realize all the more how much he had taken his sight for granted.

Elmer grabbed his cane, which he kept by the side of his bed, and stood. Today would be another day of sawing, pounding, and sanding wood. Maybe he would eventually get the hang of it without smashing his thumb underneath the hammer. And it was possible he'd even make some money selling birdhouses at the sale. But they wouldn't bring enough to support himself, much less a family. Thank goodness the lumber mill Dad owned did well enough to support the three of them and pay the men Dad hired to keep the business going when he wasn't working there himself. Otherwise, he couldn't have taken so much time off to spend with Elmer.

Elmer shook his head. *Why am I even concerned about a family? I broke things off with Deanna, and that's the end of it. There's no turning back to the way it used to be. It's over and done with. She needs to find someone else.*

CHAPTER 13

Belleville

It felt strange for Elmer to be sitting on a chair inside one of the flea-market buildings, unable to see the people walking past his table. But his ears perked up whenever anyone stopped and spoke to him. Talking to people whose voices were unfamiliar and even those he recognized made Elmer nervous. It was a good thing Mom sat beside him. Otherwise, he couldn't be here today. Dad had gone into the auction barn to see what animals were being auctioned off, but he planned to come back around noon with something for them to eat.

Elmer heard a child's laughter, and he tipped his head, wondering if Abner was nearby.

I sure do miss that little guy. Wish things had worked out as planned so I could've married Abner's mamm. I miss Deanna more than words could ever say. Elmer's heart nearly broke when he told her the marriage was off and asked her not to come around anymore.

Feeling like a sore thumb sticking out in a crowd, Elmer locked his fingers together and lowered his head, waiting to see if Deanna and Abner would stop at his table. When the child's laughter faded, he figured it must not have been Abner he'd heard.

"I sure like these colorful birdhouses. Did you make them yourself?"

"Yes, but I had a little help." Elmer didn't recognize the person's voice who spoke to him, but he figured from the gentle tone it was a young woman. It amazed him how keen his hearing had become since he'd lost his sight.

"How much are they?"

Elmer quoted the price.

"That sounds fair. I'll take two."

"Shall I put them in a box for you?" Mom asked. Elmer hoped she would take the woman's money and finish up with the sale. He did not feel ready to handle any of this by himself.

"I'm Rose Mary Renno, and my father, Raymond, owns a furniture store in the area. I'm sure you've heard of it."

Elmer gave a nod. "I've never visited the store though."

"You're one of the white-toppers, aren't you?" The young woman gave a small laugh. "I can tell from the length of your hair. Plus, you're wearing a white shirt with no suspender—not like the men in my church district do."

"Yes, we do drive the white-top buggies." Mom spoke again. Once more, Elmer felt relief. He wished he didn't feel so uncomfortable talking with people he'd never met. Maybe it was because he couldn't see the expressions on their faces. He used to be able to read people pretty well based on the way they looked at him. Now all Elmer had to go on was a person's tone of voice.

"Well, unrelated to what community you belong to, I believe these birdhouses might have a good opportunity of selling in my daed's store." Rose Mary's voice grew stronger. "As soon as I get home, I'll make sure he sees these. If you have time later today, maybe you can come by the furniture shop and talk to my daed."

Rubbing his forehead with one hand, Elmer mumbled, "Don't know if there will be time for that today. I'll have to wait and see how it goes."

"Okay, but if it turns out that today doesn't work out, please drop by as soon as you can. I'm almost sure Dad will be interested in your fine handiwork."

"Okay, thanks." Elmer wasn't sure Raymond Renno would want to sell any of his birdhouses, but it might be worth stopping at the store on the way home.

Reedsville

Blotting her nose with a tissue, Deanna made her way to the kitchen to heat water on the stove. She'd dealt with a nasty cold for the past week, and the symptoms had not let up. Abner had a cough and was sneezing too, so Deanna felt it wise not to attend the flea market today. With Christmas only a week away, she hated missing another opportunity to sell her quilted items. But her son's health came first, as did Deanna's. If she became sicker, she'd be too weak to keep up with the household chores, let alone make any more quilted items. She had a hard enough time getting them done now.

I'm at my wit's end. Deanna blew her nose as discouragement took over. In addition to Elmer cutting her and Abner out of his life, money was tight. She hadn't sold many quilts from home or at the sale day on Wednesdays this month. And those were the items that brought in the most money. It was a good thing

Deanna and Abner lived with her dad. The little bit of money she made wasn't nearly enough to support them both.

Deanna wished she could afford to have her own quilt shop in Belleville or one of the busier towns. A centrally located store drew more business, not to mention advertising, on all the bulletin boards at other nearby establishments and the local paper.

"Guess it's only a dream," she murmured, taking the tin full of tea bags down from the cupboard overhead.

Deanna tried not to envy those who had more than she did, but no one liked being poor. *I suppose*, she thought, taking a seat at the table to wait for the water to heat, *I'm feeling sorry for myself right now because I don't feel well and I miss Elmer so much.*

Deanna reflected on her friend Ruth. Although she had married the man she loved, things weren't always perfect in her family either. Her husband, Ben, had been unemployed off and on over the last few years, so Ruth sometimes sold homemade baked goods or other things at the flea market to help out. Even their daughter, Mollie, had been looking for a job in the hopes of helping her parents financially.

When the teakettle whistled, Deanna rose from her chair and shuffled across the room. She poured hot water into her cup then dropped a tea bag inside. While it steeped, Deanna popped into the sunroom to check on Abner. She found him asleep on the floor, once again holding the wooden horse Elmer had made. As she stared down at her son, Deanna's throat constricted. She'd all but given up hope of she and Elmer ever getting married, but she was determined to be a good mother to Abner whether or not he had a father.

Belleville

"We're here at Renno's Furniture Store," Dad announced as the buggy lurched and then came to a stop. "Do you want me or your mamm to go in with you?"

"No, I can manage. Just point me in the direction of the front door." Elmer pulled his shoulders back, hoping he sounded more confident than he felt. Truth was, Elmer was more nervous about talking to Raymond Renno about the possibility of selling his birdhouses than navigating his way into the store.

"Shouldn't one of us go in with you?" Mom put her hand on Elmer's arm.

He shook his head. "I'll be okay. After Dad gets me going in the right direction, just wait in the buggy with him, all right?"

"But Elmer. . ."

"Our son is right, Sara," Dad cut in. "For his sake, he needs to do this without us going inside with him."

"Okay, whatever you say, John."

Dad sounds like he understands what I need to do. Elmer couldn't help smiling as he made his way to the store using his new cane to guide him. When he entered the building, a familiar voice greeted him.

"Mr. Yoder, I'm glad you came by. I showed my daed the birdhouses you made, and he is eager to speak with you." Rose Mary paused and touched his arm. "If you'd like to take a seat in the chair to your left, I'll get Dad."

"Sure. Okay." Elmer stepped to one side and gave the chair a gentle tap with his cane to be sure he was at the front of it before he attempted to sit down. It felt like the seat, so he lowered himself into it and waited.

As Elmer sat patiently, he heard a bell jingle whenever a customer entered or left the store. Probably due to nerves, he'd barely noticed the sound of the bell when he pushed the door open. But now listening closely, Elmer concluded that the bell hung above the door. It was a good way to let the owners know when a customer entered their store.

A few minutes later, he heard footsteps approach. "Hello, Elmer. I'm Raymond Renno. Sorry to keep you waiting. My daughter told me about meeting you at the flea market this morning."

Elmer stood and held out his hand. "It's nice to meet you."

"Same here." Raymond shook Elmer's hand with a firm grip. "I was quite impressed with the birdhouses Rose Mary showed me. The workmanship is top-notch."

Elmer shifted uneasily. "Would you be at all interested in trying to sell them in your store?"

"Definitely, but I can do more than that. I'd like to offer you a job here." Raymond cleared his throat. "I don't actually mean here, but in the back of the store, where the woodworking is done. I lost a man who recently moved, so I need to hire a new person to sand some of the furniture pieces that have been cut by one of my other employees. You did a fine job sanding the birdhouse, so I'm sure you'd be capable of doing the work."

A wave of heat traveled up the back of Elmer's neck and cascaded across his face. *Does Raymond feel sorry for me? Is that why he offered me a job? I need to be honest with him.*

"I appreciate your offer, but I've never worked with wood

professionally—it's just a hobby for me. I was a farrier until I lost my sight."

"I heard about the unfortunate incident and was sorry to learn of it. While we've never met personally until now, you have worked on my horses."

Elmer tipped his head. "Oh?"

"Jah. One of the men working for me brought two of our buggy horses to your place to have their shoes replaced."

"I see." Elmer shifted his weight from one foot to the other. "I've worked on a good many horses here in the Big Valley, although some folks have hired farriers from outside the area."

Raymond clasped Elmer's shoulder. "Would you agree to work for me even a couple days a week? If you like the job and things work out well, I'd offer you a full-time position."

Elmer rubbed his sweaty palm down the front of his trousers while keeping a firm grip on his cane with the other hand for support. "I. . .I suppose I could give it a try. I'll have to hire a driver to bring me into work, of course. Unfortunately, my days of driving a horse and buggy are over." Elmer's disappointment exhibited in his voice. It was one thing to hire a driver when a person needed to go out of the area, but to be reliant on one for trips he used to take by horse and buggy was an unhappy adjustment for him. Even so, Elmer felt good about the opportunity to earn some money. *It's time for me to support myself instead of depending on my folks. And a job will give me a reason to get out of bed every morning, not to mention earn a paycheck.* For the first time in many weeks, Elmer felt a ray of hope.

"Danki, Raymond." Elmer held out his hand again. "I look

forward to working here at your store. When would you like me to begin?"

"Would tomorrow be too soon?"

"Nope, not at all. Just name the time, and I'll be here."

"We don't open for business until nine in the morning, but the fellows who make the furniture in the shop out back usually start at eight."

"No problem. I'll make sure to be here on time."

Elmer shook Raymond's hand once more, and using his cane, he found his way to the door. He wasn't sure how well he could do the job Raymond offered him, but it beat sitting around his folks' house all day, wallowing in self-pity while twiddling his thumbs.

I can't believe what just happened in there. When Elmer went to bed tonight, for once he'd have something to look forward to in the morning. "And who knows?" he murmured as he made his way to the buggy, following the sound of the horse's nicker, "I may even enjoy sanding wood all day."

CHAPTER 14

Reedsville

Christmas came and went, and here it was the middle of January. Without Elmer, the holiday wasn't the same. It made Deanna sad, but for Abner's sake, she tried to make it as joyful as possible. While her son continued to play with the wooden horse and buggy Elmer had made, he didn't talk about Elmer much anymore. Maybe, like Deanna, he'd also given up hope of Elmer being a part of their life.

Deanna paused from her pondering, keeping her focus on guiding Bess down the road in the direction of Belleville. The weather this month remained nippy, and a light dusting of snow covered the ground. But Deanna made up her mind to attend the flea market today. Even the sale of a few quilted items would help with expenses. She needed new material to make Abner a few pairs of trousers and preferred not to ask her dad for more money. He'd done enough already, letting them live with him and helping out when finances were tight.

Deanna shivered, and Abner huddled close to her, looping his arm through hers. In the partially open buggy, their heavy jackets and gloves did not shield them well enough from the cold as they continued onward. They still had about five miles to go before they reached Belleville, and by the time they got there, they'd probably feel like someone had put ice down their backs.

"*Guck*, Mammi, *schmoke*." Speaking in Pennsylvania Dutch, Abner pointed to their horse's head.

"It's not smoke, Son. When it's cold outside, you can see your breath." Deanna made an O with her mouth and exhaled. "See. Now you try it." Even inside the buggy, the rawness of the air made that possible.

Abner did the same and giggled. Apparently, he hadn't noticed the vapor before with just his normal breathing, but now Abner found it fascinating. That would hopefully keep his mind occupied for a while as he blew breath out of his mouth in every direction.

Deanna giggled. *It's amazing the simple things that amuse kids—almost like children getting more enjoyment playing with their mamm's pots and pans instead of their own toys.*

I wonder if Elmer and his mamm will be at the market today. From a distance, she had seen them the last couple of times, but Deanna hesitated to approach his table. She'd heard from another vendor that Elmer was working at Renno's Furniture Store and had also started making birdhouses to sell at the market. *I'm glad he found something meaningful to do.*

"*En kareb eppel?*" Grabbing her attention, Abner pointed to the basket of apples on the floor in front of his seat.

Deanna nodded. "Jah. We will sell the apples at the flea market." Dad's apple trees had produced abundantly this fall, so Deanna had decided to take some of the excess to the market in hopes of making a little more money.

Abner reached down and picked one out, but before Deanna stopped him, he'd taken a bite. "*Es bescht.*"

Her gaze flicked upward then back at him. "It is the best, but next time please ask before you take something, Son."

Abner took another bite then dropped the apple back in the basket.

Deanna almost scolded the boy but decided to let it go. She leaned over and picked up the apple, making a mental note that once she got to the market, she would wash any of the other apples it had touched. *I hope things go better as the day progresses, including Abner behaving himself.*

Belleville

Elmer's life had been going a bit better—at least in the area of his confidence. Even though a few mishaps still occurred, getting around had gotten easier for him at home as well as at his new workplace. He'd recently begun working four days a week for Raymond Renno, leaving Wednesdays free to take his birdhouses to the flea market. Although Mom wanted to accompany him, today Elmer had hired a driver who'd helped set up his table. It was worth the extra money he'd spent to pay the driver not to have his mother hovering around all day, treating him like a child. Mom said she wanted him to be independent, yet she often tried to do things for him that he'd learned to do himself. *She needs to find a happy medium,* he mused.

Elmer hadn't said anything to his parents yet, but he planned to move back to his own place on Saturday and would take his dog with him. Despite his blindness, he needed to be back in the familiarity of his own house and furnishings. Unfortunately, Elmer's horse had to stay because he had no use for him anymore. But he couldn't bring himself to sell the gelding. He hoped Dad wouldn't mind keeping Buster. Elmer would certainly agree to pay for his feed.

As Elmer sat behind his sale table listening to people chatter, his thoughts went to Deanna, as they so often did. *Is she here at the market today? If so, will she stop by and say hello?* So far that hadn't happened. *How can I blame her? I told Deanna to stay away from me.* Now Elmer wasn't so sure he'd done the right thing. He longed to hear Deanna's sweet voice, and he ached to hold her in his arms. Elmer missed Abner too, remembering how much fun it had been to give the youngster horsey rides. *Do they miss me as much as I miss them? I wonder what kind of Christmas they had.*

Elmer's holiday hadn't been the least bit exciting this year. He'd enjoyed Mom's meal, and getting together with his sisters had been nice, but nothing seemed the same without Deanna and her son. His thoughts had been on her most of Christmas Day.

Elmer picked up his cane and snapped it lightly against his leg. *Quit thinking like this. I can't marry Deanna, so there's no use wishing I could.* No, it would be better if he didn't hear anything from Deanna or Abner today.

Even though Elmer managed a little better on his own now, gaining the ability to be a good husband or a father to an active child appeared to be impossible. What if something dangerous occurred and he couldn't see what was happening? Without his eyesight, he'd be unable to protect Abner from getting hurt or find his way over to the child to save his life if an emergency arose.

When Elmer heard someone approach his table, he sat up

straight and pushed his thoughts aside. If someone were to buy a birdhouse, he needed full concentration—especially when it came to making change.

"Hey, Elmer. How's it going?"

Elmer didn't have to think twice. He had no trouble recognizing his bishop's voice. "All right, I guess. As you can see, I'm here selling birdhouses today." Elmer wasn't trying to be rude. He became tired of people always asking how things were going and wished it would stop. *But then if no one asked, I'd probably think nobody cared about me,* he reasoned.

"How's your new job at Renno's Furniture Store?" Henry asked, apparently unaffected by Elmer's sarcasm.

"I like it well enough. At least I've found a way to make a living."

Elmer felt Henry's hefty hand clasp his shoulder. "Good to hear. It's an answer to prayer, that's for sure."

Elmer folded his arms. "If Jesus were still here on earth, do you think He would touch my eyes and take away my blindness?"

"Jah, I believe He would."

"Guess I was born a few centuries too late. Now all I can do is pray for the strength to get through the rest of my life dealing with my blindness."

"I thought you were coming to grips with it, Elmer. You told me you were the last time we talked."

Elmer relaxed his arms and fidgeted with his shirt collar. "In some ways I am, but I can't help feeling frustrated about all the things I'm not able to do." He groaned. "I feel inferior to other men."

"Nonsense! You're still the same kind, helpful man you used to be. That hasn't changed because of your disability."

"Helpful? How am I helpful, Henry? I can barely take care of myself, let alone help someone else."

"Calm down, Elmer, and please lower your voice. Several people are looking this way."

A rush of heat erupted on Elmer's face. The last thing he needed was to make a scene. "I'm trying to take it a day at a time. Some days I can tackle more. Other days, I take two steps back." Elmer spoke much more quietly this time. "Can we talk about something else?"

"Sure, but I need to move on soon. My fraa's waiting for me across the way."

Elmer swatted the air with his hand. "Go ahead then. I've taken up enough of your time. Have a nice day, Henry."

"Okay, I'll see you in church Sunday morning."

"Jah, sure thing." Elmer had to bite his tongue to keep from saying, *I'll be there, but I won't see you. I won't see anyone from our church district because my eyes have been damaged.* No point saying what he thought though. Most folks he knew probably already believed he was a big complainer.

After the bishop moved on, Elmer leaned back in his chair, careful not to lean too far lest the chair fall over. He didn't need to end up flat on his back.

The morning went quickly as a couple of people came by and bought birdhouses. Thanks to the training he'd had at the center in Lewistown, Elmer was able to make change when the customers paid for their purchases.

Elmer took a sip of the bottled water sitting on an upright

box next to him, when another customer came to his table.

"What is it, Mommy? What are you looking at?" A girl's small voice broke through the silence.

"I'm looking at some beautiful birdhouses, Sheila. This gentleman has quite a few he is selling."

"Can I touch one of them?" the child asked.

"You'll have to ask the man if it is okay."

"Is it okay, mister?"

"Why sure." Elmer had to smile at the sweet sound of her voice and friendly tone.

"How about we buy one to hang in the backyard, Sheila? You know how you love listening to the birds at the feeder your daddy put up. Maybe next spring we can get them to build a nest in this."

"Oh boy, Mommy. Yes, please get one. But can I pick it out?"

"Yes honey, go ahead and choose one." Then the lady asked, "How much are they, sir, and are they all the same price?"

Elmer told her the cost and added, "The price is the same no matter which one your daughter chooses."

"Sheila likes this one." The woman handed it to Elmer. After the payment was made, Elmer wrapped the birdhouse in several grocery bags to protect it; then he put it in a bigger bag. "Thank you for your purchase."

"You're welcome. And by the way, will you be here each week, selling these birdhouses?"

"Probably so," Elmer answered, using his cane to back up and sit down again in the chair behind him. Then he heard the lady's daughter murmur something to her.

"Just a minute, sweetie." After responding to her daughter, the woman spoke to Elmer again. "I'm glad to hear you'll be here.

I'll most likely purchase another birdhouse as a gift for one of my friends." The lady's voice sounded friendly like her daughter's. "Umm... If you don't mind, I'd like to ask you something else."

"Sure, what is it?" Elmer waited, a bit perplexed.

"Sheila asked if she could see what you look like. Is it okay with you if she comes around to your side of the table?"

"Yes, it's quite all right." Elmer wondered what was going on, but he didn't want to hurt the little girl's feelings. Just by her voice, he could only imagine how precious this child must be.

Sheila's mother told her to hang on to the table and follow it around to the back, where the gentleman sat. When the child came to his side of the table, she bumped into his cane and knocked it to the floor.

"Here, Sheila, let me pick that up," her mother was quick to say.

"Give it to me, please, Mommy. I want to hand it back to the man." When the girl's small hands found Elmer's, she handed him the cane. "What's your name?"

"Elmer Yoder." A lump formed in his clogged throat when the realization hit him. *This child is blind.*

She touched the top of Elmer's head. Then her delicate hands moved down his face. Sheila placed her fingers on his forehead then his closed eyes, his nose, and chin. "What color's your hair?"

"Kind of a reddish brown."

"Would you like to touch my face so you can see me too? I could tell by your cane that you're blind like me." The child took Elmer's hands and placed them on her head. "Now do like I did."

Elmer did as the little girl had done and tried to imagine what she looked like. His fingers felt long strands of silky hair, which curled on the ends around his fingers; then he touched her forehead, closed eyes, and slightly turned-up nose. When he got to her chin, he gave it a tickle. "I'll bet you have blond hair and the prettiest blue eyes the color of the ocean. And I'll bet you're about four years old."

"I'm almost five. My birthday's in April." Then she squealed, "Mommy, he sees me too, like I can see him." She reached for Elmer's hand and shook it like a little adult. "Maybe we'll come again sometime. It was nice to meet you, Mr. Elmer."

Elmer smiled, but he could have bawled like a baby. "It was a pleasure to meet you too, Sheila."

"Thank you again, sir, for understanding my daughter's request." The girl's mother took Elmer's hand and shook it. "I'll be sure to spread the word to my family about the nice birdhouses you sell. We are all nature lovers."

"Thank you. You have a special little girl." Elmer's heart nearly broke, thinking how someone so young did not have the joy of eyesight. Was she born without vision, or did something happen causing the child to go blind?

I could sure learn a thing or two from this little girl. The sale of that one birdhouse will stick with me forever.

Elmer was about to reach under the table for his cooler to get the sandwich Mom had prepared this morning, when he heard another child playing nearby. Only this time, he recognized the voice. It had to be Abner's. Assuming Deanna must be close at hand, Elmer remained silent and listened.

"Hey, little boy. Would you like a piece of candy?" A lady's voice Elmer didn't recognize spoke. Then Elmer heard the rustle of paper and figured it must be a candy wrapper being opened.

A few seconds later, the boy coughed, then a gagging sound followed. Did he have something caught in his throat?

When the stranger's voice screamed, "Someone help, the kid's choking," instinct kicked in, and Elmer jumped up from his chair. Maneuvering quickly with the aid of his cane, he located the boy. Elmer knew in a split second that Abner wasn't breathing. The child could no longer cough or speak.

Wrapping his arms around Abner's waist, then making a fist and positioning it below Abner's rib cage above his navel, Elmer leaned slightly forward and performed the Heimlich maneuver. *Dear Lord*, he silently prayed, *don't let this dear boy choke to death.*

CHAPTER 15

After a customer paid for the quilt she had purchased, Deanna looked behind her where Abner had kept himself occupied moments ago. Her muscles grew tense as she mumbled, "Now where did he get to?"

Deanna's heartbeat quickened. "Abner, where are you?" Every time she brought her son to the flea market, she feared this could happen. *I need to find him now, or he could get lost in the crowds.*

Hearing some commotion two aisles over, Deanna hurried in that direction. Several people clustered around a scene, wide-eyed and pointing. When Deanna stepped between two women, she saw Elmer kneeling on the floor, holding her sobbing child in his arms.

"What's going on?" she asked, stepping up to them. "Why is Abner crying?" Deanna's voice shook with emotion as she got down on her knees and touched her son. All these weeks, Elmer had avoided them, and now he'd apparently done something to make her precious boy cry.

"The little guy choked on a piece of candy, and this nice man saved his life." The elderly woman speaking pointed at the lemon drop on the floor.

Deanna gasped. Lemon drops could be dangerous, especially for a child to eat. And how in the world did Abner get the candy?

Before Deanna could ask her question, Elmer spoke. "While I sat at my table, I heard Abner's voice. Then someone offered him a piece of candy. A few seconds later, I heard him choking, and an alarmed lady yelled about it." He paused and rubbed Abner's back as his sobbing subsided. "It was all I needed to hear, so I made my way over to him and performed the Heimlich maneuver. My daed taught me how to do it many years ago. Abner's okay now. Just a little shook up."

Deanna pulled her son gently into her arms. Then she reached out and touched Elmer's shoulder. "Danki, Elmer. I'm thankful you were here when it happened and knew what to do."

"You're welcome." Elmer picked up his cane and rose to his feet. "He should be fine now, but you might wanna make sure he stays with you for the rest of the day. It's not good for Abner to wander off by himself or take candy from strangers."

Deanna's lips pressed together. Despite her appreciation for Elmer saving Abner's life, his comment irritated her. *Doesn't Elmer realize I always try my best to keep Abner close to me?*

Relieved that the crowd had dispersed, Deanna moved closer to Elmer and snapped back through clenched teeth: "I don't have eyes in the back of my head, and when I'm busy with a customer, Abner sometimes slips away."

"Maybe you shouldn't bring him to the sale with you anymore."

Deanna bristled. *The nerve of him speaking in that tone and scolding me on how to handle my son. If he honestly cared about me and Abner, he wouldn't have pushed us away.*

"I don't have time to debate this with you," she stated. "Again, I am thankful for what you did for Abner, but I need to get back to my sale tables." Clasping her son's hand, Deanna led Abner away.

"That went well," Elmer muttered as he found his way back to his own table. "Don't understand why she got so upset. I was only pointing out the obvious."

When Elmer reached his table, he lowered himself into the chair. *Could Deanna still be upset with me for breaking things off with her after I lost my sight? Is that why she seemed so testy?*

Elmer leaned forward, elbows resting on the table. *I saved Abner's life. Maybe I'm more capable than I give myself credit for. Thanks to my job at the furniture store, plus selling birdhouses here, I'm able to provide financially. And now I've just proven that I am adapting to situations and can respond to an emergency if it's within my power.*

He rubbed his forehead, contemplating things further. *I need to speak to Deanna again, but not here at the market. Think I'll hire a driver to take me over to Rufus's place after supper this evening. I need to clear the air with her, and if she's willing to listen, I hope we can chat about a few other things too.*

Reedsville

That evening during supper, Elmer went over and over in his head how to break the news to his folks about moving back home. He

129

waited until Dad stopped talking about the weather then cleared his throat. "Umm. . . There's something I need to say."

"What is it, Elmer?" Mom asked.

"Freckles and I will be moving back home Saturday."

Mom let out a small gasp. "Elmer, you can't be serious."

He bobbed his head. "I'm getting around better on my own now, and after what happened today, I believe I can handle most anything that comes my way."

"What happened?" Dad asked.

Elmer explained about the incident with Abner at the flea market. "Because of my blindness, I never thought I could step in and take charge in an emergency such as that. But I proved myself wrong today." He reached carefully for his glass of water and was relieved when it touched his lips without spilling.

After taking a drink, Elmer continued. "For the first time since my accident, I let go of my fears and self-doubts. Coming to Abner's aid and realizing he was okay afterward felt good."

"You did well, Son." Dad gave Elmer's back a few easy thumps. "I'm proud of you—not in a *hochmut* sort of way, but because you set your fears aside and did what you could to dislodge the candy and get the boy breathing again."

Elmer lifted his chin, giving a satisfied smile. He was never one to boast or feel prideful, but he felt good about having done the right thing.

"What you did for Deanna's son was certainly brave," Mom said. "But your act of bravery doesn't mean you ought to live on your own again. What if something happened that was out of your control and no one was there to help you?"

The muscles along Elmer's jawline clenched. "Jah, it's a

fact—I'll have to face obstacles. But with God's help and the new talking phone the church ministers agreed I could get, I am ready to take the chance. So please don't try talking me out of it, Mom. I am determined to move back home, and it's gonna be Saturday. I've already lined up my driver." He rose from his chair. "And speaking of drivers, Drew Higgins will be here soon to get me. I'm going over to Rufus's place to speak to Deanna."

"I shouldn't be too long, so if you don't mind waiting, I'd appreciate it," Elmer told his driver when he announced they had arrived at their destination.

"No problem," Drew replied. "I brought a new western novel along to read, so take your time."

Elmer got out of the van and leaned back in through the open passenger's door. "Umm. . .would you mind pointing me in the direction of the house?"

"Sure, no problem." Elmer heard his driver's door open, and a few seconds later, he felt Drew's hand on his arm. "Here you go, Elmer. I'll take you right up to the porch steps. I'll keep an eye out for you, so give me a wave when you're ready to go, and I will help you back to the van."

Elmer felt like a child again, but he didn't have the time or inclination to go wandering around the yard, hoping to find Rufus Kanagy's house.

Maybe I'm not as independent as I thought. Guess I do need someone around me most of the time. Hope moving back home isn't a mistake.

Pushing his insecure thoughts aside, Elmer thumped his way

up the porch stairs. He took five steps, rapped on the door, and waited. Pretty soon he heard the door open, and a whoosh of warm air touched his face.

"Well, what do you know. Sure am surprised to see you here this evening, Elmer." Rufus's voice boomed loud and clear.

For a split second, Elmer almost lost his nerve. But then his determination to speak to the woman he loved won out. "I came to see your dochder. Is she here?"

"Deanna's out in the barn, and so is Abner. They're showing Franey Hostetler our latest batch of kittens. Guess Franey wants to get one for her daughter's birthday. Want me to walk you out there?"

"Maybe just up to the barn door. Then I can take it from there. Danki."

"Not a problem. I'll get my jacket real quick and be right with you."

As Elmer stood waiting for Rufus, he lifted his head and sniffed. Moisture was in the air—he could smell it. Elmer figured more snow was probably in the forecast.

"Okay, I'm all set. If you'll reach out and take hold of my arm, I'll lead you on out to the barn."

Elmer did as Rufus asked.

"So are you doing okay, Elmer?"

Elmer sighed. "Some days my confidence level is pretty high, but then the next, I'm unsure about everything."

"I can only imagine what it's like to have your world turn upside down in a split second." Rufus squeezed Elmer's arm, looped through his. It was one of the few times someone actually talked to Elmer without telling him how he should feel.

"I have a job now and am planning to move back to my house this weekend. Plus, I go to the flea market on Wednesdays to sell the birdhouses I make."

"Sounds like you're trying real hard to get above an unsure situation."

"Jah, I am."

The whole time they walked, Elmer held his cane in front of him, moving it slowly back and forth. When the cane hit something solid, he figured they'd made it to the barn.

"You're right here by the door now. Do you want me to go in with you?" Rufus asked.

"No, thanks. When I come out, I'll give my driver a wave, and he can lead me back to his van."

"Okay." Rufus gave Elmer's shoulder a good tap. "You take care now, you hear? It was good talking with you."

"Same here." Elmer grasped the door handle, pulled, and stepped in. While not as warm as the air he'd felt when Rufus opened the door to his house, being inside the barn was better than standing outside in the cold.

The smell of straw reached his nostrils, and he felt a cat rub against his leg. The cat's purring got louder as it moved around Elmer's right leg then his left. He heard other cats meowing, but they sounded more like kittens. He figured they were the ones Franey came to look at.

Elmer used his cane to gently shoo the cat away, then he took a few cautious steps, letting the cane be his guide. When he heard Deanna's voice, he came to a halt.

"Yost Hostetler came by last night. He wants to court me and said he has marriage on his mind."

"What did you tell him?" Elmer recognized Franey's high-pitched voice.

"Said I would give it some thought."

Elmer's shoulders dropped, like a branch falling from a tree. *I'm too late. Deanna's gonna end up marrying Yost. Why did I foolishly break things off with her?*

Elmer had two choices. He could either barge in where the women were talking and pretend he hadn't heard what Deanna said or turn around and walk out of the barn. He chose the latter. As much as it hurt to imagine Deanna marrying someone else, she and Abner would be better off with the buggy maker. He could provide well for them, and Yost had two good eyes. He didn't have to rely on anyone leading him around or taking him from place to place.

With a stooped posture and heart filled with sorrow, Elmer shuffled off. He loved Deanna enough to let her go.

Chapter 16

"What'd Elmer have to say?" Deanna's father asked when she and Abner entered the house after Franey left with her kitten of choice.

She tilted her head to one side. "You mean this afternoon at the flea market?"

"No, a short time ago. He stopped by and wanted to speak with you, so I walked him out to the barn."

She moved her head quickly from side to side. "I have not seen Elmer since the sale in Belleville."

Dad gave his earlobe a tug. "That makes no sense. I walked Elmer right to the door, and as I was heading back to the house, I looked over my shoulder and saw him enter the barn. He knew you were in there, because I told him you were showing Franey the kittens."

"How strange." Deanna touched the base of her neck. "I wonder if. . ." She let her hand fall to her side. "Dad, I need to see Elmer right away. I hope he didn't overhear something I told Franey and left because of it."

"What did you say?"

"I mentioned that Yost had asked if he could court me, and..." Without finishing her sentence, Deanna grabbed her woolen shawl from the back of a chair and wrapped it around her shoulders. "I need to see Elmer."

His brows lifted. "Now?"

"Jah. If that is what Elmer heard and it's the reason he left, I need to give him an explanation." She gestured to Abner, playing with his wooden horse across the room. "Would you put Abner to bed for me?"

"Of course, but I wish you'd wait till tomorrow. I don't like you taking the horse and buggy out after dark. It's hard to see with only the light of the lanterns on the front of the buggy. Also, when I talked to the neighbor today, he said more snow is forecasted."

She held up her hand. "I'll be fine, Dad. Even though we had a light dusting of snow this morning, the roads were dry on my way home from Belleville this afternoon. Besides, I've driven in the dark many times and never had a problem. And it's not snowing yet, so I need to get going so I can get back home before it starts up again."

"Okay, guess if I can't talk you out of it, after Abner is in bed, I'll get out my Bible and pray for your safety."

"Danki. Right now, both Elmer and I need all the prayers we can get."

Elmer made his way out to the barn. Thanks to the rope Dad had strung, it was easier and less intimidating than the first time he'd tried it on his own. After the dusting of snow they woke up to earlier today, the afternoon had brought partly cloudy conditions, but it was cold enough to keep some of the snow still lingering on the ground. His father had mentioned the full moon and a possibility of heavier snow in the wee morning hours.

Elmer paused for a minute to listen. He'd always loved the peace and tranquility of nightfall when it settled in. His mind raced with thoughts of Deanna, along with the many regrets he now had.

Elmer envisioned the full moon and still remembered how the snow sparkled on the back fields and the way stubbles of cornstalks created shadows in the moon's light.

The little blind girl at the market today came to mind. *What if that precious child was born blind? At least I have the ability to remember how things used to look and can envision my family and friends' faces. How does a blind person picture everything if they've never had eyesight at all? Guess I'm pretty lucky for that, at least.*

Elmer sighed into the night air. *Little Sheila made me think about things from a different perspective. I don't want to give up everything I enjoyed before I became blind. I just have to find a way to appreciate things differently. If that sweet child can enjoy her life, then so can I.*

A chilly breeze blew against his face, and he imagined the vapor as he blew his breath into the air. Elmer cocked his head in the direction of a sound he always reveled in hearing. A barred owl hooted in the distance, and seconds later another one answered. He smiled, listening to the nocturnal birds conversing back and forth with each other. One sound was deep as it called: *Whoo. . . whoo. . .too-whoo.* The other owl called back in a quieter tone: *Whoo. . .whoo. . .too-whoo.*

Elmer stood a while longer, listening and hoping the nature

sounds would help ease his rapid thoughts. The owls eventually quieted down, but in the distance, Elmer heard what he felt sure was a coyote howling. "Now that's something you don't hear often. Maybe it's howling at the full moon."

Shaking his head, Elmer asked himself: *Would I have even noticed that when I still had my eyesight?*

Elmer had always found contentment and joy hearing the sounds of nature but even more so now than before the accident. Tonight, he fought hard not to let another setback take over or dwell on his many regrets. *How can I be around Deanna again if she's courted by Yost? And Abner—will he end up getting close to the buggy maker like he once was with me? What if Deanna's little boy forgets about me altogether after Yost is in his life?* Elmer lowered his head. *I made a mistake pushing Deanna away, and I'll regret it for the rest of my life.*

Grasping the rope, Elmer moved toward the barn, needing to get his mind off things. The best way to remedy depression was to keep busy. He needed to make extra birdhouses to take to the market next week in case Sheila's mother returned with more requests.

After Elmer entered the barn and felt his way to the work-table, he picked up the cut and sanded pieces of wood and began nailing them together. *Once I move back home, I'll have to sell my farrier tools. Then maybe Dad will help me get a workshop set up inside my own barn.*

With fingers clenched tightly, Deanna drove Bess down the darkened road toward John and Sara Yoders' place. She went over and over in her head the conversation with Franey and what Elmer likely had heard.

"I can only imagine what he thought," Deanna mumbled, more determined than ever to speak with him tonight.

Thankfully, not many vehicles were on the road this evening, so she kept Bess at a steady pace, all the while her thoughts on Elmer.

It sure seems like everything has gone against us, but I won't let Elmer's blindness keep us apart anymore. He has to listen to me this time. Oh, I hope it's not too late and Elmer will believe the words I'm about to tell him.

By the time Deanna pulled onto the Yoders' driveway, she'd fully rehearsed what she wanted to say. After climbing down from the buggy and securing her horse, she made her way up to the house, using a flashlight to guide the way.

Deanna's heart pounded as she knocked on the door. *What if Elmer doesn't want to see me? What if he sends me away like he's done numerous times since he lost his sight?* Deanna squared her shoulders. *I'm not leaving until I tell Elmer what he didn't hear.*

The door opened, and Elmer's mother greeted her. "Deanna, this is a surprise. Most folks don't come calling after dark on a weeknight. Is everything all right?" Sara's voice held a note of concern.

"Everyone's fine at our house. I came to speak to Elmer. Would you please tell him I'm here?" Deanna pulled her black shawl tighter around her shoulders to block the cold.

"Elmer is in the barn, working on another set of birdhouses." Sara stepped out the door and joined Deanna on the porch. "We heard what happened to your little *buwe* at the flea market today."

She touched Deanna's arm. "So glad to hear Abner's okay."

"Jah. I shudder to think what would have happened if Elmer hadn't jumped in and dislodged the candy blocking my boy's airway. He may very well have saved Abner's life." Deanna turned her head in the direction of the barn, where the light from a lantern shone in one window. "It's cold out here, and I should let you go before you freeze to death. I'm going out to see Elmer now."

"Certainly—go right ahead."

Sara ducked back into the house, and Deanna carefully made her way across the yard. When she reached the barn and opened the door, she called, "Elmer, may I speak to you? It's me—Deanna."

Hearing Deanna's voice, Elmer dropped the piece of wood he held. *What in all the world is she doing here? I hope Abner's okay.*

"I'm back here at my workbench," he responded in a loud voice. Several seconds later, Elmer felt her small hand touch his shoulder. "Why are you here, Deanna? Is everything all right with Abner?"

"He's fine." Deanna stepped in front of him. He felt her warm breath on his face. "I came to see you, Elmer."

"About what?" Elmer tried not to let on how conflicted he felt in her presence, especially with her standing so close. He still loved Deanna, no doubt about it. But he couldn't speak the words. Not after what he'd heard in Rufus's barn.

Her hand tapped his arm a few times. "I came to talk some sense into you and hopefully make you see that there's no good reason for us not to get married."

Elmer's chest tightened. "Don't see how that's ever gonna

happen now that Yost will be courting you."

Deanna's hand fell away from Elmer's arm, and she clasped his shoulders with both hands. "My daed said you came by our place earlier this evening and that he'd helped you find your way to the barn."

Elmer's head moved slowly up and down.

"Did you hear me talking to Franey—telling her Yost asked about courting me?"

"Jah. So I left." The words almost stuck in Elmer's throat. "After what happened with Abner today, and me dislodging the candy, I'd reached the conclusion that maybe I could take on the responsibility of marrying you and raising a family." Elmer paused, searching for the right words. "I wanted to ask you to marry me all over again till I heard about you and the buggy maker." He lowered his head. "Figured he'd make you a better husband, so I just walked on out of the barn. I was not gonna interfere with your decision about Yost."

Deanna's cold fingers touched Elmer's chin, and she tipped his head upward. "There is no me and Yost. I only said I would think about his request." She pressed her forehead against his. "It's you I love, Elmer, not Yost. Even if I had allowed him to court me, I would never agree to marry a man I didn't love."

Dampness formed in Elmer's eyes as he reached out and touched the curves of her face. "Will you marry me, Deanna?"

"Jah, of course. My wedding dress is made and hanging in my bedroom, so nothing stands in our way except talking to the bishop and setting a date to have our plans to be married published in church."

Deanna's sweet voice and declaration of love nearly melted

Elmer's heart. "Our wedding day can't come soon enough."

Elmer leaned in until his lips met hers, and then he sealed his love with a kiss as gentle as butterfly wings. *Thank You, God*, he silently prayed, *for blessing me with a woman of such determination. Please guide and direct us in the days ahead, and give Deanna, Abner, and me many good years together.*

EPILOGUE

Deanna stood inside the living-room door, watching her husband and son sitting side by side on the floor. Abner's hands clutched his wooden horse and buggy, and Elmer held a book.

"Tell me what you see on this page, Son." Elmer tapped Abner's shoulder.

Deanna smiled, listening to her boy describe a fat pink pig rolling in the mud.

Elmer turned the page. "What animal do you see here?"

"A horse!" Abner leaped to his feet. "Horsey ride, Daadi! Horsey ride, please!"

"Okay, little man, climb up on my back." Elmer got on his hands and knees.

Abner didn't have to be asked twice. He hooped and hollered as Elmer, neighing like a horse, crawled around the living room with Abner on his back.

The furnishings were sparse in this room, and Elmer had memorized the layout of his home well, so he didn't bump into any of the chairs.

So many good things had happened since they'd gotten

married last month. Deanna's dad and father-in-law created an area in the barn for Elmer's workshop. And several men from their white-top community came together and built a small addition to the barn where Deanna now had her quilt shop. This allowed Deanna and Elmer to work closely in case he needed her for something. Abner loved helping Elmer too, even if it was only to hand him things.

Remembering the dream she'd once had where Simon had given his blessing, Deanna continued to watch a few more minutes before clapping her hands. "I hate to interrupt your fun, boys, but supper's on the table, and it's gonna get cold if we don't eat soon."

"What are we having?" Elmer huffed and puffed as he continued his trek around the room.

"Baked cabbage—your favorite."

Elmer smacked his lips. "Sounds good." He helped Abner off his back and felt around for his cane before he stood. Taking Abner's hand, he led him into the kitchen.

After taking a seat at the table, Elmer reached for Deanna's hand. "God has blessed us in so many ways, and we have a lot to thank Him for. Shall we pray?"

Deanna closed her eyes and bowed her head. *Thank You, Lord, for my husband, son, and the food on our table. Please show us how to be an instrument of encouragement to others—especially those who have needs.*

Deanna's Baked Cabbage

6 cups cabbage
6 tablespoons butter
6 tablespoons flour
1 tablespoon salt

½ teaspoon pepper
3 cups milk
1½ cups cheese, shredded
½ cup breadcrumbs

Preheat oven to 350 degrees. Shred cabbage and cook for 8 minutes in simmering water. Drain and put in lightly greased casserole dish. In separate pan, melt butter and stir in flour and seasonings. Add milk and stir until mixture is combined. Pour over cabbage. Top with cheese and breadcrumbs around the outer edge. Bake for 20 minutes.

New York Times bestselling and award-winning author Wanda E. Brunstetter is one of the founders of the Amish fiction genre. She has written close to ninety books translated in four languages. With over ten million copies sold, Wanda's stories consistently earn spots on the nation's most prestigious bestseller lists and have received numerous awards.

Wanda's ancestors were part of the Anabaptist faith, and her novels are based on personal research intended to accurately portray the Amish way of life. Her books are well read and trusted by many Amish, who credit her for giving readers a deeper understanding of the people and their customs.

When Wanda visits her Amish friends, she finds herself drawn to their peaceful lifestyle, sincerity, and close family ties. Wanda enjoys photography, ventriloquism, gardening, bird-watching, beachcombing, and spending time with her family. She and her husband, Richard, have been blessed with two grown children, six grandchildren, and two great-grandchildren.

To learn more about Wanda, visit her website at www.wandabrunstetter.com.

ROSE MARY'S RESOLVE

by Jean Brunstetter

Chapter 1

Belleville, Pennsylvania

Rose Mary hurried over to her father's furniture shop. She'd chosen a purple work dress to wear, and her hair was combed back neatly in a bun, not a strand out of place. This morning, Rose Mary would start training with her older sister, Linda. If she proved to learn the ropes over time, she'd take Linda's position at the front desk.

Rose Mary and Linda had celebrated their March birthdays recently; her only sister had turned twenty-one and Rose Mary was now nineteen. The Renno family was going through changes. In the fall, Linda would marry Isaiah Miller and move away from home. And Mother's older sister, Sally Petersheim, had moved in with them after becoming a widow. Aunt Sally and her deceased husband didn't have any children to leave their place to, so she sold their house. Rose Mary's mother, Susan, insisted Aunt Sally come live with the family.

It was different having her auntie there. For the most part, everyone seemed to take the transition in perfect stride, where some families might have troubles with such an adjustment. As long as the grown-ups set a good example, it was easy to follow suit.

Rose Mary entered the furniture shop and found Dad in his office. She stepped in and looked at Dad's name tag: RAYMOND RENNO. His rugged hands wrote in the ledger on the desk.

Dad smiled up at Rose Mary and laid his pencil down. "Linda has stepped in the back. Are you ready for your first day?"

"Jah."

Her father stood, came around the desk, and gave her a hug.

Linda came in holding a couple of dust rags. "We can start dusting everything in the showroom before the customers start coming in."

"That's a good idea," Dad agreed, pulling his fingers through his thick brown beard.

Rose Mary followed her sister out of the office and began to wipe off each piece of furniture. Knick-knacks sat on most of the tables, pictures that were for sale adorned the walls, and numerous other decorating items were displayed throughout the showroom as well. Dad's store was the most visited place in the Big Valley and the largest. In the back of his showroom was another building where some of the pieces were crafted. Other items, such as the dining-room sets and the larger furniture, would be brought in by truck to sell.

At nine o'clock, Dad unlocked the front door. Not long after a car pulled in, Linda sat at the counter, and Rose Mary slid a stool over and took a seat. The little bell jingled as the customers walked in.

The older couple smiled when Linda greeted them with, "Good morning. If you have any questions, please feel free to ask."

"Thank you," they replied.

The two of them chatted softly while they looked at the

different items. Not long after, another car came into the lot, and a woman entered the shop.

Linda leaned over and whispered, "How about if you go with the older couple? That way, if they need some help, they'll see you there."

"All right," Rose Mary agreed.

Even though she headed toward the couple, the lady coming in caught her attention. She was brightly dressed in a hot pink shirt and white pants and was carrying a school bus–yellow purse. "Good morning." The English woman gave a nod.

"Good morning," Linda replied.

"Say, your pieces look real nice." The woman brushed her hand over one of the end tables. "Sure wish I could take some of this furniture back home with me to Oregon."

"I've never been to Oregon. What part of the state are you from?" Linda leaned forward behind the counter.

"I'm from the coastal part of the state, and we can get a lot of rain." She laughed. "That's why I'm so pale."

"Oh, so you are visiting the area?" Linda asked.

"Yep. I'm enjoying my trip so far." The lady continued to shop.

Rose Mary watched the older couple looking at what the showroom offered. She also listened to Linda and how easily she spoke to the customer. *Maybe in time I'll learn to be more assertive and fill my sister's shoes. Being involved in this business seems to run in our family.*

Susan had fed the boys, along with her husband, and they'd done the morning chores and readied themselves for the day. The spring season was in full force with trees and ground flowers in bloom. In just a couple of months, her sons would be out of school for summer break. *I can remember how fun summer breaks were for me. Going camping with my family, spending the night with my friends, and sometimes sleeping under the stars on the front porch. Summer is such a special time of year.*

Susan looked at the walls of her kitchen with a fixed expression. "I'd sure like to get this room painted. It's the last room to do."

Sally entered the room and went right to the sink. "What did you say, Sister? I didn't catch what you said."

"Oh. . .I was talking out loud to myself." Susan watched her brown-haired sister as she squirted and rubbed dish soap on the lenses of her glasses. If it weren't for Sally's glasses and the hint of gray sprinkled in her hair, they could have almost been mistaken for twins. "With Linda's wedding coming up in November, I'd like to get things spruced up."

"I'll help you any way I can." Sally rinsed off the suds before drying the glasses with her apron.

Susan took a seat at the table. "I've got everything reserved, including the mobile kitchen and the walk-in cooler. Linda has the menus figured out and her helpers chosen. She's even picked out the material for the wedding dress."

"You'll want to paint this room soon. Is there anything outside that needs any touching up?" Sally joined her at the table.

"Jah, the front and back porch railings and benches will need a fresh coat of paint." Susan fiddled with the pepper mill. "We'll have to get the animals out of the barn at some point to pressure wash it a few times. The horses will have to stay out until after everything is taken down from the wedding."

"Your yard will look nice with some extra added flowers in pots and hanging baskets." Sally smiled.

Susan set the mill down. "You've got a good point. The more flowers in our yard, the better."

"It'll be nice to hear how well Rose Mary enjoys her first day at the shop. You and Raymond must be quite happy she's joining the business."

"That's for sure. My daughter is growing up, and she gives us joy. And I'm happy you are living here with us." Susan patted her sister's hand. "It's like old times being able to chat with you and go places together."

"It was hard leaving my home at first, but I've been blessed having you, Raymond, and the children to keep me going strong." Sally teared up.

"Here, Sister." Susan handed her a tissue. "That's what family is for."

Susan paused then added, "I'd like to make up some of those cheesecake brownies. Do you want to help me?"

"Of course." Sally dabbed her eyes and got up.

The two women checked the recipe card and gathered the ingredients. While they measured out flour, sugar, and other parts of the batter, they visited about the past.

"Remember the time I tried to make chocolate-chip cookies and didn't add the leavening?" Susan blended the sugar into the cream cheese.

"Yes, each batch was flat as could be, but our mom figured it out." Sally mixed together the cocoa batter.

"She sure did and fixed the rest of the dough by adding in some leavening to make the rest like they should be." Susan grabbed a bowl. "I do miss Mom."

"I do too."

"We should take a ride over to Dad and Mom's and visit them someday this week," Susan suggested.

"I am glad our brother, Matthew, and his wife live next door to our folks." Sally greased the glass pan. "What would we do without family?"

"The Lord likes us to take care of one another, and from that we are truly blessed." Susan added the eggs into the mixture. "How's the oven doing? Has it come up to temperature?"

"Jah, I believe so." Sally mixed together the crust ingredients and pressed it in the bottom of the baking dish, and Sally added the batters to the dish.

Team work was the kind of thing Susan enjoyed. She and Sally would be working together more on things now that her youngest daughter worked at the shop. "Rose Mary might be tired since this is a different kind of day for her. Usually she's here helping us with the cleaning and baking." Susan popped the dish into the oven, set the timer, and left it on the kitchen table.

"I'm tempted to go peek in on her and see for myself how she's doing." Sally grabbed the sponge and wiped off the counter.

"That sounds like you, Sister—always curious about everything."

"I can't help it. Maybe one day I'll do something challenging."

"I hope you do, and I'll support you with it." Susan put the remaining eggs in the refrigerator. "After the brownies are done baking, maybe you could help me make a green salad for supper."

Sally washed out a bowl in the sudsy water. "Sounds good, and if we make enough extra, we could have it for lunch."

Susan grabbed a clean towel from the drawer and dried the utensils. "I think that's a good idea. More is always better than not enough."

They finished the dishes and worked on the nice-sized salad they'd have for two meals. Susan couldn't help feeling blessed. *Everyone is healthy and everything is going well so far in my family's lives.* She glanced out the window. *But there's always a storm ahead after it's been calm for so long. Lord, let us be ready for the next trial You have for us. Amen.*

Rose Mary walked to the house from the furniture store with her father and sister. They said they were happy with her first day at work. Midday, after they'd eaten lunch, Dad took Rose Mary back to the shop and introduced her to the crew as a new employee. It was a nice experience getting acquainted with the staff. Rose Mary liked that her father employed a blind gentleman. Elmer Yoder had worked as an employee for some time. She couldn't help standing a little taller and knowing her father must have high hopes in her abilities. Rose Mary believed she'd started a new page in her life. It was wonderful to be a part of something her father had made happen years ago. She couldn't wait to share her day at supper with *Mamm*, Aunt Sally, and her brothers.

When they entered the house, the aroma of cooking ham and potatoes permeated the air. "Something sure smells good, *Fraa.*" Dad followed Rose Mary into the kitchen and stood beside Mom.

"Do you need any help?" Rose Mary asked.

"We're close to serving supper." Aunt Sally worked on mashing the potatoes but paused to add more milk.

Linda came in and washed her hands. Rose Mary did the same.

"The table is mostly set, but someone could add anything else we'll need." Mom stirred the sugar into the meadow mint tea.

"Since we're close to eating, I'll get out of the way and go wash up in the other room." Dad winked at Mom and headed out of the kitchen.

Mervin and Harvey rushed in from outdoors. "Hey, Mom! Look what Harvey caught out by the garden." Mervin pointed to his brother.

Harvey opened his hand slightly. "Do you see it, Mamm?"

Wiping her hands on her apron, she grinned. "Oh, it's a cute little green tree frog."

"Yep, it's a quick little fella. I'd like to keep him as a pet."

"Have you showed your dad yet?" Mom asked.

"Not yet." Harvey peeked into his hand. "Where is *Daed*? I'll show him what I have."

"He went to wash his hands."

Mom went past Rose Mary and set the pitcher of sweet tea and cold milk on the table. After her brothers showed their father the frog, Dad told them to find something to put the critter in until after dinner and instructed them to wash their hands.

Everyone took their seats at the table and bowed their heads for silent prayer. Soon they were passing the food.

"How was your first day at work?" Mom smiled at Rose Mary.

"It went well. I helped dust off most of the furniture before Dad opened the store."

"I'm glad we don't have much furniture to take care of in our own house." Mom grinned and took a bite of her vegetables.

Dad nodded as he cut a piece of ham.

"I helped the customers if they asked any questions." Rose Mary took a bite of potatoes.

Linda forked a piece of ham into her mouth. "I think she'll catch on fast working in the showroom."

"I can't wait until I'm old enough to work in your store, Dad."

"The way my children are growing, it won't be long." Dad gave Mervin's shoulder a tap.

"I'd like to work there too."

Dad looked over at Harvey and tussled his sun-lightened hair. "Don't you worry, Son. I'll have something for you to do."

Rose Mary couldn't believe she was now working and earning a wage. She wondered what to do with her first check. She might want to open a bank account right away so she wouldn't be tempted to spend much of it. But she did have a more pressing problem: her boyfriend, Tom Yoder. He'd been seriously thinking of going English. Rose Mary was put off by his ongoing efforts to convince her to follow him. She'd tried to break off their courtship, but he wasn't taking no for an answer. *I hope to keep myself so busy Tom Yoder will give up on me.*

CHAPTER 2

Rose Mary and her friend Marlene were out in the buggy running errands. First they took care of some banking, where three weeks earlier Rose Mary had opened checking and savings accounts with her first paycheck. She enjoyed putting money away for the future rather than spending it on needless things.

Next the two friends shopped for fabric for a dress Marlene was going to make, and then they picked up some personal items for Rose Mary.

"Let's get some lunch soon," Marlene suggested. "Our favorite lunch place stays open until two." Her auburn hair peeked out from her bonnet, and her arms were covered with little moles and freckles.

"That sounds good. My breakfast has worn off, and I'd enjoy a sandwich." Rose Mary shifted on the bench. *I hope we don't run into Tom while we're out today. At least with Marlene with me it would be easier to keep a visit short.*

Marlene bumped her arm. "Hello. . .Rose Mary, what are you thinking about?"

"Just hoping we don't run into Tom while we are out and about."

"You did say you'd called off the courtship." She clicked her tongue at her horse, Clyde. He picked up his pace while she looked at her friend.

"I tried, but Tom didn't want to hear any of it."

"Maybe you should try a little harder then, because if you don't hold firm, he might persuade you to leave your Amish roots and go English."

Rose Mary shook her head. "No way!"

Marlene kept the gelding moving along.

Rose Mary's fingernails dug into her palms. *I don't know why I'm having a hard time saying no to Tom. It doesn't help that he is so pushy. When I'm with him, I feel like I don't have a mind of my own.*

The restaurant came into view, and they pulled into the lot, parking in front of the hitching rail. Marlene secured the brake, and Rose Mary climbed out then tied Clyde to the rail. Both of them grabbed their handbags and walked to the door.

"I'll buy lunch, Rose Mary, so don't worry about getting out your wallet." Marlene held open the door.

"Thank you." Rose Mary stepped inside the restaurant and followed her friend to the wall where a blackboard hung. The choices were written down in different colors indicating specials, house favorites, and desserts. Marlene chose an iced tea and chef salad, while Rose Mary ordered a soft drink and a turkey and swiss sandwich.

They visited until their orders were ready. Shortly after they had prayed silently, Rose Mary noticed Tom's rig driving into the parking lot.

Oh great. Rose Mary sat stiffly, waiting for him to enter the establishment and wondering how things would turn out.

Linda sat at the counter in the furniture shop while Mom took her lunch break. Today she envied Rose Mary, taking part of the afternoon off to have some fun with Marlene. Linda enjoyed her job at the store and the money was nice, but it was difficult to get away from work when the business was open six days a week. They opened promptly at nine in the morning and closed at five in the evening. They were closed for most holidays, as well as for weddings and funerals in their community.

Linda rubbed her stomach. "I can't wait to take my lunch break when Mom returns."

"Your mamm packed mine this morning, so I'm gonna take my break in the back room pretty quick." Dad used a hankie to clean off his readers. "There should be more German potato salad left and sandwich makings."

"I'm holding out for the yummy salad. Mom mentioned yesterday we'd be having haystack for supper today." Linda added more business cards to the holder in front of her.

Elmer Yoder came through from the back of the store. He used his red-tipped white cane to move along the pathway toward the front entrance. "Hello, Raymond. I'll be leaving for my dentist appointment soon. The desk I've been sanding on is about as smooth as it can be."

"Okay, Elmer, I'll take a look at it soon. You have a good appointment, and we'll see you tomorrow."

Elmer waved and turned around. "All right then. See you in the morning."

Linda liked her father hiring a person with a disability.

Sometimes businesses wouldn't do that, but she figured people deserved an opportunity to try. Elmer supported a wife and a stepson, not to mention upkeep costs for his home. In addition to working at the store five days a week, he took some of the birdhouses he made to the flea market every Wednesday.

The little bell jingled over the door. "Good afternoon." Linda smiled at the couple who entered.

"Hello." The woman looked through the candleholders and grabbed up some different colors. "Look, hon, wouldn't these look nice in our living room? I think they may match my tablecloth too."

He nodded.

Linda could see the man wasn't too interested in shopping until he noticed the inlaid checkerboard table sitting off to the side. He stepped over to it and knelt down, giving the table an easy brush by his hand. "Look, dear, I've always wanted one of these."

His wife gave a silly grin and walked over to him. "How much are they wanting for it?"

He told her the price. "I may have to take this home."

"Okay, hon, but where will you put it?" She shifted the items in her hands.

"I have a place in mind."

They were still shopping when Mom entered from the back. "Are you ready for lunch?"

"Yes, I'm going to enjoy the salad." Linda rose from the stool.

"There's plenty left in the refrigerator, and I'm brewing more sweet tea."

"Okay, I'll see you after my meal." Linda moved out from behind the counter and watched the couple looking farther in the store.

"I've got this. You go have a nice lunch." Mom left the counter and headed back to the customers.

Rose Mary chewed on a large bite of turkey sandwich. She tried not to mash down the bread despite her vise grip. As Tom approached the table, she broke out in a nervous sweat. *I wish it were possible to shrink and disappear right now.*

"Hello, Rose Mary. Hi, Marlene." He stood beside them, wearing a big grin.

Marlene nodded, but Rose Mary continued to chew until she'd swallowed her food. "Hi, Tom." She wiped her mouth and then forehead. "You can have a seat if you'd like."

His lanky form stood over her for a moment before he grabbed a chair from an unoccupied table and slid it next to Rose Mary. "Sure is nice running into you here today. What are you two girls up to?"

Rose Mary looked about the room, noticing how much the tables were filling up. She would've liked to have said what was on her mind, but this wasn't the time to do it. Instead, she filled him in on what they'd done so far.

Tom brushed at his pant leg. She couldn't help wondering what was up.

"I took my car in to be fixed." His blue eyes danced with obvious delight. "It will be good as new when they've finished it." He cleared his throat. "I'd like to take you out for supper next Saturday, up to State College. I know you like going to the Quaker Steak & Lube."

Rose Mary looked over at Marlene as her eyes widened. *I feel cornered. He knows I don't want him to keep courting me.* Rose Mary bit her lip. She looked away briefly and then back at Tom.

"All right. If you'd like to come by Saturday to pick me up, I'll be ready to go." She mustered a smile for him.

"That sounds good. I'll be by about four o'clock. I'd better go get my to-go order." Tom stood and slid in his chair.

"Have a good lunch, and I'll see you on Saturday." Rose Mary watched Tom go up to the counter and pay for his food. He waved at her before going out the door. She was glad he didn't try to eat with them. She needed some quality time with her friend today.

"What just happened here?" Marlene whispered.

Rose Mary took a long drink, leaned close to her, and spoke in a soft tone. "You know what happened."

"I would've never believed what I witnessed unless I was sitting right here to see it. Tom will never take no for an answer if you don't get assertive with him. And if you're not careful, he will convince you to go English with him."

"We've been over this before, Marlene. I won't go English. And going out with Tom is not a big deal. It's just supper."

"Okay, but if he tries to persuade you, don't say I didn't warn you."

Rose Mary nodded. "I know. So, if we're done here, we can leave and let someone else have this table." She hoped this discussion was over. *Marlene worries too much. I won't let Tom sway me to do anything I don't want to do.*

"Okay, I'm ready to head out. That salad was delicious, but I could use some fresh air." Marlene got up and took her purse.

Rose Mary stood and grabbed her things, following Marlene out to the buggy. Soon they were heading out of the parking lot and on the way to the hardware store to buy some paint for Rose Mary's mother.

"I'm sorry you ran into Tom earlier," Marlene said a bit later as they headed for home. She tapped the reins, and Clyde picked up his pace.

Oh no, not this again. I wish she would drop the subject. "It's okay. I'm going to have a nice meal and try to have a decent time. You have nothing to worry about." Rose Mary's tone was less than enthusiastic. Truth was, she wasn't absolutely sure she could stand up to Tom once and for all. It had always been hard for Rose Mary to say no when she didn't want to hurt someone's feelings.

She squinted, seeking inner answers to her situation. *Or maybe my problem is that I'm afraid people won't like me if I don't go along with their ideas. I need to find the courage to deal with Tom once and for all.*

"It's too bad I can't come along." Marlene pulled a piece of bubblegum from her bag. "But since I'm not seeing anyone right now, I can't exactly go on a double date with you."

"It'll be okay, but thank you for trying to be supportive." Rose Mary flipped her apron. "I wish he would have asked me in private. I could've turned him down without an audience to disapprove of my actions."

"Yeah, I have to say Tom did have you at a disadvantage. Especially being in a public place."

Rose Mary saw her driveway coming into view. "I'm glad we could spend some time together."

"Me too." Marlene guided the horse and buggy close to the

house. "I'll help you take the paint up to the porch." She set the brake and hopped out of the rig.

Rose Mary went around back to pick up a paint can. She also gathered a couple of other bags and headed for the porch.

Aunt Sally opened the front door. "Hello, ladies. Thank you for picking up the cans of paint for us. Now the kitchen can be done in no time."

"Mom will be happy to get the project finished," Rose Mary commented. "I'll be heading over to the furniture store to relieve her in a little bit."

"Here's the other can of paint." Marlene handed it to Aunt Sally then turned to Rose Mary. "I'll see you in church on Sunday, and we can visit for a while afterward."

"Sounds good, Marlene. Thanks again for driving everywhere today." She gave her friend a hug.

"My pleasure. See you later." Marlene headed for the buggy.

Rose Mary waited until her friend got in, then she watched as Marlene turned the rig around. "See you Sunday," Rose Mary called, waving as Marlene pulled out of the driveway.

She carried the can of paint into the kitchen and set it next to the other one. Aunt Sally wasn't in the room, so Rose Mary ran the bags up to her bedroom. She set them on a chair and headed back downstairs. "I'm going over to the shop."

"Okay, Rose Mary, we'll see you at suppertime," Aunt Sally said from the kitchen.

Rose Mary closed the front door and walked toward the store. The warm sun touched her face, and it felt soothing. Mom came out to greet her. "Hello, Daughter. How was your outing?"

Rose Mary didn't want to say anything about how she

regretted seeing Tom or how she'd be going on a date regardless of her good judgment. Her folks had already made it clear they disapproved of her seeing Tom. "Marlene and I had a nice time together."

"That's good." Mom gave her a hug. "A couple came into the shop after you left—the husband was interested in the checkerboard table."

"Jah, did he buy it?"

"He did." Mom winked. "Your father sure likes to make those tables and is even happier when someone buys them."

She smiled. "We picked up your two cans of paint, and they're in the kitchen."

"Thank you." Mom squeezed Rose Mary's shoulder. "Well, I best be getting over there. It won't be long before Sally and I will need to start supper."

"Okay, see you later, Mamm." Rose Mary waved and went into the shop.

"Hey, how's Marlene, and how did it go?" Linda asked as she added some chair gliders to the bin close to the door.

"Marlene is good, and everything went well. We ran a lot of errands, making time for lunch and some shopping." Rose Mary gave a brief smile.

Linda wadded up the empty glider bag. "You aren't convincing me that your day went so well. Your tone says otherwise."

Since Dad wasn't to be seen and there were no customers at the moment, Rose Mary decided to spill the beans to Linda.

CHAPTER 3

State College, Pennsylvania

Tom was sure he'd done a smart thing by inviting his girl out for supper. The weather wasn't too bad for an April evening. He'd given Rose Mary a bouquet of flowers at the door to soften her disposition. Tom looked over at her and thought her golden-brown hair was pretty. The scent of her perfume reminded him of fresh flowers.

He wondered what she was thinking as he pulled his car up to the Quaker Steak & Lube. She was looking off and hadn't paid much attention to him. *Rose Mary needs to see things my way, that's all there is to it. Leaving the Amish way of life would be good for both of us. There'd be a lot fewer restrictions, and no one would fault me for driving a car.*

Tom opened her car door and held it until she got out. *I'm the perfect guy for Rose Mary. She just doesn't see it yet.*

They were greeted by the hostess, who picked up two menus and led them to a table in another room. When they were seated, Tom looked up at the car suspended from the ceiling by cables. "I like how they did that. Maybe it would be fun to do it in my garage someday."

Rose Mary furrowed her brows. "With an old carriage? That would be silly."

"No, with a car like this one." He laughed.

A waitress came up to their table, took their drink orders, and let them continue to look over their choices.

"I've saved plenty of room to eat here this evening." Rose Mary studied the menu. "Just look at all the choices."

"I think those all-you-can-eat hot wings are good, but they serve them on Tuesdays." He looked at her and set down his menu.

The woman returned and placed their drinks in front of them. "Do you know what you'd like to order, or would you like to have more time?"

Tom looked over at his date. "I'm ready to order. How about you?"

Rose Mary nodded.

"Okay." He sat up straighter. "I'll have the Bacon Love Burger and fries."

The waitress wrote on the notepad. "And what would you like to order, miss?"

"I'll have the House-Made Pulled Pork Sandwich and fries too." Rose Mary handed the menu to their waitress.

"Those sound like good choices. I'll put in your order right away." The lady smiled as Tom handed her his menu.

Based on Rose Mary's serious expression, Tom knew he'd have his work cut out for him this evening. "I'm sure glad my car is running like it should again." He took a sip of his soda. "I think it's far more relaxing without a driver involved taking us places. Don't you, Rose Mary?"

She tapped her finger against her chin and looked up. "I suppose."

"Rose Mary, if you could drive and go places without having to call someone to take you any distance from your parents' house, it would be more convenient. And look at the places we could go together."

"To be honest, it's not hard to hire a driver. Besides, there's no worrying over the upkeep of your own vehicle." She set her beverage down and rested her hand on the table.

"I understand the Amish ways are what you are used to, but there's a big world out there waiting for us." He reached over and took hold of her hand. "I can help you learn to drive if you'd like."

Rose Mary shifted in her seat, avoiding his gaze. "I'm not comfortable learning how to drive." Her tone was sincere. "I don't mind using a horse and buggy to get around. In fact, I enjoy the slower pace."

He brushed his thumb against her fingers. This wasn't going so well. "After we're done eating, let's take a drive to see what else we can do while we're in town."

"All right."

"It's too bad you work six days a week." He leaned forward, smiling. "I'd like to take you out more often."

Her cheeks reddened. "Daed runs the business like clock-work. The more hours we can serve the public, the better it is for them and us."

"This place sure does a good business. It seems to always be busy whenever I've been here." Tom looked about the room.

The waitress brought their food and asked if they'd need anything else. Tom looked at his empty glass and asked for more soda.

When the lady left to get his drink, the two prayed silently before enjoying their supper. Tom was hungry and dove into his burger and fries. He looked over at Rose Mary biting into her pulled-pork sandwich.

Soon their waitress returned and set his drink down then left to take care of another table. The silence was a little awkward, but at least they were together. Tom finished his mouthful of food. "How's your sandwich?"

"It's good. I like the roll they use for it." Rose Mary took another bite.

Tom thought about how he and Rose Mary first started courting. They'd both attended the same singing one evening and afterward stood outside the building talking. It was more of a friendship at first, but later the relationship grew stronger. Tom sensed a different approach was needed to get her to try the English way though. Since she didn't want to drive, maybe Rose Mary would rather dress in English clothing. This might be a way to get her more interested in becoming English.

Rose Mary cleared her throat. "Tom, didn't you hear me?"

"I'm sorry. My mind was wandering. What were you saying, Rose Mary?"

"I was asking how your food was." She nibbled on one of her french fries.

"It's tasty, and I'll be full in no time eating this half-pound hamburger." He dipped some fries in ketchup and ate them. Tom wanted this evening to last as long as it could, and winning Rose Mary was at the top of the list of what he wanted to accomplish.

Rose Mary got through supper, although it was awkward. Tom seemed to be all over the place—sometimes polite and other times pushy. She didn't want to learn to drive a car even if Tom would be the one to teach her.

Rose Mary could imagine what Marlene would think about Tom trying to convince her to drive. She knew her best friend wasn't on board about her continuing to date him. Her sister, Linda, shared this view of Tom and urged Rose Mary not to see him anymore.

Rose Mary didn't want to be weak and let Tom sway her to go against her better judgment. She didn't share his desire to go English. Even though the non-Amish way was intriguing sometimes, in Rose Mary's heart it was not enough. She had to stay true to her convictions and quit trying to please him. Tom was fun to be around. He'd always had interesting things to say and had been generous with his gifts. Those qualities had drawn her to him in the first place. But were they enough?

They finished their meal and went to his car to take a drive. Tom suggested they head downtown, where the shops and stores were located. Rose Mary thought it would be nice to look around and hoped that being in public would keep Tom from speaking about going English.

He found a parking spot. "I can't get over how busy this town is on the weekends." Tom shut off the engine and got out of the car.

Rose Mary waited for him to come around the vehicle before heading into the Barnes and Noble bookstore. "We can have a good look around in there, and it would be a great way to burn off some supper."

"It's a big store, so we might work up some room for dessert." He chuckled.

"I can't even think about dessert." Rose Mary stepped through the automatic doors with Tom.

They both headed down the same aisle, looking at some of the selections.

He cleared his throat. "I'm going to take a look at the magazines. Maybe we can get one of those special coffees before we go."

"Okay." Rose Mary watched him walk off, then she ambled down the aisle, looking at the various books. She read the back covers of some enticing fiction titles before moving over to the cookbook section. The pictures in the first one she looked at made each recipe look inviting.

Rose Mary noticed a few college girls standing at the end of her row, chatting quietly. She continued to look through the book, but when she looked their way again, they were staring at her.

"Look," said one of the students. "There's one of those Amish girls. You know, those plain kind of people who live out on some smelly old farm." She laughed before turning away and moving on with her friends.

Rose Mary didn't say anything even though those girls weren't polite to her.

Not too long after, Tom reappeared. "How's it going?"

"Well, I think I've found a book to take home." She held it up to him.

"A cookbook." He sniffed the air. "I'll buy this for you, and then we'll get some of those good coffees I'm smelling."

"You don't have to pay for this. You've already paid for our supper, and you want to get us coffees."

"It's my treat today. Don't worry about a thing." Tom's smile grew. "I've got it covered."

Rose Mary allowed him to pay for the book, and then they got coffee. He wanted to sit at one of the tables. She hesitated, seeing the college girls not so far away.

"What's up, Rose Mary?" He took a seat.

She sat down and explained quietly what the college girl had said.

"Too bad she acted so rude." He took a drink of his mocha latte. "How about we go to the clothing shop when we're done here?"

"What for? It won't solve anything that happened earlier," she whispered.

"If you try dressing like the English, they won't act like that around you." He leaned closer to her.

Rose Mary felt herself weakening. With those girls in the store, she wanted to be anywhere else. "Okay, I'm ready to leave if you are." *What would it hurt to go look around at some clothes with Tom? I just won't buy any.*

Belleville

After supper, Susan sat in the living room with Sally. Her husband went out to the barn with the boys to build some shelves.

"I don't like the idea of Rose Mary out with her boyfriend. Since my daughter told me he's been toying with the idea of wanting to go English, I'm worried." Susan rocked her chair with a strong cadence.

Sally looked at her with a soft expression. "Rose Mary is a smart young lady."

"I can't help wondering if he might win her over if she keeps on dating him."

"We will keep praying for her." Sally stood up from the couch. "I wouldn't mind some herb tea. Would you like some too?"

"Yes. Thank you, Sally."

"I'll get it started and check on the coffee level too. Maybe Raymond would like a cup when he returns from the barn with Mervin and Harvey."

Susan watched her sister walk out of the room. She began to rock in her chair then closed her eyes. *I wish my worrying over Rose Mary could make things better. I need to pray for my daughter and give it to the Lord.*

Susan quit rocking and gazed out the window at the busy bird feeder. She couldn't help being amused by their constantly competing for the food and eating all the seed they could while perched. *Those little guys don't seem to be worried about a thing. Guess I could learn a lesson from them and try not to worry so much.*

Getting up, Susan joined her sister, who had just measured coffee into the filter. As Sally turned toward her, the coffee can slipped from her hand. It hit the floor, and grounds shot out everywhere.

"Don't worry, Sally. I'll help you." Susan went for the broom and dustpan.

Sally bent down and picked up the container. "I'm sorry." She set the can on the counter. "There isn't enough left for coffee tomorrow morning."

Susan swept the coffee grounds into a pile. "Not a problem.

We have another can."

Harvey came in the kitchen door. "What's on the floor? Is it dirt?"

"No, Son, it's some spilled coffee we're cleaning up." Susan smiled. "How's the work going in the barn?"

"*Gut.* I've been sanding, and Mervin is helping Daed stain the wood." He grabbed a glass and filled it with water. "I got pretty thirsty out there working."

Sally started the coffeepot. "I'm glad it's going well. How about you take a couple of water bottles with you in case someone else is thirsty?"

Harvey set his glass in the sink then went to the refrigerator and pulled out two waters. "I'd better get back to it."

"When you're done out there," Susan said as she put the cleaning tools away, "we've got pound cake with berries to have for dessert."

"Mmm. . .sounds good, Mamm." Harvey shut the door behind him.

"Our tea water is ready," Sally said. "I'll get it poured."

"While you're busy, I'm going to see if the berries need any more sweetening." Susan washed her hands and pulled a bowl from the refrigerator.

"I'll take our tea to the living room." Sally carried the cups out of the room.

Susan lifted the lid and drew out a spoonful of berries. After a taste, she decided to add a little more sugar. Being alone in the room, she bowed her head. *Lord, be with Rose Mary, and help me to lean upon You instead of my own strength. Amen.*

CHAPTER 4

The end of April offered more pleasant flowers in Susan's yard. It was almost lunchtime, and Susan wanted to help her sister prepare their meal. She'd loaded the dried laundry in the basket and carried it into the house. Susan dropped off the folded clothes in each room and put them away. The last stop was her youngest daughter's room.

She stepped into Rose Mary's bedroom and opened the closet to put away her dresses. A bag fell from its spot and spilled open. A shock wave spiraled through Susan when she saw the contents were tops and a pair of jeans. *What is Rose Mary doing with these? What would make her get English clothes?* With trembling hands, she picked up the bag and put the items back inside. Part of Susan wanted to confront her daughter. But on second thought, she decided not to say anything right now. The clothes sported their tags, which meant they hadn't been worn.

She went back to the kitchen to help out with lunch and tried not to appear troubled by what she'd found. "What can I do to help?" she asked.

"Could you slice some bananas for this fruit salad?" Sally asked as she added some raisins. "We're having a busy day, and let's not forget this evening we'll be going to the baby shower for Wanda."

"If you prefer, I can drive us there."

"Thanks." Sally washed the strawberries. "I hope Wanda likes what I'm giving her for her first *boppli*."

"Wanda will love that cute sweater you made with those adorable matching booties." Susan smiled then glanced around the room. "I think the paint job we did on the kitchen walls looks good."

"I agree." Sally added the sliced bananas to the bowl. "The paint color you picked out brightens the room."

"I'm pleased with the result," Susan admitted. "And thanks so much for helping me to finish it."

"No problem." Sally snacked on a few of the raisins.

"Linda is coming with us this evening."

Sally tilted her head. "How about Rose Mary?"

"I'm not sure if she'll be going." Susan wanted to get lunch on the table and eat something to calm her nerves. She figured it was much needed after the shock she'd gotten from finding those English clothes in Rose Mary's closet. *I'm sharing my findings with Raymond when he and I are alone this evening. I wonder how stunned he'll be.*

The English woman Rose Mary waited on wanted to ship a piece of furniture back to her home in Texas. The lady spoke in a thick Texan accent, which was fun to listen to. Rose Mary called her father over to assist with the needed information for the customer. Dad rang up the bill for the hutch, and the customer handed him her credit card.

"I am so glad I found y'alls' place. I can't wait for this to arrive at my door in a couple of weeks." The woman put the card into her purse.

"Rose Mary, you can go ahead and put the sold sign on the hutch." Linda tore off the receipt and gave it to the customer to sign.

As she labeled the hutch, Rose Mary noticed a buggy pulling into the parking lot. She recognized Tom's rig and wondered why he had come. It was almost time to close for the day, so Rose Mary stepped out to see what he wanted. "Hello there."

"Hi, Rose Mary. How's it going?"

"Okay."

"Can we talk a few minutes?"

"I guess so."

He led the way toward the back of the building.

"I wondered if you'd have time this evening to hang out." Tom adjusted his straw hat.

Rose Mary wasn't in the mood to go anywhere with him and was glad she had a legitimate excuse.

"Sorry, but I have other plans. I'll be going to Wanda's baby shower this evening."

Tom's shoulders drooped. "I'd like to get together before I go to Lancaster to stay with my uncle for a while." He stepped closer to her. "I'll be helping with work he needs done around his place."

"When would you leave?" She looked over and saw Linda outside, watering some hanging baskets.

Tom grabbed her hand and held it. "In a couple of weeks. My dad said he can cover for me at our family's goat farm while I'm away."

"That's good. I'm pretty sure it would be hard on my dad if Linda and I couldn't help out in the shop." Rose Mary noticed her sister looking their way.

Tom smiled and waved at Linda. "Hello."

Linda gave a smile that slipped as she continued her chore.

Rose Mary squeezed his hand playfully to lighten the mood. "Maybe we can get together one evening before you go."

"Sure, sounds great." His face brightened. "How about next week about this time?"

"Okay, it should work out for me. But I'd better get to the house and help with supper." She let go of his hand.

"All right, then I'll see you next Saturday." He walked along with her.

As they rounded the corner, Linda reeled up the hose. She looked over at them with a somber expression. "I'm ready to head over. Are you coming, Rose Mary?"

"In a minute." She stepped away from Tom. "I'll see you later."

"Okay. Have a nice time at Wanda's baby shower this evening." He turned and headed for his buggy.

As they walked toward the house, Rose Mary sensed her sister's disapproval.

Linda stopped walking. "So why did Tom stop by today?"

Rose Mary halted. "He let me know he'd be leaving to go work for his uncle in Lancaster."

Linda smiled. "Good thing he's leaving. He is no good for you. Tom is trying his best to win you."

Rose Mary sighed. "Look. I've got this under control. He wanted to go out with me this evening, but I told him it wouldn't work."

"Yes, because of Wanda's baby shower. Otherwise, wouldn't you have gone with him?"

"Maybe not. I'm stronger than you think." Rose Mary's hand came up to her hip as her conscience took over. *If you were strong, you wouldn't have let Tom buy those English clothes for you.*

"I hope so for your sake. I wonder what Marlene thinks of him." Linda crossed her arms.

"Let's not bring her into this right now, okay?"

"I guess she'd agree with me. Especially since you don't want to discuss this." Linda's form grew rigid.

"You are blowing this out of proportion. Besides, he will be leaving in a couple of weeks, and things will subside." Rose Mary patted her sister's arm. "You worry too much about me, but I'm glad you care."

Linda uncrossed her arms and smiled at Rose Mary. "Let's try to worry less and pray more."

Rose Mary gave Linda a hug. *If my sister feels this way about Tom, I can imagine what my folks are feeling these days.*

After the evening meal, Susan dried and put away the last of the dishes. Raymond wandered into the kitchen, looking for a toothpick.

"If you're not busy, I'd like to speak to you in private." Susan took the dish towel and draped it over a chair back.

"This sounds like something serious. What happened?" Raymond took the toothpick from his mouth.

"I'd like to talk in our room if you don't mind."

"Of course."

When they entered their room, Susan took a seat on the bed.

Raymond closed the door and sat next to her. "Okay, what's troubling you?"

"Earlier today, while I was in Rose Mary's closet putting clean laundry away..." She paused.

"What happened?"

"I started hanging up her dresses, when a bag fell to the floor and its contents spilled out." Her brows wrinkled. "There were English clothes in that bag."

Raymond shook his head. "I wouldn't think our daughter could be wearing them. I haven't seen any signs of it myself."

"I haven't either. But the clothes are in her possession, and she could decide to wear them." Susan frowned. "I'm afraid Tom might be influencing her."

"He came by the furniture store today and spoke with Rose Mary before I closed shop." Raymond gave Susan a hug. "We'll pray for our girl and keep being watchful of things. Hopefully, our daughter will lose interest in him."

Susan remained silent, sheltered in her husband's embrace. She didn't want him to let go.

Raymond is such a caring man and a good provider. She felt surrounded by his love and care.

Raymond leaned over and kissed Susan's forehead. "You are special to me. Don't ever *vergesse* it."

"I won't forget." She released his warm hand and stood up. "When we're ready for dessert, there's plenty of fruit salad left over to enjoy or chocolate cake."

Raymond rubbed his midsection. "I might be ready in a little while to have something with a cup of *kaffi*."

"I guess I'll head to the living room to see if Sally would like some coffee too."

Raymond rose from the bed, headed to the door, and paused. "I wonder what the boys are up to. Harvey spotted a bunny over by your garden earlier."

"Maybe Mervin and Harvey can chase the silly rabbit away from my vegetables. I don't need it getting into my plants and eating everything we have." Susan followed him out of the bedroom.

As they entered the living room, Harvey bounded in from outside. "We found some baby *haas!*" he announced.

"How many baby rabbits did you find, and where are they?" Sally asked.

With rosy cheeks, he responded, "Three."

"What's going on?" Rose Mary came down the stairs. Linda followed behind with her baby gift and placed it by the front door.

Mervin came in from outside. "I saw three baby bunnies in their nest."

"So we heard." Dad grinned.

Harvey looked over at Dad. "They sure are cute. I wish we could make pets out of them."

Susan shook her head. "My garden can't support a bunch of bunnies and our family."

"Come on, I'll show you where the nest is, by the woodpile." Mervin led the way.

Harvey sprinted ahead of him with the rest of the family following behind. When they got to the spot, Harvey pointed. "See."

Susan protected her eyes from the sun. "I'm sure their mother is around here somewhere."

"They sure are small." Rose Mary smiled at her brothers.

"I wish they could be pets." Harvey looked at Dad.

"They're wild, Son." Raymond patted his shoulder.

"Let's leave these bunnies alone, and in a while we can get out the desserts." Susan looked at her family.

"I'll help you, Mom, when we're all ready for it," Rose Mary offered.

Susan put an arm around her daughter's waist. "I am always happy for anyone's help." She headed to the house with Rose Mary at her side.

CHAPTER 5

The next church service fell on the first Sunday in May. After church and the meal that followed it, Rose Mary pulled Tom aside. "I need to speak with you in private."

Tom nodded and led her across the property. When they were out of earshot from the others, Rose Mary took a deep breath. "Tom, I think it's time to call off our relationship."

"Not this again. We've been down this path before, and we ended up right back together again. What makes this time any different?"

"This time I mean it. I need my own space." Rose Mary crossed her arms as she checked to make sure they were alone. "I'm not comfortable with going English like you seem to be, and I don't want the clothes you bought me."

"Why are you doing this now, when I'm leaving town to help out my uncle?" Tom's brows knitted together. "Your timing is unfair. I don't understand your thinking."

"It's the way I'm feeling about us. It's not working for me."

"If you feel this way about you and me, then fine. We are done. Oh, and you can do whatever you want with the clothes." He huffed and walked off.

Rose Mary watched his steady gait move in the direction of his friend. She thought it best to go another way. Near the house, she found a bench swing and took a seat, hoping to be able to relax. The gentle breeze played with her bonnet ties as she gazed at the flowering shrubs around her.

Tom hadn't taken her news well, which wasn't a big surprise. She hoped this time he got the message. If the look on his face was any hint, he appeared to be finished with their relationship too.

Rose Mary felt utter relief that she had finally gotten the courage to say no. Sometime next week she would take the clothes to the thrift shop in town.

Marlene found Rose Mary and took a seat in the chair swing. "Are you okay?"

"I think so. I broke things off with Tom. Our courtship is over."

"Are you sure?" Marlene spoke in a soft tone.

"Yes. At least Tom won't be around to try changing my mind." Rose Mary stared off in the distance.

"I see. But maybe you'll change your mind by the time he returns from Lancaster." Marlene pushed against the grass to get the swing moving.

"As far as I'm concerned, Tom is available to any girl who is interested in him. Please don't lose faith in me." Rose Mary uncrossed her arms. "Let's change the subject. I'd like to do something fun before the day is over."

"Hmm. . . Ice cream can help ease a wounded soul. And even if it doesn't, what can it hurt?"

"That sounds good to me." Rose Mary stared toward the buggy lot. "I see Tom is leaving."

"Speaking of leaving, since I rode with my folks, I'll need to go when they're ready."

Marlene pulled sunglasses from her purse and put them on.

"Why don't you come over to our house later?" Rose Mary smiled. "Maybe I can talk Dad into making homemade ice cream."

"I'd like that." Marlene stood up from the swing. "I'll go check with my folks to see if it's okay if I come by this evening."

Rose Mary felt torn. Part of her couldn't help feeling blue about ending the courtship with Tom. The other part of her cried out, "You're free of his influences! Be happy."

Would Tom follow through becoming English and leave the Amish way of life? Rose Mary hoped nobody would think she'd swayed him to do such a thing.

When Marlene returned, she sat down and announced, "I can come over."

"Oh good."

Marlene remained quiet for a while and then asked, "Do you think Tom will go English?"

"I wondered the same thing a bit ago." Rose Mary watched Melvin and Harvey sitting with some other children under the shade of a tree.

"I hope someday I'll find a nice fellow to court, but he can't be wanting to go English." Marlene swatted at a pesky fly buzzing her head.

"You will, my friend. Give it a little time." Rose Mary crossed her ankles. "Any fellow would be blessed to have you for his girl."

"Thank you, Rose Mary."

She nodded. *If Tom were to change his mind and join the church, would I want him back?*

⚭

It'd been a little over a week since Rose Mary broke up with Tom. She hadn't heard a word from him and figured he'd finally gotten the message. She'd been busy most of the day at her father's store with a busload of tourists who'd descended on their business.

After work, Rose Mary decided to help with chores outside, giving Mervin a break. She went out to the barn with her brother Harvey to feed and water the horses. Her youngest brother was a lot of fun. Harvey liked carving wood, a hobby he'd discovered a year ago. His latest creation was a rooster and hen.

After they'd finished feeding and watering the buggy horses, Rose Mary talked her brother into taking a break at a table next to the barn. Rose Mary was listening to Harvey talk about school when the sound of a small plane interrupted. When its engine popped, cutting in and out, they looked up and could see it descending toward their field.

Rose Mary jumped up. "Look, Harvey! It's landing in our field!"

Harvey headed around the back of the barn. "Come on, Sister. Let's go see!"

"I'm right behind you."

Gasping, she watched in amazement as the plane came down and bounced along the terrain. A deep spot caused the plane to stop abruptly, and it tipped forward against the prop. Then it righted itself as the engine wound down.

Stunned, Rose Mary and Harvey waited for the pilot to exit the plane. But the plane sat silently with no sign of movement inside.

Her heart pounded. "We'd better go and see if whoever is inside needs help."

They rushed over to look in the window. Rose Mary saw a young man with neatly cut, light brown hair slumped forward in his seat.

"I'll try to open the door." Bumping into her, Harvey twisted at the handle until it released with a clunk.

The young man raised his head and moaned.

"Are you all right?" Rose Mary asked anxiously.

"I. . .I'm not sure."

Harvey pointed. "He's got a cut on his head."

"Let me see." She stepped in beside Harvey for a closer look.

"Yes, you've got a cut and a slight bump there." Rose Mary looked at the young man.

He put his hand up to his head and winced when he saw blood on his fingers. "I'm sure it's nothing to worry about. S—sorry for landing on your property." He shook his head slowly. "My name is Kevin Presley."

"It was exciting to watch." Harvey gave a wide grin. "I can't wait to tell my friends about this."

Kevin pulled a tissue from his pocket and dabbed at the wound. Then he moved his legs toward the open door. "How bad does my plane look?"

Rose Mary explained what she'd seen during the airplane's landing.

From the house, Mervin rushed up to them. "We heard it come in."

Dad and Mom hurried after him.

Kevin shifted in his seat. "I'd better climb down to inspect the plane."

191

Rose Mary shook her head. "You should stay there."

"My sister is right. You shouldn't try to do much," Harvey interjected.

Dad and Mom did a brief check of the pilot's injury.

"This is Kevin Presley," Rose Mary said then looked at Kevin. "These are my parents, Raymond and Susan."

"I'm sorry for landing in your field," he apologized. His gaze dropped to the floor.

"Don't concern yourself about it. How are you feeling?" Mom asked.

Kevin lifted his head and looked at her with striking blue eyes. "I'm mostly shaken up, but other than the cut on my head, nothing else hurts."

"Why don't you come inside the house to rest and see how you feel later," Dad suggested.

Rose Mary nodded. "I think taking him to the house would be a good idea too."

"I'll be happy to accept your hospitality." Kevin smiled.

Dad held out his arm. "You can lean on me and Mervin as we head to the house. Come help me, Son."

Once inside, Mom asked Kevin to take a seat on the couch and put his feet up.

A few minutes later, Linda and Aunt Sally arrived home from the market. They came inside carrying the groceries to the kitchen.

"Has anyone noticed a plane out in our field?" Linda called.

"Jah," her brothers answered in unison.

Linda and their aunt joined them in the living room. Rose Mary filled them in on what had happened and introduced Kevin.

"I need to check the plane out soon to assess its damage," Kevin said.

Dad shook his head. "That can wait till you're rested."

"Let's get the rest of the groceries and put them away." Aunt Sally motioned to Linda, and they returned to the kitchen.

"Are you sure you won't need to be checked out by a doctor?" Mom's brows drew together.

"No, I'll take it easy," he replied.

Rose Mary felt concern for this handsome Englisher.

Mom looked over at her. "Maybe somebody should get this young man an *eis packe* for his forehead."

"I'll go get the ice pack." Rose Mary headed for the kitchen.

As she entered, Linda said in a hushed tone, "I would have never imagined a plane landing in the field."

"Neither would I." Aunt Sally put the milk away in the refrigerator.

Rose Mary grabbed the ice bag. "I'm glad we were around when his plane landed. Otherwise, he'd have had nobody to help him."

"You're so right," Aunt Sally agreed as she carried some paper products to the pantry.

Rose Mary wrapped the ice bag in a towel, then she brought it out to him. "Here you go."

"Thank you." He lay back and placed the ice on his forehead. "What's your name?"

"Oh, sorry, I forgot to introduce myself. My name is Rose Mary Renno, and my brother Harvey was there when your plane came down."

"I live in State College, and I took the Piper Super Cruiser out for a spin." Kevin closed his eyes. "I never thought the

193

plane would act up like it did."

"Is there anyone you need to call right now?" Dad inquired.

"I'll have to let my parents know at some point." He opened his eyes. "I need to rest first."

Rose Mary felt curious about Kevin's response to her father's question. It made no sense that he wouldn't want to call them right away. No doubt they'd be worried about him.

"Well, you rest there, and you're welcome to have supper with us." Mom gave a warm smile.

"Thank you very much." Kevin adjusted the ice pack.

If Kevin stays longer, I might get to find out some things about him, Rose Mary mused then chided herself. *Why do I care what this stranger does or doesn't do?*

Kevin had dozed off but was awakened by a sweet voice.

"We've set up a room for you upstairs to spend the night. My folks thought it might be better if you wait till morning to check out your plane and get it repaired." Rose Mary stood by the end of the sofa. Her brown eyes looked ever so serious.

"Thanks, but I feel like I'm taking advantage. Your family is going through a lot of trouble for a perfect stranger."

"My parents are that way. They like to help out someone in need, so you're not taking advantage at all." She shifted her weight and pointed at the coffee table. "I brought you a glass of water in case you're thirsty."

"Thank you again." He lifted the ice pack off his head.

Rose Mary smiled at him then looked toward the kitchen. "We'll be eating in a little while. Maybe you'll feel up to having some fried chicken and a couple of side dishes."

"Sounds good." Kevin heard sounds of cookware being used in the other room. He also heard the women speaking in Pennsylvania Dutch, though he didn't understand a word of what was spoken.

She cleared her throat. "I should go and help out in the kitchen."

Kevin nodded and replaced the ice bag on his forehead. *These Amish are incredible. So much different than my own family. Something feels right about being here with them. Their way of life seems so laid back.* He reached under the towel to check his cut. At least it wasn't bleeding, and the cold had taken some of the discomfort away. Lying there, he thought about what might be broken on the Cruiser. Hopefully, it was nothing serious. He wasn't ready to face his father yet. They weren't getting along these days, and Kevin wasn't thrilled with the crop-dusting business, like his dad.

He closed his eyes. *I need to find my own passion in life. Why can't my father see that pulling me into this is pushing me away from him?* Despite Kevin's headache, he'd text his folks a message to let them know he was all right but wouldn't be home tonight. His father would be fuming over this. Kevin felt sure of it. And his mother, as usual, would deal with the disharmony in the house. What pulled his mind away from that was the smell of chicken being cooked. It made his mouth water.

Harvey came in and looked over at Kevin. "How you doing?"

"I'm feeling better than I did when I landed earlier."

Harvey plopped in one of the chairs. "What was it like to land in our field?"

"It was bumpy, and I stopped pretty fast when the plane

hit the low spot. But before that, when the Super Cruiser was sputtering in the air, I knew it was time to land as fast as I could." Kevin spoke with feeling. "It could've been a lot worse if I hadn't."

A teenage boy with subtle brown freckles peered into the room. "Hey, Harvey, Dad needs both of us to let out the horses and bring in the expectant mare."

"Okay." Harvey looked at Kevin. "I need to go help my brother, Mervin." He got up from his chair and followed his brother out.

Rose Mary's aunt entered the room. "Would you like a fresh ice bag for your forehead?" She held a different one.

"Umm, sure." He gave her the old one.

The woman looked a lot like Rose Mary's mom. Kevin watched her switch out the small, spent bag for the new one, rewrapping it in a towel.

"Here you go—good as new." She brushed her hands against the black apron covering the front of her dress.

"Thank you." He offered her a smile before she headed out of the room.

Raymond came in and took a seat in the recliner. "My boys should be about done taking care of the horses. I've been getting some looks from passersby seeing your plane parked out in my field." He chuckled. "The people who know I'm Amish and live here must be chomping at the bit right now, wondering what's going on."

Kevin couldn't help smiling at what Raymond said. He seemed to be enjoying the novelty of this situation. Kevin hoped he wouldn't wear out his welcome with these dear people. He was also intrigued with Rose Mary. She seemed nice, and what a pretty girl. Kevin wouldn't mind visiting with her if the opportunity presented itself.

Focusing on his present problem, he looked on his phone for local repair places and found one. Once they got the plane, Kevin could go by and check on the repair progress. He wanted it fixed and in better shape than before.

Tomorrow, I'll take care of things myself. The plane will be taken out by truck, and repairs will be made. I think using a local place would be better than hauling the plane back to State College. Kevin rubbed his throbbing temples. *I can only imagine what Dad will say when he gets my message.*

CHAPTER 6

It had been three days since Kevin arrived at the Rennos' place. He got up at six o'clock and dressed before leaving his room. *I must be back to my old self because I'm up at my usual time.*

When Kevin heard muffled voices, he opened his door. Kevin crept along the hallway and stopped before the wall ended by the stairway. He listened to Raymond reading something in Pennsylvania Dutch. *Should I head back to my room or stay here a little longer to find out what is going on?* The closing of a door behind him brought Kevin out of his thoughts.

"Good morning." Rose Mary smiled, holding on to a book. "Come downstairs with me. We're doing our morning devotions. I have my Bible to follow along."

"Are you sure it's okay? I wouldn't want to intrude on your family's worship time."

"You won't be. We do our devotions every morning, but since you weren't up in time, you've missed out on the last couple."

I could look at her all day long. She is so pretty. He gave a gentle sigh. *She probably has a boyfriend, and Rose Mary wouldn't be interested in an English guy anyway.*

199

He followed her to the dining room, where they took their seats at the table with the rest of Rose Mary's family.

"Good morning." Each family member greeted him.

"Morning," Kevin replied. He glanced around at the plain room he sat in. The space didn't have outlandish decor, like he'd seen in a lot of homes. Kevin thought it looked nice and well kept.

He waited in silence while Raymond explained what they were doing. Rose Mary's father told him he'd speak English instead of Pennsylvania Dutch. Raymond read through a section of scriptures from the Bible. When he was through, he grabbed a devotional booklet, setting it on the table next to him. Rose Mary's father flipped open the marked page and read it. Kevin couldn't help being drawn into the story, which summarized Psalm 27. It made what the scriptures were about a lot clearer. Kevin craved hearing the Word, and it brought clarity in his own life. *What would it have been like to grow up in a household like this?* He glanced at Rose Mary's folks.

When the devotions were finished, they prayed silently like they did before meals.

A few minutes later, Kevin's phone vibrated. He looked to see who'd called him. It was Dad. Kevin stepped out of the room and sent his dad a text about when he would be coming home. His avoidance with talking in person wasn't right, but Kevin had at least let his dad know he was in Belleville—safe and staying with a nice family. Also, the plane needed repairs to make it airworthy, and when they'd been completed, he would fly it home.

Kevin wanted a better relationship with his father, but it was difficult pleasing him. He was desperate to make good on taking care of the Cruiser. And Kevin wanted more time on his own to figure out what he needed in his life. His father kept a tight grip on him, which at times was hard on Kevin.

Not long after they'd finished devotions, Raymond asked Kevin if he'd like to come out to the barn. He put away his phone and followed Raymond and his two sons out the door. In the red building, Kevin watched Mervin and Harvey both grab some hay from a bale. Together they went into the horses' stalls and fed them. Raymond grabbed at a coiled hose on the ground and pulled the end of it to the closest stall. Then he passed it through to Mervin, who filled up the horse's water container. The silly horse kept putting his muzzle into the stream and sending splashes onto the boy. Mervin laughed; it didn't seem to bother him at all.

Harvey peeked in. "Belle always likes to do that."

"What's the name of the other horse?" Kevin pointed to the second animal while he stood against the stall enclosure.

Mervin turned off the hose and passed it back to Harvey. "Her name is Sugar."

"I can't help saying this, but that sounds sweet." Kevin grinned. "I'm sure you've never heard that comment before."

Harvey nodded. "Yep, I've heard it."

Raymond came with a bucket. "My boys are right; that horse's name does get us some funny comments."

"Okay, ladies. I brought you both some sweet oats." He poured the dried mix on top of the hay in each stall. Both animals whinnied in response.

"What does that stuff smell like? It sure makes the horses act happy."

Raymond came over with a little bit left in the bucket. "Feel

201

free to take a whiff if you'd like."

Kevin dipped his head near the rim of the container. "This stuff doesn't smell good to me. In fact, I don't see why the horses get excited over it."

"That's because you aren't a horse." Raymond dumped the rest of the grains into the last feeder and closed the stall door behind him.

Although Kevin had never been around horses that much, he felt comfortable with Sugar, and she seemed to be at ease with him as well. It was strange, but everything Kevin had done around here made him feel at ease.

After the horses were taken care of, they toured the barn and visited.

Linda came into the barn and announced that breakfast was ready. They headed in and washed up. The food had already been placed on the table. *These people are so accommodating and treat me so well.*

Rose Mary took a seat across from Kevin. The table sported plenty of food for everyone to eat. She loved bacon and eggs and hoped Kevin would like her version of scrambled eggs. Rose Mary liked to mince some onion and gently cook it with butter before adding the egg mixture. Aunt Sally made scones to go with the seedless raspberry jam she and Mom had put up in jars last summer.

Dad cleared his throat. "Let us silent pray."

Rose Mary closed her eyes and wondered what Kevin thought so far about their Amish ways. She wondered if his family prayed before eating. *I think Kevin is nice, and he seemed to be listening to the devotions my father led earlier.* A gentle nudge from Aunt Sally brought her thoughts back.

"Rose Mary, could you pass the *oier*?" Her aunt waited.

She took a couple of small helpings of the eggs and passed them to Aunt Sally. "Sorry for holding things up."

Dad tugged on his long beard. "Not a problem. No one has ever starved at our table yet."

"How was your first time out viewing the horses?" Rose Mary looked over at Kevin.

"I have to say the barn is set up nice, and I enjoyed seeing how to take care of the animals. The horses do get pretty excited about the sweet oats they get fed."

"Kevin didn't think the oats smelled that good," Harvey spoke up.

"That's because he's not a horse." Dad sipped on his cup of coffee.

The family laughed. Kevin blushed during the teasing, but it was all in fun.

Rose Mary thought he looked sweet with his rosy complexion.

Linda talked about having Doris make up the bride-and-groom wall hanging for their wedding. She picked out the colors from her wedding dress, attendants, food servers, and helpers. Linda sounded excited as she explained about the nice glassware she'd bought to use. Mom brought up getting the painting started on the front and back porches.

"I can start on it after work," Rose Mary quickly replied. "But I might need some help with the high places."

"Would it be all right if I helped? I've painted on my folks' house and didn't have any complaints." Kevin glanced over at Rose Mary's parents.

They looked at one another and shrugged. Her father grinned. "I've got the paint out in the small shed by the house. I'll set it out if you are willing to get started before I start work this morning."

"I can begin painting whenever you're ready." Kevin took a bite from his strip of bacon.

"When I'm done at the furniture store, I can help him paint too." Rose Mary looked over at Kevin and smiled.

"Then that's what'll happen," Dad responded. "The place will be looking better and better for Linda and Isaiah's wedding in the fall."

Kevin asked for more scrambled eggs, and Rose Mary grabbed them from the spot next to her. "Here you go."

He reached out to get the bowl. When his hand came in contact with Rose Mary's fingers, her heartbeat picked up its pace. She couldn't help being drawn to him. Maybe nobody but she could tell. *I can't wait to join Kevin later, even if it is to paint on parts of the house. I'd like to get to know him better.*

After work, Rose Mary left the store, almost skipping toward the house. She reached for the door and went in the back way. Mom and Aunt Sally appeared to be enjoying some sweet tea over ice in the kitchen. Rose Mary often thought of it as a ritual they liked to do after most of the chores were done.

While rummaging through her bedroom drawer, Rose Mary decided to get Kevin and herself glasses of iced sweet tea. Finally, she found a gray dress with stains on it. "This will make an impression on Kevin," she mumbled. Rose Mary breezed through the wardrobe change and slipped on some flip-flops. She then grabbed a black scarf from her top drawer and tied it into place on her head. Looking at her reflection in the mirror, she thought, *I look pretty plain, but at least getting any paint on this dress won't be a problem.*

As she descended the stairs, Rose Mary saw Mom in the living room, putting some books back on the shelf. "I think our houseguest has been looking through our selection of *buch*. Your father did tell the young man it was okay to do so."

"Can you tell if any of the books are missing?" Rose Mary stepped up to her.

"Mmm. . . It looks like a spiritual book is gone. Hopefully, he'll get something from it and enjoy the verses."

Rose Mary leaned closer to Mom and whispered, "When you were courting, did you ever go out with anyone outside of our community?"

Mom shook her head. "No, my family's ways were strict, so I chose to court the young men from my own community." Mom continued dusting. "I'd like to think we've taught you the right ways as well."

"Don't worry. I think I'm in good shape with how things are going."

Mom fell silent. She started to dust on a higher shelf then turned to look at Rose Mary. "You look like you're ready to do some work."

"I'm going out to help Kevin scrape and paint the railings on the porch."

Mom turned again. "Your sister and I will be happy. The improvements around here are a welcome change before the wedding."

"I better get busy then." Rose Mary stepped from the room

and went to the kitchen to grab two glasses of iced sweet tea.

Once outside, she held the beverages and scanned where Kevin had scraped off the old paint. He'd gotten quite a bit of the preliminary work done. Rose Mary perceived him as a hard worker, and he looked kind of cute in her father's old work shirt and trousers. Kevin almost looked Amish. *If only he was.*

"Hi, Rose Mary." He climbed off the ladder. "I'm sure it looks much worse now than when I started."

"No problem. Here's a glass of ice-cold sweet tea for you." Rose Mary passed him a glass.

Kevin took a quick drink. "Thank you. This does hit the spot."

"I'm glad you like it." She also took a sip and set down her glass. "I could start painting where you've already scraped away at the loose stuff." She pointed at the railing.

He nodded and took a couple of long drinks, emptying his glass. "Okay, I'll pop off the lid. Your dad set this stir stick here."

Kevin grabbed a common screwdriver and began prying the lid loose. Soon it popped off, and he stood up. "I'll get back up on the ladder and keep scraping until it's finished."

Rose Mary grabbed the stick and dipped it into the full bucket. She was careful not to stir too hard and have the paint leak out over the can. It took awhile to mix the paint completely, so while she worked, she peeked up at Kevin as he scraped away at the loose paint. *What should I say to him? I feel tongue-tied.*

Before she could think of anything, Kevin stopped scraping and looked down at her. "How did the rest of your day go at the furniture store?"

"Busy, especially after lunch. A passenger van pulled in with a small group of tourists.

"How many people?" He stepped down and rested his elbows on top of the ladder.

"Nine. One of the couples bought a sideboard. The Hendersons are from New York and seemed pleased to find that piece for their home." Rose Mary took the stir stick out of the paint. She carefully scraped it on the inside rim of the can then laid it on some newspaper.

"Did you ring up their order for the sideboard?"

"Linda helped, and I think I'm getting the hang of it, thanks to Dad and my sister." She couldn't help boasting.

"That sounds good. I hope my work out here on this porch will be good too. I'd like your parents to be happy with my efforts, since I volunteered to do the job."

"Don't give it another thought. We'd have to do an awful job on this to get them upset." Feeling a bit more relaxed, she picked up the brush and dipped it about a third of the way into the paint. "I'll start here on this railing."

"That'll work. I better climb back up and get busy." Kevin moved up the ladder.

I look frumpy in what I'm wearing, but my skill with the brush will look impressive. Rose Mary thought about lunch as she applied the paint to the railing. The rest of the family had other plans, so when she had gone home to eat, Kevin had joined her. *How cozy the two of us were sitting alone and eating toasted cheese sandwiches, along with Mom's homemade broccoli-cheese soup and crackers.* Rose Mary remembered how Kevin had enjoyed his lunch. It amused her when she noticed how he wasn't shy about going for seconds.

She watched him working. *If I ask more questions, I wonder what Kevin will tell me about his life.*

Chapter 7

A week had passed since the Cruiser had been hauled in for repairs, and Rose Mary had eaten her lunch with Kevin at the house every day during that time. Throughout the week, Kevin called the mechanic and checked on the progress.

Rose Mary joined Kevin at the dining-room table again for a sandwich and some German potato salad she'd made.

"This meatloaf sandwich is good, and your homemade salad is delicious." He took a big bite of the creamy dressing chock-full of eggs, pickles, and green onions that coated the potatoes.

"I'm glad you like it." Rose Mary couldn't help smiling. She truly enjoyed Kevin's company. He was like a breath of fresh air. Even though he appeared modern, he seemed old-fashioned to her too. She liked to visit with him, but the conversation leaned toward her and the family.

"If there's time today, would it be okay for me to see your dad's business?" Kevin wiped his mouth with a napkin.

"Sure. I think you may enjoy seeing our shop." Rose Mary bit into her sandwich.

"I've asked your dad about the furniture store. He mentioned that, besides the showroom, there's the shop in the back." He drank some water. "I can't wait to see it."

They ate for a few moments in silence. It wasn't awkward to her, because Kevin seemed to be content eating his lunch, until he paused and looked at her. "I do have a request, but it's about a different topic."

"What is that?"

"The gentleman working on the Cruiser would like me to come by soon."

"So, you would need a ride?"

"Right."

"We should be able to provide for you." She took a sip of her water. "You'll be traveling the way we Amish do, by horse and buggy."

Kevin shrugged. "I don't have any problem with that. It'll be a new experience."

Rose Mary liked this English fellow and hoped the feeling was mutual—although she didn't know why, since nothing could come of it. Kevin would be leaving soon.

Susan came out of the office and saw Linda at the counter doing a little reading.

"I can see you're having a nice break between customers. How are you enjoying the story?"

"It's great. I can see why you asked me to take a look at it." Linda set the book aside.

"I'll be heading back to the house now." Susan reached for the door.

"That's good, because I think Rose Mary is enjoying her lunch breaks a lot. She returns here afterward with an obvious spring in her step."

"I'll remind her to return to the store, and you'll have your break too." Susan turned and went out the door.

The more time Rose Mary spent with Kevin, the more intrigued and frustrated she became. While he had plenty of questions about her world, he didn't share much about his own home life. Rose Mary noticed he liked home-cooked meals. He'd also commented a couple of days ago that his clean clothes smelled good from being dried out on the line.

She and Kevin were just finishing their lunches when Mom came in. Looking at Rose Mary, she asked, "Is your lunch break about over?"

Rose Mary glanced at the wall clock. "Yes, it is. I'll need to get going so I can relieve Linda."

"That would be good. How was your lunch?"

"It was very good." Kevin placed his fork on the plate.

"I agree. Lunch was filling and good." Rose Mary cleared their dishes.

Mom followed her into the kitchen and watched while she rinsed off the plates and forks. Kevin came in afterward with their glasses and set them near the sink. "When should I come over to see the shop?"

Mom turned to retrieve a cookbook and began thumbing through the pages.

Kevin waited near the sink for Rose Mary's response. "How

about you come over in about a half hour. Then I should have some dusting finished."

"Okay, that works for me." Kevin nodded.

Mom seemed to be engrossed in the pages she looked through. Rose Mary thought it funny how she stayed put there. *My mother must think I need a bodyguard. I wonder what she'd say if I took Kevin by myself in the buggy to his repair shop.* Rose Mary rinsed off the glasses and dried her hands.

Susan walked out to the garden on the way back to the furniture store. She found Sally busy staking up the tomato plants. "How's it going?"

"It's going well," Sally responded. "I've got this last one to finish."

"The garden is looking nice, and the plants are thriving in this warm spring sun."

Sally stood and rubbed her back. "I can't wait until we can pick fresh, ripe tomatoes from these plants. When I had a garden back home, it was smaller than this because there were only the two of us at home, so. . ." Sally's shoulders drooped a bit.

Susan reached around her sister's waist and hugged her.

"I was getting a little homesick, but I'm fine." Sally smiled, showing her dimples. "I am happy here with you and your family."

"We are blessed to have you with us." Susan released her and moved toward the path.

"Where are you headed?" Her sister knelt down next to the tomato plant.

In Dutch, she answered, "I'm troubled about Rose Mary, and I need to speak with Raymond. I think there's a problem with my daughter and the new Englisher."

"I've got the same feeling myself." Sally grabbed some twine from the spool and cut off a fair amount.

"Rose Mary is at the store, and Linda is in the house right now getting her lunch." Susan looked in the direction of the house then toward the furniture store. "I better go. I'll see you in a while."

"Okay." Sally continued with her work.

Susan trotted down the path until she reached the gravel parking lot. No customers were at the store yet, so this was a good time to speak with Raymond. Susan walked into the showroom, where Rose Mary was dusting. "Everything is looking nice, Daughter. I'll be in there chatting with your father."

Rose Mary nodded and went back to polishing an end table.

Susan went into her husband's office and closed the door.

"Did our daughter have another lunch date today with Kevin?" Raymond inquired.

"Of course. It has become a daily thing with them." Susan pushed up her sleeves. "I hope this doesn't lead to anything serious. You know it hasn't been long since Rose Mary broke up with Tom."

"Rose Mary and Kevin are just friends. I do realize things can happen, but who knows yet where it will lead?" He tugged at his beard. "Our daughter didn't stay with Tom because he wanted to go English, remember?"

"I do remember." Susan gave a heavy sigh. "But we must recall how I found those English clothes in Rose Mary's closet."

"Yes, Fraa, but she hasn't worn any of them so far, right?" His chair creaked as he leaned back. "We shouldn't get too worried yet. When Kevin gets the repairs finished, he will fly out of our lives and back with his own family."

"You think it will be so simple? I don't." Susan frowned. "If she falls for this flyboy, we'll have our hands full for sure."

"He is a nice-looking young man and has been curious about some of the things we do."

Susan shook her head. "You sound as though you're giving Kevin a free pass."

"I don't see it as that, but each of us deserves a chance to prove ourselves." Raymond rubbed the bottom frame of his reading glasses.

"I should let you get back to working on the books. I'll be heading to the house soon."

"Okay, I'll see you when I'm done here for the day."

"Oh, I'm making one of your favorite dishes for supper—lasagna with extra cheese, the way you like it." She winked.

"I can't wait until we eat this evening."

Susan headed for his door. "Thanks for chatting with me about Rose Mary."

"You're welcome." Raymond gave a wave in response before she left.

I'll be upping my prayers about my younger daughter. Susan nearly tripped on an uneven paver, which halted her thoughts. She couldn't get over her husband's flexibility when it came to this young English man. *At the right time, I'll speak with Rose Mary about my concerns.*

∽

Later that afternoon, Kevin got into the buggy with Mervin and Rose Mary She sat in the driver's seat, holding on to the reins. With a gentle swish of the leather straps, the buggy lurched forward.

This was his first time in a buggy, and he was excited. This event compared to going on a hayride or when Kevin was a child and got to ride the ponies at the fair. It also gave him a chance to spend more time with Rose Mary.

Rose Mary got the mare trotting down the road. The hooves hitting the pavement made a unique, rhythmic sound. Kevin enjoyed the gentle flow of air coming through the open windows.

Mervin waved at some young Amish boys in a yard as they passed, and Rose Mary acknowledged the buggies that approached them, traveling the opposite way.

This opened a whole new world to Kevin, and he enjoyed witnessing it. It seemed more like the old western days, which had long since disappeared.

They'd traveled several miles from the house, and he used his phone to give directions. Kevin looked at the names of the roads to keep track of which way they needed to go. Soon, the small airport came into view. "There it is. That's the place we'll pull into, and I'll go talk to the mechanic."

Rose Mary guided the horse and buggy up to the office. "We can wait for you out here."

"All right. I'll go in and see what is happening." Kevin climbed out of the rig and went into the building.

A woman sitting behind the desk spoke on the phone. Kevin

215

waited, looking around the room. Its walls were plastered with photos of planes.

The woman hung up the phone and smiled at him. "How may I help you?"

"I talked to Barry earlier, and he asked me to come by about my Piper Super Cruiser." Kevin stood waiting.

"You can have a seat while I go get Barry from the hangar." She motioned to a chair.

Kevin took a seat. He hoped the plane might be ready. He picked up a magazine on flying and thumbed through the pages. Then he grabbed a golfing publication and did the same. Kevin became bored while waiting, so he got up and walked over to the window. He looked out and thought about the contrast. There stood the horse and buggy he had arrived in. Yet he waited for an airplane to leave in.

The woman entered the room and stood by the open door. "I'll take you to Barry."

"Okay." Kevin followed her a short distance before he saw the mechanic.

"Hello there. I'm sure you are interested in how things are looking so far." Barry wiped his greasy hands on a rag.

"Definitely, but I'm guessing she's not ready yet." Kevin squinted against the sun.

"Nope, not yet. Your prop is on order." The mechanic stood with his hands resting on his hips. "This is a beauty and in nice shape. What year again is your plane, Kevin?"

"It's the 1956 PA-12." Kevin laid his hand on the fabric-skinned hull.

Barry nodded with a smile. "Yep, sounds right. I like the

brown-and-orange striping on it."

As their conversation ended, the woman interjected, "I talked on the phone with the parts supplier, and he told me it will be at least a few more days until we get the prop here to install."

Barry looked over at the Super Cruiser then back at Kevin. "I'll show you what I've done if you've got some time."

Kevin thought about his friends sitting out in the buggy waiting for him. "Would it be okay if I got my friends so they could come out here and wait?"

Barry nodded.

"Let's go back to the office," the woman suggested as she led the way. "You can go get your friends and come through the office."

Kevin returned to the buggy and invited Rose Mary and Mervin back to see the plane in the hangar. Rose Mary secured the horse to a post, and they followed him through the office and into the tall building where the Piper Cruiser sat.

"What do you think of this place?" Kevin looked at both of them.

"It's great." Mervin played with the brim of his straw hat.

"It kind of reminds me of a huge barn in some ways." Rose Mary looked toward the rafters up high.

Kevin chuckled. "Yes, one could put a lot of farm equipment in here, right, Mervin?"

He smiled up at Kevin. "I think so."

Barry walked over and greeted them. Then he and Kevin went to look at the work he'd done so far. Repairs were coming along well. Next week looked good for getting the plane flying again. *I'm determined to see this matter through*, Kevin thought. *I need to show my father I can do things on my own.*

217

CHAPTER 8

Rose Mary got up early and joined her family in the dining room. When they'd eaten breakfast and cleaned up, she stepped outside for some fresh air. Kevin came out the door and took a seat on the porch near her. "Another nice morning, but today I'll be leaving for State College. The Super Cruiser will be ready to fly this afternoon."

Rose Mary smiled at him and looked out toward the back field. "Let's take a walk around the yard. We can visit before I need to head off to work."

Kevin rose to his feet and patted his stomach. "I wouldn't mind, given the big breakfast I ate. I'm gonna miss these good, home-cooked meals."

As they began to walk, Kevin talked about her family's practice of reading from the Bible and having devotions every day. He'd been showing an interest in the scriptures and asking questions about God. Rose Mary could see Kevin seemed curious, and he'd mentioned he would like to go to church.

Kevin led the way, and with Rose Mary close behind him, they headed for the green maple. "This old tree is sure a focal point in your yard, and it provides a lot of shade." He rested his hand upon its surface.

"I can't believe it's been two weeks since you landed in our field." Rose Mary took a seat on the swing hanging from one of the huge branches.

"I would have never guessed in my whole life I'd meet a family like yours and be so welcomed by them." Kevin's eyes engaged hers. "Also, I've enjoyed your parents, and I like your family's values."

"It's been nice getting to know you." She smiled as she rested on the swing. *If only we could spend more time together. Guess it's just a silly, foolish dream.*

"And I, you. I've dreaded leaving." He looked toward the house. "But I can't stay here forever."

"I'll miss seeing you too." Her eyes filled with tears.

"Rose Mary, would there be. . .would you have a problem with me continuing to see you? I mean, even when I'm at State College, if I were to drive down here so we could see each other."

She brushed at a tear. "I wouldn't have a problem with seeing you again."

"I'm glad you feel that way. It will make having to leave you today a little easier." He stepped away from the base of the tree and came closer to her.

Rose Mary looked up at him. "I best go back to the house and get a couple things done before work."

When she went to stand, Kevin reached out and helped her up. He continued to hold Rose Mary's hands. "I'm relieved you have agreed to keep seeing me, and I'm looking forward to going for more buggy rides."

Rose Mary's face warmed. "I can take you on all the buggy rides you'd like, Kevin, just say the word."

I can't believe this is happening. I feel like I'm floating on a cloud. Kevin is so kind and polite. He's nothing like pushy Tom. Rose Mary looked into his eyes but felt a twinge run up her back. *I'm delighted about this, but my folks. . .will they be pleased?*

Before heading to the furniture store, Linda came up the stairs to finish getting ready. She heard Rose Mary humming in her room. Linda decided to stop in and chat for a few moments. "Don't you sound chipper this morning."

"I can't argue with that. We took a nice stroll around the yard earlier, talking."

Linda shook her head. "You mean with Kevin?"

"Yes." Rose Mary swept the broom along the mopboard.

"You seem to be getting chummier with him." Linda closed the door behind her and took a seat in a chair. "I'm a little confused about you two."

"Like I said before, we took a walk and visited. How can it be confusing to you?" Rose Mary looked back at the mopboard and continued to sweep it.

"I get what you said. But why are you bothering to get to know this guy, anyway?"

"Because I think he's different and sort of a needy soul." Rose Mary paused from her work.

"True, but he isn't Amish and isn't churched either. What would there be to talk about between you two?" Linda shifted on her seat.

"If you must know, we talked about the Bible."

"You've got to be kidding me." Linda tried to stifle a laugh.

Her sister looked away and frowned. "It's the truth. You don't have to believe me."

"You can't blame me, Rose Mary, for worrying about you."

"There's nothing to worry about."

Linda stared out the window. *I love my sister, and I want what's best for her.* She turned back to see Rose Mary set the broom by the wall.

"He is a nice person, and I think I'm getting to see the real side of Kevin." Rose Mary's voice rang with assurance.

Linda crossed the bare bedroom floor and gave her a hug. "Okay, I don't want to *fecht* with you. But since you haven't denied my earlier comment about him, then I must be right."

Rose Mary stepped away from Linda and glanced over at the alarm clock. "I don't want to fight either, so let's please drop this issue and focus on getting ready for work."

When Linda saw the time, she headed for the door. "I'd better hurry and finish getting ready. I'll see you in a bit."

Linda went to her room. She hadn't put in enough hairpins this morning, so her bun had come loose. Linda stood in front of the mirror and brushed her long brown hair. Then she began working in some hair spray to help smooth back her hair into a ponytail. Soon, Linda coiled her hair into a tight bun and pinned it into place. She picked up her white prayer *kapp* and put it on. *Lord, please help me to say the appropriate words to Rose Mary. I hope she can make the right choices for herself. Amen.*

Reedsville, Pennsylvania

When they arrived at the small airfield, Kevin let Harvey climb into the pilot's seat. He showed Rose Mary's brother how to push the lever for the flaps to move up and down on the tail section. Mervin watched what his brother did and asked if he could try it too.

Kevin asked Harvey to move to the backseat while his brother climbed in the front to be shown what to do. Mervin smiled as he sat in the pilot's chair. Kevin showed the boys the gauges and explained what they were for. He looked over at Rose Mary and smiled. "How about a quick flight before I go—just you and me?"

She gasped. "Really?"

"Of course. I'll take us up."

"Are you gonna do it, Rose Mary?" Mervin spoke up.

"I'm nervous, but I'd like to try it." Rose Mary looked at her brothers. "Would you two mind waiting for me while I go flying with Kevin?"

The boys shrugged their shoulders.

Barry, the mechanic, walked over and stood by them. "Me and the boys will watch you go up in the plane. She is running great now—good as new."

"Let's take it out." Kevin couldn't wait to see Rose Mary's reaction. He'd also be getting to spend a little more time with her before saying goodbye.

Kevin helped Rose Mary step on board and get seated, wearing a safety belt. He got in and closed the door of the plane. Soon they were cleared for takeoff, and the small plane taxied down the runway.

When the Piper Super Cruiser left the ground, Rose Mary let out a holler. "Whoa! This is exciting! Now I know how it feels to fly."

Kevin laughed. "It's a fun aircraft to fly, and it doesn't move too fast either."

He thought about his father's expensive, single-seated, AT-502 air tractor and how much faster it flew. A pilot needed to be skilled to fly in and out of people's fields. Common obstacles such as buildings, trees, and power lines could cause great damage if hit. His father worked hard and kept insisting Kevin should follow through with being trained.

"This looks like my parents' place, am I right?" Rose Mary pointed.

"Yes, it is." Kevin turned the plane into the direction of the house. "You should have a better view now."

"I never would have imagined I'd get to do something like this in my whole entire life." Her voice rang with delight.

"We'd better head back to the landing strip. I'm sure your brothers are anxious for your return." Kevin headed the plane back toward the field. After landing, he wrestled with saying goodbye to Mervin, Harvey, and Rose Mary. One thing helped: knowing he would get to see Rose Mary again.

State College

During the short flight back to his hometown airport, Kevin went over what to say to his parents when he returned. He wanted to show them he could be responsible and manage things on his own, but when he'd left a couple of weeks ago, Kevin had been upset and caused his parents unnecessary worry. He would do his best to apologize for it.

Kevin made time to think about what he wanted in life. Before leaving his home and landing in Belleville with the Amish, he hadn't been happy. But being with the Rennos gave him a clearer understanding of everything. Kevin learned that simple, meaningful things counted and could make a person feel good.

When the town of State College came into view, Kevin checked with the tower, and they gave the go-ahead to land. The Piper ran well, and not much later, he taxied over to a nearby hangar. He'd stepped out of the airplane when a mechanic named Ed, who did work on the planes, came over to Kevin. "Where have you been with the plane?"

"A couple of weeks ago, I needed to land it in a field." He stood by the opened cockpit door.

Ed moved around the plane, looking at it and rubbing his chin. "This prop isn't the same one you flew out of here with, is it?"

"You're correct, Ed. It got bent during the rough landing and had to be replaced." Kevin placed his hand on one of the blades.

"How did she fly coming home for you? Any problems?" Ed asked.

"Nope. The plane handled well, and the engine ran fine all the way here." Kevin glanced toward the parking lot and saw his father's truck pull in. "I'll talk to you later, Ed. I need to see my dad right now."

"No problem." The mechanic headed off.

When Kevin approached his father and saw his reddened face, he figured Dad was upset. "Your mother has been worried sick about you being gone so long."

"I sent a text, letting you both know I was all right." Kevin straightened his collar.

His father's green-eyed gaze landed on the keys Kevin held.

"I need to see my plane, and where did you take it to be fixed?"

"I stayed in Belleville this whole time, and the Piper got fixed in Reedsville." He followed his father over to the craft.

His father walked around the plane and stopped in front of it. "This is new. What else got fixed on her?"

"Here's the invoice of the work the other mechanic did in Reedsville." Kevin pulled the folded paper from his jeans pocket.

His dad's booming voice grew stronger. Kevin tried not to let his father get the better of him. "The plane began to have problems after I left here. The engine kept cutting in and out, so I put her down in a big field." Kevin looked away then back again. "I apologize for leaving you and Mom when I felt upset and also for making her worry about me."

"You are lucky the plane and you didn't wind up in bad shape." His father seemed to be calming down with his tone softening a bit. "Your mom and I brought your car back to the house, so you'll need a ride home from here." His dad gave him a quick hug. "You did good with the plane, Son."

Kevin liked to hear his father say those words. Though he wasn't sure how long it would take for Dad to get upset about something else. Kevin asked if he could drive them home, and Dad said okay. Driving along, the radio played some country-and-western music. It didn't take more than fifteen minutes to arrive at his folks' place. Kevin parked the truck in the garage, and they headed into the house.

Kevin smelled dinner cooking as Mom came over to him with a big hug and then pulled back. "I've been worried about you. You seem to be okay. Nothing hurt, right?"

"Just a little wound on my head where I bumped it on my landing in the field in Belleville." He moved his hair away to show the mark.

She reached up and touched near the spot. "I'm glad you are all right." Her blue eyes shimmered with tears.

"I'm sorry, Mom, for making you worry so much about me while being away."

"It's okay now, Kevin. Are you hungry?" His mother patted his back.

"I'm getting there." He smacked his lips. "Something does smell good."

"It's a tuna casserole I whipped up. You know me; I don't like to cook often." She headed toward the kitchen.

His father rolled his eyes. "I thought we'd be going out for a bite this evening."

"I'm glad we are staying in for a home-cooked meal. I like to eat in rather than having to order restaurant food." Kevin stood in the dining room with his father.

"I think I'll read the paper until the food is ready." Dad wandered off in the direction of the recliner.

Kevin thought he'd talk with his mom more privately in the kitchen while she got things ready, so he headed in that direction.

"I'd like to tell you about my adventure." Kevin leaned against the counter.

"Okay, I'm listening." Mom sat at the kitchen table. "Take a seat here by me."

Kevin pulled out a chair and sat next to her. He told his mother about the Rennos and their hospitality. Mom seemed intrigued about the whole story until Kevin revealed the part about liking the Amish way of life.

"You've got to be joking," his mother scoffed. "You can't be serious."

"Well, here's more, Mom. I asked Rose Mary Renno if we could see each other again."

"An Amish girl?" She shook her head. "Why would you want to do that?"

"I know what I want to do, and crop dusting isn't it." He looked away from her.

"You can't be serious about this. Why would you throw away the training you've received?" His mother's voice sounded strained.

"I never wanted to do this sort of thing, but Dad convinced me that I'd like it." Kevin sighed.

"You must have bumped your head harder than you thought to be talking like this. Your father will get upset, and you know it." His mom slid her chair back.

"That's why I'm sharing this with you right now and not Dad."

"He will be very disappointed about this, Kevin. I'm stunned myself by what you've said, but I'm glad you are okay from the ordeal." She stepped over to the oven to check the meal. "Let's change the subject, please. I've got a green salad in the refrigerator and some rolls on the counter that I'll be putting in the oven to warm."

"Okay. I'll go wash up in a little bit and sit with Dad in the living room." Kevin stood.

Mom picked up the pile of paper plates, utensils, and napkins sitting ready for dinner. "Would you mind placing these on the dining-room table on your way through?"

"No problem." Kevin reached for them and carried the items out to the table.

I figured Mom would react this way, and I can't blame her for how this might hurt. He headed to the bathroom. *I'm not ready to tell Dad yet. I hope Mom doesn't say anything to him.*

CHAPTER 9

Belleville

Two weeks had gone by since Kevin had flown back to State College. Rose Mary checked the hour from a nice, woodcrafted wall clock. It was about time to close the store for the day. Kevin was coming to see her this evening, and she couldn't help feeling overjoyed. She'd seen him last week when he'd come by to visit everyone. Rose Mary thought about how handsome Kevin looked and pictured his face in her mind.

Linda took a seat, brushing against Rose Mary's arm. "What are you doing this evening?"

Rose Mary smiled widely. "Well. . .a special someone will be coming by to see me."

"Are we talking about Kevin Presley, by any chance?" Linda folded her arms.

"Of course."

"I can't believe you are allowing him to keep coming around."

"Don't let it bother you. We will be fine. He respects my ways and our family's too."

"Mom seems funny with you and him seeing each other." Linda looked toward the back of the store where their father stood talking to a customer.

"Well, Mom wasn't happy with Tom either, but Dad's been okay about me having Kevin over so far. He hasn't said anything negative whatsoever."

"I don't know if our father would have let me get away with that." Linda's mouth slackened.

"How would you know? Anyway, you found Isaiah Miller, and he is perfect for you." Rose Mary gave her sister's arm a squeeze. "Besides, I haven't gotten a marriage proposal from anyone yet."

"It will happen one day for you. You'll make a fine catch for any guy." Linda patted her shoulder. "Just make sure you're thinking clearly where Kevin is concerned."

The little bell jingled over the front entrance of the store.

"Hi, Marlene, I'm glad you're back." Rose Mary hopped off the stool from behind the counter.

"Hello, and I'm happy to be back." Marlene hugged her. "I thought I'd come by and see how you are doing." Her cheeks were reddened. "I road my scooter over for some exercise today."

"How did your visit with your aunt in Lancaster go?"

"It was great to see her and the rest of the family. They're doing well, and their neighbor's wedding was lovely." Marlene leaned against the counter.

"Hello there, Marlene, how was your trip?" Rose Mary's father came up front with the customer he'd been helping.

"It was great and a lot of fun." She spoke in Pennsylvania Dutch.

Linda took the price tags from her dad and rang up the customer's purchases. When she finished, Dad told Rose Mary she could go ahead and leave with Marlene.

They stepped outside in the early-summer air and were greeted by bright pink petunias standing in old wooden barrel containers.

"What are you doing this evening?" Rose Mary played with a head covering tie as she watched Marlene pick up her scooter. "Why I'm asking you is because a certain fellow I've met will be by here to see me later."

Marlene walked her scooter back beside Rose Mary. "Are you meaning Tom?" They headed toward the house.

"Nope, someone new. He isn't from here. His name is Kevin Presley, and he lives in State College."

"Wait, then this guy isn't Amish, is he?" Marlene stopped abruptly.

"No, he's not." She fidgeted. "He's English, and he flies a plane."

"Are you serious, Rose Mary?" Marlene's eyes grew large.

"I'm speaking the absolute truth." She looked toward the house. "If you'd please stick around, I'd like to introduce you to him."

"I guess it would be okay." Marlene laid the scooter on the lawn. "How are your parents acting about this English fellow?"

"Let's walk to the garden and sit on the bench." Rose Mary led the way. "Dad hasn't seemed too worried about any of it, but my mom appears not to be so happy. Let me say, she doesn't stay long in the same room when Kevin is there. It's like Mom is trying to avoid him."

"Has he given her a reason to feel that way?" Marlene sat down beside her.

"No, of course not. Kevin is kind and polite around all my family." Rose Mary paused. "I hate to ask you this, but I could use a favor."

"What is it?"

"Would you mind hanging out with me and Kevin? Maybe if you were with us, my mother would be less upset over me seeing him again."

"Umm...you've got a point. I'll stay and help you out." Marlene sighed. "But I'm curious about how long you will keep seeing him."

"I'm not sure yet, since I'm seeing him once or twice a week. Both our schedules are too busy to do more." Rose Mary's stomach growled. "Guess I'm getting a little hungry. How about we go to the house for something to drink and snack on? I know my mom would like to see you and ask about your trip."

"Okay, sounds good to me. I could use something cold to drink, and visiting with your mom would be nice."

State College

Kevin had just changed into some fresh clothes in his room, when his mom knocked on the door.

"Come in," he called.

His mother entered, wearing a look of concern. "Where are you headed this evening, Son?"

"I'm going to Belleville to see Rose Mary."

"Are they all right with...I mean is her family okay with you coming there and seeing their daughter?" Mom's face tightened as her brows drew together.

"So far they've seemed fine with me there. Why?"

"I don't know much about the Amish, but don't they like their children to date other Amish?" She took a couple of steps closer to him.

"Sure, it's their way, but I like Rose Mary. She's a breath of fresh air."

Mom reached out and held his shoulder. "But face it, you don't have a future with her, dear. I don't see why you are pursuing this."

"I'm taking this one day at a time. When I'm ready, I'll let Dad know what I'm doing." Kevin patted her arm. "I need to finish getting ready to head out of here pretty quick."

"I'll let you do that, and I'll try to keep a lid on things here with your father." She let go of his shoulder and gave a long sigh. "But he is getting antsy about you learning to fly the air tractor."

"I know, Mom. I'd like to talk about this later."

"Okay." She held up her hand. "I hope you have a nice evening with the young lady you'll be seeing."

"Her name is Rose Mary."

"Okay, okay. You and Rose Mary have a nice evening then."

"Thank you." Kevin felt relieved when she left the room.

Mom was somewhat in his corner, so half the battle was won. Kevin knew when he decided to tell his father about hanging out with an Amish girl, he would not be too happy. He shook his head and looked in the mirror. "My father wants things his own way."

Kevin combed his hair and headed out to his car. The garage door stood open, and he heard someone, probably Dad, rummaging through something. Kevin moved quickly to get into his car and head out of the driveway. In his rearview mirror, he saw his father come out of the garage, but Kevin kept right on going. Dad would ask questions, and if Kevin admitted he was heading to Belleville again, Dad would put his foot down and say to forget about this girl. But regardless of what his father thought, Kevin didn't want to walk away from his growing friendship with Rose Mary.

Belleville

Once Kevin pulled in the driveway and up by the barn, he noticed Rose Mary and another young woman outside by the front porch. Rose Mary led the other girl over to him and introduced them to each other.

Kevin wondered if Marlene knew much about him and Rose Mary. He missed her, and she looked so pretty in her green dress this evening.

Rose Mary asked Kevin if he'd be interested in going for a drive. She offered to take out the buggy. Kevin couldn't wait to go and wanted to help her get the carriage out from the barn. Once the rig stood ready, Rose Mary secured it to the hitching rail and led Marlene and Kevin into the house. He met up with Raymond in the kitchen snacking on an apple. "Hello, Kevin." He shook Kevin's hand. "I see the buggy is out, and the horse is hooked up. What are you up to, Rose Mary?" Her father ran a thumb up and down his suspender strap.

"We're going for a ride, and then I'm taking them to the store." Rose Mary picked up her purse.

He sipped at his beverage and set it down. "Be careful and have a good time."

"*Danki*, Daed." Rose Mary gave a warm smile.

Kevin followed the girls out of the house and closed the door behind him.

Once they'd climbed into the buggy, Rose Mary got the rig

going onto the road. "It's such a nice evening. We should get some hot dogs and rolls from the store and cook them over a wood fire out back at my house." Rose Mary jiggled the reins.

"Sounds good to me." Marlene laughed. "Maybe some s'mores too."

"I'll buy the food at the store since you are supplying the mode of transportation and the place to have supper," Kevin offered.

"If you insist, then that is what we'll do."

As the buggy moved forward, he saw a yellow carriage. He pointed to the other buggy. "Is there a reason their rig is yellow instead of black like yours?"

From the backseat, Marlene responded: "They are a more progressive Amish than we are. We black-toppers are much more traditional in our ways."

"In another part of the valley, there are the white-toppers," Rose Mary interjected. "They're stricter than we are and more old-fashioned."

"How so?" Kevin questioned.

"For example, they don't have indoor plumbing," Marlene explained. "They have a tradition of painting their front doors blue. Also, the white-toppers' barns have no paint on them. Very plain, for sure."

"It's interesting how much difference there can be in other Amish communities." Kevin shifted on the seat as Rose Mary nodded.

Kevin listened to the girls talk about Linda's upcoming wedding. It sounded like a lot was involved—planning the meals, desserts, and the amount of food needed for their guests.

After a while, they reached the grocery store. Rose Mary

pulled up to one of the hitching rails provided for the Amish. They climbed out of the carriage and walked into the store. Kevin grabbed a basket for Rose Mary, and the three of them started shopping.

"Look who is here." Marlene nudged Rose Mary and pointed. "It's Tom."

A trickle of sweat rolled down Rose Mary's cheek. "Umm, he is looking our way now. This is a little awkward."

"Maybe I'll go talk with him for a little bit while you and Kevin shop. Are you okay with that?"

"I don't mind. You go right ahead." Rose Mary watched Marlene head over to Tom.

Kevin wasn't sure what seemed to be happening here, but he hoped to find out. He walked with Rose Mary to get what they needed. When they'd gotten everything, they made their way to the checkout line. Kevin noticed Marlene standing in about the same spot, talking with the guy named Tom. He wondered if maybe Marlene and Tom were more than friends.

The clerk rang up the amount and waited. Kevin pulled out his wallet and paid the lady. Kevin and Rose Mary picked up a couple of bags and left the store.

"Marlene must have a lot to say to the fellow in the store." Kevin stepped up to the buggy and slid the bags inside for Rose Mary.

"It's probably some catch-up conversation. Tom's been away to Lancaster for many weeks, helping out his uncle with odd jobs around his place." Rose Mary stood by the horse, patting its neck. "And Marlene took a trip as well, visiting her aunt and family."

"Those two are both single, right? Or am I wrong?" Kevin tilted his head.

"Yes, they are not seeing anyone." Rose Mary looked past him. "Oh, here she comes now."

"Sorry I took so long chatting with Tom. I didn't realize how much time went by." Marlene sported a sheepish smile.

"Did you talk about your trips by any chance?" Rose Mary began untying the horse from the rail.

Marlene climbed into the buggy. "Yes, he talked about the work he'd done at his uncle's. Then I shared about my trip too."

Kevin listened and tried to figure out the whole picture. He got into the rig after Marlene. She spoke some Pennsylvania Dutch, and Rose Mary responded in the same manner. Kevin wondered what these two were talking about, since they were going to great lengths to shield him from hearing.

Rose Mary looked over at Kevin. "I'm sorry for talking in Dutch and leaving you out. It is easy to do at times when you're embarrassed about discussing something. Tom used to court me."

"I see." His eyebrows rose. "And don't worry about it. I accept your apology."

"Thank you." Rose Mary got into the buggy.

"Let's get going. I'm hungry," Marlene spoke up.

Kevin couldn't help wondering what had happened between Rose Mary and Tom and why they weren't courting anymore. He gripped the edge of his seat. *What if she changes her mind about this guy, and he wins Rose Mary back?*

CHAPTER 10

As Rose Mary mowed the front yard, she caught sight of Tom's car pulling into their driveway. *I wonder why he's here.* It had been a couple of weeks since she'd run into him at the store. She continued to push the machine alongside the last swath she'd cut. *Marlene shared with me some things she and Tom talked about when we all saw him at the store.* Rose Mary stopped walking and watched as Tom got out of his car. *He should've called to see if I had time to talk to him today.*

She shut off the mower. "Hello."

"Hi, Rose Mary. I came by to talk to you about something. Can we visit in private?" He glanced around the yard.

"All right. Come with me."

Tom followed Rose Mary over to the corral. She saw Aunt Sally taking some clothes off the line behind the house. Her aunt waved in their direction, and she and Tom did the same. He removed his hat and held it close to his leg. "I want to begin by saying Marlene told me about your new boyfriend. I heard he isn't Amish. Is this true?"

"Yes, Kevin is English, and he is a friend."

"Do you like him?"

"Well, yes, but—"

"This is unbelievable, Rose Mary." He shook his head. "I'm not getting it, because we broke up on account of me wanting to go English. But I've changed my mind on that foolish notion. I will be selling my car soon too."

"You have changed your mind? I'm sure your family is happy about this."

"My family is also happy about me wanting to join the church." His brows lowered. "I can see you're not in any hurry to do the same."

Rose Mary tried to compose herself. "I'm not ready to join the church yet. I've got plenty of time ahead." She adjusted her scarf. "I'd like to know what made you change your mind about not going English."

Tom let out a long breath. "While staying with my uncle, Martin, we did a lot of talking. He is Mennonite and has been for a good number of years. But he started out Amish. When he was around my age, he made the choice to leave his community. My uncle followed through with it, thinking it was a wise thing."

Rose Mary listened to Tom tell more of the story of how his uncle held on to some regrets because he'd left the Amish faith.

"I thought to myself at first things would be so much better out there. But my uncle let me know there are always consequences in wanting more than is truly needed." Tom lifted his foot and rested it on the fence rail. "I realized I'd gotten selfish. I wasn't myself around my family or friends anymore. I didn't like that guy very much; I really was not happy."

"I appreciate your sharing with me what happened in Lancaster and also why you changed your mind." Rose Mary stepped away from the fence. "I'm curious. Do you like Marlene?" she asked.

A deafening silence hung in the air as they stood facing each other.

"I'm okay with it, honestly."

"I've talked with her some, and she seems pretty nice."

"She's a good person. I think the world of her. Marlene has always been there for me."

"We'll see how things work out in the days to come." He took his foot off the fence. "Now, I've got to ask you, why are you hanging out with this Englisher? Do you think he's cute, or is it because he flies a plane?"

"Kevin's a nice fellow, and he's searching for answers. He's not a Christian but seems hungry to know about the Bible."

Tom frowned. "That didn't really answer my question."

Her face warmed. "I do think he's cute, and flying a plane is fascinating, but I just enjoy his company."

"Has he said much about his family?"

She looked out toward Harvey blowing bubbles by the house. "Not much. He'd mentioned he was an only child. Also, Kevin said he and his dad don't get along very well."

"Maybe you should forget about him. He might not be able to be helped." Tom gave a shrug.

"I'm going to ignore what you've said. Furthermore, I think Kevin is worth trying to help. And if he asks, I'll do my best to teach him about serving the Lord."

"Okay, I'll back off." Tom moved away from her.

"If we are through here, I need to get back to mowing. I'm glad you stopped by and we could air out our thoughts."

Tom got back into his vehicle. As he made a right out onto the road, she noticed Kevin's car turning around in the neighbor's driveway and leaving in the opposite direction. She called and raised her hands to get his attention, but he sped off. *This isn't good. I hope he doesn't think I'm seeing Tom again.*

State College

Kevin drove up to his folks' garage, turned off the car, and stayed there. *What was I thinking, dropping by like that?* Kevin couldn't believe Tom was at Rose Mary's place. But it wasn't like she expected Kevin to come by today. *Has she been dishonest with me? I've been leery of this very thing happening.* His shoulders slumped as he placed the cell on the dashboard. Kevin then reached over to the passenger seat and picked up the new TracFone he'd purchased for Rose Mary to use. Kevin thought he would surprise her with it, but he was the one getting a shock.

Feeling hurt, and with his ego bruised, Kevin got out of the car and slipped the cell phones in his pockets. As he walked on to the house, he didn't see any sign of Dad's truck. *Bet my folks went out for dinner as usual.*

Unlocking the back door, he went in. Sure enough, the house sat quiet and no one was at home. *At least I can mull things over in peace.* Kevin took a seat on the overstuffed couch. He retrieved his phone and looked up a couple of churches not far from their home. Kevin figured it would be nice to start attending a service. He found the hours of one church that offered two services on Sunday. Kevin would decide which one and attend this Sunday. He wondered if his parents might join him. *I'll ask them, but regardless of their decision, I'm going.*

Kevin thought about Rose Mary. They planned to get together in a couple of days, but after seeing her with Tom, Kevin didn't know what to do. Should he follow through and go to Belleville again? *Or I could wait and confront her on the phone when she calls to see why I didn't show up.*

Kevin's stomach rumbled, so he went to the kitchen for something to eat. He made a sandwich and sat at the table to pray before eating. *If I were at the Rennos' place, they'd have some good food to enjoy.*

He ate in the peacefulness the quiet house provided. *Instead of making a rash decision, I should sleep on it and decide what to do in the morning.*

Belleville

It was a nice evening as Susan stood in the kitchen, baking some pies with Sally. She wanted to contribute some items for the upcoming auction and knew Raymond would donate some nicer items he and his crew put aside for the sale.

She still wanted to talk to her daughter about Kevin and what she thought about Rose Mary seeing him. She looked up at the kitchen battery clock. Rose Mary had mowed the lawn earlier, and Susan wondered what she was up to now.

"We've got these six pies ready to bake." Sally wiped her floured hands on a dish towel.

"Thank you for your help. I'd like to make up some sticky buns too." Susan took a seat at the table.

"Do we have what we need for those?" Sally grabbed a note-pad and pen.

"I should check." As her sister went to the recipe-card holder, Susan opened the cupboard and sorted through her dry goods. "Oh, I'll need some more brown sugar, yeast, and pecans."

Sally wrote on the notepad. "Okay, I've got it down. Will we need any butter or milk?"

"Let me see." Susan opened the refrigerator. "Umm. . .yes, we'll need those too. Thanks for helping me out."

"No problem. I'll take myself to the store. Would you like to come with me?"

"I've got some things to do. I'll go with you on the next run to the store." Susan grabbed the hot mitts and slid them on her hands as her sister picked up her purse and headed out.

Susan lifted the cookie sheets with the pies, put them into the hot oven, and set the timer. *I don't understand how my husband can be so calm about our daughter and this Englisher.*

Raymond came into the kitchen with his metal commuter mug. "I've got a collection of dirty coffee mugs from my office needing to be washed."

"Okay, I'll take care of it."

"Is your sister going somewhere? I saw Sally heading for the barn with her purse."

"Yes, she's going to the store."

"All right then, while you are there, I could use a new pair of tweezers. You know me and wood—we can't stop getting under each other's skin." He chuckled.

"I'm not going with Sally. I'll stay here to bake these pies."

"You didn't have to bake any pies today. There's a couple of days yet before the auction. What's up?"

"I. . .I was going to talk to our daughter about the young man she is seeing."

"Not this again, Fraa. I said we need to let Rose Mary handle things. She will be fine."

"There's no guarantee everything will be fine." Susan folded her arms.

"Rose Mary has a good head on her shoulders, and you should allow her to come to us if she needs to. Please go to the store, and I'll pull the pies out of the oven when the timer goes off." Raymond rinsed out the mugs in the sink.

"Okay, you win. I'll go with Sally to the store. Please don't forget the pies though." She pulled off her apron and draped it over the kitchen chair.

"Also, don't forget my tweezers. I've got some slivers to dig out of my hands."

Susan went into the washroom and cleaned up. Then she headed outside to catch up with Sally before she left. Susan made it to the building's entrance when she saw her sister leading the horse out of the barn.

"Did you remember something else for me to add to the grocery list?" Sally asked.

"I do need to pick up a pair of tweezers for Raymond."

"I can do that."

"I'm going with you." Susan helped her back the horse to the front of the buggy and attach the forks in place.

"What about the pies baking in the oven? Who's watching them?"

"Raymond is," Susan replied.

"I'm a little confused. What's up?"

"Okay, I'll confess. I wanted to stay home so I could talk to Rose Mary about Kevin. But my husband found out and said for me not to say anything. So here I am."

"Like I've said before, your daughter is a smart young lady. Most often, children sooner or later come to their folks when there is a need or a question."

"Honestly, I'm not fond of this situation. I wish she'd find an Amish fellow to court." Susan got in and sat by Sally.

"There is power in our prayers." Her sister got the carriage going.

"You're right." Susan bowed her head. *Lord, I need to pray and trust in You. I give You Rose Mary, Father, to work in her life. Thank You. Amen.*

CHAPTER 11

State College

Today at the airport, Kevin had worked his typical schedule of loading and off-loading many of the planes' cargoes. After his shift ended, he'd gotten into his car and headed straight for home. Kevin couldn't wait to drive to Belleville to see Rose Mary. A couple of days had passed since seeing Tom at her place. Kevin wanted to see Rose Mary again, but he wasn't sure how to tackle the topic of seeing Tom at the Rennos', and Kevin couldn't move forward unless this issue was cleared up.

Once at home, he needed to get some things accomplished—like grabbing his clothes from the dryer. Kevin threw the damp items in before breakfast this morning but neglected to get them out before going to work. *I shouldn't expect my mom to take care of it.*

Kevin walked through the house. He hadn't seen any sign of his folks yet, but Kevin could tell by a few open windows that someone was there. He took the stairs down to the basement where his clothes were.

"Hello, Kevin." Mom pulled some laundry from the washer. "How was your day?"

"Not bad. I worked up a good sweat outside, but then the weather has gotten warmer." He brushed away some moisture from his forehead.

"I reran your clothes that were left in the dryer this morning. They were wrinkled." She pointed to the hung-up shirts and pants.

Kevin hugged her. "Thank you for doing that. I apologize for leaving those clothes behind earlier today. I'll try not to do it again."

"I'm not worried about it. Sometimes we forget things." Mom started the dryer. "Have you got any plans for this evening? Your dad and I will be going to the steak house for dinner, and you're welcome to join us."

"Not this evening, but thank you. I'm going to Rose Mary's place, and I'm giving her the TracFone I bought."

His mom grabbed a cleaning wipe from its container. "Why would you buy her a phone? Doesn't Rose Mary's family have a telephone?"

"Their phone is in a shed out by the driveway."

"What a funny place to have a phone—and not very convenient."

"That's why I bought her this kind of phone. Most Amish don't have telephones in their homes. And sometimes different families share the same phone shed." Kevin collected his clothes. "I enjoyed an interesting time seeing how the Amish live."

"Of course, it makes perfect sense since you stayed with that Amish family for a couple of weeks." She wiped off the counter and inside the entire sink.

He hesitated. "Mom, I've been wondering if you and Dad

would like to go to church with me this Sunday. I've been wanting to start attending and would like you both to come."

"I would like to Kevin. I'll discuss it with your father, but I don't know if he'll be for it." She threw away the used disinfectant wipe.

"I'd appreciate your company since it is my first time going."

"I have to ask you. What brought this on, Son?" His mother stepped closer to him.

"It has to do with Rose Mary and her way of life. The Rennos are a devout Christian family who live a simpler style of life."

"You seem quite taken by them." She offered Kevin a gentle smile. "And I'm seeing a change in you that's for the good."

"I feel different about myself, and I want to continue working toward a better way."

"A change in the right direction is always good. I'm wondering how your father will feel about you making changes that could affect our lives here. He'll no doubt have a hard time with this."

"Dad will not be happy with me seeing Rose Mary because she's Amish." Kevin's shoulders slumped.

"Let's give it some time. I'll try to smooth things over with your father. It will not be pleasant, but he will have to come around at some point." Mom reached over and patted his arm. "Let me know when you are about to leave, so I can tell you goodbye."

"All right." Kevin went up to his room and put the stuff away. He hoped the evening with Rose Mary would go smoothly. *I can't wait to see her. I'm wanting to, as the Amish say, court Rose Mary. I wonder when I propose the idea if she'll be okay with it.*

251

Belleville

Rose Mary hummed as she carried in the rugs she'd shaken outside by the wash area. Mervin and Harvey came into the utility room and showed her the tree frog they'd found. Harvey told her it would make a nice pet. Rose Mary agreed, but she asked her brothers to make sure Dad was okay with it. They smiled and walked out of the room with the frog.

Rose Mary wanted to see Kevin later. She couldn't help worrying Tom's presence the other day might have upset him. Rose Mary didn't want there to be any bad feelings between her and Kevin. She hoped he was the one for her, but time would tell how things would play out.

After she laid the mats back in their places, Rose Mary stepped outside to look at the garden. Mom came over from filling up the bird feeders. "The vegetables seem to be taking off."

"We'll have plenty of corn, it looks like." Rose Mary squinted with the sun facing her.

Mom held a hand up to her eyes, shading them from the intensity. "What are you up to this evening?"

"I will be seeing Kevin." *I'm hoping.* Rose Mary turned toward Mom.

"I can see you are taken with this young man. Is he reading any materials that are helping him find the Lord?"

"Kevin said he enjoyed our devotions in the morning and learning about the Bible. And he's made mention how much he likes my family and our ways of living." Rose Mary's gaze went back to the garden.

"I have your best interest at heart. I want you to have happiness with your decisions and make wise choices for your future."

"I think I'm doing that so far, and I feel good about my life."

"You're not getting serious about him, I hope."

"No, Mom. Kevin and I are good friends." *But I wish we could be more.* Rose Mary walked back into the house with her mother. They met up with Aunt Sally in the living room.

"Are the bird feeders filled?" Her aunt rocked in the chair.

"Yes, and the seed bags are put away too." Mom took a seat on the sofa next to Rose Mary.

"Mom, do you think I should ask Kevin if he has a Bible?"

"Sure. I don't see why not."

"It seems like a million years ago since I've courted." Aunt Sally kept rocking. "Time sure can slip by."

"I think there's plenty of time to start looking around." Mom winked. "A special fellow is out there for you, Sister."

Aunt Sally blushed. "Now don't start up about that stuff. I'm not in any big hurry to get married again."

"Okay, but I like to check up on you to be sure of any changes going on. I'd be unhappy if you began courting again and I didn't know about it," Mom teased.

"If I decide to start looking around for a beau, don't worry, I'll tell you." Aunt Sally slowed her chair to a gentle pace.

"I can't wait for supper." Dad stepped into the room. "Do I smell meatballs?"

"Yes, we have those, noodles, green beans, chow-chow, and cheesy hash browns too," Mom replied.

"It was nice of Marlene to bring us the chow-chow from her trip," Aunt Sally commented.

Linda stood by the entrance. "I've got the table set. I hope Rose Mary made up more sweet tea."

"Did it this morning. It's in the large red container like always." Rose Mary smiled.

"I'm getting hungry hearing about supper."

"Mervin, you are always hungry like your brother." Dad winked at Mom. "By the way, where is Harvey?"

"He's outside with a ladybug." Mervin got up and headed for the hall.

Aunt Sally rose from the rocker. "We made a couple shoo-fly pies for dessert."

With a schoolboy grin, Dad nodded. "I know because I peeked at them."

Aunt Sally headed to the other room. "I'll check on the green beans and the rest of the food."

"I'll go with you." Rose Mary joined her aunt in the kitchen.

Rose Mary enjoyed her family's banter. It comforted her to be a part of it. She felt blessed and hoped Kevin could experience this in his life too.

Kevin arrived at Rose Mary's home and knocked on the door. Susan answered and invited him in. He was led to the living room and took a seat on the couch. *I remember lying here after my not-so-great landing with Dad's plane.*

Kevin waited for Rose Mary. It sounded like her voice speaking Dutch in the kitchen, maybe helping with after-supper chores. *The house sure smells good from dinner. I wonder what they ate.* Kevin sniffed at the air.

"What are you doing?"

He turned toward Harvey, who'd joined him in the living room. "I'm trying to guess what I'm smelling."

Harvey tilted his head. "Really? So what are you smelling?"

"Food." Kevin gave a wide smile.

"You waiting for my sister?"

"Yes. So what did you do today?"

Harvey looked up toward the ceiling. "I got chores done for Daed and Mamm. And I've been outside catching a lot of different bugs."

"What have you caught so far?" Kevin leaned forward.

Harvey held up a canning jar half full of grass. "A couple of spiders, some grasshoppers, and a ladybug. I did have some other ones, but I let 'em go. I like these ones better."

"What are you two doing?" Rose Mary asked when she entered the room.

"Looking at my bugs in the jar." Harvey rotated the container and continued to look inside.

"I'm done in the kitchen, so we can go for a walk if you'd like." She looked over at Kevin and smiled.

"That sounds nice."

They headed out the front door and walked toward the big maple tree. "I saw you the other day when you left without stopping by." Rose Mary waited for Kevin to catch up.

"Yes, it was me, and I left, like you said." He leaned against the old tree. "I thought when I saw Tom. . . Well, I got to thinking maybe he was trying to get back with you."

Rose Mary shook her head. "He did come by that day unannounced. But Tom came to talk about what made him decide to

stay Amish. He inquired about us though. I told him the truth—
we are good friends."

Rose Mary filled Kevin in on the conversation and Tom's
interest in her friend Marlene.

What a relief this news is. "I have something for you." Kevin
pulled the TracFone from his pocket. "I got you this. It's set up
to use."

"My own phone? Did it cost a lot?" She held it and looked it
over.

He shrugged. "Not that much. I can show you how to use it.
The TracFone is an easy electronic device for most users."

Rose Mary looked up at Kevin. "This will be nice for me."

He showed her how it worked and gave her his number. *I need
to ask Rose Mary about taking our friendship further, so here goes.* He
cleared his throat. "There's something I want to ask you while we
are alone here." Kevin reached for her hand.

"What would you like to ask me?"

"I would like to date you on a regular basis." His face warmed.
"I guess you call it 'courting,' right?"

She nodded. "I'd like that, Kevin."

His heart fluttered as he held on to her hand. *This is great!*

They continued to visit and share some things going on in
their lives. Kevin wished the day could last and hoped it could
keep going on. *I wonder how long it would take me to learn Pennsylvania Dutch.* Kevin looked out toward the open field. *I bet Rose
Mary would say anything is possible with the Lord's help. But can
He truly help me through my relationship with Dad, by repairing the
bridge across the chasm that exists between us?*

CHAPTER 12

A few weeks drifted by since Rose Mary received her TracFone. She could see it was a nice convenience to carry in her handbag. Rose Mary called Kevin more often, and it was nice not to have to sit in the cramped, old phone shed. Now she could talk from anywhere. And she sensed Kevin enjoyed it too. During their talks, he had opened up and told Rose Mary more about his home life. She felt bad hearing that he and his father didn't get along. It was hard to believe Kevin was expected to follow in his dad's footsteps even though he wanted something else.

Rose Mary brought out one of the birdhouses Elmer Yoder had made and placed it on a rectangular quilted runner that went nicely on the handsome dining-room table in their showroom. They'd sold one yesterday to an English man. It was a birthday gift for his wife.

She glanced out the glass front door of the furniture store and watched a gentle breeze moving the pink flowers in their wooden pots. It was about twenty minutes before her lunch break. *I wish I could be having a cozy lunch with Kevin today.* She suppressed a yawn. *That'll teach me to stay up talking to him*

257

on my phone late in the evening.

Rose Mary stepped over to her purse and made sure the ringer was shut off. So far no one knew of the TracFone in her possession. She hoped to keep it that way. Rose Mary cringed. *I'm being so dishonest. I need to start setting a better example, but I really want to keep the phone.*

She walked around the showroom and spoke in a quiet voice. "Since there are no customers right now, I should do a little dusting." She went to where they kept the rags and wood polish and got to work. Rose Mary continued polishing until her sister entered the store.

"Hello, Rose Mary. I'm back from my dentist appointment."

"How was your cleaning?"

"The cleaning went well, but they found a small cavity on one of my back teeth." Linda grimaced.

"Sorry to hear that." She stopped working. "I need to go to our dentist for a cleaning too."

"I hope you don't have any cavities."

"Me too. I'm not fond of getting those shots to numb my mouth."

"I'm with you on that." Linda looked toward the entrance. "I think I'll get some glass cleaner and paper towels to wipe the fingerprints off the front door."

"Good eye."

"Do you have any mints? I'm sure my breath is gross right now."

"Yes, there are some in my purse." Rose Mary began dusting.

Linda stepped behind the counter and retrieved the handbag, setting it on the counter. She rummaged a few seconds and pulled out the TracFone. "Uh, what are you doing with this?"

Rose Mary stood like a statue. "Umm. Kevin got it for me."

Linda returned it to her purse and picked up the mints. She popped one into her mouth and put away Rose Mary's handbag. "Why would you want to use it?"

Rose Mary looked around the room, hoping no one was within earshot. "It's handy to have. And I can call Kevin anytime I want."

"You seem to really like this guy. Aren't you worried about him pushing his ideas on you—like the phone you have in your purse?"

"Kevin's not like that. He's never tried to push anything on me. But I've been considering what you've said, and I know it isn't right to be deceitful."

"It's a good thing you haven't joined the church. Our ministers wouldn't look the other way on this." Linda frowned. "Especially since it involves an outsider like Kevin."

"That is true. I need more time to sort out my feelings."

Their conversation ended when Dad came in from the back of the store. He asked Linda about her appointment and they chatted.

Rose Mary had gotten caught with the phone in her purse. *I've received a wake-up call from my sister. Marlene was easier on me with this issue. Although not happy, she didn't bring the ministers into our conversation.* Rose Mary put away the dusting supplies. *It's time to take my lunch break. I hope Linda won't say anything to our folks about my TracFone.*

State College

When Kevin got home from work, he went to his room to organize paperwork. He sat at the desk filing receipts from the bank and other places for the month. Kevin found the TracFone receipt and gazed at it. *This was a good purchase. I'm glad Rose Mary likes it, and now I can talk to her more often.* He placed the paper on his desk and checked emails on his phone.

When he'd finished, Kevin jumped into the shower. Afterward, he dressed in a fresh shirt and his new denim pants. He opened his bedroom door, and a few minutes later his father stepped in. Kevin took a seat on the bed and put on his shoes.

"How are things going?"

"Okay."

Dad glanced over at the desk. "Looks like you've been doing some paperwork."

"Yep."

"What's this?"

Dad picked up the TracFone receipt.

A cold chill ran up Kevin's spine. *Oh boy.*

Dad scratched his head. "Kevin, why'd you buy this kind of phone when you already have a better model to use?"

"I got it for a friend."

"Which friend?" His voice rose.

"A girl. Her name is Rose Mary and she lives in Belleville."

"The girl lives in Belleville? Is she from that Amish home you were staying at?" Dad's face reddened.

"Yes, I'm seeing her a lot, and I'm hoping, if it's possible, we might have a future together."

"You can't be serious! How can there be a future with someone like that? Their ideas seem so different from ours, and their mode of transportation is from my great-grandfather's era."

"I enjoy being around Rose Mary and her family."

Dad blew out a breath and started to rant. "I think you should call this off. Things are changing around here. Your mom's been trying to get me to go to church. This isn't right. What has happened to you, Kevin? Whatever it is, it's rubbing off on your mother now."

"You're right, and I like the change."

"Well, I don't. You need to concentrate on learning to fly the air tractor and making a good living crop-dusting for the big farms in the area like me." Dad stood with his arms crossed.

At that moment, Mom entered the room. "What is going on in here? I heard raised voices down the hall and can feel the tension in this room."

"Your son is being unreasonable. He has been seeing an Amish girl in Belleville. His mind is full of silly ideas." Dad looked over at Mom. "You didn't know Kevin was seeing this Rose Mary, did you?"

"Yes, I've known about it for some time," she admitted.

"How could you let him do that? Kevin doesn't need this kind of distraction right now. He should be following through on his task." Dad's arms fell to his sides. "Why aren't you supporting me with what I think is best for him?"

"Do you want your son to be happy?" She stepped closer to her husband.

"Of course I do. That's a silly question."

Mom spoke calmly. "Then you need to listen to him and let Kevin choose his future."

Dad threw up his hands. "You both don't get it. I know what is best. You two should listen to me."

Soon Dad walked out of the room. The tension left with

him. Mom came over and hugged Kevin. He could tell his father wasn't ready to change his mind. How long would this take? he wondered.

Belleville

Rose Mary drove the buggy over to Marlene's place after dinner. It was good to see her friend and get out of the house for the evening. When she pulled in by the house, she spotted Marlene with her brothers at a picnic table. Her friend stood up and came over to the buggy. "I played a friendly game of checkers but lost the match to Ben."

"Is Ben playing well against Tristan?" Rose Mary set the brake and climbed out.

"Not sure. Let's go put your horse in the corral."

"Okay." Rose Mary followed.

Once Belle was taken care of, the girls headed toward the house. "Let's go talk up in my room when we get the chance," Marlene whispered.

She nodded.

"Hi, Rose Mary," the boys said in unison.

"Hello. How's it going?"

"I'm winning," Ben responded.

Tristan pinched the bridge of his nose. "He always wins."

"When you're done with checkers, how about playing catch?" Marlene suggested.

"Good idea. Let's do it, Ben."

"All right, after this match." He made a move and took another game piece off the board.

262

"We'll leave you two alone to play."

Upstairs in Marlene's bedroom, Rose Mary took a seat on a chair. Marlene sat across from her on the bed. "I can't believe I'm seeing Tom. It's a little strange since he was your old boyfriend."

"I think it's great you two have hit it off. Now we can double date and that'll be fun."

"I don't know about that. I'm not real comfortable with the idea."

"How come?"

"I'm worried about you dating a guy who isn't Amish. Remember how Tom was thinking about going English?"

"Yes, but this is different."

"How so?"

"Because we're just friends, and this is my time to have a little fun. You've got nothing to worry about."

"Since you put it that way, I suppose going on a double date will be all right. Besides, I don't have to worry about being the third wheel anymore. That in itself is a welcome change. Tom is sweet, and I think he's cute too."

Rose Mary smiled. "I like to see you being so cheerful. You deserve to be happy."

"Thank you." Marlene stood up and walked over to her dresser. "I bought some new books when my mom hired a driver to go up to State College for some shopping."

"Those look like a couple of good novels."

"One is a romance and the other is more suspenseful in nature." Marlene put the books back on the dresser and sat back on her bed.

"Speaking of books—I got Kevin a new Bible."

"That's a good gift. I take it he didn't have one?"

Rose Mary wiggled her feet. "Nope. I asked him about it, and he doesn't have one. So now he'll have his very own to read. He's coming down this weekend. How about we go out together?"

"Sure. Since Kevin has a car, he can do the driving."

"Makes sense. I'll find out now." Rose Mary pulled her phone from her purse and punched in Kevin's number.

It wasn't long before he picked up. She smiled, hearing his voice. "Would you like to go out this weekend?" Rose Mary waited for his response. "Good, me too."

Marlene got up and moved toward her bedroom window.

"I'm at Marlene's house. We got to talking about going out on a double date with her and Tom. How does that sound? Uh-huh. . .right. Sure. I can let you know more details."

"What's he saying?" Marlene drummed her fingers on the windowpane.

"Would you mind driving? Or we can take my horse and buggy." She concentrated on what he was saying. "Are you sure? Okay, I'll call you later. Bye."

"What are the plans?" Marlene stood beside Rose Mary's chair.

"Kevin doesn't mind taking us wherever we decide to eat on Saturday. We need to figure out what time we want to go."

"Sounds like fun. I can't wait until this weekend." Marlene grinned.

"I agree. I'm looking forward to us going out." *I hope Kevin and Tom will get along all right.*

CHAPTER 13

Kevin and Tom waited outside by the house while the girls ran in to grab their things. *The last time I saw Tom was when I was about to stop by Rose Mary's house.* Kevin sat on a bench, wondering how this evening would go.

"So, there's your car. Not a bad rig." Tom moved over to look at it.

Kevin got up and followed him. "Thanks. It gets me around, but they can be expensive to keep up."

"I agree, but I'm not going to worry about my car much longer."

Kevin looked at him. "How's that?"

"I'm putting it up for sale soon. I've set aside enough money to get myself a buggy." Tom pushed a hand into his pants pocket.

"That'll be a big change, won't it? I mean, going from a vehicle with speed to a horse-drawn mode of transportation is a huge difference."

"True, but I'm ready. Besides, I'll be working on joining the church to be Amish."

"I thought Rose Mary said you're Amish and you go to church."

"I've been raised Amish, but I have to decide if I want to stay that or be English. Also, I have to attend classes first with other Amish young people. Then we'll attend a special church service when we've completed the classes. At that time, we are baptized and welcomed into the Amish church."

"Sounds interesting." Kevin rubbed his chin. *He seems happy and content with his choice.*

The girls came out of the house. Rose Mary looked nice in a teal-colored dress that brought out the color of her eyes. Kevin couldn't keep from staring at her natural beauty.

"Have you two decided where we should go have dinner?" Rose Mary asked.

Tom smiled. "No, we started talking about our cars. Then it ended up about me joining the church."

"Okay, but where should we go eat? I'm getting hungry."

Kevin opened the car door for Rose Mary. "It doesn't matter to me. Anywhere's fine."

Tom followed suit. "Should we let the girls choose?"

"I think we should."

Once inside the vehicle, the girls named pizza places, burger joints, and some Mexican restaurants as they pondered what they'd like to eat.

Marlene spoke up. "Maybe a steak would be good this evening."

"That does sound good," Rose Mary agreed. "What do you fellows think?"

Both men agreed.

"Let's head to State College," Kevin suggested. "I know a place that serves some great steaks."

State College

At the restaurant, Rose Mary and her friends waited to be seated. She noticed the place maintained a warm ambience and modern decor. Rose Mary sat across from Marlene. She liked being next to Kevin. *I wonder how long this will last. Eventually, I will have to make a choice about joining the Amish church. When that time comes, I will need to break things off with Kevin.*

Their waiter came over to the table and passed out menus. "I'll give you some time to decide on your drinks." He smiled and stepped away.

"I wouldn't mind a soda." Marlene looked at the choices.

Tom brushed a strand of hair off his forehead. "I'm going with the same."

"What should I have? Maybe I'll get an iced tea." Rose Mary set her menu down.

"I don't want any more coffee. I've already had two lattes today." Kevin looked at Rose Mary. She grinned back at him.

The waiter returned and took their drink orders. "Are you ready to place your meal orders yet, or should I come back?"

"Are we ready, you guys?" Rose Mary asked.

They all nodded. Everyone at the table ordered a steak with variations of potatoes and salads.

I can't wait to give Kevin his gift later, Rose Mary thought. *But I should get him a card to go with it.* "When we're done with supper, maybe we could stop by a store," she suggested.

"Okay, I'm fine with that." When their waiter brought a pitcher of water to pour into their glasses, Kevin passed over his glass for the man to fill.

"I wouldn't mind going into the store with you. I'm sure I'll find something there I don't need." Marlene laughed.

Tom grinned at her.

The waiter brought their drinks to the table. "I'll bring you warm bread when I return."

"Thank you." Rose Mary picked up her iced tea and took a sip.

Marlene set her soda aside. "I can't wait to start taking classes in the fall to join the church."

"I'm looking forward to it too. I hope the classes won't be too hard." Tom grimaced.

"Are you joining the church together?" Kevin questioned.

Rose Mary sat playing with her spoon. "I'm thinking about it."

Kevin sipped his drink. About then their waiter came with a basket of warm bread.

Rose Mary thought Kevin looked so handsome with his wavy brown hair and chocolate-colored eyes. *I hope he won't care when I give back the cell phone. I can't keep using it anymore.* Rose Mary wondered what Kevin was thinking about as he sat there staring at his nearly full glass.

"How's work going?" She nudged his arm.

"Fine. There's never a shortage of planes needing cargo loaded and off-loaded."

"I think that would be a way to build up some muscles." Tom laughed.

"You're right. How about you? How's your job?"

"My family owns a goat farm. We raise our stock for dairy products."

"Then you must like goat's milk and cheese," Kevin commented.

"Oh yes. I like it more than cow's milk."

"I've never tried any goat products." Kevin glanced at Rose Mary. "Have you?"

"Many times. I like goat cheese on my pizza."

Kevin's eyebrows rose. "Hmm, you've got me curious. Maybe I should try it one of these days." He reached for her hand under the table.

Rose Mary leaned closer to him. "I would enjoy baking you a pizza. We need to do that sometime soon."

"Okay. You name the evening, and I'll be there." Kevin gave her hand a gentle squeeze.

Rose Mary couldn't be any more content than with her friends getting along with Kevin and everyone having a nice time. They continued chatting until their meals arrived and they paused for silent prayer.

Rose Mary hadn't eaten a steak in a while, so this was a treat. The meat was tender and juicy with a good flavor. Everyone else seemed to be enjoying their food too. *I wonder what Kevin will think of his gift,* she asked herself once more.

After supper they left the steak house, and Kevin drove them along, looking for a place that would suit the girls' needs. "I can't eat another bite. My stomach is full, and I'm glad I passed on dessert."

Tom moaned. "I ate the warm berry cobbler because it's one of my favorites."

"I'm glad to have skipped the sweets. I wouldn't want to be miserable like Tom," Marlene said.

"My dinner was good," Rose Mary said. "So good that I ate the whole thing." She opened her window halfway, enjoying the cool evening breeze.

Kevin glanced at Rose Mary then back at the road. "Let me know where you want to stop."

"So far nothing looks good," Rose Mary replied.

A few more blocks passed by and more places came into view. "Oh look." She pointed. "That drugstore coming up will work."

Kevin pulled the car into the lot and parked. "Okay, ladies. I hope you find what you're looking for."

Marlene got out, closed her door, and waited. Then Rose Mary got out. "We shouldn't be long. Do you want anything?"

"I don't. You girls take your time."

She nodded and closed the door.

Kevin watched them go into the business. "I hope I don't fall asleep because of all the food I ate."

"If the girls stay in there too long, we might be out cold, snoring." Tom chuckled.

Kevin wondered what they'd do after this. Maybe they could go up to the shopping mall in Altoona instead of State College's mall. Kevin figured a change of pace would be nice. There was also Whipple Dam State Park, twelve miles away. The lake had a nice three-mile path people could hike around.

Kevin stared out toward the edge of town. *I don't want the day to end. I want to be with Rose Mary as long as I can.*

Belleville

That evening after Rose Mary and Kevin said goodbye to their friends, she invited Kevin into her house. "I've got something to give you."

"Okay."

She unlocked the front door, and he followed her into the house.

Rose Mary asked Kevin to take a seat in the living room. "My family is at our friend's house for supper and games, so we can talk privately."

"I wondered why the house seemed so quiet."

"I'll be back with your gift." She headed upstairs.

In her room, Rose Mary filled out the card she'd bought. She wrote a heartfelt note inside and slid it into its envelope. Then she placed the sealed card into the Bible. Rose Mary made ready a foiled gift box for Kevin's Bible. She took a quick look at her reflection in the mirror then went downstairs, carrying the box behind her back. She asked Kevin to close his eyes. "No peeking, and please hold out your hands."

Kevin did what she asked.

"Here you go. Now you can look." Rose Mary sat next to him.

"What is it?" Kevin unboxed his gift. "Oh wow! It's a Bible. My very first one too." He smiled widely. "Thank you."

"You're welcome. I hoped you'd like it. There's a lot to read inside."

He thumbed through several pages. "You're right. I've got plenty here to keep me busy."

Rose Mary could see how happy Kevin was. She figured she'd make the moment even better. "Would you like to take Belle or Sugar out for a little jaunt?"

"I sure would. I'll help you get the horse ready." Kevin stood.

"I'll need to put my gift away in my car." He picked up the Bible and put it inside the box. They headed out of the house, and Rose Mary locked the door. Kevin went to his car and put the gift inside, securing his vehicle.

"Okay, are you ready?" Rose Mary retied her apron. *Kevin can read my note in the card later.*

"Yes. Let's take a buggy ride."

They went into the barn to see which horse was left. Sugar whinnied at them and bumped the stall door with her hoof. "All right, girl. You seem eager to get out and need something to do. Well, don't you worry, Sugar, we'll take care of that." She grabbed the harness gear off the holder.

Kevin came into the stall with Rose Mary. He stepped next to the mare and patted her flank. "She sure is a beautiful animal."

He helped Rose Mary get Sugar ready. Then she placed the bit in the mare's mouth and slipped the head gear into place. "My dad takes good care of them. These horses know when they've got it good."

"I bet."

Rose Mary tugged on the harness. "I'm done here with Sugar. I'll let you step out first, and then I'll lead her to where we can finish this."

Rose Mary waited for Kevin to step from the cubicle, and then she brought the horse outside. She held Sugar and pointed. "Would you mind pulling that open buggy over here?"

"No problem. I'll get it." It wasn't long before the horse was hitched to the buggy. Rose Mary and Kevin climbed in. With a lurch, the buggy rolled along, and Sugar stepped onward in good form. They headed down the road for a nice evening ride. Not far along, Rose Mary heard a thud on the floor of the buggy. "Oh, it's my TracFone. It fell off the seat." *I'm giving Kevin the phone when we return to my house.*

"I can hang on to it for you," he offered.

"That'll be fine." She glanced to the right and waved at her neighbor, who was watering her flowers.

Kevin cleared his throat. "It's a nice evening. Bet we'll see lightning bugs showing off their little lights in a while."

"I think they're so pretty."

Kevin ran a hand through his short hair. "I've always enjoyed them. I have many fun childhood memories of catching them and watching the little guys light up a jar."

"Yep, they are a sure hit for kids and some adults too. By the way, when you get some time, I did put a little note in your Bible."

"Oh, I must have missed that." He smiled. "I sure like riding in the buggy. It's relaxing."

"Yes, but there are times when it can get a little scary." She jiggled Sugar's reins to get her moving quicker. "Last week Mom and I visited a sick lady from our church. On the way there, a car crossed over the middle of the road."

"Really, what happened?"

"Mom swerved toward the ditch so he didn't hit us." She glanced at him. "I didn't know what was going to happen in those few seconds, but we were spared. The driver corrected the car and avoided us. Mom slowed the buggy, and we crept along for a few minutes before we got going again."

"Why didn't you tell me this?"

"That kind of thing happens. If we could make drivers pay

attention to the buggies, it would help, but it's out of our hands." Rose Mary sighed. "We pray for God's protection."

Kevin nodded.

Rose Mary drove for a while and showed him where Tom lived and then a bit later where their bishop's place was. Kevin also got to see the property and the new house that would soon be finished for Linda and Isaiah. They drove on and enjoyed seeing the fireflies coming up from the ground. But with it getting darker, they decided to turn around and head back.

Kevin seemed relaxed as he leaned back in his seat and talked about the Amish ways. When they pulled into the yard, he helped put away Sugar and the buggy.

"I had a nice time with you tonight." He touched Rose Mary's hand.

"I had a good time too."

Kevin reached into his pocket and got out the phone. "Oh, before I forget, I'd better give this back."

"Sorry, I don't want it back. My sister caught me with the phone, and it made both of us feel bad. I've been hiding it and being deceitful, sneaking around with it. I can't do it anymore."

"But it was a gift, and you said you liked it."

"I know, but I should've never accepted it from you. Sometimes I've made choices that I later regret."

"I can't change the way you feel." Kevin shoved the device back into his pocket. "I'd better get going. I'm beat. The day has caught up with me."

"Okay. I should get inside. I noticed Mom peeking out the window. She's probably wanting me to come in." Rose Mary stepped back.

Kevin reached out and took her hand then let it go. "Goodbye, Rose Mary." He turned and made a beeline for his car.

"Kevin? Good night." She watched him drive away until his taillights disappeared. *That didn't feel right. Was he meaning goodbye for good?*

CHAPTER 14

State College

Over a week had gone by since Kevin saw Rose Mary. He'd gone to church the other day with his mom. Kevin's dad didn't go and found reasons why he couldn't attend. The obvious issue was his father wanted to play golf on Sundays. This bothered Kevin. And he felt bad for his mother when she'd mention how nice it would be if Dad would come with them. Kevin reassured his mom they'd continue to go, and one day Dad could see it would be good to attend church too.

Today after work, Kevin pulled into his parents' driveway and thought he'd wash his car. *I'm already dirty enough from work, and when I've finished cleaning the car, I'll get a shower.* Kevin got the supplies he needed to take care of the job. Soon he took the hose and sprayed water over the vehicle before getting the bucket of soap ready.

Dad pulled up to the house and came over to him. "I sure had a busy day with the air tractor. I've been crop-dusting some corn-fields. It went well." His short, gray-brown hair showed beneath his baseball cap.

"That's good."

"Washing your car?"

"Yep." Kevin sprayed the car some more. "It's overdue, and I'm going to vacuum it out too."

"I know mine could use a washing. Maybe when you're done, I'll come out and get started on my truck."

"Okay." Kevin poured some soap into the wash bucket and added the water. He dipped the wash mitt into the bucket and worked on the car.

As he worked, Kevin thought about the last time he'd seen Rose Mary. *I miss her so much.* He dunked the wash mitt again in the bucket and scrubbed the hood. *I thought she'd like the phone I got her, but that turned out bad. I'd hoped things could work out between us, but I'm not the right man for Rose Mary. Spending time with me has deterred her from joining the Amish church. Since we have no future together, I shouldn't have taken up her time or allowed myself to fall for her.*

Determined to clear his head, Kevin removed the mitt and rinsed off the car. After he'd washed the vehicle, Kevin took some clean rags he'd set aside to dry it. He had to admit his rig looked nice and shiny. Too bad he couldn't drive it down to Belleville and take Rose Mary out for a meal. He rapped the top of his head. *I've gotta quit thinking about her. She'd never want to go English, and I—*

"I guess I'm next to clean my truck," his dad said as he came out of the house.

"Everything is ready for you to use." Kevin stood back to admire his work. "I'm tired, but I'm going to vacuum the inside of the car. Maybe I'll start with the mats."

"That's fine, but can you move your car? I'd like to park where you're at."

"Sure. No problem." Kevin got in his vehicle, started it, and moved over by the side of the garage, where he dried the car with the rags. He went into the garage and brought out the shop vac. The cord dragged along the ground and got hung up on something, so Kevin went to fix the problem. When he came out to the car, Dad was busily hosing off his truck.

Kevin opened the car doors and pulled out the mats. He gave them a shake and watched the dust fly. Then he wheeled the vacuum over and switched it on. Kevin cleaned the front and back floor. *Boy, there are a lot of rocks in here. Some of these came from Rose Mary's driveway, I'm sure.*

Not long after he shut off the machine and set it aside, Kevin reached into the glove box and pulled out the TracFone that was once Rose Mary's. A vision of her lovely face came to mind. *If only there was some way. . .*

Dad stepped over. "Are you finished with the vacuum?"

"Uh, yeah."

Dad stared at the TracFone in Kevin's hand. "Hey, isn't that the phone you gave that girl you're seeing?"

"Yep."

"Then what are you doing with it instead of her?" Dad hovered over Kevin.

"Rose Mary gave it back to me. She didn't want it anymore."

Dad rubbed his chin. "Sounds like she's a smart girl. I've noticed you haven't been going down there lately."

"No, I've been hanging around here when I'm not working. But I might go out with some friends later." Kevin put the phone in his pocket.

Dad smiled. "It's for the best, Kevin. You'll see what I'm

talking about. Things should get better."

Kevin shook his head and continued to clean out his car. *I'm miserable without her. How long until it does get better? Wish I'd never landed in her parents' field.*

Belleville

Rose Mary sat behind the counter and yawned. Linda was home today with a migraine and wasn't able to come in to work. It was hectic without her sister there to help run things, but Rose Mary managed.

Dad came out of his office wearing a smile. "You did good today and handled the customers like a professional."

"Thank you, Daed."

"That English couple took their time deciding on which of the hutches they wanted to buy." Her father walked behind the counter and picked up the receipts for the day. "I've noticed Kevin hasn't been around lately. Has something happened?"

"I believe so, but I'm not quite sure why." *I'm being dishonest again. Kevin might be upset about me giving back the TracFone, but I'm not divulging that to Dad.* Rose Mary collected herself and continued. "I went out to the phone shed and left a message on Kevin's phone, asking him to call me. So far I've heard nothing back."

"I'm sure he'll call you when he gets the chance." Dad squeezed her shoulder. "It's about time to close up for the day."

"Yes, and I have to say I can see how much my sister does. But I needed a busy day like this to prove I've got what it takes."

"Like I said before, you did a good job, and I'm happy with

how well you pitched in." He turned over the CLOSED sign on the door. "I hope Linda is feeling better. No one likes a migraine."

"I agree." Rose Mary moved closer. "I'll head to the house and check on her. And I'll see if Mom and Aunt Sally need my help with supper." As she headed out the door, her shoulders slumped. *I wish Kevin was joining us for the meal this evening. What if I never see him again?*

When Rose Mary entered the kitchen and found Mom and Aunt Sally drinking sweet tea again, she smiled and greeted them.

"Hello, Rose Mary. How was work today?" Her aunt sipped her beverage.

"It was busy." She plopped in the seat across from her mom.

"I noticed a good amount of car flow in and out of the lot today." Mom pushed a plate of chocolate chip cookies toward her. "Care for a treat?"

"Sure, that sounds good. Then I want to go see how Linda is doing."

Aunt Sally took a cookie too. "Your sister came in here a few minutes ago to get some juice. She said her headache wasn't as bad, but she thought she'd lie down awhile longer."

"I don't blame her." Rose Mary nibbled on her cookie. "Something smells good coming from the oven. What are you making?"

"There's a ham baking right now," Mom replied.

"Would you need any help with supper?"

"I'm sure we can find something for you to do." Mom winked. "You can do me a favor and get a couple of canned pickled beets from the basement."

"Okay, I'll fetch them as soon as I get something to drink." Rose Mary got up and retrieved a glass from the cupboard. "What else are we having for supper besides the ham? There's some of my German potato salad left over from last night." She poured some sweet tea in her glass.

"I'm thinking mashed potatoes or rice pilaf with the ham."

"Oh, that does sound good." Rose Mary sighed. *At least I can try to eat away my sorrows with good food tonight.*

"What's the matter, Daughter?"

"I'm tired and a little bored."

Mom patted her hand. "I figured you and Kevin might have something planned. It's been awhile since we've seen him around here. I'm rather surprised."

"Has Kevin been working overtime at the airport?" Aunt Sally poured herself more tea.

Rose Mary sat slumped in her seat. "I don't think so. I called him the other day and left a message. I've not heard anything. Maybe I'll walk out now and see if he's called back yet. When I come back inside, I'll get the pickled beets."

Once outside, she walked down the driveway to the phone shed. *Should I be feeling this nervous? What should I do if Kevin hasn't returned my call? Should I keep trying to contact him or let it go?*

CHAPTER 15

State College

Kevin sat on the sofa, watching television and sulking. He wasn't doing much otherwise except working and moping around the house. It was early Saturday morning. Kevin's routine was to get up, shower, and eat. He might look like he was ready to do something, but lately brooding around the house had become a daily pastime. Every day he thought about Rose Mary, wishing yet again that things could be different. He'd made a lot of mistakes in his life, but falling for her was the biggest one of all. The only thing he'd accomplished by courting her was making himself miserable when he had to tell her goodbye.

Mom came into the living room in her pajamas and robe. She looked at Kevin and plopped down on the couch facing him. "I need to talk to you." Her head was encased in a silky yellow covering she slept in. The steel-blue eyes of his mom seemed to coincide with her mood.

He picked up the manual for the air tractor, muted the game show that was on, and turned to her. "About what?"

She folded her arms. "It's been a couple of weeks since you've gone to Belleville. Kevin, I've never seen you so depressed and

283

sulking around like this."

He sat with the crop-dusting information on his lap. "Dad seems to be content with me not seeing Rose Mary."

"You're not happy, and you need to be up front with me." She pinched her lips together.

"Up front about what?"

Before she could respond to Kevin's question, Dad came into the room with a cup of coffee and set it down. "What are you two talking about?"

"I'm doing the talking, and I want to find out what is happening with our son. He is not happy."

Kevin's dad took a seat in his recliner and looked over at her. "Why isn't he happy?"

"Okay, I'll tell you what's going on." Kevin hesitated. "I think I've been holding Rose Mary back from joining the Amish church." He released a heavy sigh. "Maybe she isn't the right one for me, but I thought she was. We had such good times together, and the more I was with Rose Mary, the more I felt drawn to her."

Mom stared directly at him. "Has she come out and said this directly to you, Kevin? That you're holding her back?"

"Well, no, she hasn't. But her friends are joining in the fall, and she isn't." He stared down at his hands. "Why else then?"

"I would have to say not every person is ready at the same time as others. Rose Mary may simply be taking her time and doing it her own way." Mom's posture seemed relaxed. "Your uncertainty says a lot. You don't appear to have all the facts, Kevin."

Dad waved her words away. "Now, dear, if our son thinks this young lady isn't right for him, then we should let him be."

Kevin sat silently, rubbing his forehead. This conversation was going nowhere, and Dad was obviously not on his side.

Mom looked at his dad with disapproval. "I've not heard our son utter those words yet. Please, Kevin, is there more you would like to tell us?"

Not really, but here goes. "Remember when I got Rose Mary the TracFone?"

Mom nodded.

"At first she liked it. But my last night in Belleville, before I left her place, she told me I could keep it." He massaged the back of his neck. "She said she felt deceitful having it and hiding the TracFone from her family. Then Rose Mary told me her sister, Linda, had caught her with it and that it made them both feel bad."

"It makes perfect sense they'd feel that way. I'm guessing Rose Mary didn't want to hurt her parents either." Mom spoke in a gentle, understanding tone. "We live differently than the Rennos, but that doesn't make their way of thinking wrong."

"What are you talking about? Don't go messing with Kevin's head. He has made up his mind. Haven't you, Son?"

Kevin held up a hand. "Wait. So you are saying, Mom, that I have every right to keep seeing Rose Mary?"

"Yes. And I think Rose Mary is good for you. Besides, didn't she give you the Bible sitting there on the sideboard?"

"True." Kevin sat there a moment and then tapped the side of his head. "In all this fretting, I've forgotten to read the card Rose Mary gave me with the Bible."

Mom's eyes darted to the book. "You better read it."

Kevin found the card inside and opened the envelope. He read the note to himself:

Kevin, I'm so glad you came into my life, and I know in my heart you are the one for me. But I have to do what's right for my family. No matter what happens, I will never forget you. With all my heart, Rose Mary.

Kevin's mouth dropped open. *Even though Rose Mary has to do what's right for her family, she believes I'm the one for her.*

"Are you all right, Son?" Mom walked up to him.

"Oh boy! This note tells me everything I needed to know!"

"What on earth are you talking about, Kevin?" Dad crossed his arms.

"I'm going to see Rose Mary as soon as I can." He came over and hugged his mother.

Kevin's father began to rant. "Dear, what have you gone and done? Go see Rose Mary? Now hold up, Kevin. Wait a minute; it's too early to go see her. You don't need to run out the door like some lovesick mule."

"You should hurry, Kevin." Mom whispered in his ear. "Maybe you should fly to her."

Kevin grinned. "Smart thinking, Mom."

"What's going on? What did you tell him?"

"Your son is going to Belleville to fix things."

Kevin grabbed two sets of keys and his wallet. Mom walked with him to the door.

"No matter what I think is best for him, it seems my son's mind is made up." Dad looked at the two of them with a sagging posture.

"I pray everything will work out when you talk to her." Mom patted Kevin's back. "I'm confident that you'll make the right decision, Kevin."

"Thanks, Mom."

"We'll have to go see the Rennos once things are worked out. It will be nice to meet Rose Mary and her family." Mom hugged him again.

Groaning, Dad shook his head. "Well, since I can't seem to stop you and you're flying there in my plane, please be careful with it, because I saw you grab the keys for it along with your car keys."

"Thank you, Dad."

Kevin went out the door, headed straight to his car, and drove to the airport. *How could I have had such doubts?*

Belleville

After devotions and breakfast, Rose Mary swept the hallway upstairs. She had time before going to work. Rose Mary hadn't heard a word from Kevin, and she'd lost hope. She opened the hallway window to allow the fresh morning air inside. As Rose Mary grabbed the broom to continue cleaning, she heard an airplane in the distance. It reminded her of Kevin. *I wish it was him.*

Moving along the hallway, she picked up the dustpan and swept up some dirt. She threw it in the garbage and noticed the plane sounded louder. Rose Mary looked out the window and caught sight of the craft. *That plane looks familiar. Could it be Kevin?* She set the broom and dustpan aside and rushed down the stairs. "I think Kevin's here!" Rose Mary hollered.

She dashed out the screen door with Mom, Aunt Sally, and Linda following. Once outside, Rose Mary looked toward the sound and spotted the Piper Cruiser.

Harvey ran up to her from the barn. "Sister, is that Kevin?"

Rose Mary smiled and laughed. "I think it is."

Mervin came from the barn with Dad, and they watched the plane as it buzzed the air.

"What's going on?" Mom walked over to Rose Mary.

"I think we're about to have company," Mervin replied.

Dad stepped over by Mom. "You're right, Son. The plane's coming in to land."

The Super Cruiser descended quickly and touched down in their field. Even bumping along, the landing went well, and the plane looked perfect. The craft slowed and turned back the way it came. It taxied toward the barn, and then the engine turned off. Kevin emerged and smiled as Rose Mary came toward him.

"This is quite a surprise." Rose Mary's face warmed.

Looking into her eyes, he gently picked up her hand. "I have so many things to say, but first, I need to tell you that I love you, Rose Mary. I'm sorry for distancing myself from you these past weeks. But we can't keep living in two different worlds, mine English and yours Amish."

Rose Mary's smile faded. "What are you saying?"

"I am saying that I want to be Amish, and I'd like to join the church with you." He caressed her hand.

Her eyes teared. "Are you sure about this?"

Nodding, he released her hand and pulled her into his arms. "I'd like to continue courting you if you'll have me."

With more happy tears, she replied, "Yes, Kevin. That would make me so very happy."

Her family stood a few feet away, hearing Kevin's news and

watching the two of them together. They came over to greet Kevin and welcome him with open arms. Today was a new beginning for her and Kevin, and Rose Mary resolved to help Kevin with his goal of becoming Amish. She could hardly wait to see what their future held.

EPILOGUE

Two months later

Rose Mary smiled as she sat beside her sister at the bride and groom's corner table. Linda radiated happiness and natural beauty. "Just think. After the meal, you and Isaiah will be opening your gifts from your family and friends." Rose Mary leaned in close.

Linda's brown eyes twinkled. "It will be a lot of fun to see the new things we've gotten. And even nicer to put them to good use in our new home."

"I can't wait either. The servers will be bringing out the hot food pretty soon. I can smell the delicious aromas." Rose Mary glanced toward the entrances of the tent where the wedding meal was being held.

She thought about the morning and her mom flittering around the house. Rose Mary could only imagine her nervousness. Mom tried to make sure things were in good order for the bride-to-be. And she'd done a good job too, because everything had turned out so well.

She felt honored to be one of her sister's witnesses. Someday maybe her turn would come.

Rose Mary couldn't help stealing glances at Kevin. He smiled back at her while chatting with Harvey and Mervin. *I can only imagine what they're talking about.*

The newly married couple looked so sweet sitting there together with glowing faces. *They are a good match, and it's obvious how much they love each other.*

Rose Mary couldn't help thinking how things worked out for her and Kevin, as well as a few others in the family. She got to meet his parents and see where he grew up. Rose Mary could see the contrast with his parents and hers. Kevin had recently become a Christian, and she hoped his folks would find the Lord in time.

Kevin lived in a little place he had rented since he'd moved to Belleville. He was learning about the Amish ways, including speaking Pennsylvania Dutch and getting accustomed to dressing plainer.

His dad finally came around and gave Kevin his blessing. His mother was happy about that as well and also with her husband deciding to attend church. They had agreed to help Kevin with finances until he was working full-time at the furniture store.

Rose Mary sat toying in her mind about her future and wondering if a year from now she and Kevin might be getting married. In the meantime, she would enjoy every moment they spent together and would do all she could to help Kevin adjust to the Amish way of life. Rose Mary lifted a silent prayer. *Thank You, God, for all You do. Please guide us in the days ahead.*

Rose Mary's German Potato Salad

1 teaspoon sugar
½ teaspoon salt
¼ teaspoon dry mustard
Dash pepper
2 tablespoons vinegar
1 cup sour cream
½ cup thinly sliced
    cucumbers or onions

2 to 3 slices bacon, fried
    and cut into small
    pieces
4 boiled potatoes, cut in
    chunks
Paprika

Combine sugar, salt, dry mustard, pepper, vinegar, sour cream, cucumber or onion slices, and bacon pieces. Pour over warm potatoes and toss lightly until coated with dressing. Serve warm with a dash of paprika.

Jean Brunstetter became fascinated with the Amish when she first went to Pennsylvania to visit her father-in-law's family. Since that time, Jean has become friends with several Amish families and enjoys writing about their way of life. She also likes to put some of the simple practices followed by the Amish into her daily routine. Jean lives in Washington State with her husband, Richard Jr., and their three children but takes every opportunity to visit Amish communities in several states. In addition to writing, Jean enjoys boating, gardening, and spending time on the beach. Visit Jean's website at www.jeanbrunstetter.com.

LEILA'S LONGING

by Richelle Brunstetter

CHAPTER 1

Belleville, Pennsylvania

Leila Fisher stretched her arms above her head, squeezing her eyes closed as she rotated her legs off the mattress. Opening her eyes, she hummed and reached over to her nightstand. "Here we are. My trusty notebook." Placing it on her lap, Leila flipped over the cover and skimmed each page sketched with flowers and scenery in graphite until stopping at an incomplete page with her thumb.

After getting dressed and picking up a pencil from her nightstand, Leila dragged the point across the page with stagnant movement. *Gonna draw a little bit of grass right here, but I should go back to that field today if I want a better reference.* Leila flipped the pencil over and erased some of the places she wasn't satisfied with, sweeping away the eraser bits with her palm.

"Leila, are you up?" A voice spoke from behind the door.

Closing her notebook, Leila got up from the bed and went over to her dresser. "*Jah*, come in."

The door creaked open. Peering in was Leila's older brother. "*Guder mariye.*"

"Good morning, Leon."

"Checked up on *Mamm* yet?"

"Not yet, but I was going to after I was done getting ready." She plucked her hairpins one by one and placed them in her palm. "I'm actually surprised you're here early today, since you don't have to work with *Daed* until later."

Leon tugged at his shirt collar. "I didn't have the best night. I may have fallen off my bed once or twice."

She lifted her *kapp*, flipped it in the air, and caught it. "Maybe you and Judy need a bigger mattress."

"Honestly, I get more restful nights when I sleep on the couch." His gaze bounced around the room. "I also wanted to check up on Mamm. She hasn't been overdoing it with the housework, has she?"

"I've been helping her as best as I can." Leila headed over to the door where Leon stood. "I gotta get myself ready. Can't be late to open up the store today, especially when there's things to be done before then."

"Do you have everything packed for school, Henry?" Darla Fisher handed her youngest son his hat from the wall hook.

"Yes, Mamm." He looked up at her with wide, blue eyes. "Has Leon left with Daed already?"

"Not yet. But they'll be leaving soon, so you better hurry before it's too late."

Giving her a quick hug around her hips, Henry scurried out of the living room.

Darla couldn't help but giggle, watching her son's hair bounce as he left. *My son is eager as always.* Darla cupped her protruding stomach as she lowered herself into the rocking chair. *Bearing a child never becomes easier, no matter how many times it happens.* Pressing her feet against the braided throw rug, she rocked the chair while her eyelids fluttered shut.

"Mamm, are you falling asleep?"

"No, Leila. I'm resting my eyes." Darla opened her right eye. "Are you heading over to the store soon?"

"Jah. Just need to carry out the box of stamps and ink pads to restock the shelves."

"I'll be over there as soon as I can."

Leila knelt in front of Darla and took her hand. "I know you're wanting to move around, but you should stay in the house and rest from now on. I don't wanna see you in any pain from pushing yourself. Besides, I can run things in the store. At least I'll try."

Curling her fingers around her daughter's hand, Darla smiled. "All right, Leila. And I'll try my best to refrain from doing so much. You have been doing a good job around here, keeping your father and brothers in line."

"They've been doing a good job keeping themselves out of trouble." Leila tucked a loose strand of auburn hair behind her ear. "Even Henry. One of these days, he'll be working at our father's sawmill."

Darla giggled, taking her other hand and placing it on top of her daughter's. "I appreciate everything you've done for all of us, Leila. You will make a wonderful wife and mother someday."

"Wife?" Leila shuddered as a flush crept across her cheeks. "Very funny, Mamm. I'm no good when it comes to that kinda thing."

"What kind of thing?"

"Being desirable," she muttered.

"When the right guy comes along, he will see you as desirable." Darla gave her daughter's hand another pat. "You better get a move on and open the store. I know plenty of people will be coming in for today's Friday sale."

"Jah, you're right. Let me know if you need anything."

"I will." She let go of Leila's hand.

As Leila walked out of the room, Darla's husband and oldest son came in.

"We're heading out." William tugged on the single strap crossing his left shoulder.

"Okay, dear. I hope you and Leon have a nice day."

William leaned over and gave her a kiss on the forehead. "We'll be home as soon as we can. Make sure Leila helps you out with things you can't do."

"William, I'm not completely useless, you know."

"Never said you were. I just want to be sure you don't overdo it." He stroked her face with his thumb. "I've seen you go through this before, and I know you prefer grinning and bearing rather than telling me how you're really feeling."

"Oh William. I'm fine."

Leon and her husband said their goodbyes before heading out the door. Darla pulled up from the rocking chair and went over to the window, watching them load supplies into the yellow-topped buggy.

"That'll be seven dollars and sixty-one cents." Leila picked up what the customer brought to the counter and placed the contents into a paper bag. "Will there be anything else?"

"No, but thank you."

After receiving payment, Leila handed the paper bag over. "Thank you. Have a good day."

"You too."

When the customer closed the door behind her, Leila's skin became unbearably warm. *I wish it wasn't so hard for me to deal with customers. Communication with strangers is difficult for me. Maybe I can't do this without Mamm after all.*

Leila left the front counter and went over to the table near the window. *The day is almost over anyway, so maybe I won't have to converse with anyone else.* There were stacks of construction paper, including stamps and ink pads, and a box filled with a variety of embellishments for her choosing. Taking a sheet of paper from the pile, she folded it in half, unfolded it, and then folded the other side. Afterward, Leila picked out an ink pad in a shade of light blue and then reached for a stamp with her eyes closed.

"Ah-ha! Here's a stamp." Her eyes fluttered open. The picture printed on the stamp was an intricate design of a butterfly. She placed the stamp on the ink pad, then pressed it on the paper. She carried on constructing more cards. Cutting lengths of ribbon, she picked out specific decorative pieces to glue onto each one. Leila didn't even have to process what she did with her mind but allowed her intuition to influence her creativity.

"Leila! Teapot laid her first egg today!"

Leila whipped her head toward the window.

Outside stood her young brother carrying a white-feathered chicken underneath his arm. He jabbed his hand into his trouser pocket and plucked something out. "See? It's right here. You gotta see it up close."

"Henry, that's not—" But it was too late. Leila watched as Henry took off from the window and headed to the entrance of the shop.

Swinging the door open, Henry rushed in and came over to Leila. The chicken clucked and flapped its wings—like fanning oneself with a sheet of plywood. "Teapot, calm down." Henry attempted to get the egg back in his pocket, but as he did so, the chicken slipped from his arm and was airborne. Teapot glided past the cards hanging from the clothesline, causing each one to flutter in disarray. Some were on the floor while others landed on the shelves.

"My cards!" Leila yelped.

"Don't worry! I'll catch her!" Henry chased after the chicken. Teapot plummeted to the floor and ran around the stamp shelf, knocking over some of the stamps as her wings came in contact with the lower section. They clanked against the wooden surface. "Slow down, girl!" Henry's foot struck one of the shelves, causing him to resign from the chase. "Ow! My foot!" He bent his leg close to where he could reach.

Leila's body temperature increased, and her muscles quivered. While she wanted to give in and scold her brother, seeing streams of tears cascading down his round cheeks diminished a fraction of her anger. Leila held her breath and yanked Teapot off the floor before she could make a run for it. "Blasted chicken."

"She didn't mean it. She didn't mean to do it. I'm sorry, Leila."

"I know, Henry. It's okay." She carried the chicken as she knelt to her brother's level. "You all right?"

Henry pinched his injured foot and winced. "It hurts."

"I know, Henry. I know." Leila rustled Henry's hair with her free hand. "I'll be right back to get you after I put Teapot in with the other chickens."

Henry wiped away the tears with his arm. "No. I can get up. It doesn't hurt too bad."

"You sure?"

He nodded.

After Leila went out of the shop and put the chicken away, she walked back in. Sure enough, Henry was no longer there. What was left, however, was the mess. How could she continue to manage on her own? Not just in the store, but in communicating with people outside her family.

She picked up the cards and clipped them back on the clothes-line. *I hope every day doesn't get this crazy. I really need some help here in the shop.*

CHAPTER 2

It had been a few weeks since Leila began working in the store without her mother. Although it wasn't going as smoothly as she would've hoped, Leila refused to give up. She knew that she needed to become independent, just like her older brother. If he could establish a good life with a loved one, then she could do the same if she tried hard enough.

Leila got up prematurely as usual on a weekday and mentally prepared herself for what was to come. *It'll be over before you know it. It's only eight hours out of the day, socializing with strangers and familiar people.*

After she got changed, she headed downstairs and went out of the house. When she entered the card store and turned on the gas lanterns, she went over to the worktable and set out her supplies. It was around six o'clock, so Leila had a sufficient amount of time before any customers came in. She folded several pieces of construction paper and positioned them on the table, stopping when she heard the sound of crowing outside the window. Leila peered over her shoulder and observed the chicken that usually roosted in the flowerpot near the house.

"Flowerpot." Leila tapped the window with the stamp in her grasp. The rooster turned its head over to her, exposing the milky cornea of his left eye. He crowed once more then lowered his head and proceeded to peck at the gravel.

That chicken never wants to be with the rest of the flock. Leila looped her fingers around the handle of her scissors. *I don't blame him though. The other roosters always pick on him whenever they get the chance.*

About an hour later, a couple of vehicles pulled up to the store, meaning Leila would have to stop making cards until she had her lunch break. She had plenty of restocking to take care of and some more cards to assemble, so she figured it would be best for her to eat lunch in the store today. Fortunately, the store was about forty feet away from the house, so grabbing something to eat wasn't difficult.

Near the end of the day, Leila was about to close the store when a customer came in and plucked a card from the clothesline. Leila handed the young woman the bag and thanked her for the purchase. A few minutes after the customer left, the shop door opened again. "Leila, I'm back from school!"

She held her arms out wide as her brother ran over, squeezing her waist. After embracing him, Leila let go with one arm and took off Henry's straw hat, tousling his hair. "You goofball."

"Hey, no fair." He giggled, reaching up for his hat. "Wait until I grow taller. Then I'll steal your kapp."

"Oh no. I'm in trouble." She tugged the hat over his head. "Seven-year-olds grow like weeds, so you'll be taller than me in no time."

Henry grabbed on to Leila's arm and held it, looking straight at her with his striking blue eyes. "Are Daed and Leon done working yet?"

"Not sure. Maybe you should check with Mamm and see when they'll be finished at the sawmill today."

"Okay, but I gotta check if Teapot laid any more eggs first." Releasing Leila's arm, Henry trotted to the door and reached for the knob.

"Make sure to feed Flowerpot the leftover spinach we have in the fridge. I don't think he's had enough food to eat, so he'll surely enjoy it."

"Okay." As Henry opened the door and stepped out, he stopped and paced a couple of steps back. "Ah! Sorry, miss. I didn't see you."

"No, it's fine. I was in your way."

Leila's insides twisted like a tattered rag. *That voice sounds familiar. I hope it isn't who I think it is—*

"Leila! It's so *gut* to see you."

The young Amish woman who stood by the doorframe was someone Leila went to school with about six years ago. Back when they were in sixth grade, she and Leila were inseparable friends.

"G–good to see you too, Hannah." Although Leila looked forward to having a nice supper once she closed the shop, she had lost the urge to eat. She returned to the counter, hoping she wouldn't have to converse any more than necessary.

Hannah went over to the shelf of stamps filled with an assortment of woodland creatures, gazing at them for what seemed like centuries. "How lovely. You have a great collection to choose from."

"Danki." Leila tried not to look at her, but there weren't many places where she could focus her eyes, so she diverted her attention to the counter's surface. Leila squeezed her fingers and breathed lightly through her nose.

"Where are the stamp pads?" Hannah asked, holding her stomach.

Leila hadn't noticed before that Hannah's belly was visibly prominent through the fabric of her violet dress. *She's already married to someone and expecting a child too?* Leila held her breath as she discerned a pulling sensation in the gut.

"The stamp pads, Leila. Where are the stamp pads?"

"Ah! I'm so sorry." Leila pointed in the direction of the shelf where the stamp pads were located.

"Danki."

As Hannah went over to the other side of the store, Leila pressed her fingers against her forehead. *Calm down, Leila. You're making this worse than it actually is.* Although her thoughts were reassuring, her body's reactions contradicted them. She wasn't okay with this situation whatsoever. Leila was afraid of being in the same room with someone who knew her when she was younger.

Leila wasn't like most people when it came to social interaction, and it had been that way for plenty of years. When she'd first learned to talk, Leila approached others cheerfully, without becoming nervous about speaking. But because she didn't know when to contain herself, her behavior became overwhelming for the other children. This made Leila a target for ridicule, and she was often picked on by some of the kids she was friends with.

By the time Leila was in sixth grade, her trust in others became meager. She began to second-guess what she said and distanced herself from the other kids for fear of getting hurt. That is, until she saw Hannah, who sat by herself on the first day of school. With the little bit of courage Leila could muster, she approached Hannah and welcomed her to the schoolhouse. Hannah was from the black-top community, and she had switched schools because her family moved to Belleville from another area in the state.

They were close friends until they reached eighth grade and Hannah made other friends. Leila wasn't comfortable but tried to save face by not saying anything to Hannah. They hung out with one another less often, and Leila was by herself most days during school. At recess, Leila would find a quiet place away from the other kids and draw in her notebook. It kept her mind from thinking about how lonely she felt.

After a while, Hannah approached Leila and said the words she'd feared would come. *"I don't want to be friends anymore."*

"I'm ready to pay for my items, Leila." Hannah's piercing voice drew Leila's thoughts aside.

Leila pressed her stomach against the counter and swallowed. "Okay." She plucked the stamp pad and the two stamps and rounded up the prices. "So how have you been doing?"

Hannah gave an incredulous stare, which made Leila feel more ill at ease. "I'm fine, I suppose. I mean, I've been better, but you know how married life is, right?"

"Not really."

"What? You're not married yet? How could you not have found someone? You're such a sweet and kind girl. Any guy would be fortunate to have you as his wife."

Don't be ridiculous, Hannah, Leila thought. *You of all people know that couldn't be further from the truth.* "Th–thank you." She proceeded to calculate the amount and then stuffed the items into a bag. "That'll be fifteen dollars and eight cents, please."

As Hannah reached for her bag, Leila held out her hand and waited. Her fingers trembled a bit but not so much where Hannah could point it out.

"Here you go." She dropped the money in Leila's hand. "So, what have you been doing with your life?"

"Working here."

"But have you been courted by anyone? Had any love interests?"

"Never gave it much thought." Which was a lie, but that wasn't something Leila would admit to Hannah.

"I kind of envy you in that regard. Marriage is a struggle, especially when you have to plan how you're going to raise children."

Leila handed her the bag. "I'm sorry, Hannah."

"You still haven't broken that habit, huh?"

"W–what habit?"

"Apologizing for no reason." She took the bag from Leila and turned from her. "Have a good evening, Leila."

Pinching her lips together, Leila waited for Hannah to walk out of the shop. Once she was out of sight, Leila trotted over to the chair at her worktable and crumpled as she sat.

So that's why you stopped being my friend; is that it? Leila's eyes were wet as she blinked. *I know that isn't the only reason. I'm just a mess from every angle. That's why. . . That's why no one would want to marry me.*

Butterflies flittered along the hills of the field. Their wings complemented the hues of the sunset, which gave Leila a sense of tranquility. The warmth of the late-spring day added to her restfulness. Leila tipped her head back. *If I had to stay in this same spot for the rest of my life, then I would be happy for all of my days.*

The sun wouldn't be in the sky much longer, so Leila raised the notebook positioned beside her thigh and opened it. Thumbing through the pages, she found a vacant sheet to sketch on. Leila seized her pencil and outlined the scenery ahead of her, jabbing the point against the fibers before each stroke. Drawing the grass and weeds dispersed through the field was simple, but illustrating insects and wildlife was more of a challenge. The butterflies never stayed put long enough for her to sketch out the finest details of their wings. But Leila was fine with that since she loved being challenged creatively.

When she plopped the notebook and pencil on the ground, a couple of birds glided close to her left ear, catching her off guard. They headed off to the west, one flying close behind the other. The warmth emanating from her skin prickled every inch of her face, yet her heart grew thoughtful. *I wonder if that could ever be me someday. If I could finally fly off on my own with someone.*

Leila peered at her notebook. *Whether I keep to myself or not, I'll continue being an intrusion on other people's lives. Even Hannah is still annoyed with me after all these years. Not only that, but she found someone to marry and is already pregnant.*

Sighing, she picked up the notebook and pencil and hoisted herself up, brushing away the soil from her dress. *At least my family accepts who I am. If I can never be betrothed to anyone, then I'll be content with what I have rather than hoping for something that may never happen.*

The sky's brightness decreased with every stride as Leila

headed to her home. She would've stayed in the field for another half hour if she didn't have the responsibility to prepare her family a meal for supper. Despite Leila telling her mother not to worry about cooking, she would still lend a hand. Fortunately, Mom would only do a few of the smaller tasks, such as setting out the utensils and pot holders to place on the table. This gave Leila more reason to get home sooner, because if she wasn't there promptly, her mother would attempt to put the meal together herself.

"I'm home!" Leila called as she entered the doorway to the kitchen.

Mamm shuffled into view, holding her stomach. "Welcome home. Did you enjoy some time to yourself?"

She nodded, gripping the spine of her notebook. "Very much so. I needed it after a long day." Staring in the direction of her bedroom, Leila kicked off her shoes. "I'm gonna put my things in my room and start making tonight's supper."

"Before you start the meal, Leila, I need to speak with you for a moment. Could you sit with me in the living room once you're done?"

"Sure. I'll be there in a bit." She leaned over and clutched her shoes with one hand then went over to her mother and gave her a quick hug before leaving the kitchen.

Once Leila stowed away the shoes in her closet, she dropped the notebook on her bed, and it bounced off the cushion. Leila studied the cover, scrutinizing the scuff marks on it. She'd had the notebook for about a year, so the dings didn't surprise her, but they bothered her in a way she couldn't describe.

Leila shut the bedroom door when she walked out, turning her head toward the entrance of the living room. *Hopefully,*

Mamm isn't going to deliver any terrible news.

"There you are, my daughter. Have a seat anywhere you would like."

Leila strolled to the chair across from her mother and perched on the cushion, crossing her ankles.

"I wanted to let you know that you have been doing a great job maintaining your work in the shop. You have shown a lot of dedication, and I am very pleased." Her mother's eyelids lowered, offering a subdued dimple on her cheek. "I can't believe how much you children have grown over the years. I remember when I first held you in my arms, with your beautiful red hair already so thick on your head."

Leila leaned over, with elbows propped against her knees. "Mamm, we were all able to grow as we are now because of you and Daed. You both have always been there for us and taught us how to function. Even Henry. He's still in school, but he's a *schmaert* kid."

"I suppose that's true." Her mother's brows drew closer, and her eyes were no longer in Leila's line of sight.

"What is it, Mamm?"

"I feel like you haven't been doing much other than work in these recent weeks. You wake up before everyone else does and head into the shop without having any breakfast."

"I have breakfast. Sort of. I sometimes bring something to snack on."

"I'm concerned you're overdoing it. I don't want you to do so much work in the store to the point where you no longer have time for yourself."

"I have plenty of time to myself. Making cards isn't only work for me. I enjoy it. And I give myself time to draw something once I'm done with my chores."

"I mean not interacting with people your own age."

Leila brought her hand up to her throat. "I. . .I don't know what you're getting at."

"I think you should attend one of the young people's gatherings and make a friend or two so then you can socialize with others and not always stay here."

"B–but Mamm, I can't do that. I have to keep up the store every day. Having to restock shelves, make more cards, calculate income, and many other tasks I can't neglect."

"Leila."

"Yes, Mamm?"

"You don't work in the store on Sunday, and some of the events take place only on Sundays."

Defeated by my lack of paying attention to details, Leila mused, spreading fingers against her collarbone. "Even so, I still have to do the tasks you're not capable of doing in your condition."

"It's only one day out of the week, Leila." Her mother spoke with a soothing tone. "I heard there's a young people's singing at a neighboring black-top community. You love singing when we're at church, don't you?"

Leila searched for another way to avoid her mother's request, but a fraction of her didn't disapprove of the idea. She enjoyed singing at services, and even if her voice wasn't noticeably loud, Leila always joined in with enthusiasm. But talking with people intimidated Leila to no end.

This is happening way too fast. What if it goes horribly wrong and I can't recover from it? Leila pulled her head back, pushing her shoulders forward. "I don't know if it would be a good idea, Mamm."

"You have tonight and tomorrow to think about it." Her mother rose from the chair. "I only want you to be happy, Leila. I don't want to force you into something you don't want to do."

"I know. I'll consider it."

"There's always next Sunday too."

"Jah. That's true, Mamm."

Leila got up from her seat and headed to the kitchen, where she knelt down to grab a couple of pans from one of the lower cabinets. Next, she picked out some vegetables from the shelf above the block of ice in the chest fridge and carried everything to the counter. *By attending the singing events, I'm only putting myself at risk. But what if I become friends with someone and I end up trusting them too much?* Leila pulled a knife from the drawer next to the sink. *I don't want to put myself in that situation again.*

CHAPTER 3

Aden Troyer wiped the sweat from his neck, glancing out past the forest of trees enclosing the area. While the sun wasn't right overhead as it had been a few hours before, its heat still had him sweating through his indigo shirt. "This is probably the hottest it's been out here all month."

"Aren't you glad we only have to work a couple more hours, Aden?" Samuel, a close friend of Aden's, hitched the horse to the log lying on the leafed path. "The sun is getting a tad bit unbearable for me."

"Could always consider some indoor work if you can't take the heat." Aden went over to the horse and took ahold of the reins. "What do you have going on after work anyway?"

"I have a date this evening. A double date, actually. You could join us if you were courting someone."

Holding tightly to the reins, Aden followed the horse in the direction of the log pile. "Come on, Samuel. You know I'm not exactly the courting type."

"But haven't you told me you were interested in some of the girls from the singing events? Like Carol, for instance? You two are always hanging around each other when you have the chance."

"Carol is a nice person. Her voice is pleasant, and she has pretty blue eyes." Aden shook his head. "But I can't picture myself being married to her. She's more of a friend than anything."

Samuel's jaw slacked. "I don't know how you do it."

"Do what?"

"Resist the opportunity to be with a beautiful woman." He scratched at his bare jaw.

Aden rolled his eyes yet snickered in response. Once he reached the log pile, he tugged the reins to halt the horse then bent to unhitch the sizable branch. Samuel held down one end of the branch as another worker attacked the other end with a saw.

"Whoever I find to court is in God's time, Samuel," Aden said, holding the horse's reins. "When I find the right one, He'll let me know."

"Guess I can't argue with that response." His friend stood up and patted Aden on the back. "Don't worry, bud. You'll find her."

"I'm more worried about not getting our work done for today."

Aden proceeded with the routine of unhitching the branches once he led the horse to the log pile, trying to limit the amount of chitchat with Samuel about courting. *I don't get why nobody sees why I don't want to rush into a relationship.*

Once the workday had ended, Aden set out for home with Samuel since his buggy was in need of some repairs. Aden's horse had dragged the buggy into a ditch a couple of days ago, which damaged the front axle and the wooden reaches. He tried not to stress over it and was thankful it hadn't toppled over. His father had been willing to assist him with the repairs in the meantime, but his mother reprimanded him for his recklessness. Aden found his mother's reaction rather strange, since he was usually attentive to his buggy whenever he took it out.

Aden directed his gaze to the hills surrounding the valley. It would be about ten miles until he got home. He wanted to lead a horse and buggy along those hills. Giving a bemused smile, he tapped his hands on the frame of the buggy like a woodpecker pricking a stump.

"Could you stop with the tapping? It's getting on my nerves."

He lowered his hands, placing them on his knee. "Sorry about that. My hands have nothing better to do. It would be one thing if I had ahold of the reins—"

"You're not driving my buggy into a ditch."

"Hey, that was one slipup. It's not like I do it all the time."

"I'm not going to risk it."

Sighing, Aden leaned his arm on the side of the buggy. "If it weren't for that truck driver speeding too close to Chance, he wouldn't have gotten spooked. Normally, nothing scares my horse, but that was the one exception."

"I suppose I could let you drive the rest of the way."

Aden raised his eyebrow. "There's a catch to your generous change of heart, isn't there?"

"You'd be right." Having pulled the buggy to the side of the road, Samuel pointed at him. "I'll trade you seats if you ask Carol out tomorrow after church."

"Are you serious? I already told you, she's just a friend." He instinctively leaned away with his hands up, palms facing his friend.

"You say that, but I see it as you needing a little bit of incentive. You say you're waiting for God to give you an answer, and I say I'm the sign you're looking for."

"Harsh."

"Do you want these reins or not? Your choice, Aden."

His focus fixated on the reins, Aden jutted his chin and slumped in his seat. "I suppose it wouldn't hurt."

"That's the spirit."

Aden snorted out dismissive laughter. "I'll tell you now that either she'll say no or we'll date once and that'll be it."

"Or you could be married by next year with a baby on the way." As they switched seats, Samuel nudged him and displayed a wide grin, showing his somewhat crooked teeth.

"Don't push it, Samuel."

"And with the event being held at your family's barn tomorrow, you can surely impress her to the point where she can't refuse."

He flicked his hand at Samuel and then concentrated on the road as he started the horse back on their way. Although he was a little riled up, Aden tried his best to act as if he wasn't bothered too much. The clicking of the horse's hooves against the pavement soothed him for the time being. *I gotta take things as they come. Maybe courting Carol wouldn't be such a bad thing, that is, if she even says yes.*

Leila massaged her eyelids as she sat up in bed. She had slept profoundly, and her dreams were vivid and calm. But her sense of peace fled when she remembered it was Sunday morning.

"I can't believe I'm going to do this." She stood and lethargically made her way to the closet. Leila skimmed through the clothes until she found one of the dresses she wore for church. It was a dark shade of purple, and a black apron was draping from the hanger. Laying the clothes on her bed, Leila went over to the mirror and pulled her fingers through the strands of her hair.

She had informed her mother the night before that she would attend her first singing event later this evening. Because she had learned that Hannah was already married, Leila thankfully didn't have to worry about bumping into her. For that matter, she hoped most of the people she'd gone to school with were already married.

Especially him, Leila thought. *I don't want to see him ever again.*

When she was fifteen years old, Leila had become interested in a boy her age who'd gone to school with her from the very beginning. She hadn't been romantically interested in anyone else before then, but given how kind he was to her over the years, fondness began to ensue. While Leila was alone most days, he would talk to her during breaks. She showed him the sketches in her notebook, and he encouraged Leila to draw. He made those lonely days a tad more bearable.

But when she began to have feelings for him during that last year of school, Leila started to be more talkative and joyous whenever he was around. Every chance Leila had to talk with him, she expressed how much she appreciated having him around. She became too comfortable, and that made her vulnerable. One day at school, Leila gained enough courage to admit she liked him more than other people.

"Wake up, sleepyhead!"

Leila's thoughts halted, and she turned toward the closed door. "I'm awake, Henry! I'm getting ready!" She went to the bedroom door and opened it. *"Guder mariye, mei bruder."*

"Good morning." Henry bounced his head up and down, his

hair moving like grains jostled by heavy winds. "I'm excited for breakfast. You make the best breakfast in the world!"

"Oh, is that all I'm good for?" Smirking, Leila kneeled down to her brother's height and placed her hands on his shoulders. "If anyone else offered to make you breakfast, you would replace me at the drop of a hat."

"No, not ever." Henry reached his arms around Leila and gave her a hug. "You making yummy food is just a bonus."

She returned the hug and tousled his hair. "I know, goofball. I know."

After getting herself presentable for church, Leila went to the kitchen to prepare breakfast. Her mother was already there, cutting up fruit. Usually, Leila would have intervened and taken her place, but she let it slide since the activity wasn't strenuous.

About a half hour later, Leila set a plate of fresh pancakes on the table. Their gratifying scent of cinnamon wafted through the entire dining room. "Breakfast is served!" she called.

Her mother shuffled behind Leila, patting her on the shoulder. Leon and their father emerged from the living room with ravenous expressions. Henry came in through the kitchen door leading outside, stepped behind Leila, and grabbed at her dress.

"This all looks very good." Leon pulled out one of the chairs from the table. "Especially those *pannekuche*. You went all out, Sis."

"I agree with your brother." Her father's tone radiated joy. "I'm very fortunate to have you help your mamm."

Leila shrugged. "It's nothing really."

"Isn't Judy going to join us?" Mom gave Leon a wide smile.

"She wasn't feeling up to it. Judy wanted to be here, but. . ." He ran his hand through his hair. "She'll be fine. I'll be heading back home after we eat, and we'll meet the rest of you at church."

"All right. Hopefully, she'll feel better soon."

"Judy isn't sick, Mamm. She was just exhausted from working two extra hours yesterday."

They all seated themselves to pray in silence before setting the meal in motion. Weaving her fingers together, Leila lowered her head to pray.

The church service was comparable to other Sundays. The ambience created by hymns sung in unison was Leila's favorite part, but this Sunday it was also a reminder of what was to come. Once church ended, most of the people got up from their seats, but Leila was firmly planted, seizing the side of the wooden bench. A sliver of wood pierced her finger.

"Are you doing okay?"

Leila glanced up at her brother. "Do you want the honest answer or the convincing lie?"

"Well, you're a terrible liar"—Leon sat down next to her—"so I want the convincing lie."

She snorted. "You got me. I'm not gonna lie to you." Leila brought her hands to her lap. The sliver was lodged in the outer part of her index finger. "The thing is, I'm really nervous about going."

"You have a choice, Leila. You don't have to go to the singing event if you don't want to."

"But that's exactly it." She swallowed the thickness lodged in her throat then smacked her lips. "How could I expect to live stably when I struggle with communication? You know, something normal people can do? How can I expect to find someone if I can't overcome it?"

He patted her back. "You shouldn't feel like you need to rush into it either."

"Leon, you married Judy before you were twenty years old." She rolled her shoulders forward, resting her elbows on her upper legs. "And you guys seem very happy together. So much so that I can't help feeling envious."

"Really? That's why you feel that way?"

"That's part of it. There are many reasons why a person acts the way they do. Most would believe there's only one root to the problem."

"But a plant has more than one root."

"Exactly, and there are bigger roots to cut through as well." Leila got up from the bench. As she pivoted away from Leon, she heard him mumble a response under his breath.

"What was that, Leon?"

He bumped the side of the bench. "I said, sometimes I'm envious of you too."

Biting her lips, she wanted to ask him why he could possibly be envious of her, especially when he had everything she could only hope to have. But instead, her mouth trembled, and a sudden frigidness dispersed from her core. *Leon doesn't know what he's talking about. He found someone who loves him for who he is.*

As Leila walked away from the row of benches, she peered over her shoulder and caught a glimpse of Judy heading over to Leon. *I can only hope someday I'll find a soul mate.*

CHAPTER 4

Leila stepped down from her buggy, almost tripping from the loose gravel beneath her feet. Meekly approaching the home, Leila's heart stuttered in her chest as she observed the young people in the front yard. Some of the groups were young teens, while others looked to be around her age. A few were just getting out of their buggies.

You can do this, Leila. You're making this a big deal when it shouldn't be. Leila nodded to herself.

She passed through the gates, moving her head from side to side in attempt to figure out which way to go. The garden next to the house drew Leila's attention. She hurried to the area and stood in its presence with admiration. Two sections of garden were separated by the lawn, like an emerald path, with rows of flowering plants in warm shades. Both sections of flowers mirrored each other, which made the garden symmetrical overall. Leila became engulfed in the sight of it all.

I wish I would have brought my notebook along. Leaning over, she extended her hand to one of the plants and scooped a crimson blossom. *Our garden is pretty good, but it doesn't compete with this family's. They must be very diligent and organized.*

"Do you like the garden?"

Leila jumped up and straightened her spine. She turned to the person behind her.

"Sorry for scaring you." The girl covered her mouth. "It just makes me feel happy when someone admires my hard work."

Leila bit the tip of her tongue. The girl who stood in front of her appeared to be around sixteen or seventeen years old. Based on what she had said, she was one of the family members who lived on this property.

"Y–you planted all of this?"

"Uh-huh. My mamm allowed me to be creative and come up with the layout, so I diagrammed it on paper and then the rest followed."

Leila's scalp prickled underneath her kapp. "T–that's good. It looks very nice." *You're stuttering again, Leila. Stop doing that. She'll think something's wrong with you.*

"By the way, my name is Sue Anne Troyer." She held out her hand and grinned. "But you can call me Sue if you want. It's much easier to do so."

"I'm Lila. I—I mean Leila! Leila Fisher." As much as she desired to make a run for her buggy, Leila tentatively reached out and shook Sue's hand.

"Nice to meet you, Lila Leila." Sue's rosy face displayed a sense of amusement. "Is this your first time being at our place? We've held singing events in our barn before, and I've never seen you. Did you recently move to this community?"

"N–no. I work most of the time and never had the chance to go to any of the events."

"Where do you work?"

"In a shop next to my home."

"Oh, really?" Sue tilted her head. "What kind of shop?"

"It's n—not much. Just stamps and homemade cards." *Why is she wasting her time with me? Can't she go talk to someone more interesting?*

"Do you make the cards all by yourself?"

"Well, my mamm worked in the store with me. But since she's in a family way, I've been taking care of things."

"Aww. I'm sorry you have to work there without anyone. Doesn't it get lonely?"

I'm used to being alone. That isn't the issue. Leila inhaled through her nose. "It's mostly overwhelming. Since there's no one who can run the cash register as I make the cards, I have to stop what I'm doing whenever customers come in. It would be nice to have some assistance. I just don't know anyone who would be willing to do so."

"If I wasn't working at the window-and-door shop, I would love to do it. I enjoy making crafts, and having card making as an occupation would be a dream come true."

Leila moistened her lips. *Should I bring up that I draw in my notebook? She probably wouldn't care about it. Besides, I don't know her well enough anyway. Should I ask Sue something about herself? Wouldn't I be imposing on her life if I did so?* Pressing her lips together, Leila made the choice not to speak.

"So, you say this is your first time at a singing event, right?"

Leila nodded.

"We've already played some games, but I can show you around."

"T—that's okay."

"Nonsense. Besides, this is my family's place, and you and everyone else are considered guests. It's the least I can do." Sue took hold of Leila's hand. "Come on. We'll be starting pretty soon, so we should head over to the barn."

Leila's other hand curled into a fist as she was being led to the barn. *I could've waited a little longer to attend a singing event. Maybe two or three months. Or a year. Two years?*

Once they entered through the barn doors, Leila was awestruck with how massive it was on the inside—especially since the outer structure made it seem much smaller. It was considerably immense in comparison to her family's barn. Rows of long tables with backless wooden benches stretched in front of her, and an empty table was probably where the food would be served.

"Pretty nice setup, huh?" Sue released her hold on Leila's hand and swung her arms as she kept walking.

"Yeah, it's really nice." Leila was impressed by the size and the layout of the barn, and it smelled like it had been thoroughly cleaned. Other than church, Leila's family had never held a social event on their property, and Leila could see why. With her family being so small, not to mention the property itself not having much space, it would be difficult to host a large number of people. As it was, whenever it was their turn to have church, Dad and her older brother put up a tent in the yard in order to accommodate everyone.

Sue halted then spun around and looked at Leila with her dark brown eyes. "I'm going to help bring the food out for everyone to eat. You can stay here and socialize with someone you don't know, or maybe you already know someone here you can talk to."

As uncomfortable as she was conversing with Sue, Leila felt somewhat at ease with her. *I can't stand around by myself, and there's no way I would go and talk with anyone.* She rubbed her forehead. *And I won't have anybody to sit with either.*

"Wait." Sue snapped her fingers. "Would you want to help bring the food out? We could use some extra hands."

"Okay, sure." Leila felt grateful for Sue's offer.

"I can't believe that happened, Aden." Carol's head flinched back. "You could've gotten seriously hurt if your horse went into the road after getting spooked."

"Jah. Definitely not what I was expecting to happen this week. But God was looking out for me, and Chance only did what a startled horse might do." Aden leaned to his right and patted Samuel on the back. "My buggy got damaged, but my terrific pal right here has been getting me to work on time."

Samuel puffed out his cheeks. "And risked the possibility of having my buggy damaged too."

"Nah. I'd never do that. Like I said, I'm usually careful when I drive, but this was unexpected."

Carol closed her eyes and giggled. She then gazed at Aden, sweeping a wayward strand of blond hair back under her kapp. "So, are you excited to sing pretty soon?"

Aden gave a throaty laugh then winked at her. "That's why we're here. I can never get enough singing from church. I can't get enough food either."

"Actually, Carol, Aden wanted to show me the repairs on his buggy real quick before we head over to the barn."

"All right. I should go be with the girls before we eat." Turning away, she peered over her shoulder and waved before pressing on toward her friends. "See you both pretty soon."

When Carol was no longer in earshot, Samuel's head snapped toward Aden, and he scowled. "Don't forget, we have a deal."

"Do we?" Leaning toward Samuel, Aden put his hands in his pockets and shrugged. "I don't remember."

"Yes, we do. And you better follow through with asking Carol on a date."

"Wow. No need to doubt that I'll back out. I'll ask her afterward."

Samuel sighed. "I know it feels like I'm pressuring you, but I can't shake off this feeling you're going to end up with no one. No wife, no kids."

"I get what you're saying. But as I said before, it's in His time, not mine." Part of Aden wanted to tell Samuel he should be focused on his own relationship rather than stressing over Aden's.

The scent of a potluck meal drifted through the air, and Aden didn't hesitate to inhale. "Okay, Samuel. We should probably get some grub. I'm starving."

"All right." Samuel folded his arms. "Don't forget."

"Don't worry. I won't."

The two of them followed the rest of the group into the barn. Aden was prepared to sample everything on the serving table. He went to the young men's tables, joined Samuel at a table with some of their friends, and chatted until it was time to pray and dish up their food.

After the women had served themselves and sat down, Aden saw his sister at the end of one of the tables. *There's Sue, being talkative as usual.* He wondered who his sister was conversing with. Too many people blocked his view. He made the effort to get a good glimpse of who it was. When he did, his curiosity was piqued. *Who is she? I've never seen her before. Maybe she just moved to Belleville.*

Leila had savored every moment of singing among people her own age. The event was comparable to church services, except it was shorter and didn't have a sermon. Church lasted for more than three hours most Sundays. While they sang, Leila held her chin high and her shoulders back. She couldn't contain her exhilaration. But now it was over, and she'd been reintroduced to reality.

"Did you enjoy yourself, Leila?"

"It was. . .actually more fun than I expected it to be."

"Glad to hear that." Sue got up from the bench. "You should come to the next one with me. I usually go with my brother, but I could pick you up in my buggy if you want."

"Is your brother here tonight?"

"Uh-huh. He's older than I am, but we don't have any difficulties getting along with one another. He's basically my best friend. Do you have any siblings?"

"Yeah. I have two brothers."

"Are they here tonight? I would like to meet them."

"One of my brothers is married." Leila released her grip from the bench seat and stood. "And the other is in second grade."

The two continued their conversation as they left the barn. Leila's shoes skidded against the blades of grass with every step she took. She gazed at the stars in the dark sky and felt the chilled night air brush against her skin.

"Oh! What am I thinking?" Sue stopped and faced Leila. "You should at least meet my older brother before you leave. I think you would like him."

"Hey, Sue!"

Sue perched on her tiptoes. "Speaking of which, he's right behind you."

Leila whirled around, flooded with nervousness as he strolled toward them.

"Who's your friend?" His softened features in the dim light complemented the hospitable tone of his voice. Leila noticed he wasn't towering over her, yet he managed to make her feel smaller than he.

"Aden, this is Leila. Leila, this is Aden."

"Nice to meet you, Leila."

"N–nice to meet you." As she shook his hand, Leila made the mistake of looking directly into his eyes. The moonlight reflected in his lapis-blue eyes.

"So what community are you from, if you don't mind me asking?" His gaze seemed to wander as he spoke, almost as if he were surveying her.

"The y–yellow-top." Leila's senses were acute as she fidgeted with her hands. *Why do I feel even more uneasy than usual?* If Leila's body were a thermometer, the top would've shattered from exceeding the temperature limit. Under normal circumstances, she would be able to manage herself better, but talking with Aden amplified her nervousness.

"Haven't seen you around before. Did you just move here?"

She rubbed her clammy palms against her apron. "No, I—"

"This was her first time attending a singing event," Sue explained. "And Leila said she had fun. She even liked the garden I planted near the house."

He looped his thumb around the single suspender crossing his torso. "How old are you, Leila?"

"Nineteen. I'll be twenty in August."

"So, we're almost the same age."

"Aden!"

"Hey, Samuel."

Samuel? Leila's senses heightened even more. She scratched at her neck with the nubs of her fingers. *That's the name of the boy I knew from school.*

"What are you doing over here?"

Leila ducked her chin when she recognized the face staring at her.

"Oh. . .umm. . ." Samuel leaned over to Aden, decreasing the volume of his voice. "Why are you talking with her?"

"What do you mean?" Aden responded.

"This redheaded girl is kind of weird. Trust me, I would know. And you're supposed to be talking with Carol. Not her."

"Samuel—"

"I can hear you, you know, but you're right." Leila bit her quivering lip. "That's why you humiliated me in front of your friends when we were younger, right?"

"You wouldn't leave me alone. What else was I supposed to do?"

Leila was hit with an instant onset of nausea. *Then why did you bother speaking to me in the first place?* she wanted to say, but such a retort wouldn't do any good. Although Leila was on the verge of tears, she smiled in attempt to put on a brave face. "Then I'll leave." Leila turned and walked to her buggy. She held on to her quaking shoulders, catching something else Samuel said, but the ringing in her ears tuned it out.

I knew coming here would be a mistake, and I was right to believe something would go wrong.

CHAPTER 5

Darla gripped her husband's hand as they waited outside the door of the doctor's office. She wasn't feeling well and had finally gathered the courage to express her concerns about the pregnancy to William.

"I'm so afraid of what is wrong with me. I've tried to do everything the same with this pregnancy as the last ones."

"I'm here with you, and I'll stay right by your side throughout this. You can count on me, *Fraa*," William spoke soothingly to her.

"Thank you for supporting me. I don't know what I'd do without you." Darla gripped the arm of the chair.

"Please try not to worry. You'll get the proper care here. The doctors will treat you and give us good instructions, and soon we'll have a healthy new child." William squeezed her hand and smiled.

Darla brought her hands up to her temples while closing her eyes. *Oh Lord, help me to gain strength and healing as I carry this life inside me. I need You so much right now. I've slacked on my praying, but that'll change as of today.* Her eyes remained closed. *Help me,*

oh Lord. I want to do everything possible to have a healthy pregnancy.
Thank You, Jesus. Amen.

Darla looked up and blinked as a woman sat across from her with an infant. She spoke gently to the baby girl in what Darla presumed to be Spanish. The woman fussed with the blanket and cuddled the baby. It was endearing to watch her so involved with the child.

William got up from his seat. "I'm going to find a vending machine and get you some water while we are waiting."

"Thank you. I could use a drink right now." Darla rested her hands in her lap as he left the room.

Watching William disappear around the corner, Darla wondered how much longer she'd have to sit there. She looked across the room where the office help worked behind a sliding glass partition. They kept busy answering the phones and running back and forth for yet another yellow file. She soon saw her husband return with bottled water.

William twisted the top and handed the bottle to her. "It'll be okay. I'm sure the doctor will give some answers."

"I hope so." She took a long sip of the needed water.

The waiting room had gotten busier, causing Darla's stomach to quiver. "I wish they would call us in soon. All this waiting is hard to bear." She sighed. "I just want to know what is happening with me and the baby."

William leaned in close to her. "I understand."

An attendant came out and called their names. When she noticed Darla raise her hand, the woman came over and asked for a couple more things to add to the paperwork.

"You won't have to wait much longer. We'll call your name again shortly." The lady stepped away and walked back through the door.

"That's good to hear, right?" Darla's husband patted her shoulder.

"Yes, I can't wait to be helped." She took another sip of water.

Darla wasn't sure what to think, especially when this was the first time she had ever experienced something out of the ordinary. She went through her other pregnancies with no complications, so why would her fourth pregnancy be any different?

As she placed her hand on her tummy, Darla's breaths slowed while her eyes fluttered shut. She wouldn't know what to do with herself in this situation without William, and his supportive presence eased her worries ever so slightly.

"This hen has an egg under it." Henry tugged on Leila's sleeve, pulling her in the direction of the egg-laying hen.

"All right, Henry." She followed her brother's lead and crouched down to look. "Could be. She hasn't budged from her spot since this morning." A slight whistle slipped through her teeth when she spoke. Tugging her bottom lip, Leila placed the basket next to her and reached in, scooping the chicken and lifting her from the nest.

"See? She does have an egg under her."

"And you were right." The hen flapped her wings, so Leila pinned them down with her thumbs. "Could you hurry and grab it? She doesn't like me holding her too much."

Henry stretched his arm under the chicken, grabbing the egg and bringing his arm to his chest. "Okay, Leila. You can put her down now."

Leila did so with ease. The hen caused a ruckus but calmed down when Leila picked up the basket and scooted away from the nest. Leila stood, turning to her brother so he could place the egg in the basket.

After they finished collecting the recently laid eggs, Leila and Henry headed out of the barn, greeted by beautiful weather. Summer came closer every day, which meant her young brother would be out of school for a few months until late August.

"Excited for school to be over?"

"No, not really."

"You enjoy spending your time hitting the books, huh?"

"That's not it. I mean, I like learning about things. But it's fun to play with my friends during recess. And to eat with them when we have lunch."

She clutched the handle of the basket. "I see. That must be nice. But don't you become tired of the same old routine every day?"

"Sometimes. When I have a bad day." He fidgeted with his fingers, evading Leila's gaze as they stood near the wall of the barn. "I do get into fights. Not with fists but with words. I say I'm sorry, and usually things work out."

"Henry, I hope you don't apologize when you're not the one who starts the argument."

"But I say things too. It's not nice."

"You're right. It isn't nice at all."

It had been over a week since Leila went to the singing event. Whenever she had a moment to herself, she remembered what Samuel had said to her. Then her thoughts would wander back to when she was in school. She had been picked on many times, yet she never retaliated in the way her brother did.

But when Samuel had reacted so badly to her telling him she liked him, Leila couldn't contain her frustrations. And seeing him again had pushed those painful memories to the front of her mind. *It would be easier for me to function if I could forget all the moments I regret.*

"Hey! Get away from Flowerpot!"

Leila's eyes darted to the commotion near the front yard. One of the roosters had gotten out again, and he puffed out his neck feathers, lowering his head while facing the blind-eyed rooster. Henry ran over to the two roosters.

"Henry! Don't get in the middle of it."

"But he's hurting him."

"You could get hurt too." When Leila caught up to her brother, she watched as the roosters collided against one another. Her fingers and toes tingled as she placed her hand on Henry's shoulder. *With Mom being in the condition she's in, I certainly don't want anyone getting hurt. I hope her doctor's appointment goes okay and it isn't anything serious.*

Since it was Wednesday morning, after all the eggs had been gathered, Leila decided to head to the flea market to see if any craft items were available. Leila grabbed her bag and left her bedroom. She walked over to her parents' room, pushing her palm against the partially closed door. Leila peeked in through the gap. "Mamm, I'm gonna go buy some things from the market."

"All right." Her mother rolled over to face Leila, eyes squinting as she yawned.

"Need anything? I could bring back some natural remedies

from Big Valley Dry Goods if that'll help."

"That's all right, Leila. I have everything I need." She sat up on the mattress and smiled. "Besides, the doctor said I only needed to lie down for a while to rest my body. So nothing to worry about."

"I'm glad." Leila went over to the bed. "Even so, are you sure you don't need anything before I leave?"

"I'm sure. And your older brother is going to stop by here in about an hour, so I can ask him for help if I need it."

"Okay." Leila leaned forward and kissed her on the forehead. "I'll be home soon."

When Leila arrived at Big Valley Dry Goods, she got out of her buggy and fastened the horse to the hitching post. She grabbed her bag and pulled out her list. "Let's see." She unfolded the paper and mumbled each of the items she had listed. After Leila finished, she looked up. An older English couple stared at her with slack expressions. She was about to apologize but caught herself in time. Leila hurried past the couple. *Good job, Leila. You didn't apologize for no reason this time. It isn't a crime to talk to yourself.*

Leila browsed the array of products on the shelves as she pushed the cart along the aisles. As usual, Leila had found a few more things she didn't have on her list and placed them in the cart. It was a good thing none of the items needed to be refrigerated.

When she found the craft area, Leila moved over to the shelf with decorative items. *Exactly what I was looking for.* Eyeing the rolls of ribbons, Leila picked up the ones she wanted and dropped

Leila's Longing

them in the cart. She moved over to the next shelf but stopped when she realized someone stood there.

"Oh, I'm sorry!" a young Amish girl yelped. "I'll move out of your way."

"No, you don't need to do that," Leila protested. "I—I wasn't paying attention. I'm sorry."

"It's okay." The girl's hazel eyes softened, but her body appeared stiff. "I was looking at some of the crafts. It seems like a lot of fun."

"Y—you've never made anything before?"

"Not in a while. I've been trying to find some work to earn a bit more money, but. . ." The girl tucked her arms to the side, dipping her chin. "I haven't been too successful."

An idea came to mind, and Leila's stomach quivered at the possibility of going through with it. She definitely needed some sort of help in the card shop at home, but how was Leila going to bring it up when she didn't even know this girl?

"I'm sorry you haven't been able to find any work." Leila thumbed her ear.

"It's fine." The girl shrugged, shuffling her feet as she moved away from the shelf. "So, what are you buying?"

This is my chance, Leila thought. "I—I was picking out things for making cards."

"You make your own cards?"

"Jah, I do. It's a lot of fun." Rubbing the back of her neck, Leila stepped back from the cart to browse the shelf. She wasn't even searching for something else to pick out. Leila just needed to direct her attention elsewhere to distract herself from how nervous she felt.

The girl tilted her body toward Leila and blinked. "Are you

341

making the cards for a birthday? Or for Christmas, maybe?"

"Sorta. I actually make them in a shop next to my home and sell them with the rest of my inventory."

"Really?" The girl's posture perked up. "You make homemade cards for a living?"

"That's right."

"Amazing!" The girl's eyes gleamed as a smile emerged. "It must be nice to make crafts with the other people working there too."

Leila pressed her lips together. "Actually, it's only me working in the shop at the moment. I used to work with my mom, but she isn't in any condition to do so right now."

"Oh, I'm sorry to hear that."

"No, it's okay. It's been stressful running the shop on my own, but I'm managing." *What are you saying, Leila? Don't pretend everything is okay when it isn't.*

"Well, I should get going. It was nice talking with you. Umm. . ." The girl cleared her throat. "I never asked you your name, did I?"

"L–Leila. My name's Leila Fisher." She extended her hand, and thankfully, the girl shook it.

"My name is Mollie Hershberger. I live in Reedsville."

"Oh, are you a white-topper?"

"Yes. My community drives the white-topped buggies." Letting go of Leila's hand, Mollie turned away. "It was nice to meet you, Leila. Hopefully, we'll see each other again."

"W–wait, Mollie!" she called. "Would you like to work in the shop with me?"

Mollie hurried back to Leila and pressed her palms to her cheeks. "I would love to."

"I still have to ask my mom if it'll be okay, but I think she'll be fine with it."

After discussing more with Mollie about working in the shop, they said goodbye to one another and Leila went to purchase her items. Even though she had only just met Mollie, something about her made Leila feel comfortable—more so than with some other people she talked to. Leila looked forward to getting home and informing her mother about the new person who would hopefully be working with her in the store.

CHAPTER 6

"That'll be five dollars and twenty-seven cents, please." Mollie held out her hand as the older woman gave her the payment. From her worktable, Leila watched Mollie run the battery-operated cash register. Even though Mollie had been working in the shop for only a week, she had mastered sweeping and dusting off the shelves, as well as helping Leila make the cards when no customers were in the store. This was her first time running the cash register.

Mollie showed diligence when it came to her work. It eased some stress when Leila felt the need to check on her mother. And with Henry almost being out of school, Leila would have to consider how to manage him without her mother being active. Her father could possibly take Henry to work with him and Leon, but that wouldn't be an everyday solution.

Leila cut a length of ribbon from one of the rolls she bought the day she met Mollie. The color reminded her of lavender petals.

"Looks like the coast is clear for the moment." Mollie brushed off the apron draping against her blueberry-colored dress. "What do you want me to do now?"

"I guess you can work with me for a little bit. I'll take over the cash register once we have our lunch, and you can make some cards and then move on to stocking the shelves that need more stamps."

"Sounds good to me." Mollie sat in the chair across from Leila at the worktable. Plucking from the pile of construction paper, she placed the sheet in front of her and folded it.

Leila stopped gluing embellishments on the front of the card to watch Mollie fold the paper precisely along the edges. "You're really good at this, Mollie."

Mollie's hands flinched away from the table, and she placed her arms to her sides. A hint of pink crept across her face. "I—I am? I mean, I try my best."

Seeing someone else get easily flustered gave Leila reassurance that she wasn't the only person who dealt with nervousness.

When it was time for lunch, Leila and Mollie headed out of the shop, and Leila locked the door. She put a sign on the window that indicated they'd return in an hour.

"So where are we going to eat today, Leila?"

Leila was about to respond when she thought how much easier it would be to eat inside the house rather than outdoors in the heat. But she wasn't sure if she was comfortable enough with Mollie to have her in the home for a long period of time. It wasn't because Mollie came off as untrustworthy, but Leila was worried about disturbing her mother.

"I can unlock the shop so we could eat in there for today. It'll be nice and cool with the battery-operated fan."

"Okay, sure." Mollie gave a smile, but it diminished rather quickly. "But before that, may I go in the house and use the restroom?"

"Uh, jah. I'll come inside with you to get our lunch from the kitchen."

While Leila had been avoiding having Mollie come into the house, not allowing her to use the restroom would have been rude. She walked ahead of Mollie and went to the front porch. Before she opened the door, Leila turned to her and brought a finger up to her mouth. "My mamm is still resting in her room, so please make it quick, all right?"

"Don't worry. I wouldn't want to disturb her."

"Thank you, Mollie." Leila turned the knob and nudged the door open. Fortunately, the bathroom wasn't a long distance from the front door. She headed to the right side of her house, past the entryway of the living room.

"Your house is spotless," Mollie whispered. "And the living room is well furnished and homey."

Leila had heard from her father a while back that the white-toppers used outhouses, but she'd never seen it for herself. All Leila knew was her yellow-top community was more progressive in comparison to the other two communities in the Big Valley. She was uncertain by how much, since there were many similarities among the three communities.

When they were at the bathroom door, Leila pivoted to face Mollie. "Meet me in the kitchen when you're finished. I'll set the food out so we can make some sandwiches."

"Will do. I'll be out soon."

After Mollie shut the door, Leila hustled down the hallway to her parents' bedroom. *I wonder if Mamm needs anything before I head back out to the shop.* A clunk from behind caused Leila to stop in her tracks. Looking back, she realized she had knocked over the framed family tree Mom had made that had hung on the wall.

"Oh great." Leila dragged her feet along the wooden floor, picking up the embroidered cloth from the frame. Part of the frame detached from one corner and struck the floor.

I'll take care of this later. No need to stress over it now, Leila thought while picking up the cloth and frame. She rose and hurried to her room with the items. *If anyone notices the family tree is gone from the wall, I'll have to explain. But I'm sure I can put it back together.*

Leila entered her room and went to her bed to place Mom's handiwork on the mattress. She took a moment to admire the carefully stitched names of her parents and siblings inside the silhouette of the tree. Her mouth quivered at the notion of becoming skilled enough to embroider well. Leila worked sufficiently with a pencil and a notebook, but she wanted to learn the art of cross-stitch and more elaborate embroidery.

"Is everything okay?"

Hitching a breath, Leila did a double take to her partly opened door. "Mollie, I told you to wait—"

"I know, but I heard a crash and was worried something horrible happened, so I wanted to check on you."

"Don't worry about it. Everything's fine."

"I'll go wait in the kitchen."

"All right. Be there in a bit."

Mollie disappeared from view, and Leila heard her footsteps heading away from the hallway. Leila's vision flitted to her window then to her shelves, stockpiled with notebooks, and again to the family tree on the bed, a sure sign of stress. *Calm down, Leila. Keep yourself together. You're just hungry. You'll feel better after lunch.*

Leila looked at the frame one last time, planning in her head how to mount it together again. Then she closed the door of her room and went to her parents' room, making sure to turn the knob slowly so she wouldn't disrupt her mother if she was asleep. She peeked in through the opening, and sure enough, Mom lay sleeping with her mouth gaping. Leila held in the urge to snicker. Her mother appeared so peaceful.

She shut the door and headed down the hallway, making a beeline to the kitchen. Mollie stood by the sink, twisting the knob back and forth, seemingly infatuated with the spout of rushing water.

Leila snorted. "Found a way to amuse yourself?"

Jerking her hand away from the knob, Mollie's hands fell to her sides as her cheeks turned rosy, complementing her olive-colored skin. "I'm sorry."

"Don't be. I kept you waiting." Leila went into the separate room to get the food out of the chest fridge. She squeezed the condiments between her arm and the side of her body, carrying the meat and bread with her hands to the counter. "We better hurry and make our lunch. We have plenty to do before the workday is over."

Aden opened the front door and hurried out of the house to look up at the sky. The evening breeze cooled his body as he sat on the porch steps and gazed toward the heavens. His vision adjusted while he absorbed the sight of one cluster of stars to the next, listing each constellation in his head.

Aden had admired the stars since he was a little kid, and his love had grown as the years progressed. He sought solace every night when he viewed the stars from his bedroom window. Someone was watching out for him, and becoming engrossed in the splendor of constellations was a reminder to give his worries to God.

But Aden couldn't stop thinking about what took place at the singing event a few weeks ago. Although what transpired didn't involve him, Aden felt somewhat responsible for allowing his friend to say those things to Leila. Yet a small part of him wondered if Samuel's actions were warranted. Maybe Leila wasn't as nice as he thought. If Aden were to talk about it with Samuel, then he might have a better understanding of why Samuel had spoken that way.

Aden's elbow prodded his upper leg as he leaned to one side. *I didn't get to talk with Leila like I wanted. I could've gotten to know her if we had had a moment alone.* He shook his head. *What am I thinking? I only met her once, yet here I am unable to get the vision of her out of my head.*

Not only was he thinking of Leila, but the fact that he'd broken his promise to Samuel had also lingered in his mind. Here Aden was supposed to ask Carol out, yet he couldn't bring himself to do it whenever he saw her. He kept thinking of Leila's amber strands and eyes that called to mind the rich color of mahogany. Her presence accentuated those physical qualities he admired. Aden could tell something about Leila was different from other people, and his thoughts gravitated to her as they did to the stars.

"Hey, Aden."

Aden swiveled his head to look over his shoulder. His sister stood by the front door with a ladle in her grasp.

"Supper is about ready. Are you coming in or not?"

He smiled. "I'll be there in a bit."

Sighing, Sue walked over to Aden and sat next to him on the steps. "I know something's on your mind, Brother. When was the last time you refused to budge from your spot when food was available."

"True as that is. . ." He swallowed. "I can't stop thinking about the one girl."

"You mean the one Samuel made that nasty comment toward?"

"Jah. Samuel tends to say the first thing that pops into his head. Most people are more discreet when it comes to relaying their opinions about other people, but he isn't like that."

"If you ask me, it comes off as being rude." Narrowing her eyes, Sue tapped the ladle against her stocking-covered knee. "Especially when I got to spend some time with Leila. She's timid but very nice, and she was willing to help serve the food for the singing."

"And because of Samuel, she won't be coming to another one." Aden's stomach roiled. "Leila, she makes me feel something, and I can't exactly describe what it is." Rubbing the middle of his forehead, he looked toward the bottom step through his fingers. He noticed a flicker near the step, realizing a firefly was perched on the edge.

"Do you feel attracted to her?"

"It's more than that, Sue." Aden mumbled a laugh. "All I know is, I want to see her again."

"Well, maybe you can. You just have to ask around, and then you can find the address of the store where she works."

"But what about Samuel?"

"What about him?" She lowered her head, wrinkling her brows. "Look, I know he's your closest friend, but don't allow his opinion of someone to sway your perception of them. It's best to figure out who a person is by taking the time to know them yourself." Sue hit the ladle against her knee again. "I may not be a good judge of character, but Leila is not someone I'd consider two-faced. She seems. . .I don't know how to put it into words."

"Misunderstood, perhaps?"

"More or less. We all are to an extent, but I can tell she's had it rough."

"Ruff like a dog?" Aden snorted as he watched his sister react to his response. He couldn't avoid smirking when he saw how unamused she was.

"Sure, Aden. Sure. You're hilarious." She batted his shoulder with the ladle. "Now, come on. You can stare at the sky after we finish eating."

Rubbing his shoulder, Aden stood from the steps, continuing to fixate on the night sky. *I wonder what I would say to Leila if I were to see her again.*

CHAPTER 7

"I don't want to talk about it, Aden." Samuel grabbed a full water bottle and gulped the liquid down completely. He threw the container near the log pile.

Aden fumbled with the reins as he waited for the log to be unhooked from the horse. "But I want to know why you would treat such a timid person in that way. It don't make a lick of sense."

"Now's not the time to talk. I don't know if you've noticed, but we're at work right now."

"Then you can tell me over lunch."

"I'm not getting into it while I'm enjoying a delicious meal." Samuel laughed, though there was a hint of edge to his laughter. "You've been asking me for the past week. Why do you want to know so badly?"

" 'Cause you never explained why you think Leila is weird. Or why you supposedly did something to hurt her."

"Look, I was young then, and I'd rather not get into it." He spoke forcibly. "And you were supposed to ask Carol out and never did, even after I let you drive my buggy while yours was out of commission."

Aden sucked in his cheeks. "You only let me drive for a few minutes."

"And for good reason, since you didn't do as promised and are still a sad, single loner as a result."

"Ouch."

"What are you two yapping about?" one of the English workers asked.

"It's nothing." Glancing sidelong at Aden, Samuel went over to the worker. As he walked away with him, Aden heard his friend say, "I told Aden we should be focused on our work, but you know how he is. He'll find any reason to slack off."

Aden clenched his teeth to avoid saying something he would regret. He was offended by Samuel's comment, considering his friend had told him that he was thorough with his work. Samuel was right about one thing, however. This wasn't the appropriate time to discuss the subject. Aden didn't feel any other time would be suitable either.

Since he wasn't going to get what he wanted from Samuel, Aden was set on going to the shop where Leila worked once he was given the go-ahead to have his lunch break. He wanted to know her better, and what better way to do so than by being in her company?

"So, you don't use milking machines on your cows?" Leila asked Mollie while digging a handful of chicken feed out of the bucket.

Mollie shook her head. "We do it by hand."

"It must be difficult to milk cows without any pumping mechanisms." Making sure the feed didn't fall between her fingers,

Leila cradled it in her hands as she made her way to the entrance of the chicken run.

"Nah. It's better to do it the old-fashioned way."

Mollie unhinged the gate, and Leila pushed it open with her elbow. The chickens rushed over to them, clucking and demanding the feed Leila held.

Mollie stopped midstride. "Your family has a lot of chickens."

"My litte brother adores them. Almost as much as I did when I was his age." Leila knelt down and extended her hand to the chickens. A few approached with hesitation, eyeing her as they moved closer. But others ran over as if they'd been without food for days, which wasn't the case since Leila had taken care of them earlier that day.

They pecked at Leila's palm and between the crevices of her fingers where bits of grain had wedged. While a few of the chickens were soft when it came to their pecking, a couple compressed the top part of her palm with their beaks.

Leila jerked her hand away and winced. "Ow! That one got me good."

"Your hand is bleeding! Are you okay?" Mollie reached for Leila's arm but shakily retracted her hand.

"Relax, Mollie. It looks worse than it actually is." Leila applied pressure with her thumb near the punctured area. More blood squeezed from the needle-sized hole, and she wiped it away with her thumb. "It doesn't hurt, but I'll need to clean and bandage my palm so it won't get infected."

"I'll come with you."

As they crossed the lawn, up against the house stood Flowerpot, the lone rooster, pecking at the ground below a bird feeder.

His head tilted upward, and he trilled out a lengthy crow that echoed throughout the property. Then he lowered his beak to the grass and proceeded to nip between the blades.

Leila admired the chicken. While he spent most of his days in solitude, Flowerpot typically had a commanding presence that none of the other chickens had. It was as if he possessed empowerment from being the odd one out of the group. Then out of the hedge below the feeder, a couple of chicks appeared from the green, chirping and scraping their feet in the gravel. They were close to becoming fully grown chickens, yet they peeped as if they'd just emerged from their shells.

Leila hummed. "Looks like Flowerpot is making friends with the younger chickens."

"Why does he usually hang out around the house and not with the others in the chicken run?"

"He got into a fight with one of the other roosters, and since he was relatively smaller in size back then, that rooster got the upper hand and Flowerpot became permanently blind in his left eye." Leila pushed on her palm again. "After that, the same rooster continued to pick on him to the point where he was driven out of the coop. He's been wandering our property ever since."

"I see." Mollie crossed her arms as she observed the rooster. Her pale pink lips parted. "Why'd you decide to name him Flowerpot?"

Leila laced her fingers around her other hand. "Because he started roosting in the pot near our home."

"Well, it suits him. He's a pretty tame chicken from what I've seen."

"Until he wants food, that is." Leila couldn't hold in a snicker.

"Or if he sees a stray *hund*."

Mollie giggled. "Who doesn't get fussy when they are hungry or when there's a stray dog around?"

Leila brought her hand up to view the punctured palm. Fortunately, the bleeding had slowed down, but it was still crucial to sanitize it.

"After I get my wound cleaned up, we should probably head back to the shop."

Aden jerked on the reins and steered the horse to cross the street, making sure to look both ways before having Chance move forward.

Must be the place over there. Aden had asked around and providentially found the address for Leila's shop.

The muscles in his neck spasmed as he drove the buggy up to the store. *Maybe this isn't a good idea. I don't want her to believe I'm obsessing over her, which I'm not.* The blood rushed to Aden's face. *Or maybe I am.*

He sprung out and landed on the gravel, peering down to avoid tripping over his own feet. He then secured his horse to the hitching rail. Turning toward the shop, Aden fabricated an explanation as to why he had come to the store. He figured he could purchase a few stamps and say they were for his sister, which wouldn't be too much of a lie since she used stamps on occasion. And at least he would have the end of his lunch break as a reason to leave if things became too awkward.

But would conversing with Leila while she's working be appropriate? She may not appreciate it. And what if Leila's not by herself in the store? Lifting his straw hat from his head, he rubbed his temples. *I'm not going to miss eating for nothing, so I should commit.* He pulled the hat back on his head and went over to the entrance of the white-painted building. Straightening his posture, he opened the door of the shop.

"Welcome. How may I—"

Sure enough, the first person to greet him was in fact Leila herself. She carried a box in her arms but soon placed it on the floor. Her long fingers touched her parted lips as she lowered her gaze.

"Afternoon, Leila. Remember me?"

"Ah, of course. You're Sue's brother." When she looked up, her brown eyes darted side to side. "Aden, right?"

He winked at her. "You got it."

Leila turned away, and her gaze seemed fixated on the cash register Aden had walked past when he first came in. "I'm sorry. Kinda slipped my mind for a moment."

"Who is this guy, Leila?" A young Amish woman came into Aden's view from one of the aisles. She had a box in her arms but placed it next to one of the shelves.

"Uh, Mollie, this is Aden Troyer. I met him and his sister at one of the singing events."

Aden offered his hand to her for a handshake. "Nice to meet you, Mollie."

"N—nice to meet you too."

He noted the way Mollie's hand trembled as she brought it to his. *She's sort of timid like Leila.* After shaking her hand, Aden shoved both hands into the pockets of his trousers. "So, where are you from?"

"Reedsville."

"Ah, a white-topper, I'm guessing."

"J–jah. That would be correct. I hope you don't see that as a bad thing."

"Nope. Not at all. I know people from all three communities. Even some Englishers. We all walk different paths, yet those paths can have similar obstacles."

"Yes, exactly!" She bounced onto her tiptoes but then quickly covered her mouth. "I didn't mean to shout, but I'm glad you see it that way."

As Aden continued to talk with Mollie, he peered over at Leila and noticed she was seated near the window. His stomach sank. *I wanted to talk with her, but here I am talking to Mollie instead. Is this a habit of mine, breaking promises? Even ones I make to myself?*

Leila carried on with one of the cards she'd been working on. She surely wouldn't have guessed Aden would stroll into her store. It gave the impression of being intentional, considering he didn't appear surprised she had greeted him.

She lifted her chin from her worktable, surveying the discussion ensuing between Aden and Mollie. *Those two are getting along quite nicely. They actually look kind of cute together.* While Leila smiled because of her thought, her stomach clenched at the possibility. But why? Leila didn't know anything about him that would warrant jealousy.

Tilting her chin, Leila opened one of the ink pads and pressed the stamp she held in a forceful manner. *Even if you knew anything*

about him, what makes you think he would want to get to know you?
Grunting in her throat, Leila peeled the stamp from the ink pad
and examined it to see if the entire pattern had been covered.

"Seems like your work requires precision."

Startled, Leila raised her head, inadvertently making eye
contact with those vivid eyes that mesmerized her weeks ago.
Her body heated up, registering she had gone too long without
responding to Aden. She lowered her head, twiddling ribbon
around the tip of her index finger. "I suppose."

"It does. I've been doing it for a few weeks, but I still struggle
with it. Leila is too good."

"Mollie, what are you saying? You're a natural." Leila let go
of the ribbon and scratched her shoulder. "As for me, I've been
making cards since my mom opened this shop."

"Does she still work with you?" Aden asked.

"Not since she became in a family way. I couldn't handle it
on my own, which is why I'm thankful for Mollie being here and
making all of this a little more bearable."

"I'm thankful you gave me the opportunity to work."

"Wow. Look at all of those cards." Aden eyed the clothesline
dangling above their heads. "Did you make these cards yourself?"

"N—not all of them. Mollie made some too."

"Leila made most of them. Mine are at the end of the clothesline over there." Mollie pointed in that direction.

"Would you mind if I take one off the line?"

Leila rose from her worktable, pinching the inside of her bottom lip with her teeth. "Okay. Help yourself."

Stretching his arms, Aden removed one of the clothespins to
detach the card he supported in his other hand. Once his arms

fell, he held the card out in front of him. An inner gleam in his eyes intensified the already exceptional blue color. Opening the card, Aden turned to Leila, giving a wide smile. "You put a lot of time and care into what you make. It's impressive. These cards are certainly beautiful."

"D–danki. I can clip the card back up there."

"Actually, I'd like to purchase it, if you don't mind."

"Oh. Of course." She rubbed at the ink stain on her arm. "But I'm surprised you're picking out a 'get well soon' card. Is someone you know not feeling well?"

"No. I just liked the way it looked, and. . .I was wondering if I could watch you finish the card-making process."

Leila had a difficult time comprehending Aden's interest in her work. She was uncertain whether his interest was sincere. Aden and Samuel were friends, after all, and rooted from her past were Samuel's and his friends' words of ridicule. She pressed her lips flat then narrowed her eyes. "How come?"

"I appreciate craftsmanship of any kind."

Which wasn't a rational explanation to Leila. "Why'd you come all this way to my shop?"

"I—I wanted to buy some stamps for my sister." Clutching the homemade card, Aden glanced at Leila and then looked away. "I'm sorry. You're probably still mad about what went down a few weeks ago, right?"

A flare of adrenaline shot through Leila. "I know people have motives, and I wouldn't be surprised if you came all this way just to make a fool out of me and then talk about it later with your friends."

"That's not why I'm here. I just—" Removing his hat, Aden

361

released a deep sigh while shaking his head. His dark hair glistened in the light radiating from the window. "Look, I may not know what went down when you two were younger, but I'm not Samuel. I don't think any less of you for being upset, all right? I don't agree with what he did, and I certainly don't condone that kind of behavior."

At that moment, Leila accepted Aden's words as authentic. She felt a hint of doubt, since he seemed like he wasn't relaying all his thoughts to her. But Leila was content with him being straightforward about Samuel. A sudden weightlessness enveloped her, and all the tension was released from her body. *I almost yelled at him when I shouldn't have. That wouldn't have ended too well.*

"There's another reason I'm here."

I hate it when I'm right. Leila thumbed her ear. "What is it?"

"I wanted to invite you to come to another singing event."

She shook her head. "I don't think it would be a good idea."

"Don't worry; I'll keep Samuel off your back. My sister really wants to see you again. And your fun shouldn't be ruined because of someone else. Sue told me you had fun last time, so I wish you'd go to this one too."

"But I have so much going on here, and my mamm needs me."

"Just think about it, okay?" His smile wavered. "We can come pick you up if you'd like."

Normally, Leila would continue to draw excuses or search for any reason to excuse herself from answering questions. She looked back at Aden, licking her lips before speaking. "All right, I'll think about it. But I'll drive myself."

"Fair enough."

Rubbing the bandage on her palm, Leila sat back in her chair. "If you want to watch me finish this card, it's fine." She gestured to the empty seat next to her. "You can sit down if you want."

Aden accepted the offer and seated himself next to her. At that moment, another customer came in.

Mollie patted her hand on the worktable. "I'll head back over to the register. Have fun, you two."

Leila resumed her card making, and while at first her heart pounded from being watched, she began to relax as she and Aden conversed. They mostly talked about making cards, and Leila was untroubled with keeping it that way for the time being.

CHAPTER 8

It astounded Leila that a month had gone by fairly quickly. It was already the latter part of July, and the sun's rays intensified over the valley.

Leila had the window open in her room, and the sunlight cascaded over the bedsheets as she lay there with her notebook. She was sketching a rose by memory rather than by reference, as she normally would. Leila had been doing that more often to develop her skill.

As she lightly outlined the petals with graphite, Leila thought about being with Aden during the last singing events. She relished every moment, especially since Samuel never intruded when she was with Aden and Sue. Samuel would walk away when Aden called Leila over or when she approached. Having people ignore her was something Leila had struggled with for years, but it was certainly better than confrontation.

Leila pressed the pencil eraser against her cheek. *How can I resolve the issue with Samuel if he's not willing to work things out? I feel terrible for Aden, because without me around, he wouldn't have a problem with his and Samuel's friendship.* Leila twiddled the pencil with her fingers. *Once again, I make other people's lives more of a hassle than they need to be.*

Placing the notebook on her nightstand, Leila pressed off the mattress and marched out of her bedroom. *I wonder if Mamm is awake from her nap yet. If she is, I better make sure she doesn't attempt to make dinner again.*

Leila's mother's health had improved during the past weeks, but the doctor recommended she rest as much as possible. Even so, Leila wasn't aware of the extent of her mother's condition. She'd asked several times but was always told her condition wasn't anything serious. Regardless, Leila prayed for her mother every night and for her new sibling to be well when he or she was brought into the world.

She peeked into her parents' bedroom. No sign of Mamm there. Leila wondered if she might be outside on the porch. Her mother often went there after waking up from a nap.

Opening the front door, Leila saw her sitting in the swinging seat, bending her knees to rock it. She could see Mamm's kapp sliding off her head, but she lifted her hands and grabbed the ties to pull the head covering in its rightful place.

"Evening, Mamm."

"Leila, my daughter. Would you come sit with me before making supper?"

"Of course." Leila went to the swing and sat.

Her mother patted Leila's shoulder. "I wanted to ask you how things have been going with the young man you hang around with."

"Oh, you mean Aden Troyer." Leila averted her gaze. "Well, I know he works eight hours a day as a logger. He is a year older than me, but I'll be his age next month."

"Leila, I've heard all of this before. What I want to know is, how do you feel toward him?"

"I feel. . .comfortable, I suppose. Why do you ask?"

"I'm curious to know if something's going on between you and Aden, since you have been going to the events after church with him."

"Mamm, I am with his sister as well." Leila curled her hands around her middle. "Aden and I are only friends."

Mamm prodded Leila's shoulder. "From what I've noticed, you two appear to have respect for one another. And it seems he focuses on you, especially the one evening when he stayed to talk with you so long."

Leila recalled that night often. Sue hadn't felt well that Sunday and hadn't attended. For the first time, Aden had offered to take Leila to the singing event in his buggy, creating the first time they were alone with one another. She had asked Aden why his horse was named Chance, and he'd grinned. He explained that the horse was the runt out of the bunch and that his father had told him that it wouldn't survive after a month. But Aden kept caring for the runt, and sure enough, the horse developed into a stallion. Hence, Aden's horse was named Chance.

"Leila, are you listening to your poor old mother?"

"Ah, sorry," Leila whispered, avoiding her mother's eyes.

"You were thinking of him, weren't you?"

"You can't prove it."

"I don't need to." Her mother giggled. "It's written all over your face."

Slumping her shoulders, Leila accepted defeat rather than

defending herself. She was well aware that her mother saw Aden as a potential lover. Leila wasn't certain if she had any romantic feelings toward him or not. It was difficult to differentiate her usual nervousness from a sensation of love. Or was that only an excuse to avoid her actual feelings?

"Good evening, my wonderful wife and daughter." Leila's father stepped onto the porch.

"Welcome back, Daed."

Mom gave a gentle smile. "Yes, welcome home."

Gazing toward the buggy shop, Leila noticed her brother wasn't anywhere to be seen. "Where's Leon? Figured he would be here with you after work like he usually is."

"He hurried to his home today for some reason. Didn't say why."

"Maybe he's bringing his wife over for supper." Leila's mother pushed her glasses against the subtle bump on her nose. "How was work today, William?"

Seating himself in the chair across from Leila and Mom, her father leaned back and intertwined his fingers. "Nothing too exciting. Just examining and sorting the raw logs that were unloaded."

As they conversed on the porch, Leila saw a buggy coming up the road. "Leon is heading this way."

"Wouldn't doubt that. Guess he and Judy want to have supper with us tonight."

Leon and Judy walked up to the house. "Evening, everyone." Leon grinned.

"Joining us for supper, I see."

"Yes, but before that, Judy and I want to say something." Leon grasped Judy's hand. "I'm not sure if any of you noticed, but Judy and I have struggled with our marriage for a while now."

Leila's skin tingled. She had no idea Leon and Judy were having marriage problems. *Did anyone else not realize they were struggling in their marriage, or was it only me? Would it be better not to ask that sort of question?*

"But there was a reason Leon and I were so frustrated." Judy's shoulders quaked as she lowered her gaze to the porch. "We were wanting to have a baby for two years with no result."

Dad's neck bent forward. "Where are you two going with this?"

"Basically, Judy and I continued praying, and—"

"Our prayers were finally answered." Judy caressed her stomach.

"Oh my goodness." A stinging sensation prickled Leila's chest as she covered her mouth with her hands.

"I can't believe this." Mom got up from the swinging chair and wrapped her arms around Judy. "I'm so happy for you two!" She embraced Leon next, patting him on the back.

Leon chuckled. "We're pretty happy too."

"Of course, you would be." Letting go of Leon, Mom turned to Leila's father. "Our first grandchild, William. Can you believe it?"

He patted Leon's back. "This is *wunderbaar* news."

Leila watched as her parents grouped with Leon and Judy, exchanging hugs and praises. Although she wanted to join in with them, she was caught up in the moment and couldn't move.

"Are you sure you and Aden aren't courting?"

"Mollie, please."

369

"He comes by to visit you in the shop sometimes twice a week. And he always looks at you with those pretty blue eyes of his."

"He's looked at you before too."

"Not in the way he does with you. You have also gone to some singings with him."

"My mamm was just asking about Aden yesterday. And as much as I enjoy his company, I don't think we'd ever have a future together." Leila trailed a finger along the scratches on the reddened wood of her windowsill. Lifting her hand, Leila rubbed the tip against her thumb, muttering, "Dusty."

Leila was aware that Aden had been drawn to her ever since they met. But after finding out he was best friends with Samuel, she'd harbored some doubts. She was still uncertain why Aden was interested in her, considering she didn't have the greatest experiences when it came to courting.

"What's in here?"

Leila glanced over at Mollie, knowing she was referring to her notebook lying on the nightstand. Hurrying to pick it up, Leila held the notebook to her chest. "Nothing special."

Mollie's body tilted slowly toward Leila. "It must mean something to you. Otherwise, you wouldn't act so secretive about it."

"I'm not being secretive, I. . ." The muscles in Leila's arms twitched. "You wouldn't be interested in what's in it."

"I asked, didn't I? So yes, I am interested—if it isn't anything too personal. If that's the case, then I understand why you wouldn't want to show me."

"It's not that I don't want to show anyone what I have in there. It's just. . ."

Even though Leila had been teased in school for sitting alone with her notebook, Mollie wasn't coming off as if she was mocking Leila. It seemed as if Mollie was genuinely interested by what was inside.

Struggling to find the right words, Leila dragged the notebook down her torso. "Do you really want to see?"

Mollie nodded.

Leila handed the notebook to her. She watched as Mollie sank into the mattress, placing the notebook on her lap. Her jaw clenched painfully while Mollie lifted the cover to expose the pages inside. *This was a terrible choice. She's going to make fun of me for such a useless hobby.*

"Oh my!" Mollie slapped a hand against her cheek. "These drawings are so good."

"You think so?" With her heart racing, Leila sat down next to Mollie.

"Jah. I knew you were a creative person, but I didn't know you were into drawing." She traced the fibers of the paper with her nail. "I very much like this one with the butterflies in the field."

"Danki. I sketched that at the beginning of this summer."

"Why were you so hesitant to show what was in here?"

Her posture stiffened. While Leila was prepared to dismiss the question, she figured it would be okay to be honest with Mollie. "Will you promise me something?"

"What is it, Leila?"

"Please, don't think of me in a negative way after I express to you why I didn't want to show you my notebook." Leila exhaled then took the notebook from Mollie. "I know it seems silly, but drawing helps me deal with some of the situations I'm going through right now. When I was younger, having a notebook next to me was my way of escaping from the world and having a sense of control in my life."

She got up from the bed and placed the notebook on the nightstand, directing her attention back to Mollie. "I attempted to share what I'd drawn with friends at school, but they said I was silly for investing my time in something so pointless. Making friends was difficult for me because I always felt like an outsider, and drawing was my way of coping." Leila stared at her stocking-covered feet. "But since no one wanted to see my drawings, I decided to keep them to myself."

"It wasn't right for them to do that, Leila."

"Or maybe it was." She laughed. "I was never good enough for anyone."

"What about your family? Don't they care for you?"

"My family has been very supportive of me throughout the years. Without them, I would truly be alone in this world."

"That isn't true at all. Because even if you have no one on earth to support you, God is looking over you, and His presence provides us with contentment."

The thickness in Leila's throat wouldn't go away no matter how much she swallowed. Even though what Mollie expressed was something she was fully aware of, she had a hint of doubt in her soul. She'd been too trusting of others when she was young, which caused her to be suspicious of disloyalty. No matter how nice she was to others, she didn't receive kindness in return. That was why it was easier for her to not even try.

Yet here was Mollie providing her with the things Leila had always wanted from a friendship. Encouragement, devotion, and loyalty—so much so that Leila didn't believe she deserved it.

"Leila, I want to thank you for being honest with me. You've also been so generous, offering me a place to work. I don't know what I would be doing now if it wasn't for your kindness." Mollie pulled on the ties of her kapp. "And I should be honest with you too."

Leila tilted her head. "What are you talking about?"

"I want to invite you over to my house."

Leila's excitement mounted. She'd never been inside a white-topper's house before. She'd heard from others who had but was eager to see what Mollie's home looked like.

CHAPTER 9

Reedsville

The day after Mollie extended the invitation to visit her house, Leila sat on the seat inside a white-topped buggy rolling down the side of the road. Mollie had put her on the spot yesterday with the invitation, but since Leila planned on closing the store to restock homemade cards, it worked out.

"There's my home over there." Mollie lifted her arms, with the reins still in hand, pointing toward the property.

Leila saw the barn first, noticing the outer structure wasn't painted like the barns in Belleville. She had heard from her father that the Amish in the white-top community didn't typically paint their barns, but Leila had never seen it for herself.

She had been through the area of Reedsville with her folks, but she hadn't paid too much attention to the differences between her community and the white-toppers. And since the black-toppers were similar to the yellow-top community, Leila figured the white-toppers would be as well. She had seen them at some of the shops in Belleville and at the weekly flea market. Leila was aware that they dressed a little differently than the other two communities, but she'd never been friends with a white-topper before nor had she visited any of their homes.

The *clip-clop* from the horse's hooves on the dirt path should've calmed her nerves, but Leila's veins pulsated. She didn't know what to expect in this uncertain territory.

Licking the top of her mouth, Leila turned to Mollie. "Are you sure this isn't too last-minute? I don't want to intrude."

"Don't worry. I asked my parents yesterday, and they don't mind."

Leila leaned back on the seat, gazing at the house at the end of the dirt path. The first thing that caught her attention was the vines hanging from the front of the home, trailing down from the roof and dangling just above the railing of the porch. She noticed a man in front of the house. It appeared as if he might be getting ready to head over to the buggy shop.

"Hello, Daed."

"Welcome back, Mollie. Glad you made it here safely." He went up to Mollie and patted her back then turned to Leila. "Ah, you must be Lila. Good to meet a friend of my daughter."

Leila's scalp prickled. "A—actually, it's Leila."

"My apologies. I haven't heard a name like yours before." He threaded his thumbs through the band of his chestnut trousers. "Make yourself at home, Leila."

"We'll be in my room," Mollie called as they headed for the house.

As Leila followed Mollie inside, she saw the stove against the wall and realized they had entered the kitchen. She noticed the mason jars aligned in neat rows, each one filled with fruit.

"Some of the jars have red raspberries in them, which are actually the berries hanging from the roof outside." Mollie opened the door leading to the porch. "Come, I'll show you."

Poking around the blue frame of the doorway, Leila watched as Mollie went on her tiptoes to pluck the dark berries from the vines. Then she lowered herself, turning to Leila with the berries in her hand.

"Would you like to try one? They're really sweet."

Leila took a berry, slipping it into her mouth. Her taste buds erupted with overpowering sweetened flavor. "These are delicious!"

"It's one of the reasons I like this time of year. You can't get these in winter." Mollie reached up and picked a few more berries. "Now that we have a snack, we can go to my room."

They left the kitchen and walked into what Leila assumed to be the living room. The only reason she assumed it was the living room was because of the couch in the middle of the floor. The room was quite bare of furniture and devoid of any wall decorations. *No wonder Mollie commented about the furniture in my living room.*

When they entered Mollie's bedroom, Leila's eyes trailed to the splotches of white paint on the window glass, near the corners of the frame. She then observed the rest of the room, seeing the single bed in the corner. A quilt lay at the end of the bed, and from what Leila could tell, it was in a classic diamond pattern.

"I know it isn't much, but it's a place to sleep."

"I—I don't see it that way." Leila regretted not wording her sentence correctly when Mollie's tanned complexion seemed to have drained from her face. Scrubbing a hand over her mouth, Leila spoke again. "I—I mean, about it not being much. I think it's suitable."

Mollie held her palm up. "You're very kind, Leila. But maybe we should go somewhere outside instead."

She walked past Leila then motioned her out of the room. Leila wanted to tell her she didn't mind the room at all, regardless of what Mollie may have thought of it, but she kept her thoughts to herself.

Mollie took Leila to the back of the house, where she opened the door out to the lawn. Not much was outside, though there was an immense field beyond the yard.

"This is my favorite place even during the cold months, because the snow makes everything seem pure."

"I have a couple of special places I like at home too." Leila laced her fingers together. "Kinda like the one place you saw in my notebook."

"I suppose that's what inspired me to bring you here today." Mollie lowered and sat among a grouping of small yellow flowers, crossing her legs. "You and I aren't too much different, Leila. We both retreat somewhere to be alone with our thoughts. As you're probably aware, my home isn't as nice as houses like yours. My family has been struggling with finances ever since I can remember, and these recent months have been worse."

Leila sat down next to her. "Is it like that with every family in your community?"

"Actually, there are some who are pretty wealthy or financially stable." Mollie pulled a couple of the flowers from the grass. "My family isn't, however, and after my daed was let go from work, my mom had to sell some crafts to keep us on our feet. She sells some of her embroidered patterns as well as canned goods at the weekly flea market."

"Your mom does embroidery?"

Mollie nodded. "She taught me how also." Placing the flowers in front of her, Mollie exhaled. "Anyway, that's why I was searching around for work. I wasn't too successful here, and I wasn't getting anywhere in Belleville until I ran into you."

Leila wasn't sure how to answer her, especially knowing that most people didn't respond properly whenever someone talked about their problems. She wanted to alleviate Mollie's pain but feared she might say the wrong thing. Leila didn't want to tell her things would get better, because she couldn't promise such a thing. Nor did she want to say that it could always be worse, since that would be stating the obvious.

Instead, Leila squeezed Mollie's shoulder. "I don't know what you're going through with all of this, because I'm not in the situation." Her mouth twitched as she smiled at Mollie. "But you're doing your best, and sometimes that's all you can do."

Mollie's posture perked up. "Yes, you're right."

The air grew silent, and Leila realized why Mollie had plucked the flowers from the ground around them. She began tying the stems together.

"So, about you and Aden. . ."

"Again, Mollie?"

"Yes, because it isn't a secret that you two are very close."

"I really don't want to get into it."

"You do have feelings for him, don't you?"

"I'll only tell you if you promise to teach me how to embroider sometime."

Mollie squinted her eyes. "That request came out of nowhere, but I guess if it'll get an answer from you, then sure."

Leila lowered her chin to her chest. "I suppose I feel something."

"Then you should let Aden know how you feel."

"Just because I have feelings for him doesn't mean I should act on them." There was a harsh pulse in her throat. "It hasn't worked out for me before."

"I'll be honest. I haven't had the best time with love either." Mollie's movements were rhythmic as she kept tying the stems. "But if the opportunity is given to me, I'll take it, because you never know the outcome unless you are willing to give it a chance. And if it doesn't work out, then there'll be other opportunities."

Mollie rose to her feet, draping the flowers along Leila's shoulders. "Think it over, and if you're still unsure, then pray about it. Ask God to give you insight into what you should do."

In that moment, Leila realized she didn't pray as often as she should. She would pray before a meal, but she didn't consistently ask God for guidance. Part of it was from relying too much on herself and focusing too much on whenever she had messed up in the past.

Leila stroked the petals from one of the flowers with her thumb. *I can see why You brought Mollie into my life, Lord. It wasn't just for an extra pair of hands in the card shop.*

Belleville

Leila had a hard time focusing on what she was working on in her notebook. She couldn't help but think of what Mollie said to her the day before, and Leila was now left with thoughts of possibly being in a relationship with Aden. She had prayed long and hard for what seemed like hours, yet Leila still didn't know if pursuing a relationship with Aden would be a good idea. First,

Aden was friends with Samuel, and even though he didn't speak with him much during the singing events, Aden had told her that they worked together. Leila felt responsible for putting a wedge between them by hanging out with Aden. That would only become worse if Leila and Aden started courting.

Second, they were from separate communities. While it wasn't uncommon for black- and yellow-toppers to be together, there would be an issue if one of them converted to the other community after having already joined the church, that is, if the relationship were to get to that point.

Why am I even thinking about this right now? I haven't even known him for two months, yet I'm contemplating events that are far off in the future, if there at all. Leila tossed her pencil and closed the notebook. The clink of the pencil falling to the floor made her feel slightly better. *Maybe being with Aden wouldn't be so bad. But what if he rejects me?*

Getting up from her bed, Leila went over and picked up the pencil. *Then again, you're used to rejection, so why are you so fearful of it now? I must really care about Aden to be this worried about losing his companionship.*

Because there wasn't a singing event scheduled for this Sunday evening, Leila wondered if she should take the initiative to visit Aden. But what would she say to him? What would she want to say? And whatever Leila wanted to say, she would have to say quickly so she could get home and make supper.

She placed the pencil on her nightstand next to her notebook. Rolling her shoulders back, Leila shook off the chill that came out of nowhere. *I don't know what I'm going to say to Aden, but perhaps God will provide me with the words.*

∽

A short distance from Aden's house, Leila was set on going through with seeing him. She wasn't sure what she should say about her feelings, but she tried to not overthink it. She wanted to give her fears of rejection and uncertainty over to God.

When she guided her horse into the Troyers' driveway, she saw Aden and Sue on the front porch. Their attention was on each other until Leila approached the house.

"Hey! Aden, look who it is." Sue grasped the railing and jumped up and down.

Aden turned toward Leila, giving her a grin and a wave of the hand.

Leila's ears felt unpleasantly warm as she walked up to the porch. *How am I supposed to talk to him with Sue around? Or could it be a good thing? I can talk about something else and avoid discussing uncertain feelings.*

"What a pleasant surprise." He winked. "What are you doing here on this fine evening?"

"I..." Leila kicked at her ankle. *I have nothing to talk about or any excuse to be here. This was a horrible idea.* "I just stopped by to visit."

Sue came down the steps and wrapped her arms around Leila. "How's your mother doing?"

"She's been doing well."

"I'm glad to hear that." Sue's dress flittered like a flag as she hurried up the steps to the front door. "As much as I would like to chat, I need to help our mamm get supper started. We're having haystack tonight, so prepare your stomach for some delicious sustenance, Aden."

382

As soon as Sue went into the house, Aden walked down the steps and stood in front of Leila. "If you wanna come in and eat with us, you'd be welcomed."

"I probably shouldn't. It's too short notice."

"And you visiting wasn't short notice?" Snickering, Aden prodded Leila's arm in a playful manner.

She couldn't help but laugh too. "I have to make supper at home, so I can't abandon my family."

"What about later on this week?" His glowing cheeks went well with his toothy smile. "How about Friday night?"

Leila pressed her lips together. "I don't know, Aden. I want to, but I usually make cards and restock the shelves after the work-day. And I have my mother to look after."

"Just think about it, okay?"

Her belly fluttered as she examined his facial features. Although she felt somewhat guilty for not giving him a straight-forward answer, the way his nose scrunched up almost caused her to giggle. *How can I say no to such an adorable face?*

"All right. I'll think about it."

Aden nodded, sliding his hands into his pockets. "And I'll come visit your shop this week to receive your answer."

CHAPTER 10

Leila stepped out of the buggy in the midst of the humid evening, with her stomach grumbling in protest for food. Or perhaps it was from how nervous she felt. Leila couldn't believe it was already Friday and she'd just arrived at Aden's house.

When she'd returned home the previous Sunday evening, Leila was relieved she hadn't expressed her feelings to Aden. She didn't want to ruin her friendship with him. And although what had happened with Samuel was years ago, Leila didn't desire a rehash. Part of her wondered if she and Aden were to stay as friends and nothing more.

Leila told Mollie about everything the day after while working in the shop and admitted how she lost the nerve to tell Aden her feelings. Mollie expressed disappointment but also support, hoping the best for Leila in what might ensue this evening.

Though who was to say anything would happen? She was only going to have some good food and be in the company of Aden's family for the evening.

"Leila!" Sue hugged her. "It's so good to see you."

"Good to see you too."

"Come inside. You're going to love what my mamm and I are making tonight. It's one of my personal favorites."

Leila followed as they went up the indoor steps, which led to a short hallway in the open portion of the home.

"Mamm, Leila's here!"

"Hello, Leila. Nice to see you again." Mrs. Troyer held a washcloth in her grasp as she turned from the sink. "How's your mother doing?"

"Very well. In fact, it won't be long until my sibling will be here. Only about four more months."

"That's good to hear."

"Aden should be back from work soon. Unless he gets held up with something there."

"That could happen. I'm just thankful my job doesn't involve logs." Sue plucked at her sleeve. "Imagine all the slivers in my skin."

Chuckling, Mrs. Troyer wrapped the washcloth around her hand. Her blue eyes, similar to Aden's, glimmered behind her frames. "Did you close your shop early today to be here for supper?"

"No, but my friend is staying in the store to work on some cards for me." Leila held in a breath momentarily, which bottled up in her chest as she smiled. *I never would have thought I'd refer to her as a friend. But I guess she really is my friend, isn't she?*

"Leila, I want to show you what I've been working on up in my room."

"Don't you have to make your favorite dish?"

"Yes, but not yet. It's too soon to make supper." Sue grabbed Leila's wrist and led her up the stairs.

When they entered the room, Sue let go of her hand and hurried over to the corner. Stamps and ink pads as well as folded-up construction paper lay scattered on the floor.

Sue bumped Leila's shoulder. "I started making cards recently." She slid her back against the wall as she sat down. Sue held up a stamp. "I have created homemade cards before, but after my brother brought home some of the stamps from your shop, I tried to create one for the fun of it."

Leila tipped her head to the side, stopping midstride as she stared at the mess on the floor. She didn't know how to process this situation. She couldn't influence others, yet Leila was witnessing someone being motivated because of her.

"But I mostly got inspired by the card Aden brought home with him. He was trying to keep it hidden from me, but I saw it in his room and loved the design."

Leila remembered the card. "I don't know why he picked that card in particular. It was a 'get well soon' card, and from what Aden told me, he wasn't planning on giving it to anyone."

"I think it has something to do with his interest in—"

"Sue! Your brother's home, and we need to start preparing supper."

"Okay, Mamm!" Sue jolted up and jumped over the stamps and ink pads. "Aden will be thrilled to see you again. I'm sure of it."

"By the way, what exactly are you making this evening?"

"It's a surprise, Leila. You'll see."

Leila headed downstairs, and before reaching the bottom, she saw Sue and Aden bickering over something she couldn't distinguish.

"Evening, Leila." Aden grinned.

"Good evening."

"How was work today, Aden?" Patting her brother's back, Sue raised both of her eyebrows.

"The usual. I wrote it all down in my 'log' book."

Sue rolled her eyes. "Ignore him. I need to get supper ready. You're both probably starving."

"Aren't you?" Aden took off his straw hat.

"Of course. That's why I'm making my favorite meal."

"Need any assistance?" Leila asked.

"You're the guest. Just enjoy yourself." Sue gave Leila a quick hug and darted to the kitchen.

Leila was left alone with Aden, standing face-to-face in the middle of the home.

"So, we could sit in the living room if you'd like."

"Uh. . ." Leila looked outside to the hills where the sun was just overhead. "I kinda want to hang out outside if you don't mind. It's really nice out there today."

"You have a point. I guess we could—"

"*Ach, nee!*"

Leila glanced over to the kitchen area. A rectangular box sat upside down on the floor. Looking up, she noticed Sue attempting to roll up a long length of foil, smoothing it out with the edge of the counter.

"That's not how you roll up unraveled foil, Sue."

"How else are you supposed to roll it up? The foil's going to clump regardless."

Aden turned his attention to the kitchen and rubbed a hand through his hair. "We should go somewhere else. Actually, could you wait for me outside? Gotta get something from my room real quick."

"All right."

Watching as he went up the stairs, Leila felt a sense of faintness she couldn't ignore. She wanted to pretend it was from an empty stomach, but she knew better. *What if he truly is interested in me?*

"Where is it?" Aden wondered while feeling the items underneath his bed. When his fingers trailed along a metallic piece, he'd found what he was looking for. Lacing his hand around the handle, Aden pulled; the case's surface abraded the floor under the bed. "I haven't shown her this yet, but I think Leila will like it. She is a creative person, after all."

Aden patted his hand on the case, probing it as his muscles grew tense. *I could use the moment to tell Leila how I feel about her. But I don't know if she feels the same as I do. She's got a knack of keeping her emotions hidden. What if I end up embarrassing myself? What if I end up embarrassing her?*

Gritting his teeth, he stood up and leaned over to pick up the case. *I am thankful Leila has gotten comfortable with me over these few months. I just don't want to ruin what we have by allowing my feelings to interfere. And while we've been around one another, she seems to hold back from being open about things. Doesn't she trust me enough to know I wouldn't judge her for being herself? I suppose I'm gonna have to open up more if I want Leila to open up to me.* He hesitated but then proceeded to carry the case out of his room.

Leila sat on an ivory-colored swing positioned near the garden, teetering a little as the wooden seat skimmed beneath her like a sheet of ice.

"Hope you weren't waiting too long."

"Nope." Crossing her ankles, Leila gave Aden a smile as he came closer. "Looks like you have an instrument in that case."

"You'd be right." He placed the case on the lawn, flipping it over.

"I didn't know you played anything."

"Well, I figured why tell you when I can show you instead?" Unclipping the case, Aden opened it and pulled out a glossy, russet-colored guitar. The reflective exterior could have almost been a mirror.

She got up from the swing and knelt next to him. "How long have you been playing?"

Aden answered, speaking like an old person. "Ever since I was a wee lad. Those were different times back then."

"Pfft. Come on." She nudged his arm, letting out a laugh. "Can't I get an answer?"

"That is about as on the nose as I can get it. But maybe you can guess from how I play."

His fingers twiddled the strings. Leila watched as Aden's left hand shifted along the frets effortlessly, and each chord pulsated her eardrums. She hummed with a note from the individual chords Aden played with a pick held between his thumb and index finger. Suddenly, the resonant sound of the instrument was no longer dancing around Leila's ears.

"What would your guess be, Leila?"

Pursing her lips in thought, Leila rose and went back to the swing. "Fourteen?"

"Close. You're halfway there."

"How is that close?" She let out a throaty laugh, not caring how obnoxious it may have sounded.

"Seven years old. My grandfather gave me a child-size guitar for my birthday. Been playing ever since."

"I'm impressed by how well you play."

"I can tell by the way you were humming along." A genuine smile developed on Aden's face.

"Could you play some more?"

"We have a little bit longer before we eat, so sure." He picked up the guitar and strummed the strings from top to bottom. "Any song requests?"

After having silent prayer at the table, Leila and the Troyers served themselves as the food was passed. There was so much Leila saw cascading along the surface—steamed broccoli, toasted rolls, beets, and of course the main dish—chicken casserole.

Leila wasn't a big fan of casseroles, but she couldn't deny that what Sue created was delicious. The texture was pleasant and the taste savory—especially the tenderness of the chicken. But it made Leila feel somewhat guilty since Henry loved chickens and would never eat one.

Disregarding that fact, Leila enjoyed the conversations among the Troyers. She'd only spoken a few times when asked about her mother or work but was amused by their personal stories. Sue mentioned how a customer knocked over one of the windows being displayed, and it almost toppled on them. Thankfully, neither of them was injured because Sue pushed the customer out of the way.

Aden then went on about work, and Leila's negative thoughts sprouted whenever he mentioned Samuel. She wanted to get rid of those thoughts, but her mind raced through everything at that moment. Sitting still, Leila attempted to keep interested in the current conversation.

"And some of the logs get hauled to the sawmill where Leila's dad works." Aden lifted a fork carrying a chunk of casserole to his mouth.

"Ah. So that's what he does, huh?" Aden's father turned to look at Leila. "Does he own the business, young lady?"

"Jah. And my older brother works with him."

After that question, Leila phased out of the conversation. Her thoughts shifted from Aden to her past with Samuel, as well as her own insecurities and other issues spiraling within her mind. She twisted her fork in what was left of the casserole to distract from her thoughts, but it was ineffective.

"One of our friend's daughters is planning to get married to someone from the yellow-top community." Aden's mother gave a condescending smile. "Honestly, it's less of a hassle keeping marriage within the communities."

Mr. Troyer nodded. "Some young adults don't know the difficulties of switching to another community and how much it affects everyone in the family. Hopefully, their daughter is aware of that, because I wouldn't know what I'd do if one of you kids decided to join the church of a yellow- or white-top community."

Leila's voice wavered as she rose from her seat and picked up her clear plate. "Excuse me. I may have eaten too much."

After rinsing off her plate and utensils in the kitchen sink, Leila went out the front door and sat on the steps. The hairs on the nape of her neck stiffened, and the humid air wasn't helping much with lowering her body temperature. *I was foolish to even have considered telling him how I felt. There're too many issues, and I knew being from separate communities would be a problem.* Leila covered her face with both hands, but she saw between her fingers something moving across the second-to-bottom step. The long-legged spider walked along the step with an elongated leg tapping along the front. It was similar to a blind person with a walking stick, which reminded her of the blind man she saw selling bird-houses at the flea market. It stopped, motionless, then proceeded to crawl forward.

"Are you okay?" Aden approached her from behind.

Pulling her hands away from her face, Leila propped her arms on the porch and rolled her shoulders back. "Mmm... Fine. Needed some fresh air is all."

"Wanna know something funny?" He sat next to Leila, brushing his hand briefly against hers. "I come out here pretty much every night, and I sit until bedtime."

"Why is that?"

"I've always been intrigued by the stars." Aden pointed toward the night sky. "See the grouping of stars right there? That's a common one most people know."

Leila leaned to the side in the direction where he pointed, gazing with focus. "The Big Dipper."

"Right."

She leaned away from Aden but then gasped. "Wait, I get it now. I know why you chose that card out of all the ones in my store."

"Y–you do?"

"It's because of the design of the card, right? It was covered in star shapes, and it had a verse from the Psalms in relation to the night sky." Leila closed her eyes, tipping her head back. " 'When I consider thy heavens, the work of thy fingers, the moon and the stars, which thou hast ordained; what is man, that thou art mindful of him? and the son of man, that thou visitest him?' "

Aden's eyes gleamed as he rubbed his hands together. "That's from Psalm 8 from what I recall."

"So that's what Sue meant. That you have an interest in the stars." Bobbing her head, she muttered, "It all makes sense now."

Aden touched her arm. "Is something wrong?"

"Plenty is wrong, Aden." She swallowed. "The reason Samuel and I are not on good terms. . ." Leila wasn't sure if she could continue speaking. "When Samuel and I were younger, we were actually friends. Not best friends, but at the time, he was the only person I knew who I considered as such. I was kind of a loner growing up. Guess I still am a loner, now that I think about it."

Aden cast a sidelong glance but fastened his lips.

"Anyway, as I grew fond of him, I. . ." Leila held her stomach as it roiled. Maybe she did eat too much for dinner. "This is embarrassing to say out loud."

"There's no need to be embarrassed."

"Yeah, there is. I ruined your friendship with your best friend."

"That wasn't your fault. Samuel's the one being irrational. You can't blame yourself."

She jammed her heel on the edge of the step. "But it is my

fault! If I never confessed that I liked him, then he wouldn't have a reason to hate me."

"You like Samuel?" Aden was strangely quiet.

"Used to. I don't anymore, but he never liked me. Not even as a friend." Leila pressed her hand on her eyes to fend off the tears that wanted to come. "After I confessed my feelings to Samuel, I overheard him and his friends saying things like, 'Don't tell us you like that weirdo.'"

"Didn't you say anything back to them?"

"I did, and I quickly regretted it. I wasn't the type to defend myself whenever any of the kids teased me. Yet that wasn't enough to stop me from yelling at him. Didn't do me any favors. I was left with remorse and wished desperately to go back and prevent myself from confessing to him."

Leila swallowed to lessen the twinge in the back of her throat, but she wasn't anticipating Aden to embrace her all of a sudden.

"You can't punish yourself for not knowing the outcome of a choice you make. Yes, you should learn from your previous choices, but don't believe the same choice will lead to the same result." He wrapped her in both arms. "There's always an exception to those outcomes as well as there being multiple factors that could drive the result to be different."

Releasing Leila, Aden squeezed her shoulder. "Should you deny yourself the opportunity to be true to yourself when it comes to how you feel about someone?"

Leila tried to keep looking in Aden's eyes, but the warmth in his gaze caused her to break away. She pushed the knuckle of her index finger on her lower lip. "I suppose not."

"Glad you think so because there's something I've got to tell you." Aden's chin trembled as he leaned over to Leila's ear, whispering, "I find you as fascinating as the stars in the night sky."

Leila's ears burned underneath her kapp. "I–I'm not sure what to—"

Before she could say any more, Leila felt his soft lips melting into the hollow of her cheek. She had to fight the urge to flinch back, not because she hated the gesture, but because she didn't know what to do with any of this. Yes, she wanted to be with Aden, yet she wasn't sure if it was appropriate for them to be together under the circumstances.

"Aden, this is. . .I can't exactly describe how I feel right now." Leila pushed on Aden's shoulders to have him meet her gaze. "What about your parents? We're from different communities, and I think they're only okay with us being friends."

"That's too bad then." He placed his hand on hers. "I'm not denying myself the opportunity to be with someone I care about."

All of this was unfolding without warning, and undertaking it in one evening could do a person in. Leila wondered if she should tell Aden that she needed some time to think things over. Then again, what if this is what God intended for her future? What if Aden was who she was meant to be with?

Leila released a sigh then wrapped her fingers around his hand.

"So, you okay with us courting then?" Aden's cheeks were red enough to see in the dim lighting of the night.

It was rather amusing to Leila that, although Aden appeared confident most of the time, he got nervous like she did.

Leila giggled. "Yes. And thank you for caring about me, Aden." *I can only hope your parents don't mess things up.*

CHAPTER 11

State College, Pennsylvania .

It was in mid-October when Aden suggested he and Leila hire a driver and go to State College on a date. They were interested in checking out a farm with a pumpkin patch and corn maze. As Aden sat with Leila in the backseat of their driver's vehicle, his mind was fixed on how he wanted to express how much Leila meant to him but was uncertain how to go about doing it.

He was taken off guard when Leila placed her hand on his. His eyes shifted to the left, not wanting to look right at her, seeing her attention directed to the car window. Aden intertwined his fingers around hers. He smiled while shutting his eyes. *You can do this, Aden. Even if she rejects you, she'll do it gently. Nothing to worry about. You know God is looking out for you.*

Rows of vehicles were lined up in the parking area near the farm. It took some time to find an open spot to park, but a truck pulled out of one nearest to the pumpkin patch.

Getting out of the vehicle, Aden waited for Leila to scoot over to his side. He shut the door when she got out. Aden patted the top of the maroon van. In some ways, he wished he could have a vehicle to drive. He had to admit that a car was a more efficient way to travel. But he wouldn't trade his old buggy for a car. "Thanks for driving us here, Randy."

"No problem. While you guys do your thing, I'm going to pick out a couple of pumpkins to take home to my family."

Leila's brown eyes glistened as she blinked a few times before speaking. "You sure you're okay with waiting for us?"

"Yeah. I have nothing else planned for today." Randy stood with his arms crossed over his leather jacket.

When Randy headed off toward the pumpkin patch, Aden turned to Leila. He noticed a blush tinting her cheeks.

"You're very comfortable with people," she observed.

He stuffed his hands in his pockets. "The best way to make connections with others is by not worrying too much about what they may think of you."

"What if you have been open with others, yet certain people can't stand being around you?" Her expression crumpled like a piece of paper.

"It's good to question your behavior and actions. But if you're blaming yourself for the way others treat you and not for the way you treat others, then you shouldn't worry about it." Removing his hands from his pockets, Aden shook his head. "If they don't want to be around you for being yourself, then you're not gonna get a genuine friendship from whoever you're attempting to appease."

Leila crossed and uncrossed her arms.

"I know you withhold a lot of who you are to protect yourself. But those moments where you're open are the moments I enjoy about you the most." His breath hooked in his chest when tears dribbled down her rose-tinted cheeks. "Hey, are you okay? I didn't mean to—"

"No, Aden. I haven't been okay." Leila's laughter trembled, but her dimples surfaced like craters as she let out a dense breath. "But with time, I know I will be."

Leila's tears caused him to feel vulnerable as well. He reached his hand out to her. "Let's go find some pumpkins."

With their hands linked, they walked toward the pumpkins. All kinds of people were getting their pumpkins—whether with their kids or with friends.

"This one's perfect." Leila leaned over to pick up the pumpkin. "Have you ever tried cutting up a pumpkin before?"

Aden held up his figurative cane and delivered his old man impersonation. "Not since I was a wee young lad."

"Pfft. Not that again."

"Aww, come on. It's some of the best material I have." He gave a forced sigh then chuckled. Leila liked his attempts at being funny. Aden chose a pumpkin. "Since I reached a certain age, I sort of stopped. My sister, however, loves to bake pumpkin pies, so she still does. Honestly, I never mind it. It's amusing to cut the pumpkin and scoop the seeds out."

After they picked out their pumpkins, they went to find Randy and put the pumpkins in the car. Randy sat in the driver's seat and said something about taking a nap. Then Leila and Aden went over to the corn maze where other people had entered. They followed a group but eventually deviated from the path. It had been more than an hour since they'd gone into the corn maze. Aden was sure of it. Leila walked next to him, poking his arm. "I can't believe we've gotten lost."

"We should've brought an object to leave on the ground. I'm sure we've walked by this area before—at least twice."

Quickening her pace, Leila walked in front of him and halted at the wall of corn. "This corn maze is captivating, isn't it? I can't imagine how much preparation went into it."

"Jah. Hopefully, we'll find our way out."

They walked through the maze awhile longer. Aden tried to time himself accordingly—no one else around at the moment, but he grew somewhat faint.

"Leila, could we stop for a second?"

She turned. Slender strands of her auburn hair draped along her forehead. "What is it?"

"I wanted to say that I've cherished the moments we've shared, and I don't. . ." He rubbed his hand down his pants leg. Aden felt like he was having palpitations. "I don't ever want to let go of what we have. I never thought I'd find someone like you, and now that I have—"

"Aden, I know what you're going to say." Leila bit her lip. "I have a habit of hiding how I feel. I always felt like it was easier not to talk about things that are on my mind. But like you said, it's better to be honest with yourself as well as with others. I am worried that our being together will create obstacles in your relationships with your parents or friends."

"That doesn't matter to me. It's not as bad as it may appear to you." His hands quivered as he reached for Leila's, holding them up. "My parents know you're a good person. They're just overprotective. As for Samuel. . . You shouldn't even worry about him."

"I know." Her pupils appeared dilated as she inhaled a breath. "So, you can go ahead and say what you wanted to say to me."

His pulse hammered in his wrists as he separated his hands from Leila's. Aden touched the delicate skin on her cheek, bringing himself closer to her. He wished he were taller, but it was rather pleasant to see her eyes from his level. Aden tipped his head alongside the light-toned surface of her face. "I love you, Leila."

Leila's breaths evaporated against his lips. "I love you too."

That was all Aden needed to bring his lips to hers.

Belleville

On the way home from State College, Leila held Aden's hand again. She was thankful to have finally found someone who understood her. To have someone who loved her for who she was.

"I can't wait to get back and cut up our pumpkins."

"Same here, Leila." He squeezed her hand.

It wouldn't be long until they pulled into her driveway, but Leila didn't want this day to end. Part of her wanted to be back in the corn maze, having Aden's confession on a never-ending loop.

"Wait! What's going on?" Elevating her body from the seat, Leila looked out the windshield to see an ambulance outside her home. She dropped the pumpkin on the middle seat then unclipped her seatbelt. "We've gotta get in there now!" She tore out of the car and hastened up the steps.

"Leon, what happened?" She hurried over to him.

"It's Mamm. Sh—she went into early labor with hard contractions." Leon rubbed his forehead. "We found her on her knees in pain."

"Where's Daed?"

"In the ambulance with Mamm, but they only allow one person. Henry is at a friend's house."

Leila's stomach clenched. She wanted to pretend she had misheard what her brother said.

"What's going on?"

She pivoted around. "Aden, we need to get to the hospital in Lewistown. Can Randy take us there?"

"I'm sure he will." Aden ran to the car.

Dear Lord, Leila prayed, *please let Mamm and the* boppli *be* okay.

CHAPTER 12

Faces Leila recognized from the area had gathered near the opening of her mother's grave. Leila's heart felt frozen, and the tips of her fingers were numb. It had been three days since her mother's passing. When Leila and Aden arrived at the hospital, they were informed that Mom had experienced postpartum hemorrhage, which was caused by the uterus not contracting sufficiently. Her mother had lost too much blood, and her soul had withdrawn from the body only an hour later.

Leila got to say goodbye, but she still couldn't believe Mom had died. The scene remained vivid in Leila's mind: the vitality of her porcelain skin and the bruising on her lower hand where they placed an IV in her vein. Despite all that, Mom's smile was as radiant as it had always been.

Yesterday, with the coffin at their home, others came to pay their respects and view Mom one last time. The coffin exposed the upper part of her body, and Leila could only think of how her mother gave the impression of purity clothed in white. Friends and neighbors had come to their home, all dressed in black attire, sitting in silence in the living room and kitchen. Having so many people in the house at one time was overwhelming. Mollie and Aden came to give their condolences and provide her with support. It helped Leila to have her friends there during that time.

Her body stiffened when a hand touched her shoulder. Leila felt certain it was her father but didn't check since she was too focused on what was happening in front of her. One of the ministers read a customary hymn as the pallbearers piled the soil over the casket.

Leila's vision was obscured by a dreamlike haze. She blinked and looked at her father. Tears trickled down the hairs of his beard. Henry held Dad's hand, rubbing his eye with an unsmiling face. Leila felt the pain emanating from them. Grieving was a good thing, but that sense of disbelief was burdensome. Even with all of this happening, it didn't seem real. She wanted to hug her mother, missing how safe she'd felt whenever she was around. She wanted to hear Mom's endearing laughter again. Never had Leila realized until now how someone's passing could affect the lives of those who remained.

When they covered the grave with the last bit of soil, Leila looked down at the tiny sibling in her arms. Months ago, Mom had chosen the name Elsie if the baby was a girl. The infant's petite lips stretched open, letting out a noise, but her eyes remained closed. Leila brought Elsie close to her chest. *I'm thankful you made it into this world. You are loved, little Elsie. I'll do everything I can to show how much I love you.*

The following day, Leila sat in the living room with her father. Henry played quietly in his room, and Elsie slept peacefully in the bassinet. A somber tone had settled over the entire house.

Leila's eyes felt puffy. She glanced over at her father's hazel eyes, drooping as he lay in his recliner. Everyone in the family made themselves push to get through the funeral.

She thought about it when strolling through the yard in the early morning. Mom's flowers were all but done blooming, and the ones that remained were fading with the changes of fall. The garden was left uninhabited, its bare ground exposed to the elements.

Leila wasn't aware she had dozed off until she awoke to Dad closing the footrest of his recliner. The thud of the springs retracting echoed through the room.

"I must have fallen asleep." She rubbed at the crust that had formed around her eyes.

Dad leaned forward. "I was only relaxing, but I thought I heard a couple of buggies pull in just now."

"Oh, really?"

About then, some muffled chatter came from outside, followed by a knock at the door.

"I better go and see who it is." Her father stood from his chair then went over to open the door. "Hello, ladies. I wasn't expecting anyone."

Leila peered from behind her father to see who it was. The first two women she knew because they were friends of her mother's, but she'd only recently seen the other woman at church. Sarah and her sister, Jean, introduced the woman who accompanied them.

"This is our friend, Sally Petersheim. She's Susan Renno's sister and lives with her family in the black-top community." Sarah gestured with her elbow since her hands held a box with what Leila assumed to be food.

"Nice to meet you, Sally." Dad shook her hand. "Won't you please come in?"

When they came in with their items, Sarah spoke again. "We brought your family some food."

"Danki." Leila rubbed her hand on the front of her dress.

"Yes, thank you for thinking of us," Dad agreed. "You can set those things down on the kitchen table."

Jean raised her dish and grinned. "This is a chocolate pudding dessert. It'll need to stay cold."

"We have an ice-filled chest to put everything in." Leila led Jean to the kitchen. Lifting the lid, Jean placed the dessert on the top rack.

Sarah stepped over to the chest. "I made pulled barbecue pork, and it's in this container. There are also sandwich rolls in the bag I placed on the table."

Dad walked into the room. "We appreciate you doing this for us."

"Sally made a dutch apple pie this morning." Sarah's eyes trailed over to Sally, who stood next to the doorframe.

Sally held on to the pie and looked at Leila. "Would you rather it set out or be put in the ice chest?"

Dad glanced over at Sally and smiled. "If you don't mind, it can be left out."

"Okay, no problem." Sally set the pie on the table and moved over by Jean.

Sarah asked her sister if she would go out to the buggy for another box. "There's one more person who made you something to eat."

Jean went out and returned with a cardboard box. "Here's a chicken-and-rice casserole from Sally's sister, Susan."

"There's some chocolate-chip cookies in the gallon-sized baggie. Your little boy might like those," Sally commented.

Leila clasped her hands together. "We like them too."

When Henry wandered into the room, he trotted over to their father. Dad scooped him up in his arms, where the young boy melted into his father's embrace. Leila could tell Henry missed Mamm. It almost caused her to choke up, but she bit the end of her tongue. Leila needed to keep strong for her family.

The buggies were gone not long after, leaving behind all that food for Leila's family. At least some of Leila's stress had been lifted. She now had less to prepare for supper. Leila went over to the chair where her mother used to sit, tracing her finger along the arm before sitting down. *I don't know what I'm going to do without you, Mamm.*

Later that evening, Leila took out the pulled pork to heat in the oven. There was plenty to divide up for another evening, and Leila was thankful another meal was taken care of. She grabbed another dish from the cupboard and divided the meat between the two containers.

Dad came into the room, holding Elsie. "I came in to see if there was any coffee left, but the pot's empty."

"Would you like me to make another pot?" Leila went to the other room to put away the extra pulled pork.

"If you wouldn't mind." Her dad raised the foil, awkwardly holding the baby to peek at the pie.

Leila stepped over, pulled the foil off, and set it aside. "I think I know what you're having for dessert."

"Am I that transparent?" His lips quivered. "Your brother fell asleep in his room. I'll need help making the baby's formula. I'm going to feed her."

"All right. I'll get out the powder and mix it into a new bottle." Leila turned on the oven to heat the pork then took out the canister to mix the formula. "I can bring the bottle out to you in the living room when I'm done."

"That's fine." Her dad cradled Elsie, speaking to her with a hushed voice.

Leila got started as they went out of the room. The formula powder sometimes drifted all over the countertop, and it certainly didn't smell as appealing as cow's milk, but Elsie drank it. Leila used a funnel and poured in the powder then added the water and watched as the flour-like substance dissolved. She gave it a good shaking until the liquid was no longer clear. *This looks ready for my little sister.*

She brought out the bottle to the living room and passed it to Dad. Henry wandered into the room, yawning, and went for his father.

"Here, goofball. Come sit with me."

He hurried over to Leila, and she slid him onto her lap. They sat and watched their little sister's eyes slowly close as she sucked the formula from the bottle.

Leila whispered, "She is so sweet. Isn't she, Daed?"

"Jah. She reminds me of when you and Henry were this size."

"Not Leon though?"

"Nah, he was a fussy child. Always hungry."

Leila chuckled. She could only imagine what her parents went through whenever Leon needed food.

Henry looked up at Leila and then at the baby, but he didn't say anything. He hadn't said much since the day Mom passed away.

Dad sat on the couch for a moment but then he rose. "It would be better if I rocked her."

"She'd like that." Leila gently bounced her brother. "I'll need to get up soon, Henry. Gotta heat up our premade supper." Leila wiggled her feet. "I can't wait to try some of that dessert. Bet it tastes really good."

"I'm in the mood for some coffee. Could you please make me a cup?" Dad asked.

Leila bounced Henry a little more. "Oh, right. I forgot."

"Could you also heat up some vegetables to go with our supper?" Dad rocked Elsie in the chair.

"Sure, I can find something in the pantry." Leila scooted Henry off her lap and tousled his hair.

In the kitchen, Leila stepped over to the pantry door. When she went to open it, her hand brushed against Mom's black apron. She stopped and lifted it off the hook. *It wasn't that long ago when she had this on.* Leila gripped the apron and opened the pantry door. The moment she entered the space, she smelled Mom's homemade lavender sachet that hung by a purple bow on a nail. She stared at all the contents on the shelves. *Mamm took such care in putting up plenty of food for her family.* There was an array of mason jars full of fruits she had canned at the beginning of the year. Mom's lovely penmanship adorned every jar. The small room felt like her. Leila closed the door behind her and allowed the tears to flow. Her chest had felt hollow for days.

Why, Lord? Why did You take her away from us? Leila knelt to the floor in fear of anyone hearing her break down. She shouldn't blame God for her mother's passing, and she should be grateful Mom was no longer suffering. But in that moment of doubt, Leila's negative thoughts were at the forefront. How long could she go on pretending that everything was okay?

CHAPTER 13

A month had passed since the funeral, and the days were growing colder. Leaves had piled up in the yard, so Leila went to rake during her and Mollie's lunch break. Mollie sat on the porch with Elsie in her arms. Leila occasionally looked up to see if everything was okay, sometimes seeing Mollie sticking her tongue out and stretching her mouth in goofy ways. Mollie spent most of the day attempting to get Elsie to laugh but to no avail.

"Are you sure you don't want me to make you something to eat, Leila?" Mollie called.

Flipping the rake over, Leila slid off a few leaves from the prongs and dropped them over the pile. The array of shades, from red to yellow, would normally appeal to her, but instead it was a reminder that not many weeks had gone by since her mother's death.

Leila approached the porch, kneeling to Elsie's level, and gave her plump face a gentle pinch. "I'm about done. But no, I don't need anything."

After Leila put the rake away, she and Mollie went over to the shop. She fumbled for the key in her coat pocket and unlocked the door. It felt good to be immersed in warmth when they entered the store.

Mollie handed Elsie to Leila. "I've got the cash register covered."

"Thank you." Heading over to the worktable, Leila lifted her chin and looked at the cards hanging above. "I worked on some of these last night before bed, so we won't have to worry about replenishing cards today."

Not many customers had come into the shop in the early part of the day. With the weather growing cold, most people preferred to stay at home and keep warm. But that didn't stop customers coming in after they were finished with work or picking their kids up from school.

"I'm buying these stamps for when I make Christmas cards." The English lady at the cash register held one of them up. "I love this holly one the most out of the batch."

Leila was in the middle of feeding Elsie formula when the customer looked her way.

"What a cute baby! Those brown eyes are so beautiful. Just like her mom's. You have a lovely child."

"Actually. . ." Leila was on the verge of correcting her but figured it would be best not to say anything. "Thank you."

Later on, a few other people came into the store either browsing the shelves or making purchases. Elsie fell asleep in Leila's arms, breathing through her little mouth. It brought back memories of Henry when he was that little. But in those memories, her mother was holding her young brother. How sad that Elsie wouldn't have Mom to raise her up to adulthood.

Leila's thoughts went to Aden. She hadn't gone anywhere

with him in several weeks and only saw him whenever he got off work. She also worried about her friend investing too much time helping her with Elsie. Leila faced an abundance of problems to sort through, but instead of keeping them to herself, Leila spoke. "Hey, Mollie?"

"What is it?"

"Elsie doesn't have a mother to take care of her. I'm all she's got." Leila bent forward to readjust herself on the chair. "And I feel terrible about dragging you into helping with her."

"Leila, I want to be here for you and your baby sister. You were there for me when I was struggling. I'm your friend, and friends should always be there for one another, especially during times like these."

"But there's Aden to think about too. I've put him through having to argue with his parents about our relationship. Then there's..." Spots flashed in her vision, obscuring her sight momentarily. Leila pressed her forehead. "I gotta think about what's best for Elsie's future as well as Henry's. I can't even consider getting married and moving to Aden's community when I have my family to worry about. They need me, and..."

Mollie stroked Leila's back, and Leila gave in to her tears. She wiped the moisture under her eyes with her palm, not wanting to disrupt her sister's nap. *I've got to do what's right. I have to be there for my family.* Her throat and lungs grew sore, and her eyes dried from the lack of blinking. *Please understand what I'm going to do when you get here, Aden.*

Aden was glad he was done working for the day. While he no

longer had to deal with the intensity of the sun, he would have felt more comfortable in the cold temperatures if he hadn't left his jacket at the restaurant where he ate lunch. Because someone had taken the jacket from the restaurant, he had to head home to pick up another one before visiting Leila.

When he arrived at Leila's home, he saw Leila on the porch with Elsie. Henry was running around in the yard with one of the chickens. Aden hitched Chance to the post and patted the horse before heading to the porch.

"Hello, Leila." Aden leaned over and gave a little wave. "Hello, Elsie."

Elsie's pink gums showed as she smiled at him.

"Aden, can we talk?"

He rubbed his jaw as he straightened his spine. "About?"

"Some things." Leila stood, biting her lip. "Let me put Elsie in her crib first."

She staggered to the front door and went in. Aden sat on the swinging seat and clutched both hands on the cushion. Something was wrong.

"Aden!"

He turned to see Henry at the bottom of the steps with a chicken in his grasp.

"I caught Teapot. See?" He lifted the chicken over his head. "She's the fastest chicken out of all of them."

Aden chuckled and gave him a thumbs-up. "Nice one, kid. Impressive."

He heard the door unfasten and looked to see Leila push it closed.

"Follow me." Leila went down the steps and brushed her

fingers through her brother's broom-like hair. "Daed and Leon will be home soon, so please put the *hinkel* down and go wash up."

Henry put Teapot on the gravel. As the chicken bolted off to the lawn, Henry ran into the house.

Aden took a seat beside Leila on the porch. He reached over and clasped her hand. "What do you wanna talk about?"

"You know how we've talked about our future together? And how I said I would move to your community if we were to get married?"

"I remember."

"I've been thinking a lot about this, and I've been worried about Elsie. I want to do what's best for her."

"You're doing plenty for her, considering the circumstances."

"I've been concerned for you too, Aden. I know you do your best to focus on the now but—"

"Hey, Leila. I already told you that I want to be with you. Nothing else matters."

"But it does!" Leila stiffened. "It does matter."

When she lowered her head, Aden tightened his grip on her cold hand. His uncertainty bled through, and he felt weighed down. He wanted to break the silence between them but didn't know what to say that could rectify the situation.

"Aden, I can't leave my family when I'm the only one here who can take care of my younger siblings. Without Mamm, they have no one. My daed works long hours, and my brother and his wife have their own problems to worry about. It's all on me."

"When the time comes for us to decide on marriage, I can leave my community if I have to."

"I wouldn't want you to do that." Leila slid her hand away,

looking straight into his eyes. "I love you, Aden. But I don't want to continue this relationship when it can't go any further." A tear dripped off the top of her pale eyelashes. "You have your family to worry about, and you can't afford to leave when they don't want you to."

Aden couldn't prevent his body from trembling. Part of him knew Leila was right, but he could not bring himself to respond. Instead, he brought his arms around her. He was afraid she would tell him not to hug her, but Leila hugged Aden back.

"I'm sorry. I'm really sorry, Aden." Leila's chin rested on his shoulder.

Aden hitched a breath, sniffing as he hugged her tighter. "I'll miss you."

"Me too."

He couldn't believe they would no longer be together, but he had to respect her decision—no matter how bad it hurt.

CHAPTER 14

Leila trod inches upon inches in the fresh snow from last night's storm. It was near the end of January, and the wind blowing through the valley seemed to have escalated. It raised the hairs on Leila's neck. She focused her attention on the driveway, gripping the end of the shovel. If she didn't have gloves on, her fingers would most likely be frostbitten. "Can't believe it piled up to almost a foot high." Leila spoke to herself as she buried her face in the woolly scarf to evade the sting of the breeze.

Thankfully, today was Saturday, which meant Leila wasn't going to work in the store. Mollie said she would be visiting her in the early afternoon. But Leila wasn't sure that would happen now that the roads were covered by snow, especially given that Mollie would be traveling all the way from Reedsville. Hopefully, the roads would be cleared later.

Leila covered her nose with her gloved hand and dragged the end of the shovel as she walked down the driveway. *I need a break from shoveling. Besides, Elsie is probably awake by now.*

CO

"See? You just thread the needle through here," Mollie chirped as she lifted the embroidery hoop, which stretched the material. "And that's how you do a chain stitch."

Leila had been learning embroidery from Mollie for months, and she was designing a more intricate pattern to stitch. It reduced her stress, especially before she went to bed. Leila had been dealing with insomnia, but she had also been getting up to take care of Elsie whenever she awakened in the middle of the night. Sometimes, Leila couldn't get back to sleep.

Leila straightened her back, stretching the muscles in her shoulders. "Hey, Mollie. Maybe we should stop and check on Elsie."

"Good idea." Mollie placed her embroidered cloth on the nightstand. "I wonder if I should head home soon. It'll be time for supper when I get back."

Leila leaned forward to catch Mollie's gaze. "You are welcome to have supper with me and my siblings."

"Your dad is eating out again?"

"Jah, with that woman who dropped by with her friends the day after Mamm's funeral." Leila stumbled to her feet. "I've been concerned about them seeing so much of each other lately. Something tells me that Sally and Daed may be more than just friends."

"You think so?"

"Not for sure, but I have a hunch." Leila twiddled the end of the needle with her fingers. "Regardless of how I may feel about it, I'm glad he's showing signs of some happiness."

"But what about you, Leila? Don't you want to be happy?"

Leila attempted to muster up an enthusiastic response, but she couldn't pretend she was happy. She sighed. "I tried to be. . . ."

As they went to the living room, Leila remembered what she'd thought about back in October—worrying less about the future and focusing on the now. Perhaps Aden had been in her life to prepare her for when she found the right person. But another part of Leila doubted herself. What if breaking things off with Aden had been the wrong choice?

Leila strolled over to the playpen and saw that her sister was sleeping soundly. There was an unwritten rule of never waking a sleeping baby, so Leila left Elsie alone and slumped to the couch.

A short period of conversation lapsed into silence. Leila wasn't aware of how much she had sunk into the couch until she repositioned herself. Her thoughts piled up like the snow she shoveled in the morning.

"Something on your mind, Leila?" Mollie asked.

"I still love Aden, but I can't interfere with his life. If circumstances were different, I wouldn't have made the choice to break up with him." She brought her folded hands to her neck. "I don't know what to do, Mollie. Even if I wanted Aden back, I'm not sure if he'd—"

A knock sounded from the front door, which caught Leila off guard. *Maybe Daed canceled his plans this evening.* When Leila pulled the door open, she almost leaped out of her skin. "S–Samuel?"

"Hello, Leila."

She winced, feeling as if she'd been struck in the head with a hammer. "D–do you have the wrong address?"

"I would say no." He pinched the suspender showing near the

opening of his jacket. "Would you mind if I talked with you for a moment?"

As if it were perfectly timed, Elsie started crying.

"I've gotta take care of Elsie. Can't leave her alone by herself."

"But I'm here, Leila. I'll watch her," Mollie said.

Leila gripped the doorknob, feeling rather hot considering the cold from the open door creeping inside.

"May I come in? I don't know if you've noticed, but it's freezing out here."

"I suppose."

Mollie lifted Elsie from the playpen. "I'll leave you two alone. Would you mind if I went back to your room?"

"I don't mind."

As soon as her friend left with Elsie, the pressure around Leila's eyes doubled. *Why did Samuel decide to visit? Did Aden send him? No, that wouldn't make sense.*

Samuel shut the door, trailing behind him bits of melted snow from his boots. "I'm sorry about your mother passing away. It must be difficult for your family."

Leila hauled herself over to her mother's chair. "It certainly hasn't been easy."

"And you and Aden not being a couple." Samuel sat down on the couch and placed his hat next to him, revealing his light brown hair.

"It must make being friends with him less of a problem."

"Actually, just the opposite." He cleared his throat. "Aden hasn't stopped talking about you."

Leila stared at Samuel for a few seconds to process his words. "R–really?"

"Whenever Aden brings you up, he goes into great detail. He can only speak positively about you, and well. . ."

Leila watched as Samuel angled his body away from her. He had a perpetual slouch as he sat with his fingers clinging to his knees. She wasn't sure if urging Samuel to speak would be a good idea, so she clenched her jaw and waited. Having Samuel sitting in her living room drained any energy she had left. She didn't want to deal with any more stress.

"Do you know why I didn't defend you back when we were younger?"

Leila shrugged her shoulders. "Because you saw me as a weirdo who drew too much in her notebook?"

"It was because I had a hard time admitting that I liked you."

A rush of adrenaline flowed through Leila's body as she cocked her head. She couldn't believe what had come out of Samuel's mouth. "Are you serious?"

Samuel nodded but didn't look at her. "Back then, I allowed my friends to influence my way of thinking. I did like you, but when you said you liked me, I was afraid of what would occur if I were honest. That's why I told my friends about what you said—to see how they'd respond."

"Still wasn't right of you to do that, Samuel." Leila rubbed her eyes. "At least you had friends to back you up. I had no one."

"I know."

"And I thought we were friends, but then you pulled the rug out from under me."

"I made the wrong choice, and I've regretted it since."

Leila crossed her arms. "That's why you treated me terribly when you saw me at the singing event?"

"I didn't know how to approach you, so I resorted to criticizing you. For what it's worth, I'm sorry for the way I treated you. I don't expect you to forgive me, but I needed to apologize for what I did."

At his words, Leila had a moment of clarity about how she handled her emotions. She'd never forgotten what people said about her or the way others had treated her. By continually worrying about things she couldn't change, she had harbored guilt and anger within her soul. The reason she couldn't move forward was because she never forgave the people who had wronged her, and it caused her to not forgive herself either. Leila blamed herself because it was the only way she could rationalize everything that had happened to her. It was her way of feeling like she was in control.

"Samuel?"

He lifted his head.

"I forgive you." Leila had her hands loosely clasped in her lap. "I appreciate you being honest with me."

Sighing, Samuel mouthed the words *thank you* as he lowered his gaze and grinned. Seeing how relieved he was reminded her of the Samuel she'd known when she was younger.

He lifted his head. "So you and Aden aren't courting, huh?"

When Leila figured out why Samuel asked that question, she busted out laughing. "No, Samuel, and I thought you were with someone. That's what Aden told me anyway."

"We're no longer together. I've been alone for almost a month." Leila shook her head. "You had your chance, Samuel."

"I know. It's because you love Aden." Samuel picked up his hat by the brim and pulled it onto his head. "Then you shouldn't have broken up with him."

Leila rocked in the chair after Samuel left. She couldn't stop thinking about Aden and how she wanted to speak to him, to reconcile their relationship. *But I can't do that when I have the future of my siblings to think about. While things may be okay between me and Samuel now, I have to think about my little sister and brother. It seems that's God's plan for me.*

On Monday morning, Aden stirred from his sleep. When he opened his eyes, his room was shrouded in darkness. He rolled over and fought the yearning to fall back asleep. He had to get ready for work, but it seemed almost impossible for him to get out of bed. Part of it was from the wintry landscape that awaited him, but that didn't bother him as much as not being able to see Leila. Once his eyes adapted to the dark, Aden lifted the covers and began getting ready. He shambled down the stairs, hearing some commotion coming from the kitchen. Peering in, he saw his sister rummaging the pantry.

"Sorry, Aden. Was I too loud? Did I wake our parents too?"

"Nah, you're fine. The cold woke me up." Aden chuckled. "What are you doing in here at four in the morning?"

Sue shrugged. "My stomach woke me up, so I wanted to make myself an early breakfast. I can make you something too."

"That's all right. I'm not hungry yet."

"Okay." She turned her attention back to making her breakfast. "Let me know if you change your mind."

Before Aden had the chance to walk away, Sue gripped his shoulder. "Aden, don't you miss Leila?"

"I do. I've missed her so much." He grimaced.

Putting an arm around his shoulder, Sue gave him a hug. "I miss her too."

They stood in silence and then Aden confided, "I have thought about seeing her again, but I don't know if she would want to see me."

"Aden, you're being silly." Sue unraveled her arms and gave him a stern look. "Of course she wants to see you."

"How do you know?"

"Because if she didn't want to see you, she would have moved on." Her smile wavered. "You know she still cares for you."

That was the only reassurance he needed. "I'm gonna go see her." Aden hurried out of the kitchen and grabbed his coat off the rack.

Aden hurried up the steps of Leila's home, lifting his hand to the door. *You can do this, Aden.* But he couldn't find it in him to knock. *This isn't right. Leila probably wouldn't appreciate me being here.*

He turned from the door, holding his arms against his torso. What if Leila didn't want to see him? What if she was too fixated on her commitment to her siblings?

"Aden."

He turned around. She was holding the front door open with her winter clothes over her long dress. Aden wanted to wrap Leila in his arms, but he held back. "Hey, Leila. Good morning—"

She rushed into Aden's arms. It felt like an electric jolt striking him, and his pulse quickened as he clung to her. "Leila, I know you're worried about how the future will play out, but I'll leave my community. I just want to be with you."

After a while, they let go of each other, and Leila tugged her plaid scarf around her mouth. "I shouldn't overthink the future when I don't know what'll happen. I'm sorry for giving up on us."

"You don't need to apologize. You were only thinking about others before yourself. But I am willing to do the same. I'll do anything to stay with you." Aden brought his gloved hand to Leila's face. "I love you so much."

Leila grabbed his hand and pulled him close, kissing him without hesitation. Aden had seen so much growth from Leila as a person. She had learned to trust in letting things happen rather than worrying over uncertainty. His hopes soared, but there was still the problem of Mom and Dad. How would they respond when he told them he wanted to join the yellow-top community to be with Leila?

CHAPTER 15

Six months later

Leila gripped Aden's hand as they sat and stared at the stars on a lovely summer night. She couldn't believe it had been almost half of a year since they'd gotten back together. Plenty of things had happened since that winter morning.

Leon's wife, Judy, gave birth to their baby girl in late March, and it was an emotional time for the entire family. They decided to name their first child Darla, in honor of Mom.

Not long after, Leila's father admitted that he had been courting Sally for over a month, though that wasn't much of a surprise since Leila had had her suspicions. Sally visited Dad quite often, and Henry had become quite close to her. She brought goodies for him to take to school and even fed the chickens with him. It was good seeing her brother having fun and being his goofy self again.

Leila had been able to see Aden more often because of Sally taking care of Elsie. Not only that, but Judy came by with little Darla to visit on weekends. Elsie was only five months older than Judy and Leon's baby, so Leila wondered if they would become friends when they got older.

Something Leila had thought about for a while was how she'd overheard Sally and Dad talking about getting married sometime this year. Leila couldn't understand why her father would want to marry Sally less than a year since her mother's passing. As much as Leila was thankful for Sally making her father happy, she felt it was all too soon for him to remarry.

"Leila?"

Her eyes widened. *Oh goodness. Here I am worrying about this when I should be enjoying my time with Aden.*

Slanting her head, Leila pressed her lips against his cheekbone. She couldn't fathom how much merriment had filled her over the past few months. She had made friendships with people who cared for her as much as she cared for them. Although Leila thought about her mother a lot, she had come to accept her death and felt grateful Mom was in a better place. Trials and tribulations were applied to people's lives for a purpose that couldn't always be understood in the moment. Leila had concluded that her experiences had taught her to strive to do the right thing and not allow her skepticism to get the best of her.

I should be honest about my concerns with Daed and Sally. Leila pulled away from Aden, looking down at the grass.

"Something is troubling you, huh?"

"Do you think it's too soon for my daed to remarry? He and Sally were talking about getting married, and. . .I don't know. Sally is a good person and cares for Henry and Elsie a lot, but I'm not sure. . ."

"You're not sure if you can see her as your mother?"

"Jah. Sally is great, and she's done plenty for my family, but it's difficult for me to get over my mamm's passing."

Aden patted her knee. "You don't need to get over it, Leila. You loved your mother, and it's normal to feel the way you're feeling toward someone who isn't your mother."

"I miss her very much, Aden. She was the only friend I had when I was alone as a kid. She was the one who got me to go to the singing events in the first place."

"Have you talked to Sally about how you miss your mother?"

"I haven't. Even if I'm not fully comfortable with them getting married, I don't want to ruin their opportunity for happiness."

"You should share your concerns with them. Just to let them know where you stand."

"I suppose."

"Besides, we wouldn't be sitting here together right now if it weren't for Sally coming into your family's life and being so helpful."

Leila bit her bottom lip. "True."

She leaned on Aden's shoulder as she pondered everything. *I just don't know if I could see Sally as my mother. But wouldn't I ruin their relationship by expressing my concerns? Wouldn't it be better for me not to say anything?*

That evening after supper, Leila decided to speak with Sally and her father about their marriage plans. She saw Dad sleeping in the living room before she headed outdoors to look for Sally. She walked around the side of the house and found Sally holding Elsie and standing near one of the flowerbeds. Henry stood beside Sally, observing a bumblebee collecting nectar. It seemed like an intimate moment with the three of them sharing quality time.

Sally turned to Leila and smiled. "Hello, Leila. You should

come see this big bee."

Grinning widely, Henry tried to touch the buzzing insect.

"Don't put your fingers too close to it," Leila warned. "The bee can sting you."

"That's right. You can watch the bee; that's okay. But don't touch him." Sally held Elsie in a firm grip.

"I'd like to talk to you and my daed about something."

Sally's forehead wrinkled. "This sounds important."

"Yes, it concerns all of us." Leila looked toward the house. "We can go inside to talk."

"The last time I saw Daed, he was in the living room." Leila led the way into the house.

Dad still sat in his chair but was awake now. "Oh, I see everyone decided to come back indoors."

"Your daughter would like to talk to us." Sally sat on the couch next to Leila's father.

Henry went to Dad, wanting to sit on the couch with them. Taking a seat in her mother's rocker, Leila crossed her ankles and waited until they were ready.

"What would you like to talk about, Daughter?" Dad put Henry on his lap.

"It is about you and Sally. Awhile ago, I overheard you talking about marriage."

"You mean when I mentioned my niece, Rose Mary, getting married next month? She said she and Kevin wouldn't mind you all coming along with me to the wedding."

"Ah, no." Leila's blood rushed through her skin. "I meant. . . what you and Daed said about you two getting married. I know you have been courting since late winter, but it seems too soon for you to be talking marriage."

Sally remained silent. Dad looked her way and nodded.

"That is true. We've been discussing the topic." Her father tugged at his beard. "You probably weren't ready to hear us speaking that way about each other."

"I was stunned to hear it but not too surprised. You two have grown quite close these past months."

"I've been taking my time to mourn your mamm because we all need that. But it is also necessary to move on. And lately I've noticed how much Sally has become more and more a part of this household."

Leila shifted in the rocking chair, gazing at Sally's brown eyes glistening while holding baby Elsie. It was strange how Elsie's eyes mimicked Sally's.

Dad spoke up again. "I've also noticed how much you have been seeing Aden lately. The two of you seem to be getting along good, am I right?"

"Yes, we enjoy being with each other." Leila rested a hand on her chin. "Aden and I like to talk about our thoughts and interests."

"I have that with Sally too. We have a lot in common, and I only want what is best for this family."

Leila looked away, squeezing her eyes shut as she dragged her fingers down her face.

"Change for all of us will take time, Daughter. We need to pray and trust that God will help us through this adjustment. Right now, this is something new for all of us, and in time we can work through it with the Lord's help. Knowing your mamm, I know she would want me to find happiness and get married again."

Elsie began to fuss and squirm a little. "Someone is due for a diaper change." Sally rose and headed to the baby's room.

Leila had a lot to think about. Dad seemed ready to begin a new life with Sally. This would be a big change for her and the family. Leila would continue to pray for guidance and wisdom for them and herself.

CHAPTER 16

Leila went down the hallway, carrying Elsie, to check on Henry. She found him playing in his room with his toys. Henry looked over and smiled at them while holding on to a toy chicken.

She halted in the hallway, viewing the embroidered family tree hanging on the wall. Leila looked at the newly embroidered part, where she had included her little sister's name. Tilting her chin, she lightly tapped Elsie's round nose. "You're a part of our family, little Elsie."

Leila reflected on when she'd talked with Sally and her father a few weeks ago. Dad was no different. He needed to move forward with life and not be held down by the past. Sally held the key to his future and for the rest of their family. Leila had to admit Sally added warmth to the house again. Not in the way her mom had—no one could ever replace Leila's dear mother.

As she stood there, smiling to herself, a muffled knocking came from the front door. *I wonder who that could be.* She opened the door.

"Hi, Leila." Mollie smiled.

"Hello. Come right on in."

Mollie walked in with a box under her arm. "I thought I'd

stop by and show you these different samples of cards."

"Thank you. Have a seat. My daed is out and my brother is upstairs playing."

"Okay." Mollie placed the box down and took a seat.

Leila plucked a few cards from the box. "What a neat idea. This one replicates an embroidery design. It inspires me to want to try something like this."

"That's why I picked them out for you. I knew you'd like them. You can keep those."

Leila set the cards aside and sat with the baby. "Can you visit, or will you have to go soon?"

"I've got time right now, so we can talk." Mollie sank into the couch cushion. Her olive-green dress blended with the shade of her eyes. "I wanted to tell you some good news. My father has gotten a job."

"That is very good news."

"He's working for a roofing contractor and is quite pleased with the number of hours they work."

"I'm so happy for you guys. That's an answered prayer."

Beaming, Mollie's eyes followed Leila as she sat back down. "Anything new happening in your life?"

"It's the same around here. I've been less busy these days with Sally's help." She paused. "I'm hoping she'll make a good step-mother to me and my siblings. She is a good match for my daed."

"I'm sure you've prayed about it and spent time in the Word."

"I have. I pray daily for my family as well as for guidance."

"That's good." Mollie tapped her chin with her index finger. "It helps me when I read scripture and pray whenever I have some time to myself. When life gets at its worst or drags us down, reading God's Word provides guidance on good living."

Leila remembered the scripture written in the card Aden bought when he first visited her store. Psalm 8:3–4. It was a reminder that God was always looking out for her, and everything that happened in her life was for a greater purpose. Leila had let go of her past and forgiven those who had hurt her.

Later in the afternoon, before Daed went out to take care of the animals, he walked into the living room with Sally, bringing Elsie to Leila. "There she is, wide awake and ready to help you ladies out."

"Thanks for changing her diaper, Sally." She stepped over to her father and he passed Elsie over.

Sally placed her hands on her hips and nodded. "No problem."

"I'm going out and bringing Henry with me." Dad took hold of Henry's hand when he came over to him. "Okay, Son. Let's go do some work." They headed out the door, and Henry stumbled, looking back at Leila.

"That Henry is adorable." Sally chuckled.

Leila watched them head toward the barn. Then she looked down at her baby sister gazing up at her. Elsie smiled, showing a few baby teeth poking out of her gums.

"I picked up some groceries and got everything we need. Your father hinted about having a pie later on," Sally said.

"What kind are we gonna make?"

"I thought of a chocolate cream pie. We could make another kind if you'd rather."

Leila thought. "How about an apple pie? It's Daed's favorite any time of year."

"Well, let's get started on the apple since it'll take longer to make." Sally grabbed the plastic bag filled with apples from the fridge chest.

After Leila went to place her sister in her playpen, they got out all the utensils and ingredients and set to work. Leila was glad they had this time to visit.

"We also picked up some ice cream and whipping cream. Thought it would go well with the pies."

"That sounds good." Leila cut the dough for the crusts.

"These apples smell good and are in nice shape. Not a bruise yet." Sally peeled and sliced them. Sally sighed. "Being here with your family means a lot to me. Since I never had any children with my first husband, I'm new at the possibility of being a mom and stepmother." She relaxed her shoulders. "Do you still have some doubts about this? I would understand it if you did."

"I did wrestle with you and Daed being together, but I've now accepted the idea of you marrying my daed." Swallowing, Leila gazed over at Sally. "I want you both to be as happy as I am with Aden."

"Thank you, Leila, for your honesty. I appreciate it a lot."

Leila smiled. *I hope things will work out for all of us. I'd like to be a whole family again.*

"The meal was great. Thanks for inviting me to join you this evening." Aden looked over at Leila and grinned.

"You're welcome." She smiled in return.

"Since everyone is through eating, why don't we clear the table and let the dishes soak in the sink," Sally suggested. "It would be nice just to sit in the living room and visit for a while."

"Sounds good to me." Leila's father jumped up and picked up several dishes from the table. Everyone else did the same. Once the dishes were soaking, they all found seats in the living room.

Sally sat with Leila's sister-in-law, both cradling the babies in Leila's family. Henry sat on Leila's lap, and Aden visited with Leon for a while.

Aden leaned his elbow on the arm of his chair. *I'm not sure how tonight is going to play out. I want to spend the rest of my life with her by my side.* He swallowed against the lump in his throat. *I may be nervous, but I know I can do this.*

Leading the way, Aden held Leila's hand as they walked down the road. The sun was setting over the hills of the valley, and gentle winds blew as they arrived at their usual spot to watch the stars.

Aden sat on the grass, waiting for Leila to join him. "Do you know why I brought you here tonight?"

"Because it's what we do most nights when we're together."

"Yeah. I recall when it was only me sitting outside by myself." Aden cuffed his chin. "Well, Sue did sometimes. Only if there were fireflies."

Leila laughed, revealing the dimples near her mouth. "I can't blame her. They're captivating."

"Kinda like you." Aden winked. "Except you're not a flying insect."

"I hope not." She brought her hand up to her forehead, sweeping away a loose strand of hair. "So why did you bring me here then?"

"Leila, I know you're concerned for the future and what may happen, but like I said before, I'm willing to leave my community in order for us to be together."

Her eyes looked as if she yearned to say something in response, but she didn't.

"Your family is great, and I enjoy spending time with them. You don't have to leave all of that behind."

"I know I overthink everything. I get to the point where I can't even see things for the way they are sometimes. I ponder over the what-ifs, always basing it off past experiences. While it is useful for the most part, it can also hinder a person from learning from their past." She lowered her head. "I used to avoid my problems rather than facing them, but that's all changed."

He got up, rubbing the grass blades from his trousers.

She stood and faced him, staring down at her feet. "I know that you said you're willing to leave your community, but I think I should leave mine."

"Leila, you don't need to do that for me."

"But I want to." Her eyes glistened with tears when she raised her head. "Sally will take good care of Henry and Elsie. I know she will."

Aden pulled Leila into his arms, and his heart pounded fast as he hugged Leila. He felt a couple of tears trailing down his face.

As he pulled away from Leila, Aden wiped his face and she did the same. "Are you sure you're okay with joining the church in my community?"

Leila clasped his hands. "Yes. And I believe in our future, Aden."

"Then will you marry me, Leila Fisher?"

"Of course I will. Once my daed and Sally are married, we can do the same." More tears slipped from her beautiful eyes. Her smile was more radiant than ever.

Aden leaned forward and kissed her, joy filling his heart. *Thank You, Lord. Thank You for bringing me the person I was destined to be with. Leila is my other half, and I'm grateful to be with her for the rest of my life.*

EPILOGUE

Leila placed a box of homemade cards on her worktable. "There we go. Now we can get the store open tomorrow."

"Jah, and now you'll be able to follow in your mother's footsteps."

"Danki, Aden. You and Samuel did a good job building this store."

"Well, I did get some help from my father." Aden kissed the side of her face. "Do you have any doubts about leaving your community to be with me?"

Turning to face him, Leila cupped the sides of his face and kissed his lips. Pulling away, she watched as he grinned. "We've been married for a year. Any doubts I had are long gone."

Leila couldn't believe how time went by so quickly. After Dad and Sally got married, it was only a year before she and Aden were married. She had been uncertain how her father would react to Aden's proposal, but he accepted it and supported Leila's decision.

"So, how's Mollie doing running the old shop?"

Leila picked a card out of the box and clipped it to the clothesline. She'd hung the clothesline near the front door so the

441

assortment of homemade cards would be the first thing customers saw when they walked in. "She's doing good. It helps that Sally is in the shop working with Mollie as well."

With Elsie being almost three years of age, Sally had the freedom to help. Henry was now old enough to watch his sister for a while as Sally and Mollie ran things in the store.

"Oh, look who's here." Aden peered out the door. "Your brother and his wife just pulled in."

Leila stopped clipping cards and went over to the door. She watched as Leon got out of the yellow-covered buggy. It was a little disheartening for her whenever she saw a buggy from her community. However, Leila's family visited often enough so she never felt homesick.

Leon entered the shop. "Hello, Troyers." He pinched the brim of his straw hat and tipped it forward.

"Hey, Leon." Leila went over and gave him a hug. "How are Judy and little Darla?"

"They're both doing fine." Leon tugged on the collar of his shirt. "We're about to head to the flea market today and browse around for some things. Maybe get something to eat."

"Sounds like a busy day for your family." Aden shoved his hands in the pockets of his trousers.

"Jah. Judy also wants to get Darla some shoes." Leon looked over at Leila. "Speaking of children, are you excited that you'll be parents soon?"

Leila felt her face warm as she placed a hand on her stomach. "Very much."

She had been through many trials throughout the years. The treatment she received from her classmates made her believe she would never be accepted by anyone. But what she endured during her youth had not kept her from growing as a person. Leila made friends with people who appreciated and loved her for herself. By relinquishing the hurts of her past and trusting God, she was able to let go of her past and forgive. And by allowing herself to forgive, Leila had found the love of her life. All the things Leila longed for had come to pass.

Sue's Chicken Casserole

2 cups cooked chicken, cut
   in small pieces
2 cups uncooked macaroni
   or noodles
2 cans cream of chicken
   soup

2 cups milk
½ cup chopped onion
½ teaspoon black pepper
3 tablespoons butter
1 cup shredded cheese

Preheat oven to 350 degrees. Layer ingredients in large baking dish in order listed. Place in oven and bake for 30 to 40 minutes.

Richelle Brunstetter lives in the Pacific Northwest and developed a desire to write when she took creative writing in high school. After enrolling in college classes, her overall experience enticed her to become a writer, and she wants to implement what she's learned into her stories. Just starting her writing career, her first published story appears in *The Beloved Christmas Quilt* beside her grandmother, Wanda E. Brunstetter, and her mother, Jean. Richelle enjoys traveling to different places, her favorite being Kauai, Hawaii.